Rule

y Crownover lives in Colorado. She loves tattoos and
ody modification and loves to incorporate what she
es into her writing. She loves to read, particularly
y kind of great story that engages; and of course a
etty, tatted-up bad boy always makes it better.

T

T
a

Also by Jay Crownover

Jet

Coming soon

Rome

Rule

JAY CROWNOVER

A Marked Men Novel

HARPER

Harper
An imprint of HarperCollins*Publishers*
77–85 Fulham Palace Road,
Hammersmith, London W6 8JB

www.harpercollins.co.uk

A Paperback Original 2014
1

A catalogue record for this book
is available from the British Library

ISBN: 978-0-00-753629-0

Typeset in Minion Pro by Palimpsest Book Production Limited,
Falkirk, Stirlingshire

Dedicated to everyone who listened to me complain about needing a new life plan all year long. Also to those who encouraged me to just do what I do best. I try to write what I know, just a more romantic and idealized version of it, so this is also for all the real-life tattooed boys who have been in and out of my life over the years and served as inspiration for my heroes.

CHAPTER 1
Rule

At first I thought the pounding in my head was my brain trying to fight its way out of my skull after the ten or so shots of Crown Royal I had downed last night, but then I realized the noise was someone storming around in my apartment. *She* was here, and with dread I remembered that it was Sunday. No matter how many times I told her, or how rude I was to her, or whatever kind of debauched and unsavory condition she found me in, she showed up every Sunday morning to drag me home for brunch.

A soft moan from the other side of the bed reminded me that I hadn't come home alone from the bar last night. Not that I remembered the girl's name or what she looked like, or if it had even been worth her while to stumble into my apartment with me. I ran a hand over my face and swung my legs over the edge of the bed just as the bedroom door swung open. I never should have given the little brat a key. I didn't bother to cover up; she was used to walking in and finding me hungover and naked—I didn't see why today should be any different. The girl on the other side of the bed rolled over and narrowed her eyes at the new addition to our awkward little party.

1

"I thought you said you were single?" The accusation in her tone lifted the hair on the back of my neck. Any chick who was willing to come home with a stranger for a night of no-strings-attached sex didn't get the right to pass judgment, especially while she was still naked and rumpled in my bed.

"Give me twenty," I said, my eyes shifting to the blonde in the doorway as I ran a hand through my messy hair.

She lifted an eyebrow. "You have ten."

I would have lifted an eyebrow back at her tone and attitude but my head was killing me, and the gesture would have been wasted on her anyway; she was way past immune to my shit.

"I'll make coffee. I already invited Nash but he said he has to go to the shop for an appointment. I'll be in the car." She spun on her heel, and, just like that, the doorway was empty. I was struggling to my feet, searching the floor for the pair of pants I might have tossed down there last night.

"What's going on?"

I had temporarily forgotten about the girl in my bed. I swore softly under my breath and tugged a black T-shirt that looked reasonably clean over my head. "I have to go."

"What?"

I frowned at her as she lifted herself up in the bed and clutched the sheet to her chest. She was pretty and had a nice body from what I could see. I wondered what kind of game I had thrown at her in order to get her to come home with me. She was one I didn't mind waking up to this morning.

"I have somewhere I need to be, so that means you need to get up and get going. Normally my roommate would be around, so you could hang out for a minute, but he had to go to work, so that means you need to get that fine ass in gear and get out."

She sputtered a little at me. "Are you kidding me?"

I looked over my shoulder as I dug my boots out from under a pile of laundry and shoved my feet into them. "No."

"What kind of asshole does that? Not even a 'thanks for last night, you were great, how about lunch?' Just 'get the fuck out'?" She threw the sheet aside and I noticed she had a nice tattoo scrawled along her ribs that curled across her shoulder and along her collarbone. That was probably what had attracted me to her in my drunken stupor in the first place. "You're a real piece of work, you know that?"

I was a whole lot more than just a piece of work, but this chick, who was just one of oh so many, didn't need to know that. I silently cursed my roommate, Nash, who was the real shit here. We had been best friends since elementary school, and I could normally rely on him to run interference for me on Sunday mornings when I had to bail, but I had forgotten about the piece he was supposed to be finishing up today. That meant I was on my own when it came to hustling last night's tail out the door and getting a move on before the brat left without me, which was a bigger headache than I needed in my current state.

"Hey, what's your name anyway?"

If she wasn't pissed before, she was downright infuriated now. She climbed back into a supershort black skirt and a barely there tank top. She fluffed up her mound of dyed blond hair and glared at me out of eyes now smudged with old mascara. "Lucy. You don't remember?"

I slimed some crap in my hair to make it stand up in a bunch of different directions and sprayed on cologne to help mask the scent of sex and booze that I was sure still clung to my skin. I shrugged a shoulder at her and waited as she hopped by me on one foot putting on heels that just screamed *dirty sex*.

"I'm Rule." I would have offered to shake her hand but that seemed silly so I just pointed to the front door of the apartment and stepped in the bathroom to brush the stale taste of whiskey out of my mouth. "There's coffee in the kitchen. Maybe you should write your number down and I can give you a call another time. Sundays aren't good days for me." She would never know how true that statement was.

She glared at me and tapped the toe of one of those awesome shoes. "You really have no idea who I am, do you?"

This time, even against my throbbing brain's wishes, my eyebrow went up and I looked at her with a mouthful of toothpaste foam. I just stared at her until she screeched at me and pointed at her side. "You have to at least remember this!"

No wonder I liked her ink so much; it was one of mine. I spit the toothpaste in the sink and gave myself a once-over in the mirror. I looked like hell. My eyes were watery and rimmed in red, my skin looked gray, and there was a hickey the size of Rhode Island on the side of my neck—Mom was going to love that. Just like she was going to fall all over herself about the current state of my hair. It was normally thick and dark, but I had shaved the sides and dyed the front a nice, bright purple, so now it stuck up straight like a Weedwacker had been used to cut it. Both my folks already had an issue with the scrolling ink that wound around both my arms and up the side of my neck, so the hair was just going to be icing on the cake. Since there was nothing I could do to fix the current shit show looking back at me in the mirror I prowled out of the bathroom and unceremoniously grabbed the girl by the elbow and towed her to the front door. I needed to remember to go home with them instead of letting them come home with me; it was so much easier that way.

"Look, I have somewhere I have to be, and I don't particularly love that I have to go, but you freaking out and making a scene is not going to do anything other than piss me off. I hope you had a good time last night and you can leave your number, but we both know the chances of me calling you are slim to none. If you don't want to be treated like crap, maybe you should stop going home with drunken dudes you don't know. Trust me, we're really after only one thing and the next morning all we really want is for you to go quietly away. I have a headache and I feel like I'm going to hurl, plus I have to spend the next hour in a car with someone who will be silently loathing me and joyously plotting my death, so really, can we just save the histrionics and get a move on it?"

By now I had maneuvered Lucy to the entryway of the building, and I saw my blond tormentor in the BMW idling in the spot next to my truck. She was impatient and would take off if I wasted any more time. I gave Lucy a half grin and shrugged a shoulder—after all it wasn't her fault I was an asshole, and even I knew she deserved better than such a callous brush-off.

"Look, don't feel bad. I can be a charming bastard when I put my mind to it. You are far from the first and won't be the last to see this little show. I'm glad your tat turned out badass, and I'd prefer you remember me for that rather than last night."

I jogged down the front steps without looking back and yanked open the door to the fancy black BMW. I hated this car and hated that it suited the driver as well as it did. *Classy*, *sleek*, and *expensive* were definitely words that could be used to describe my traveling companion. As we pulled out of the parking lot, Lucy yelled at me and flipped me off. My driver rolled her eyes and muttered, "Classy" under her breath. She was used to the little scenes chicks liked to throw when I bailed on them the morning after. I even had to replace her windshield once when one of them had chucked a rock at me and missed while I was walking away.

I adjusted the seat to accommodate my long legs and settled in to rest my head against the window. It was always a long and achingly silent drive. Sometimes, like today, I was grateful for it; other times it grated on my very last nerve. We had been a fixture in each other's lives since middle school, and she knew every strength and fault I had. My parents loved her like their own daughter and made no bones about the fact that they more often than not preferred her company over mine. One would think with all the history, both good and bad, between us, that we could make simple small talk for a few hours without it being difficult.

"You're going to get all that junk that's in your hair all over my window." Her voice—all cigarettes and whiskey—didn't match the rest of her, which was all champagne and silk. I had always liked her voice; when we got along I could listen to her talk for hours.

"I'll get it detailed."

She snorted. I closed my eyes and crossed my arms over my chest. I was all set for a silent ride, but apparently she had things to say today, because as soon as she pulled the car onto the highway she turned the radio down and said my name. "Rule."

I turned my head slightly to the side and cracked open an eye. "Shaw." Her name was just as fancy as the rest of her. She was pale, had snowy white-blond hair, and big green eyes that looked like Granny Smith apples. She was tiny, an easy foot shorter than my own six three, but had curves that went on for days. She was the kind of girl that guys looked at, because they just couldn't help themselves, but as soon as she turned those frosty green eyes in their direction they knew they wouldn't stand a chance. She exuded unattainability the way some other girls oozed "come and get me."

She blew out a breath and I watched a strand of hair twirl around her forehead. She looked at me out of the corner of her eye and I stiffened when I saw how tight her hands were on the steering wheel.

"What is it, Shaw?"

She bit her bottom lip, a sure sign she was nervous. "I don't suppose you answered any of your mom's calls this week?"

I wasn't exactly tight with my folks. In fact, our relationship hovered somewhere around the mutually tolerable area, which is why my mom sent Shaw to drag me home each weekend. We were both from a small town called Brookside, in an affluent part of Colorado. I'd moved to Denver as soon as I had my diploma in hand, and Shaw had moved there a few years later. She was a few years younger than me, and she had wanted nothing more than to get into the University of Denver. Not only did the girl look like a fairy-tale princess, but she was also on track to be a freaking doctor. My mom knew there was no way I would make the two-hour drive there and back to see them on the weekends, but if Shaw came to get me, I would have to go, not only because I would feel guilty that she'd taken time out of her busy schedule, but also because she paid for the gas, waited for me to stumble out of bed, and dragged my sorry ass home every single Sunday and not once in going on two years had she complained about it.

"No, I was busy all week." I *was* busy, but I also just didn't like talking to my mom, so I had ignored her all three times she had called me this week.

Shaw sighed and her hands twisted even tighter on the

7

steering wheel. "She was calling to tell you that Rome got hurt and the army is sending him home for six weeks of R and R. Your dad went down to the base in the Springs yesterday to pick him up."

I bolted up in the seat so fast that I smacked my head on the roof of the car. I swore and rubbed the spot, which made my head throb even more. "What? What do you mean he got hurt?" Rome was my older brother. He had three years on me and had been overseas for a good portion of the last six. We were still tight and, even though he didn't like all the distance I'd put between me and my parents over the years, I was sure that if he was injured I would have heard it from him.

"I'm not sure. Margot said something happened to the convoy he was in when they were out on patrol. He was in a pretty bad accident I guess. She said his arm was broken and he had a few cracked ribs. She was pretty upset so I had a hard time understanding her when she called."

"Rome would have called me."

"Rome was doped up and spent the last two days being debriefed. He asked your mom to call because you Archer boys are nothing if not persistent. Margot told him that you wouldn't answer, but he told her to keep trying."

My brother was hurt and was home, but I hadn't known about it. I closed my eyes again and let my head drop back against the headrest. "Well, hell, that's good news I guess. Are you going to go by and see your mom?" I asked her. I didn't have to look at her to know that she had stiffened even more. I could practically feel the tension rolling off her in icy waves.

"No." She didn't say more and I didn't expect her to. The Archers may not be the closest, warmest bunch, but we didn't have anything on the Landons. Shaw's family crapped gold and breathed money. They also cheated and lied, had been divorced and remarried. From what I had seen over the years, they had little need or interest in their biological daughter, who, it seemed, was conceived in order to get a tax deduction rather than time spent in a bedroom. I knew Shaw loved my house and loved my parents, because it was the only semblance of normalcy she had ever experienced. I didn't begrudge her that; in fact I appreciated that she took most of the heat off me. If Shaw was doing well in school, dating an affluent undergrad, living the life my parents had always wanted for their sons but had been denied, they stayed off my case. Since Rome was usually a continent away, I was the only one they could get to so I took no shame in using Shaw as a buffer.

"Man, I haven't talked to Rome in three months. It'll be awesome to see him. I wonder if I can convince him to come spend some time in D-town with me and Nash. He's probably more than ready for a little bit of fun."

She sighed again and moved to turn the radio back up a little bit. "You're twenty-two, Rule. When are you going to stop acting like an indulgent teenager? Did you even ask this one her name? In case you were wondering, you smell like a mix between a distillery and a strip club."

I snorted and let my eyes drift back shut. "You're nineteen, Shaw. When are you going to stop living your life by everyone else's standards? My eighty-two-year-old grandma has more of a social calendar than you, and I think she's less uptight." I wasn't going to tell her what she smelled like because it was sweet and lovely and I had no desire to be nice at the moment.

I could feel her glaring at me and I hid a grin. "I like Ethel." Her tone was surly.

"Everybody likes Ethel. She's feisty and won't take crap from anyone. You could learn a thing or two from her."

"Oh, maybe I should just dye my hair pink, tattoo every

visible surface of my body, shove a bunch of metal in my face, and sleep with everything that moves. Isn't that your philosophy on how to live a rich and fulfilling life?"

That made me crank my eyes back open and the marching band in my head decide to go for round two.

"At least I'm doing what I want. I know who and what I am, Shaw, and I don't make any apologies for it. I hear plenty of Margot Archer coming out of your pretty mouth right now."

Her mouth twisted down into a frown. "Whatever. Let's just go back to ignoring each other, okay? I just thought you should know about Rome. The Archer boys have never been big on surprises."

She was right. In my experience surprises were never a good thing. They usually resulted in someone getting pissed and me ending up in some kind of fight. I loved my brother, but I had to admit I was kind of irritated he hadn't, one, bothered to let me know he was hurt, and, two, was still trying to force me to play nice with my folks. I figured Shaw's plan for us to ignore each other the rest of the way was a winner, so I slumped down as far as the sporty little car would allow and started to doze off. I was only out for twenty minutes or so when her Civil Wars ringtone jarred me awake. I blinked my gritty eyes and rubbed a hand over the scruff on my face. If the hair and the hickey didn't piss Mom off, the fact I was too busy to shave for her precious brunch might just send her into hysterics.

"No, I told you I was going to Brookside and won't be back until late." When I looked across the car at her she must have felt my gaze because she looked at me quickly and I saw a little bit of pink work its way onto her high cheekbones. "No, Gabe, I told you I won't have time and that I have a lab due." I couldn't make out the words on the other end but the person sounded angry at her brush-off, and I saw her fingers tighten on the phone. "It's none of your business. I have to go now, so I'll talk to you later." She swiped a finger across the screen and tossed the fancy device into the cup holder by my knee.

"Trouble in paradise?" I didn't really care about Shaw and her richer-than-God, future-ruler-of-the-known-universe boyfriend, but it was polite to ask when she was obviously upset. I hadn't ever met Gabe, but what I'd heard from Mom when I bothered to listen was that he was custom-made for Shaw's future doctor persona. His family was as loaded as hers; his dad was a judge, or lawyer, or some other political nonsense I had no use for. I was sure, beyond a shadow of a doubt, that the dude wore pleated slacks and pink polo shirts with white loafers. For a long moment I didn't think she was going to respond, but then she cleared her throat and started tapping out a beat on the steering wheel with her manicured fingers.

"Not really, we broke up but I don't think Gabe really gets it."

"Really?"

"Yeah, a couple weeks ago, actually. I had been thinking about doing it for a while. I'm just too busy with school and work to have a boyfriend."

"If he was the right guy you wouldn't have felt that way. You would have made the time because you wanted to be with him."

She looked at me with both blond brows raised to her hairline. "Are you, Mr. Manwhore of the Century, seriously trying to give me relationship advice?"

I rolled my eyes, which made my head scream in protest. "Just because there hasn't been one girl I wanted to hang out with exclusively doesn't mean I don't know the difference between quality and quantity."

"Could have fooled me. Gabe just wanted more than I

11

was willing to give him. It's going to be a pain because my mom and dad both loved him."

"True that; from what I've heard he was pretty much custom-made to make your folks happy. What do you mean he wanted more than you were willing to give? Did he try to put a rock on your finger after only six months?"

She gave me a look and curled her lip in a sneer. "Not even close, he just wanted things to be more serious than I wanted them to be."

I laughed a little and rubbed between my eyebrows. My headache had turned into a dull throb but was starting to be manageable. I needed to ask her to swing by a Starbucks or something if I was going to get through this afternoon.

"Is that your prissy way of telling me that he was trying to get in your pants and you weren't having it?"

She narrowed her eyes at me and pulled off the freeway at the exit that took us toward Brookside.

"I need you to stop by Starbucks before going to my parents' house, and don't think I didn't notice you aren't answering my question."

"If we stop we're going to be late. And not every boy thinks with what's in their pants."

"The sky isn't going to fall on us if we show up five minutes behind Margot's schedule. And you have got to be kidding me—you strung that loser along for six months without giving it up? What a joke."

That made me flat-out laugh at her. I laughed so hard that I had to hold my head in both hands as my whiskey-logged brain started screaming at me again. I gasped a little and looked at her with watery eyes. "If you really believe that he wasn't interested in getting in your pants, you aren't nearly as smart as I always thought you were. Every single dude under the age of ninety is trying to get in your pants,

Shaw—especially if he's thinking that he's your boy. I'm a guy, I know this shit."

She bit her lip again, conceding I probably had a valid point as she pulled the car into the coffee shop's parking lot. I practically bolted out of the car, eager to stretch my legs and get a little distance from her typical haughty attitude.

There was a line when I got inside, and I took a quick look around to see if I recognized anyone. Brookside is a pretty small town and usually when I stopped by on the weekends I inevitably ran into someone I used to go to school with. I hadn't bothered to ask Shaw if she wanted me to grab her anything because she was being all uppity about having to stop in the first place. It was almost my turn to order when my phone started blasting a Social Distortion song in my pocket. I dug it out after ordering a big-ass black coffee and took a spot by the counter next to a cute brunette who was trying her hardest to not get caught checking me out.

"What up?"

I could hear the music in the shop blaring behind Nash when he asked, "How did this morning go?"

Nash knew my faults and bad habits better than anyone, and the reason we had maintained our friendship as long as we had was because he never judged me.

"Sucked. I'm hungover, grumpy, and about to sit through yet another forced family function. Plus, Shaw is in rare form today."

"How was the chick from last night?"

"No clue. I don't even remember leaving the bar with her. Apparently I did a huge piece on her side so she was a little pissed that I didn't remember who she was, so ouch."

He chuckled on the other end of the line. "She told you that, like, six times last night. She even tried to pull her top off to show you. And I drove your dumb ass home last night,

13

drunko. I tried to get you to leave at, like, midnight but you weren't having any of it, as usual. I had to drive your truck home and then take a cab back to get my car."

I snorted and reached for the coffee when the guy behind the counter called my name. I noticed the brunette's eyes follow the hand that wrapped around the cardboard cup. It was the hand that had the flared head of a king cobra on it, the snake's forked tongue making the *L* in my name that was inked across my four knuckles. The rest of the snake wound its way up my forearm and around my elbow. The brunette's mouth made a little O of surprise so I flashed her a wink and walked back to the BMW.

"Sorry, dude. How did your appointment go?"

Nash's uncle Phil had opened the tattoo shop years ago on Capitol Hill when it mainly catered to gangbangers and bikers. Now with the influx of young urbanites and hipsters populating the area, the Marked was one of the busiest tattoo parlors in town. Nash and I met in art class in the fifth grade and have been inseparable since. In fact, ever since we were twelve our plan was to move to the city and work for Phil. We both had mad skills and the personality to make the shop bump with business so Phil had no qualms apprenticing us and putting us to work before we were both in our twenties. It was killer to have a friend in the same field; I had a plethora of ink on my skin that ranged from not-so-great to great that chronicled Nash's evolution as a tattoo artist, and he could state the same thing about me.

"I finished that back piece that I've been working on since July. It turned out better than I thought and the dude is talking about doing the front. I'll take it, because he's a fat tipper."

"Nice." I was juggling the phone and the coffee, trying to open the door to the car when a female voice stopped me in my tracks.

14

"Hey." I looked over my shoulder and the brunette was standing a car over with a smile on her face. "I really like your tattoos."

I smiled back at her and then jumped, nearly spilling scalding hot coffee down my crotch as Shaw shoved the door open from the inside.

"Thanks." If we had been closer to home and Shaw wasn't already putting the car in reverse I probably would have taken a second to ask the girl for her number. Shaw shot me a look of contempt that I promptly ignored, and I went back to my conversation with Nash. "Rome is home. He got in an accident and Shaw said he's got a few weeks of R and R coming to him. I guess that's why Mom was blowing my phone up all week."

"Kick ass. Ask him if he wants to roll with us for a few days. I miss that surly bastard."

I sipped on the coffee and my head finally started to calm down. "That's the plan. I'll hit you up on my way home and let you know what the story is."

I flicked my thumb across the screen to end the call and settled back into the seat. Shaw scowled angrily at me and I swore her eyes glowed. Really. I have never seen anything that green, even in nature, and when she gets mad they are just otherworldly.

"Your mom called while you were busy flirting. She's mad that we're late."

I sucked on more of the black nectar of the gods and started tapping out a beat on my knee with my free hand. I was always kind of a fidgety guy and the closer we got to my parents' house, the worse it usually got. Brunch was always stilted and forced. I couldn't figure out why they insisted on going through with it every single week and couldn't figure out why Shaw enabled the farce, but I went, even when I knew nothing would ever change.

"She's mad that *you're* late. We both know she couldn't care less if I'm there or not." My fingers moved faster and faster as she wheeled the car into a gated community and passed rows and rows of cookie-cutter minimansions that were built back into the mountains.

"That's not true and you know it, Rule. I do not suffer through these car rides every weekend, subject myself to the delight of your morning-after nastiness because your parents want *me* to have eggs and pancakes every Sunday. I do it because they want to see *you*, want to try to have a relationship with you no matter how many times you hurt them or push them away. I owe it to your parents and, more important, I owe it to Remy to try to make you act right even though lord knows that's almost a full-time job."

I sucked in a breath as the blinding pain that always came when someone mentioned Remy's name barreled through my chest. My fingers involuntarily opened and closed around the coffee cup and I whipped my head around to glare at her.

"Remy wouldn't be all over my ass to try and be something to them I'm not. I was never good enough for them, and never will be. He understood that better than anyone and worked overtime to try and be everything to them I never could be."

She sighed and pulled the car to a stop in the driveway behind my dad's SUV. "The only difference between you and Remy is that he let people love him, and you"—she yanked open the driver's door and glared at me across the space that separated us—"you have always been determined to make everyone who cares about you prove it beyond a shadow of a doubt. You've never wanted to be easy to love, Rule, and you make damn sure that nobody can ever forget it." She slammed the door with enough force that it rattled my back teeth and made my head start to throb again.

It has been three years. Three lonely, three empty, three

sorrow-filled years since the Archer brothers went from a trio to a duo. I am close to Rome—he's awesome and has always been my role model when it comes to being a badass—but Remy was my other half, both figuratively and literally. He was my identical twin, the light to my dark, the easy to my hard, the joy to my angst, the perfect to my oh-so-totally fucked up, and without him I was only half the person I would ever be. It has been three years since I called him in the middle of the night to come pick me up from some lame-ass party because I had been too drunk to drive. Three years since he left the apartment we shared to come get me—zero questions asked—because that's just what he did.

It's been three years since he lost control of his car on a rainy and slick I-25 and slammed into the back of a semi truck going well over eighty. Three years since we put my twin in the ground and my mother looked at me with tears in her eyes and stated point-blank, "It should have been you" as they lowered Remy into the ground.

It's been three years and his name alone is still enough to drop me to my knees, especially coming from the one person in the world Remy had loved as much as he loved me.

Remy was everything I wasn't—clean-cut, well dressed, and interested in getting an education and building a secure future. The only person on the planet who was good enough and classy enough to match all the magnificence that he possessed was Shaw Landon. The two of them had been inseparable since the first time he brought her home when she was fourteen and trying to escape the fortress of the Landon compound. He insisted they were just friends, that he loved Shaw like a sister, that he just wanted to protect her from her awful, sterile family, but the way he was with her was full of reverence and care. I knew he loved her, and since Remy could do no wrong, Shaw had quickly become an honorary member of my family. As much as it galled me,

17

she was the only one who really, truly understood the depth of my pain when it came to losing him.

I had to take a few extra minutes to get my feet back under me so I sucked back the rest of the coffee and shoved open the door. I wasn't surprised to see a tall figure coming around the SUV as I labored out of the sports car. My brother was an inch or so taller than me and built more along the lines of a warrior. His dark-brown hair was buzzed in a typical military cut and his pale-blue eyes, the same icy shade as mine, looked tired as he forced a smile at me. I let out a whistle because his left arm was in a cast and sling, he had a walking boot on one foot, and there was a nasty line of black stitches running through one of his eyebrows and across his forehead. The Weedwacker that had attacked my hair had clearly gotten a good shot at my big bro, too.

"Looking good, soldier."

He pulled me to him in a one-armed hug and I winced for him when I felt the taped-up side of his body clearly indicating some injury beyond the busted ribs. "I look about as good as I feel. You look like a clown getting out of that car."

"I look like a clown no matter what when I'm around that girl." He barked out a laugh and rubbed a rough hand through my spiky hair.

"You and Shaw are still acting like mortal enemies?"

"More like uneasy acquaintances. She's just as prissy and judgmental as always. Why didn't you call or email me that you were hurt? I had to hear it from Shaw on the way over."

He swore as we started to slowly make our way toward the house. It upset me to see how deliberate he was moving and I wondered if the damage was more serious than what was visible.

"I was unconscious after the Hummer flipped. We drove

18

over an IED and it was bad. I was in the hospital for a week with a scrambled noggin, and when I woke up they had to do surgery on my shoulder so I was all drugged up. I called Mom and figured she would let you know what the deal was, but I heard that, as usual, you were unavailable when she called."

I shrugged a shoulder and reached out a hand to steady him as he faltered a little on the stairs to the front door. "I was busy."

"You're stubborn."

"Not too stubborn. I'm here aren't I? I didn't even know you were home until this morning."

"The only reason you're here is because that little girl in there is bound and determined to keep this family together regardless if we're her own or not. You go in there and play nice; otherwise, I'll kick your ass, broken arm and all."

I muttered a few choice words and followed my battered sibling into the house. Sundays really were my least favorite day.

CHAPTER 2

Shaw

I closed the bathroom door with a soft click and turned the lock. I collapsed against the sink and ran shaking hands over my face. It was getting harder and harder to be Rule's chaperone to these family gatherings every Sunday. I already felt like I was getting an ulcer, and if I had to walk in on him and one of his disgusting bar bimbos again, I wasn't sure I was going to make it out of his apartment without committing homicide.

I turned around to splash some cold water on my face and lifted the heavy fall of blond hair off my neck. I needed to get it together because the last thing I wanted was for Margot or Dale—or Rome for that matter—to notice that something was off. Rome was one of the most observant people I had ever met and I had a feeling that even drugged up and in pain he wouldn't miss a thing when it came to his younger brother and sister, since by association I had technically been lumped into the category of surrogate little sister.

It was getting harder and harder to spend time around Rule and not just because looking at him reminded me of everything that I no longer had—which was the problem

Margot and Dale struggled with, not that the insensitive ass had any empathy for his parents. My struggle was that Rule was complicated; he was brash, mouthy, careless, thoughtless, often cranky, and generally an insufferable pain in the ass. But when he chose to be, he was charming and funny, artistically brilliant, and more often than not, the most interesting person in the room. I have been head over heels in love with both sides of him since I was fourteen years old. Of course I loved Remy, loved him like a brother, like the best friend and consummate protector he had been, but I loved Rule like it was my mission in life. I loved him like it was inevitable, like no matter how many times I was shown what an awful idea it was, what a bad match we were, what a callous asshole he could be, I couldn't shake it. So each and every time I had to have the fact that he didn't even think of me as more than a carpool driver shoved in my face it tore a little bit more of my battered heart apart.

Because my own family was such a mess, there was no way I would be half the person I was today without everything the Archers had done for me. Remy had taken me under his wing when I was a friendless and lonely teen. Rome had threatened to beat up the first boy who made me cry because I liked him and he didn't like me back. Margot had taken me shopping for homecoming and prom dresses when my own mother was too busy with her new husband to care. Dale had taken me to the University of Denver and the University of Colorado–Boulder and helped whittle down the choices logically and rationally when it came to picking a college. And Rule, well, Rule was a constant reminder that money didn't get you everything you wanted and that no matter how perfect I tried to be, how hard I worked at being everything to everyone, it still wasn't enough.

I blew out a breath that I felt like I had been holding for more than an hour and took a piece of Kleenex to wipe away the black smudges from under my eyes. If I didn't get down to the dining room fast Margot was bound to come looking for me and I didn't have a reasonable excuse as to why I was currently freaking out in the bathroom. I fished a hair tie out of my pocket and pulled my hair into a low ponytail, slicked on a sheer coat of gloss, and gave myself a silent pep talk, reminding myself that I had done this a million other Sundays and that this one was no different.

Just as I was stepping into the hall my phone rang and I had to struggle to hold back a groan when I saw that it was Gabe calling again. I sent the call to voice mail and wondered for the hundredth time in the last month why I had ever wasted a second of my time on his pompous ass. He was overly entitled, overly grabby, overly superficial, and more interested in my last name and the fact that my parents were loaded than he was in me.

I wasn't even interested in dating him—wasn't interested in dating anyone—but my parents had forced my hand. As usual, under their pressure, I folded and ended up spending more time with him than I wanted to. I had managed to tolerate him for a lot longer than I thought I would be able to. After all, Gabe was way more interested in himself than in me. It wasn't until he had started pushing for sex—making me uncomfortable by grabbing and touching things I didn't want his hands anywhere near—that I cut the cord. Unfortunately, neither he nor my parents seem to have gotten the message and I have been inundated with calls, texts, and emails for the last two weeks. Gabe was easy enough to dodge; my mother not so much.

I was shoving the phone into my back pocket when a quiet voice stopped me. "What's going on with you, little girl? I've been gone for over eighteen months and all I get is a hug and a peck on the cheek before you disappear? Where are the tears? Where's the hysterics that I'm home safe and sound? What's working in that complicated brain of yours? Because I can tell something is on your mind."

I hiccupped a little laugh and let my forehead fall onto the strong chest in front of me. Even battered and bruised Rome was the kind of guy who stood between the people he loved and anything that might possibly hurt them. He patted the top of my head and laid a heavy hand on the back of my neck. "I missed your pretty face, Shaw; you don't know how good it is to be home."

I shuddered a little and wrapped a careful arm around his waist so that I could give him a squeeze and not hurt him. "I missed you, too, Rome. I'm just stressed out. School is crazy right now, I'm working three or four nights a week, and my parents won't get off my back about this guy I just broke up with. You know I love it when we're all together. I thought your mom was going to have a heart attack when she called to tell me what happened to you. I'm so glad you're okay. I don't think this family would be able to handle losing another Archer son."

"No, probably not. I can't believe she still has you playing chauffeur for my idiot brother."

I hooked my arm through his and we started to make our way to the dining room. "It's the only way he'll come. If I have to miss it because of school or because something comes up he just blows them off. Half the time when I get to the apartment he doesn't even know what day it is and has to scramble to get out the door. Today would be a prime example of that. If I show up he feels obligated to come with me no matter what or who he's in the middle of doing."

Rome swore under his breath. "It wouldn't kill that kid to play nice with Mom and Dad once a week. He shouldn't need you to be his babysitter."

I shrugged my shoulders because we both knew that all the Archer brothers had a role. Remy had been the good

23

son, the straight-A student, the future Ivy Leaguer. He was also the one saddled with the role of keeping Rule out of jail and running interference when his twin got into trouble that he couldn't talk his way out of. Rule was the wild card, the one who lived life to the fullest and made no apologies to those he might offend or hurt along the way. Rome was the boss and the twins adored him and followed his lead through good and bad, because lord knew with the way the three of them looked, there was lots and lots of bad thrown their way. With Remy gone it wasn't a surprise to anyone that Rome had become even more protective of his remaining brother and that I had fallen seamlessly into the role of trying to keep Rule on some kind of straight and narrow path.

"It's the least I can do for Margot and Dale. They've always done so much for me and asked for so little in return. Suffering Rule's wrath once a week is a pretty easy sacrifice to make."

Something flashed in his eyes, which were so much like his brother's that it sometimes hurt to look into them. Rome wasn't anyone's fool and it wouldn't surprise me if he knew more about all the things I kept locked up than he let on.

"I just don't want you being the target of Rule being Rule. Mom needs to get over her shit and so does he. Everyone is grown now and life is too short for you to be constantly playing the peacemaker between those two."

I sighed and lowered my voice as we got to the entrance of the dining room. The table was already set and everyone was already in his regular seat. Dale was at the head of the table, Margot on his right, with an open spot for me. His left side was open for Rome, and Rule had taken the seat at the opposite end of the table as far away from both of his parents as he could get. "They need to move past the fact that he's never going to be Remy, and he has to stop intentionally cramming that fact down their throats. Until one side gives and learns how to forgive it's always going to be this way."

He pressed a superlight kiss to my temple and gave me a little squeeze back. "I don't think any of them realize how lucky they are to have you, little girl."

I let him go and went to take my seat between Margot and Rule. I tried not to wince when Rule sent a narrow-eyed look in my direction, knowing Rome and I had more than likely been whispering about him. I slid into my spot and flashed Dale a smile as he started passing the typically lavish food around. I was about to ask Rome what he planned to do with his time off when Margot had me snapping my head around in shock.

"Would it be too much of a stretch to expect you to come to brunch in a shirt that buttons and in a pair of pants that don't look like they came from a thrift store? I mean, your brother has several broken bones and was in a horrific accident and he still manages to look more put together than you, Rule."

I had to bite my tongue to stop from snapping at her to lay off him. Mostly because family gatherings were supposed to be informal and fun. I knew good and well that if I had shown up in jeans and a T-shirt she wouldn't even have blinked, but because it was him she viewed it as a direct attack on her.

He picked a couple pieces of bacon off the platter I handed to him and didn't even bother to respond to her. Instead, he turned to Rome and asked what his plans were while he was home. Rule wanted him to come to the city for a week and spend time with him and Nash. I saw Margot's mouth tighten at the dismissal and Dale's eyebrows pull down in a frown. I saw varying degrees of the same look every Sunday we were here. It hurt my chest because even in a rumpled

25

shirt and torn jeans Rule was the kind of guy who owned whatever look he was wearing. It was the same thing with the mass amounts of tattoos that covered him from head to toe and the array of metal that dotted his face here and there.

There was no denying Rule was a good-looking guy, probably too good-looking, to be honest, but he was complicated, and the beauty he possessed was buried and camouflaged under things that weren't easy to look past. Of all the brothers, he has the clearest, most arctic blue eyes, and his hair, even when it's decorated with purple or green or blue, is still the thickest and the shiniest. Even with every color under the sun dancing across his skin, of the three of them, Rule had always been the one the girls gravitated to. Just like the brunette at Starbucks this afternoon. Her name was Amy Rodgers, and I had spent all four years of high school being tormented by her and her cheerleader cronies. She dated jocks and boys who bled blue, not guys who rocked Mohawks and had their eyebrows and lips pierced, but even she couldn't resist all that was Rule Archer in his magnetic glory.

"And what's going on with your hair, son?" Dale asked. "A color actually found in nature might be a nice change of pace, especially since the whole family is together and we're all lucky to have your brother home in one piece."

I groaned inwardly and silently took the bowl of fruit Margot handed me. Now that they had teamed up on him there was no way he was going to stay quiet. Normally, he ignored his mom and shot sarcastic one-liners at Dale, but being interrupted and attacked from both sides while he was trying to catch up with Rome wasn't going to fly. Rule had a short fuse on a good day but corner him when he was hungover and being reluctantly civil at best—the fur was, no doubt, going to fly. I shot Rome a panicked look across the table, but before he could interject, Rule's voice snapped out like a verbal backhand across the face.

"Well, Pops, purple is found all throughout nature so I don't know what you're talking about, and as far as my clothes are concerned, I figure we're all lucky I bothered to even put pants on, considering the condition Shaw found me in this morning. Now, if you're both done criticizing every move I make, can I continue my conversation with my brother I haven't seen in over a year, considering he nearly got blown up by a roadside bomb?"

Margot gasped and Dale shoved his chair back from the table. I let my head fall forward and rubbed between my eyes where a headache was starting to throb.

"One afternoon, Rule. One freaking afternoon is all we ask of you." Dale stormed out of the room and Margot wasted no time bursting into tears. She buried her face in her napkin and I reached over to awkwardly pat her shoulder. I cut a look at Rule but he had climbed to his feet as well and was headed toward the front door. I shot a look at Rome, who just shook his head and lumbered to his feet. Margot lifted her head and looked at her eldest with pleading eyes.

"Tell him, Rome. You go tell him that this is not how you treat your parents. He has no respect."

She pointed a shaky finger at the door. "You tell him that this is unacceptable."

Rome looked at me, then back to his mom. "Sure, Mom, I'll tell him, but I'm also going to tell you that you had no reason to lay into him like that. Who cares if he wants to wear jeans and have hair like a goddamn Smurf? What matters is that he's here and he made an effort. Shaw took time out of her life, her busy schedule, to make that happen for you and Dad. You waited exactly three seconds before purposely picking at the scab, both of you."

Margot gasped but Rome wasn't done. "You and Dad need a wakeup call. I could have just as easily come home in a body bag instead of a cast. You've already lost one son; you need to appreciate the ones you have left, regardless of whether you agree with the choices we're making or not."

The tears came harder and she leaned her head on my shoulder. "Shaw loves coming to visit on Sunday; we should just stop asking her to bring Rule, because clearly he doesn't want to be here. I'm done trying to make him be part of this family, it just hurts too much."

Rome shook his head and both of us sighed. He followed his brother out of the room as I continued to pat Margot on the shoulder. This woman had been kind to me, treated me as a daughter when my own mother had no use for me, so what I was about to say to her came from a place of refusing to watch another family collapse in on itself.

"Margot, you and Dale are wonderful people and good parents, but you have to stop living in the past. I'm not going to come see you on Sundays anymore, not unless you figure out how to accept Rule for exactly who he is and love him anyway. I miss Remy and it was tragic how he died, but you are never going to turn Rule into him, and I can't stand by and watch you continue to try. My parents have been forcing me into a mold that hasn't fit me for years and I only wish I had enough will to refuse them the way Rule does."

I climbed to my feet and had to fight back my own tears when she looked at me with shock and dismay.

"If Remy was here none of this would be happening. You and he would still be happy together, Rule would never have started acting so awful, and Rome never would have gone off and joined the stupid military."

I had to take a few steps away because there was so much wrong with what she was saying that it nearly floored me.

"Margot, Rule was always a handful, he just never bowed to your and Dale's dictates. Rome was enlisted way before the accident. And I've told you a million times Remy was my best friend—we didn't have feelings for each other like that. I think you need to consider talking to a professional because you're rewriting history and, while you're doing it, you're losing a pretty terrific son."

"You can't honestly believe that? Rule is just as awful to you as he is to me and his father."

I bit my lip and rubbed my temples harder. "He isn't awful; he's just harder to love. Remy made it easy for you guys, and Rule never has, but he deserves the effort, and until this family can see that, I have better ways to spend my time. If I wanted bickering and bitterness I would just go home. I love you and Dale, but I see what you're doing to Rule and I will not be a part of it anymore. Rome was right; you need to appreciate the family you have and not spend your life comparing them to the family you lost. Remy was my whole world, Margot, but he's gone and Rule is here."

She crossed her arms and flopped her head down on the table. I knew there would be no getting through to her so I walked to the front door. I wasn't surprised to see Dale leaning against the kitchen counter, watching me with serious eyes.

"She isn't going to do well without you coming by. You're an important part of this family."

I tucked a few loose strands of hair behind my ear and gave him a rueful smile. "So is your son."

"Margot isn't the only one who needs to remember that, and you have to admit that hair is ridiculous."

I laughed for real this time and walked over to give him a hug. "She needs help, Dale. Remy's been gone for a while and all she wants to do is push Rule to take his place. That isn't going to happen, we all know that."

He kissed the top of my head and set me away from him. "I don't know why you're always defending that boy. He's got a hot temper and a wild streak a mile long. You're a smart, beautiful girl; you have to know how Rule's story ends."

"I don't believe in skipping ahead, Dale. I read the book all the way through. Tell Margot to give me a call when she calms down, but I'm serious about Sundays. Until it's an actual family gathering, until Rule stops being vilified for just being who he is and not who you want him to be, I'm not coming. This just hurts too much."

"Fair enough, little girl, but if you need anything you know we're just a phone call away."

"I know."

"You know he wouldn't appreciate you falling on the sword for him."

"Maybe not, Dale, but it's my sword to fall on and even if nobody, including Rule himself, can see it, he's worth it. I think so and I know Remy always thought so. You might want to try to remember that the next time he shows up with pink hair."

I made my way to the driveway and paused when I saw the brothers with their heads bent close together. Rule looked mad and Rome looked sad. It was heartbreaking and impressive all at the same time. Rule saw me first and pulled away. They said something to each other in low tones and bumped fists. Rome pulled Rule into a one-armed hug and made his way over to me. I received the same treatment with the addition of a kiss on the cheek.

"I'm gonna put as many fires out here as I can over the next week or so and then make my way to the city. I'll hit you up when I can."

"Try to convince your mom to get some help, Rome, please."

"I love you, little girl. You try to keep that jackass out of trouble for me."

I brushed a kiss across his cheek in return. "I always do."

"I didn't know it was this bad, Shaw. I've missed so much by being away."

"Families are like anything else, they take work, patience, and people willing to make it work. I'm so very glad you came home, Rome."

I moved away after another hug and tossed my keys at Rule. "I have a headache. Can you drive back to the city?"

I normally never let him anywhere near my car; he has a lead foot and no regard for other drivers on the road, but I wasn't going to make it. I felt the headache growing into a migraine and all I wanted to do was close my eyes, crawl into a soft bed, and pull the covers over my head. I got into the passenger seat and curled into a ball.

Rule didn't say anything as he turned on the ignition and headed toward home. He left the radio off and didn't even try to bother with forced pleasantries. I knew he wouldn't apologize for the scene; he never did, so I didn't even bring it up. I was drifting in and out of a little nap when Gabe's ringtone started to trill from my pocket. I swore, which was something I rarely did, and turned the stupid thing off. By now my stomach was in knots and I was seeing spots in front of my eyes.

"He calls you now more than when you were dating." Rule's voice was low and I wondered if he had any idea how much my head was hurting.

"He's a pain. I told you he didn't get it."

"Is it a problem?" I cracked an eye open because it was really out of character for him to show any concern for me.

"No. I mean it's only been a couple weeks and I think he misses the idea of me more than actually being with me.

31

I keep thinking he'll get bored or find someone else and just go away."

"Make sure you let somebody know if he becomes an issue. No girl should have to deal with that noise."

"I will." We lapsed back into silence again until he cleared his throat. I'd known Rule long enough to know he was working his way up to something and I just needed to wait.

"Look, I'm sorry about this morning. I'm sorry about a lot of Sunday mornings. You don't need to keep seeing me at my worst; in fact, it's not your job to see to me at all. I'm done with forced family fun time. It's not doing anything but driving the knife in deeper, and I see that now. This drama has been building for years and it's not fair that you're still stuck in the middle of it without Remy to back you up. He loved you to death and I've done a piss-poor job honoring that."

I was in too much pain to argue the semantics of my relationship, or rather nonrelationship, with Remy to Rule yet again. No one in the Archer family seemed to get that we were friends, best friends and nothing more. The legend of our relationship had turned into a monster that I just couldn't combat, especially when the tiny amount of food I had eaten at brunch was suddenly crawling back up my throat. I lurched forward and grabbed Rule's arm. It probably wasn't the smartest move since we were going ninety-five on the freeway, but I was about to toss my cookies in a car that cost more than some people made in a year.

"Pull over!" Rule let out a string of curse words and hastily weaved around a minivan to the shoulder of the road. I got the door open and practically fell on my knees as I lost everything in a violent stream on the asphalt. Warm hands pulled my ponytail out of the way and handed me a ragged bandanna. When I could finally breathe again, I took the bottle of water he handed me and sat back on my heels while the world tilted in a bunch of different directions.

"What's wrong?"

I sloshed the water around and spit it out on the ground away from the tips of his black boots. "Migraine."

"Since when do you have those?"

"Since always. I need to lie down in the back."

He pulled me to my feet with a hand under my arm and I realized it was the first time in years he had ever deliberately touched me. We never hugged, never brushed against each other, never high-fived or shook hands. We were strictly in a hands-off type of relationship, so my system almost revolted at the contact. I groaned as he practically shoved me back into the car. I am short, so stretching out along the backseat wasn't a big deal. Rule got back behind the wheel and looked at me over his shoulder. "You gonna make it the rest of the way?"

I threw an arm over my eyes and placed a hand on my roiling belly. "It's not like I have a choice. Just be ready to pull over again if I scream at you."

He pulled back into traffic and was quiet for only a minute before demanding, "Does everyone know you get migraines?"

"No. I don't get them very often, just when I'm stressed out or not sleeping well."

"Did Remy know?"

I wanted to sigh but I just answered, "Yes."

He muttered something I couldn't hear and I felt him, rather than saw him, look back at me. "He never told me. He told me everything, even crap I had zero interest in hearing—he never shut up about you."

He was wrong, so very, very wrong, but that was Remy's secret and even though he was gone I still would go to my grave with it. There was a lot Rule and Rome never knew about their brother, things that he was scared to share, things he battled with on a daily basis. The fact that I had migraines and was irrevocably in love with Rule didn't even scratch the surface.

"He probably just forgot about it; like I said, I don't get them very often and when you guys moved to Denver and I still had to finish high school, he probably just forgot they happened because we didn't hang out as much anymore. They've been worse the last few years." I didn't have to explain it was because Remy was gone and all the stress he balanced out for me was now my own to deal with.

"That seems like kinda a big deal to slip his mind."

"Contrary to what all you Archers have stuck in your head there was a lot more to Remy than our friendship and what was or was not going on with me."

He snorted loudly. "Yeah, right. Remy was a different person after he found you. He was always a good guy, always the best of all of us, but once you came along it was like he finally found his purpose. You gave him someone to care about without any of the bullshit baggage the rest of us had. You made him better."

My heart squeezed so tight in my chest I thought for a second everything inside me was going to turn inside out. "Well, he saved me, so we made each other better."

We fell into an uncomfortable silence again until the car stopped in front of his apartment complex. He turned in the seat and looked down at me. I peeked at him from under my arm. The blue in his eyes was all but swallowed up by the paler silver and gray. "Can you get back to University Park or do you need me to take you? I can have Nash follow us since he's home from work." It was a nice offer, one I was surprised he extended, but I had had my fill of Archers for the day, and the drive from Capitol Hill to University Park wasn't that bad on a Sunday in the early evening.

"I'll make it. It's not that far." I scrambled out of the back and had to lean on the door frame while he got out of the driver's seat. We were standing so close I could see the pulse in his throat thumping under the hummingbird tattoo he had there. "Thanks, though."

He exhaled and rubbed his hands roughly over his face. He took a step back and made sure I was looking him dead in the eye when he told me, "I'm serious about Sunday. Don't show up here next week expecting me to play nice. I'm over it."

I snapped a salute with two fingers to my brow and let my body collapse in the seat he had just vacated. "Message received. My services as chauffeur slash buffer are no longer needed, which means I probably won't be seeing you around. Try to take care of yourself, Rule, seriously; somebody has to."

I shut the door before he could say anything else and didn't even wait until he moved away from the car to put it in reverse and pull away from the apartment complex. It was a short drive to my own apartment that I shared with my best friend, Ayden.

I had met Ayden freshman year when we shared a dorm room together. She was a chem major, worked at the same sports bar I did, and totally had the patience to deal with all my endless neurotic crap. Her family background was no picnic, either, so I loved that I could always rely on her to be there for me. She was also smart as hell and it had taken her exactly zero seconds to figure the reason my social life was boring and that I could never commit to any of the guys I dated was because I was hung up on Rule Archer. So when I came stumbling in hurting, with tears in my eyes, she put me to bed without questions and closed the blinds in my room while she fetched me some painkillers and a giant glass of water.

The bed depressed when she climbed up next to me as I kicked my peep-toe heels off and tugged my belt through the loops on my slacks.

"It was bad today?" Ayden was from Kentucky and her Southern drawl rolled over me like a soothing balm.

"He was with some skank again, he had a hickey the size of Alaska on his neck, my mortal enemy from high school hit on him at Starbucks, and it took Margot and Dale less than a minute to insult his clothes and hair and remind him he is not now nor will he ever be his dead twin brother. Luckily, this time they left out his job and disregard for manners, but he blew his top and stormed out. They've all decided it's best we no longer come up on Sundays, making this the second family I've been a part of that can't figure it out and just love and appreciate one another. To top it all off, Gabe has been blowing up my phone all day and I can't think of anyone I want to talk to less. So yeah, it was really fucking bad today."

She brushed a hand over my hair and laughed softly. "Girl, the situations you find yourself in."

"Tell me about it."

"Did you give him the key to his place back?"

I moaned a little and buried my head in the pillow. "No. I totally spaced out, but it's not like I'm in any hurry to walk in on him and two girls at once again. Honestly I'll be super glad to never have to see Rule's pierced junk again."

She snickered a laugh at me and rolled over onto her back so that she was staring at the ceiling. Ayden's hair was as black as mine was blond and cut in a funky short pixie style. She had big whiskey-colored eyes and a heart that was pure gold. Besides Remy, she was the best friend I'd ever had. I loved her for not making me have to lay it all out for her to sift through—she just got it. While she might not understand how I spent my time equally loathing and loving a person who viewed me as nothing more than a nuisance, she never condemned or criticized me for it.

"That boy, he is a handful."

"I don't know, maybe the space will be good for me. Maybe time away from the whole family will finally give me the breathing room to kill the way I've always felt about him. I can't spend the rest of my life walking away from other people just because they aren't Rule."

"Well, I can't say I'm sorry to see Gabe go, but you do deserve someone who treats you amazing and loves you in all the right ways. You've earned it, because no one I've ever met in my whole life loves as freely and gives as much as you do. Seeing as those parents of yours might as well be carved out of ice, that's just a damn miracle. You're a good girl, Shaw, and at the very least you deserve a good guy."

I folded my hands together on the bed and laid my cheek down on them. My head was slowly starting to stop throbbing and all I wanted to do was take a nap and maybe work on processing everything that had happened today.

Ayden was right; I did deserve a good guy. I knew what one looked like, knew what one acted like, in fact I had been best friends with the ultimate good guy. Remy embodied everything any sane girl would want in a boyfriend and yet I had never had those feelings for him, not once. I remembered clearly the first time he had taken me home with him. I was fourteen and having a really hard time fitting in with all the preppy, rich kids my first year of high school. I know now that image and brands mattered, but back then I just wanted to wear jeans and my hair in a ponytail. Remy had been sixteen and captain of the football team. He found me crying outside the girls' locker room one day after a particularly nasty verbal beat-down from Amy and her crew. He didn't make fun of me, didn't ask questions or get all weird because I was a freshman and he was a junior. He just bundled me up and carted me home with him because I was sad and alone and he didn't want me to be either of those things ever again. He told me he could tell by my eyes that I was a kind person, that I needed someone to look out for me, and from that minute on he decided he would be the person to do it. I remembered all the warm and fuzzy feelings that came with that moment, remembered the gratitude and overwhelming joy I felt at finally having someone see how worthy and deserving of unconditional love I was, but what I remembered most was everything inside me going upside down when Rule walked into the kitchen and tilted his chin at me and asked, "Who's the chick?"

My heart stopped beating, my lungs felt like they were going to collapse, my skin was suddenly too tight all over my body, and I couldn't form a rational thought or a coherent sentence. Back then I chalked it up to a silly teenage crush; all the Archer boys were good-looking and had qualities that made them larger than life. Every girl I knew had had the prerequisite infatuation with a bad boy at one time or another. Of course, they normally grew out of it when they realized the bad boy was just an ass and they deserved to be treated better. But as time went on and things changed, my feelings never did even though it was clear they were never going to be returned. Rule only saw me as Remy's little tagalong; a spoiled little rich girl, and then as we got older, as Remy's girlfriend. That sucked because I had never been any of those things and as a result I sabotaged relationships, turned down guy after guy simply because I didn't want a good guy—I wanted the one who was damaged and blind to the way I felt.

I *was* a good girl. I was loyal and honest and I worked hard and invested a lot of time and energy in building a secure future for myself. I stayed out of trouble and went out of my way to try to be the polished and perfect daughter my parents wanted me to be, and the successful, driven woman the Archers had given me the confidence to be.

What I never spent any time being was the person that I actually felt like I was. She was locked somewhere deep inside me, suffocating and still holding on to the hope that Rule would notice she was alive. It was exhausting, and in the vulnerable moments when I was brutally honest with myself, I had to admit I wasn't sure how much longer I could keep it up.

CHAPTER 3

Rule

It was a crazy busy week at the shop. I think mostly because we were right in the thick of tax refund time and people had extra money to spend. I was booked with back-to-back appointments all the way through Saturday and even went in on my day off to work on a guy's sleeve I had started a few months ago. Nash was just as booked as I was. When Saturday night rolled around we were both ready to let loose and tie one on. Sunday morning went about the same as last week, only this time when I walked the girl to her car I didn't have to worry about Shaw bursting in on a scene I didn't want her to see. I called Rome to see when he was going to come to town, but apparently things at home weren't any better after last week so he wasn't ready to leave Mom on her own yet. I wanted to care, wanted to feel bad for her, but I just couldn't muster it up.

I was getting ready to crack open a beer and plop in front of the flat-screen to relax and watch the game, when Nash came out of his room pulling on a hoodie and a black ball cap over his shaved head. He was a few inches shorter than me, built a lot stockier, but in all actuality was a hell of a lot better looking. He kept his black hair shaved close to the scalp because he had twin tattoos on the sides of his head. His bright, bright eyes looked more purple than blue and always stood out starkly against his much darker complexion. He didn't have as much metal in his face as I did, just a hoop through the center of his nose and both ears sporting obsidian gauges. For whatever reason, he kept his hands and neck free of ink, which always made me laugh because of the stuff permanently marked on his head. We were a matched set, so when we went out together it was usually a given we wouldn't have to come home alone. Nash was a much nicer guy than I was; he just looked several degrees more badass.

"Jet and Rowdy are at the Goal Line watching the game. They wanna hang out if you're down."

Rowdy worked at the shop with us and Jet was the lead singer of a local metal band we liked—they rounded out the group that Nash and I traveled in. Going to the bar to watch the game sounded a lot more fun than brooding on the couch by myself, so I put my beer back in the fridge and shoved my feet into my black boots.

Nash drove a fully restored '73 Dodge Charger. It was a monster of black, chrome, and motor. I was pretty sure everyone in the apartment complex knew whenever we were coming or going because it was just that loud and thunderous, but it was a cool ride. I knew it meant a lot to him because he had done the rebuild mostly by himself. Nash's background was a little sketchy, but since my own was less than stellar I never really pushed him to talk about it. I knew his dad had died when he was really young and that his mom had remarried some rich asshole who, to this day, Nash refused to have anything to do with. Phil, the same Phil who let us make his shop our own, had been integral in getting Nash to adulthood without a criminal record and a whole pack of illegitimate kids.

The bar was in lower downtown, or LoDo as most people actually from Denver called it. It was a popular hangout for mostly locals and industry people, and since I hadn't been around on a Sunday in years I forgot how packed it could be when the Broncos played. The guys had a table in the back right under a massive flat-screen and already had a pitcher of beer waiting. Fist bumps and head nods for greeting went around the table and a raucous cheer went up in the packed bar as the Broncos scored.

"What up, fellas?" Nash poured us a round as we settled in. Rowdy wiggled his eyebrows up and down and motioned to a spot over his shoulder toward the bar.

"Isn't this better than family time? Nobody wants to see Mom dressed like that."

The girls who worked in the bar were all dressed in sexy sports-themed uniforms; some were supersexy cheerleaders, and some were in really small jerseys and hot pants that laced up like football pants. My favorites were the tiny referee outfits that barely covered their bottoms.

"No, they sure don't." It was nice to just chill and spend time with the guys on a Sunday when normally Sundays were the worst part of the week. It was way better than getting torn to pieces by my parents just for breathing. I felt a twinge of guilt at my selfishness, but I knew enough beer would squash it.

Jet looked up from the plate of nachos he was steadily demolishing and pointed a finger over his shoulder toward the bar. "Wait until you see the chick waiting on us. Dude, just dude, there aren't even words."

Jet's band, Enmity, was pretty big in the local scene and I knew from firsthand experience he had his pick of groupies and rock chicks to choose from. If he was impressed by a chick, then she was probably a dead ten and I couldn't wait to check her out. We chatted and pounded the pitcher away in under thirty minutes and the guys were getting louder and rowdier, but we were having a good time. We needed another round sooner than later, but I had yet to see the elusive Waitress of Hotness. Suddenly the hair on the back of my neck went up and I snapped to attention. There was a blonde making her way toward the table. Her hair was so blond it was almost white and it was in twin pigtails on either side of her head. Her startled green eyes were looking at me from under razor-straight bangs. Her mouth was a bright slash of red against a pale face I was as familiar with as my own. She had on the requisite referee outfit, complete with ruffly little black shorts and fishnet stockings. She also was wearing a pair of black boots that looked a hell of a lot like my own, only girly, and they went up seriously awesome legs to rest below her knees. While I struggled with recognition and my idiot friends leered at her, Nash climbed to his feet to enfold her in a bear hug.

"Hey, girl, what are you doing here?" Shaw gave a little squeal as she returned my roommate's hug, but her eyes never left mine.

"Uh . . . I work here. I have for a while. I normally have Sundays off, but since my schedule changed and it's busy I picked them up. What are you guys doing here?"

I knew the question was directed at me, but I was still too stunned at how different she looked to respond. Nash left an arm around her shoulder and pointed at our friends. "The guy with the chops is Rowdy—he works at the shop with me and Rule. The guy shoving his face full of nachos is Jet—he sings for Enmity and we grew up together. Guys, this is Shaw—she grew up with Rule and his brothers."

I watched with a mixture of awe and repulsion as my friends practically fell over themselves to shake the hand she extended. I still hadn't said anything and it was starting to get awkward, but she just smiled and picked up the empty pitcher and told us she would be back with another in a few minutes. All four sets of eyes followed the swish of her hair and the ruffles on her ass as she walked away. I wanted to punch everyone, including myself, in the face. As soon as she was out of earshot Rowdy turned to me and reached across the table to smack me upside the head. I swore and glared at him, but made no move to retaliate.

"What the fuck was that for?"

He shook his head and pointed a finger at me. "That's the girl you complain about driving home with every weekend? That's the girl you whine endlessly about walking in on you when you're acting the fool? That's the girl you dodge calls from and avoid like the plague? Geez, Rule, I never knew you were gay."

Nash snickered and Jet busted out in a full belly laugh. I flipped Rowdy off and narrowed my eyes.

"Shut up. You don't have any idea what you're talking about."

"No? I have eyes and that chick is killer, so either you're blind or stupid, because if I was cooped up in a car with her for two hours every week I'd be thanking God—not bitching about it."

Nash shook his head. "I can't believe you didn't know she worked here. Do you really just ignore everything she says to you?"

I glared at him. "You didn't know, either, and you talk to her when she comes over on Sundays."

"I ask her if she wants coffee, not how she makes a living. Dude, admit it, you suck."

I was going to argue but he kept going. "And she *is* hot— she's always been hot. You just don't like her so you can't see it. She looks good in all that fancy crap she's normally in, but man, in that uniform . . ."

"I like her fine." I refused to comment on her hotness or

lack thereof because it was weird. Of course I had eyes in my head so I knew logically she's a beautiful girl, but she always seemed so cold and so untouchable that I never really thought of her as attractive—more like an impressive work of art that was meant for viewing in a museum than for everyday enjoyment.

"Don't lie. You two can't stand each other."

I shrugged a little. "She's like family. You know how I feel about my family."

Jet lifted an eyebrow. "I wish my family had members who looked like that."

I rolled my eyes. "Knock it off. Stop being a creeper."

She came back with not one pitcher but two and a plate of wings. She smiled at Nash and the other guys but when her bright gaze landed on me, the shutters came down. "The wings are on me. I just can't help myself from trying to make sure you eat on Sundays." She turned away with a flip of one of her pale pigtails and moseyed over to another table full of middle-aged guys in ill-fitting jerseys. I narrowed my eyes when one of them put his hand on her ruffle-covered butt. Clearly used to it, Shaw flashed her killer grin and easily sidestepped the groper. It was such a different way to see her that when she walked past the table again, clearly intent on ignoring me, I reached out and grabbed her arm.

Her eyes flashed emerald sparks as she looked at the tattooed fingers I had wrapped around her wrist. I was surprised when a jolt of electricity shot all the way up to my shoulder at the contact. I lifted both eyebrows at her and gave her a nasty sneer.

"Do your parents know you work here? What about Margot? I have a hard time believing any of the adults you try so hard to impress know that you're prancing around here half-naked."

She scowled at me and shook my hand off. "No, my parents don't know because they've never asked, and Margot knows I work in a sports bar but she doesn't know what the uniform looks like, and I'm not even close to being half-naked. Leave me alone, Rule. My roommate works here, too, and she's giving me the look that means she's about to call in the troops. Unless you want to be carted out of here by three very big bouncers you'll keep your hands to yourself and your trap shut. I like Nash, he's always been nice enough to me, but I have no problem getting you and the rest of your friends eighty-sixed if you continue to piss me off."

We glared at each other in a hostile standoff until one of her other tables flagged her down.

"Just one weekend," she muttered so low I almost didn't hear her.

I frowned. "What?"

Those eyes blazed so much at me I couldn't even pick out one solid emotion. "Just one weekend I wanted a break from dealing with you." She flounced away from me and for the first time since I had met her I realized that maybe spending time with me was as much a pain for her as it was for me. When I turned back to my friends they were all looking at me with a mixture of pity and awe. My scowl darkened even more as I chugged back my full beer in one swallow.

"What?" I could hear the surliness in my tone.

"Dude, what's the deal with that?" Rowdy was the one who asked the question, but Nash and Jet both looked like they wanted to ask the same thing.

"What are you talking about?"

Nash lifted up his beer to hide a smile. "You both looked like you either wanted to box each other or tear each other's clothes off and go at it right in the middle of the bar. What gives with that? I thought she bugged you."

"She does. She's rich and spoiled and we don't agree on anything; we never have."

Rowdy gave me a look that outright called bullshit on my claim. "I know what I saw and there is no way you wouldn't take her if she offered it up to you."

I wanted to yell at him that he was wrong, so very wrong, because before she was any of the things that annoyed me and got under my skin, she was Remy's, and there was nothing in heaven or hell that would make me forget that. Pulling in my temper, I poured another beer and lapsed into a moody silence. I wasn't attracted to Shaw. I was just seeing her in a new environment, seeing her in something other than her fancy outfits that cost more than I made in a month.

We were almost to the bottom of the second pitcher when, silently, Shaw dropped off a replacement and a really pretty girl with supershort dark hair suddenly appeared at the edge of the table. She was tall and had eyes the color of Jack Daniel's, a mouth that would give Angelina Jolie a run for her money, and a body that was meant to stop traffic. She was wearing the same uniform as Shaw; only instead of kick-ass boots she had on a pair of spike heels that probably made her taller than Nash and Jet. There was nothing on her lovely face that came across as welcoming.

Jet sat up straighter and Rowdy, who was by far the drunkest of all of us—he had started adding shots of tequila twenty minutes ago—almost fell off his stool when she posted up at the table between the two of them. Her gaze was trained directly on me, though, so I met her look for look until she finally spoke. She had a soft Southern twang and I could swear I saw Jet fall in love on the spot.

"You're Rule." It wasn't a question so I just nodded. "I'm Ayden Cross. I live with Shaw."

I wasn't sure why that was supposed to matter to me so I kept silent while my best friend whipped his head around to glare at me. I was being kind of rude, but I was buzzed and still pissed at Shaw, so I didn't really care.

"I don't know what your deal is, but leave her alone. She doesn't need you screwing with her head anymore, so just back off."

I blinked because I honestly had no clue what this babe was talking about. "I don't mess with Shaw."

She narrowed her eyes and pointed a finger at me. "I know exactly what you do and don't do, Tattoo Boy. I adore Shaw. She's sweet, nice, and the best roommate ever. You need to just go do your troubled, bad-boy act somewhere else, she doesn't need it. . . ." It looked as if she was gearing up to lay into me even more, but something caught her eye and suddenly her eyes were glowing with gold fire. "Oh my God! I cannot believe that asshole had the nerve to show up here. I need to go get Lou." She spun on her heel and marched through the crowd, leaving me reeling. I had no clue what she was talking about but clearly something had crawled up her butt. I looked over my shoulder and felt every protective cell I had suddenly come alive.

Shaw was standing by the bar. It was crowded but her white-blond hair was unmistakable. She looked stressed and freaked out while a guy in a white polo shirt crowded her into the edge of the bar. He had a hand on her shoulder and was leaning down into her face. Whatever he was saying to her made her look like she wanted to punch him in the nuts or puke on his shoes. I'd never seen a look of panic on her face like that before; she was normally so cool and unflappable. Against my better judgment I was climbing to my feet. I wasn't the type to give two shits about a damsel in distress, and this damsel, I knew for a fact, could take care of herself. But she looked like she was struggling and, despite how I felt about her, I was going to intervene.

"I'll be back in a second."

48

Since I'm tall and have a good portion of visible skin covered in designs that cry "don't mess with me," I didn't have to worry about people in the crowded bar moving out of my way. When I got close enough her eyes snapped to me and I was pretty sure I saw relief flood into their sparkly green depths. Polo Shirt leaned in even closer to her, and I thought I heard him say something about how things were going to look when he went home alone over winter break. I saw her stiffen and try to pull away, but Polo Shirt just moved in closer to keep her pinned against the bar.

"I don't care what my mother told you, Gabe. We're over. I have no interest in going to Aspen with you or your family. Stop calling me and stop showing up where I'm at."

"Baby, we're meant for each other and once you stop being stubborn you'll see how great we could be together." I hated guys who called girls "baby." Baby was what you used when you didn't remember the girl's name or you were just too lazy to come up with your own nickname for her.

She wiggled a little more and I noticed the way the guy's eyes followed the deep vee of her revealing outfit.

"Let go of me, Gabe. I didn't want to be with you like that when we were dating, and I sure as hell don't want to be with you like that now. Leave me alone."

Polo Shirt got red in the face at her blatant rejection. He was about to lean even farther into her, about to put his other hand on her, when I reached out and grabbed her wrist and tugged her free. Polo Shirt was a good four inches shorter than me so I tucked Shaw's small frame under my arm and glared at him over the top of her head.

"Sorry I'm late, Casper." Without missing a beat she put an arm around my waist and practically collapsed into my side. I had used the nickname to tease her when we were younger because her hair was almost white and I knew she hated it. Now it sounded intimate and personal, like we had some kind of secret Polo Shirt wasn't in on.

"No problem. I've got an hour or so left of my shift. Can you hang out until I'm off?" Her eyes were pleading with me to play along but I was too busy wondering why my side felt like it was on fire where we touched.

"No problem. Who's your friend?"

Polo Shirt was glaring at me and turning an alarming shade of red. He didn't even give Shaw a chance to respond.

"I'm her boyfriend, Gabe Davenport. Who are you?"

Shaw went stiff next to me and I felt her fingers clutch the back of my shirt.

"Gabe, this is Rule Archer. Rule, this is Gabe, my EX-boyfriend, only he's having a hard time getting the 'ex' part down."

"Shaw, get away from him. What are you thinking? You can't possibly think anyone is going to believe you would go from me to someone like him, can you? Just look at him, he's a mess."

I was immune to the "someone like him" tactic—I heard it all the time—but apparently Shaw wasn't. She bristled like a wet cat and made a move like she was going to poke the guy in the chest. I wrapped her back up against my side and subtly tried to calm her down by rubbing a hand up and down her bare arm.

"I've known Rule most of my life, Gabe. I couldn't care less what he looks like because he isn't anybody's puppet, and the same thing cannot be said about you. Don't think you can stand there and judge him or me, not when you're practically stalking me and trying to bully me into a relation-ship by manipulating my parents because you know they like you. Ayden is here and you can bet your ass if she saw you she's going to go get Lou. Lou doesn't like to see his girls upset so unless you want a scene I'm sure you'll never live down, go away and don't come back. You can call my mom, talk to my dad all you want, I don't want to be with you and nothing is going to change that."

He looked like he was gearing up to keep fighting but there was a sudden surge toward the bar, knocking Shaw even farther into my embrace and I took full advantage by pulling her small frame completely in line with mine. The girl was rocking some serious curves and I wondered what in the hell I had been smoking to miss it right up until now.

"We got a problem, bro?" I asked him. She pulled away from me slightly with a scowl and put her hands in the center of my chest to get a little space.

"Yeah, bro, we do. But now isn't the time or the place. I don't have time to mess around with a peon like you. Shaw, I'll see you later. This isn't over."

He shoulder-checked me and glared as he pushed around us. I gave Shaw a squeeze and let her take a step back but kept my hand loosely at her waist. I was watching Polo Shirt walk away and trying to catch Nash's eye over her head. She let out a breath that fluttered against my throat and sent a chill running across my skin.

"Thanks."

"No problem. That guy needs to get a clue." Nash finally looked up and I jerked my head toward the door, where Polo Shirt had just exited. He gave me a slight nod, stood, and said something to Rowdy and Jet, which had the two of them climbing to their feet as well. I saw Shaw's dark-haired roommate hanging by the door with a mountain of a man. She gave my friends an odd look as they filed out the door but didn't say anything. I dug my Amex out of my wallet and put it in Shaw's hand. Her luminous eyes were watching me curiously.

"Close our tab out on that, will ya? I'll be back in just a second."

She took the card and fell back a step. I tried not to notice what it did to her breasts when she crossed her arms over her chest.

"Where are you going?"

"To run an errand."

"Leave Gabe alone, Rule. He isn't like you and Rome. He was born to be a politician—threats and intimidation don't mean anything to someone like that. Just forget about him. The idea that I would leave him for a guy with tattoos and purple hair is enough of a blow to his ego to get him to leave me alone for a while, trust me. Besides, I'll talk to Lou, the bouncer. If I tell him that Gabe is harassing me they'll eighty-six him for good."

"Look, Rome would kick my ass to Nebraska if he found out some douche bag was giving you trouble and I didn't say something, plus I hate a guy who thinks he can just do whatever he wants to a girl because he has an in with the parents. I'll be back in a second; just close our tab and hold on to the card in case you have to bail one or all of us out of jail."

I thought it was funny, but she didn't even crack a smile. She was just looking at me like I had suddenly grown another head. I needed to get a move on before the asshat left.

"It'll be fine, Shaw. Seriously, I got this."

I set her fully away from me and moved around her to follow the guys out the front door. The pretty roommate caught my eye and lifted a brow. "Maybe you have redeeming qualities after all, Archer."

I flipped her off, because, well, that's what I do. I made my way to the edge of the block, where Nash and the boys were leaning against a white Lexus. A very nervous-looking Polo Shirt was pacing back and forth in front of them threatening to call the cops, waving his iPhone around and asking repeatedly if they had any idea who his dad was. I tucked my hands

52

in my front pockets and cocked my head to the side. I could see why Shaw's parents loved this guy. He was all right looking, if you went for a dude who looked like Banana Republic threw up all over him. He actually had coloring similar to mine, dark hair minus the purple and spikes, and light blue eyes, but he oozed entitlement and vanity in a way only the idle rich can. He was custom-made to be the husband who had a piece on the side while the pretty wife smiled for the cameras during election time. While my relationship with Shaw tended to be tumultuous at best, I knew on a soul-deep level that she deserved better than whatever this slimeball was selling.

"Hey, Polo Shirt, slow down a minute. I just wanna talk to you for a second." He was in the middle of telling Nash that he was going to sue him for this or that and that his dad was a judge so they would throw the book at him when he finally noticed I had joined the party. He lowered his wildly flailing arms and glared at me.

"I know who you are, you know. Shaw might think she's clever but she has a picture of you and your brothers in her room on her nightstand. Her parents have told me multiple times about her unhealthy attachment to you and your family. Her father has even threatened to stop paying for school for her if she keeps showing such questionable judgment in who she spends time with. This little encounter might just seal the deal."

I had to give the creep credit—on my own I am a fairly intimidating guy, but he was surrounded by guys who were just as big and a hell of a lot more used to physical violence than he obviously was, but the little puke held his ground. "I don't know what her fascination with a freak like you is, but it's time for her to outgrow it. She belongs with someone like me, not someone who can't go through a metal detector without clearing out his face."

Nash snickered and Rowdy laughed outright. I just shook

my head a little and lifted my mouth in a twisted grin. "I think she belongs with someone more interested in getting into her pants than into her daddy's wallet. Shaw's a good girl and she has a good head on her shoulders. The fact she wouldn't let you even round first base in six months is pretty telling, bro. From the sounds of it, you would have better luck taking her folks on a date than her. Look, she's like family, and I don't like it when people mess with my family. This is a friendly little chat because we're on a public street and I'm feeling generous. Next time it won't be public and my generosity has a time limit. Leave her alone, end of story."

He looked like he wanted to argue, wanted to say something back, but the mountain of a human being who was clearly the bouncer for the bar came around the corner. Lou looked at the guys leaning on the car and then to the heated Polo Shirt and shook his head.

"Enough. You four go back in. Ayden told me what was going on so your tab is on me. You"—he pointed a meaty finger at Gabe—"you are no longer allowed at the Goal Line; consider yourself eighty-sixed. If Shaw doesn't want you here, I don't care how much you got in your wallet or what kinda pull your old man has, this is my house and you aren't welcome. Next time you want to get all up on one of my girls or put your hands on them, you won't have to worry about these guys because I'll make sure they never find your body, understand?"

Even I didn't question that this monster meant business, so Polo Shirt gulped and nodded his head slightly. My boys pushed off the car and Nash "accidentally" shoved into him as they made their way over to where I was standing. Gabe swore and jumped into his car. He pulled away from the curb and flipped us all the bird as he squealed into traffic. The bouncer looked me up and down and flicked his impassive gaze over our motley crew.

"You friends with Shaw?"

I mean we weren't friends, exactly, but it was as close as any other explanation so I shrugged and answered, "Sure."

He nodded. "I'm Lou. I look out for the girls who work here. Shaw and Ayden just happen to be two of my favorites. They're good girls and they work hard here—they aren't here just to show their asses and get into trouble—I respect that. I don't let anyone mess with those two; in fact, I take it personally when someone tries to."

I wasn't sure why he was telling me all this but, frankly, he was one scary mother so I kept my mouth shut and just kept making eye contact.

"Shaw is a sweet kid but she tries to do too much by herself. If that asshole keeps bothering her she'll just suffer it in silence." Now he was looking at me pointedly, so I lifted an eyebrow. "I wanna know if something needs to be done about him."

"Shaw and I aren't exactly close—she wouldn't tell me something like that. You might want to have this talk with her roommate."

"I'm having it with you, son."

I wasn't sure how to respond to that, but just as I was about to say something sarcastic, the door to the bar opened and the middle-aged guys in the jerseys came spilling out and got between us. Lou gave me one last direct look, which I took as him meaning business, and went back inside. I looked back at my friends and sorta threw my hands up in the air.

"Is this what I miss when I go out of town on Sunday?"

All three of them burst into laughter and Jet decided it was time for us to move on to another bar and I ran inside to get my card from Shaw. The guys pitched in ten bucks each for me to give her as a tip and I wound my way back to the bar, where she was talking to another waitress with honey-gold hair and dressed in a cheerleader uniform. Shaw stopped midsentence and looked at me through narrowed eyes. I grinned at her and handed her the money. "Your bouncer friend picked up our tab, but the boys wanted to make sure you got taken care of."

She handed me the Amex card back. "What did you do to Gabe?"

"Nothing." She sighed and I didn't even try to not watch the way it stretched her tiny little uniform across her chest.

"Well, thanks for intervening; I don't know what his problem is."

The cheerleader was having sex with me with her eyes, and while I was normally a fan of hot chicks doing that to me, I barely even registered her because Shaw was bending over to get her drinks, and the ruffles on her butt were suddenly the only thing I could see. She was short, so I'd never really thought about her having such great legs, but they were toned and curved just right. Given enough time, I could work up some seriously awesome fantasies involving those legs and those boots and nothing else.

"His problem is you're hot, richer than hell, have parents who are connected out the ass, and you wouldn't put out. You not only left him physically hard-up but blue-balled his visions of playing golf with your dad at the country club and sitting next to your mom at the Republican convention. You dismantled everything he was trying to build."

She flipped one of her pigtails and picked up a tray full of drinks. "I gotta get back to work. You think we can ever have a Sunday not filled with drama and fights?"

I ran a hand over my messy hair and shook my head ruefully. "Sundays have never been a great day for me. I'll catch you later, Shaw."

"Bye, Rule."

I made my way back out of the bar thinking that this had

probably been the first time since I had met Shaw when she was just a kid that I had ever seen Shaw be Shaw. It made me a little nervous that when she didn't have all her guards up and all her haughty defense mechanisms in place, she seemed so fallible, so undeniably human, so approachable, and so . . . attainable.

CHAPTER 4

Shaw

I counted the pile of money in front of me for the fifth time. I was having a hard time concentrating for a few reasons: first, the bar had gotten busy so I had stayed two hours past my shift and I was dragging; second, there were ten other girls all trying to cash out and the chatter was like a swarm of bees buzzing about purses and boys; third, Ayden kept watching me like a hawk, looking for something, but I didn't know what; and finally, Loren Decker, my post-high-school Amy Rodgers, wouldn't stop talking my ear off about Rule.

Loren was a living, breathing centerfold and was what happened when mean girls left high school and entered the real world. She was vapid, boring, and made more money than most of us combined when she was on the schedule because her job was to be flirty and come across as easy—things that were hardly a stretch for her. For some reason she was dying to get every single detail I possessed about Rule. She wanted to know how I knew him, how come he had never been in the bar before, how old he was, what he did for a living, if we were dating, if he had a girlfriend, if he liked blondes, and so on and so forth. It was endless, exhausting, and I think it bothered me that yet another bimbo was just tripping over herself to fall on him. Although I knew my feelings for Rule were my burden to bear alone, I wasn't about to offer up my slutty coworker on a platter. So I just kept grunting responses and evading all the personal questions, which unfortunately didn't stop her from rambling about how good-looking he was.

"I mean I don't normally go for guys with all those tattoos and piercings like that, but oh my God, those eyes! Have you ever seen anything like them? They're like minty toothpaste or something, so pretty! And his body, I bet he works out. I mean, I normally like a guy with a six-pack, but that tall, lean thing totally works with his look. What kind of girls does he normally go for? Are you sure he doesn't have a girlfriend? Seriously, Shaw, I just want to lick that hoop he has on the side of his lip, like, so freaking bad. I can't believe you've been friends with someone that sexy and haven't gotten a piece. That's, like, against nature."

I hadn't gotten a piece of anyone, ever, not that she needed to know that. Guys had tried and I had been tempted, but every time I was close to sealing the deal my brain short-circuited and reminded me that they weren't who I really wanted and I shut down like a light going off. I looked up at her and narrowed my eyes.

"Lore, I'm trying to do my cash-out, can this wait?"

"Just give me his number," she insisted.

I was close to losing it and ready to shove the pile of ones down her throat. Ayden must have sensed the storm brewing, because she settled in the seat next to me and leveled a dark look at the blonde. There was just something about Ayden that made people pay attention to her; whatever it was, I loved her for it.

"Lore, give the girl a break. It's not like they're besties. If you wanted to ask him out you should've done it while he was here."

She made a face that probably made guys buy her things, but made me want to roll my eyes. "I would've but he was too busy checking out Shaw's ass—that's why I asked what was going on between them. I mean, he didn't even give you a hug or anything when he left, but you looked at each other like you were about to start making out any second."

Startled, I looked up at Ayden. Since when did Rule, who normally ignored me or pretended I didn't exist, start checking anything on me out? She lifted her eyebrow.

"If Shaw runs into him anytime in the near future I'm sure she'll pass it along that you want his number or she can just give him yours if he's interested. Now, let's talk about something really important: What do you want to do for your birthday? It's only two weeks away."

I groaned and gave up on trying to get an accurate count. Instead I just handed the money to Ayden and started sorting and stapling the credit card slips, which took far less brainpower. I hated my birthday. Normally, it was a fight between which parent and stepparent I was going to spend an awkward dinner with—when they bothered to remember, that is. Last year I just got a card from Dad with a check for a grand in it and a call from my mother with a promise of something when she found time—there was never time. Ayden had ended up taking me for sushi and to see some stupid romantic comedy, and the day passed, lackluster and unremarkable. Even the Archers tended to be low-key on my birthday. I think it reminded them that another year had passed and that Remy was still gone. Rome always sent me something from whatever part of the world he was in and, to date, his were always my favorite gifts. I guess since I was turning twenty this year I should try to make a big deal about it; I just didn't want to.

"Why don't we go dancing?" Loren suggested, and I looked at her like she had grown a third head. I didn't really socialize with the girls from work, but not because I didn't like them. Some of them were really sweet, and most of them were just like me and Ayden—struggling to pay bills and balance college, but they were usually also into drinking, partying, meeting guys, going out, and doing all the things that just didn't register for me. Granted, I needed the actual income far less, but it gave me peace of mind every time either of my parents tried to use the fact they paid the bills for me as leverage to get me to do something they wanted. I didn't need any more people in the world thinking I was fundamentally broken, so I just avoided those kinds of social interactions.

"Uh . . . I don't dance."

Ayden scowled at the blonde. "Plus, who invited you?"

She blinked heavily lashed eyes and wrinkled her nose. "I thought maybe since it's your birthday Mr. Tall, Dark, and Tattooed would be around. I'm telling you ladies, I'm in stage-four lust and it can only be cured by Rule."

Ayden and I shared a look and I went back to my stapling. "No, my birthday isn't a big deal so Rule won't be around. I like to keep it low-key."

"You mean boring."

I wasn't friends with Loren; in fact I wasn't even particularly fond of her, so I was about to tell her to stick it where the sun didn't shine—which was pretty out of character for me—but Ayden just kept on talking like Loren wasn't even there.

"Come on, Shaw, let's do something fun. You know your parents are just going to stress you out, and you only turn

61

twenty once. It needs to be fun and exciting." She had a glimmer in her amber eyes and I knew she was cooking something up that I would be hard-pressed to talk her out of. I shoved the piles of paper into the drop bag and took the money Ayden handed me and did my tally. We always made good money, but for whatever reason today had been very profitable. I pulled my hair out of the ties and raked my nails across my scalp.

"Let's talk about it later, okay? I just want to find Lou to walk us out, in case Gabe decided to show back up, and head home."

She hooked her arm through mine and we made our way to the main entrance. "Do you think he would have the nerve to do that? I mean, Rule and his friends seemed pretty intent on getting the point across that he back off and Lou told him to scram or he was gonna kill him."

"I don't know, Ayd. He's acting crazy. I never would have thought he would show up here and try to be all grabby and in my face. I don't know what's going on anymore. I mean, it isn't like we had some great romance and I left him heartbroken or anything. We were lukewarm on our best days. Rule thinks he's embarrassed that I dumped him, plain and simple."

"He's probably right."

I made a face as Lou escorted us to my car. We said good-bye and headed home. I was trying so hard to make decisions that were best for everyone: I wanted Rule to have the love and support of his family, I wanted Margot to get help and stop vilifying her son, I wanted Gabe to get over his deal and just move on, and mostly I wanted to stop feeling so responsible for it all.

The next week went by in a blur. I had two tests, picked up an extra shift at work, and was doing a very complicated game of Dodge-the-Ex. Gabe also went to DU and even though he was prelaw and typically on the other end of campus, he seemed to be popping up around every corner and called me at least twice a day. I was considering getting a new number, but it seemed like such a hassle that I just sent his calls to voice mail and got really good at pretending I didn't see him.

Rome called and said Margot wasn't doing any better. She was flat-out refusing to go see a grief counselor and was now blaming Rule for the fact that I refused to come to Brookside on the weekends. According to Rome she was insisting Rule had somehow brainwashed me and turned me against her. He wasn't comfortable leaving her alone just yet even though Rule was harassing him to come to Denver and hang out. I could tell he was feeling the familiar tug I often felt of being caught between his brother and his mom. I was bummed he wasn't going to be around on my birthday, but he had so much on his plate I didn't say anything.

When the weekend rolled around I was tempted to give my Sunday shift away just to avoid one more weekend of drama, but the bar was busy, and if Rule came in with his friends I didn't see him. It was still weird not having to wrangle him for family brunch every Sunday, but when my shift was over and there hadn't been any headaches or accusations or hurt feelings, I breathed my first sigh of relief in what felt like years. I was feeling so mellow I let Ayden talk me into skipping a study group and going to grab Mexican food instead. It was the first time in forever that I just felt like me and I almost didn't know what to do with myself.

Since it was the start of a new semester and I felt like I was drowning in homework, I gave away my Friday and Sunday shifts, and I wasn't scheduled Saturday since it was my birthday and everyone at the bar knew that Lou just loved me and would murder anyone who tried to make me work on the day I turned twenty.

By the time Friday afternoon rolled around, I still hadn't heard from either of my folks so I figured I was off the hook for forced family time. I did receive a text from Margot asking me to reconsider this Sunday for my birthday. I had replied that I would gladly come if Rule was invited as well and hadn't heard anything back. Ayden was being secretive about what she had planned and it was making me nervous. I would've been happy with sushi and the movies again but she kept insisting that we needed to branch out, have an adventure and do something new. Those words and her take-no-prisoners attitude seemed like a recipe for disaster, but I was trying to stay positive because she was only trying to be nice to me.

I was walking out of my anatomy class and texting one of the girls from work to remind her that she was working my closing shift that night when I bumped into someone and immediately recoiled in fear and irritation. Gabe was standing in front of me looking as wrinkle-free and immaculately groomed as always. His dark hair looked like he had been running his hands through it nonstop and when he reached out to steady me I scrambled back so fast that I almost fell backward onto my ass.

"What are you doing?" I wanted to sound indignant and hostile, but my voice cracked and I had to clear my throat to regain my composure. His blue eyes searched mine intently and I wondered how I had ever found him attractive—now he just weirded me out.

"Uh . . . you aren't returning any of my calls and you've been really hard to pin down lately."

"That's because I don't want to talk to you or see you. Get out of my way."

"Shaw, wait." He held up a hand and dug something out of his pocket and held it out toward me. "I know your birthday is tomorrow and I just wanted to get you something to say I'm so sorry for how I've been acting. I was just crazy that you might have moved on to that freak, but your mom explained that it isn't like that between the two of you. Here, take it." He shoved the velvet box toward me and I backed away like he was holding a live snake in his hand.

"I'm not taking that from you. I'm not taking anything from you. Leave me alone, Gabe, I'm serious."

"Look, Shaw, you can't honestly believe there can ever really be anything between you and that guy. Your mom told me you've been carrying a torch for him for years and that he's never even looked twice at you. You're just not his type—you're too good for him and he knows it. Just give me another chance; we make so much sense together."

I wanted to punch him, but I just let the ice that traveled through me at his words coat all the anger I felt starting to build.

"No." I didn't say anything else, just "no," because I didn't need to explain myself or my feelings or the fact that I knew most of what he said about Rule was true. I wasn't too good for him; I was just too ME for him to see me as anything other than he always had, and I made peace with that years ago. I took a few more stumbling steps backward and then turned on my heel and broke into a full-on jog to get away from him. I think he called my name, but I didn't care; I just bolted. He was starting to really freak me out and the fact that my own mother was giving out the most intimate details of my life to him just made me want to vomit. I couldn't believe that a woman who didn't even bother to make note of when I was moving out of her house for college had noticed how I felt about Rule. If Gabe didn't knock it off I was going to have to look into not only changing my phone number but also possibly get a restraining order against him.

When I got home the apartment was empty, so like a dork I made sure all the doors were double locked and that the deadbolt on the front door was closed. I hid out in my room and did homework and wallowed in the self-pity that was threatening to drown me. I didn't consider myself an overly outgoing or optimistic person; it came from years of being overlooked at home and socially awkward at school. For a while Remy had managed to pull my head out of the privileged shell I normally cowered in. I had thought for sure that when I left Brookside and went off to college I would come into my own, but instead Remy had died and I was still trying so hard to be all kinds of things to people who just didn't seem to appreciate my efforts.

I dressed nice and minded my p's and q's so that my parents wouldn't totally forget I existed. I babysat Rule and put up with his awful behavior because I wanted Margot and Dale to remember that he needed and deserved their love just as much as Remy had. I wore a ridiculous outfit to work and put up with silly girls and drunk customers because Ayden deserved a solid roommate she could rely on. And mostly I acted like interacting with Rule, watching him plow his way through the greater population of young adult women in Denver, didn't bother me and didn't kill something inside me. And doing all these things day in and day out was starting to turn the little bits that were really me into a shadow.

I knew the reason I had initially agreed to go out with Gabe was because he, in a very vague sense, reminded me of Rule. He had dark hair and light eyes, and although he was preppy and clean-cut, he still had a little bit of mischief in him that just got past my normal reservations. I had known within the first few dates there was no spark—there never was. I was always looking for something, or rather someone, that wasn't there. Gabe was polite and comfortable until he realized I didn't want things to get physical. Six months was a long time to string someone along, I knew that, but it didn't justify the bizarre obsessive behavior he was showing now, and it was just one more burden I felt I had to shoulder.

I was so ready to just let it all go. I changed into a pair of sweats and curled up on the bed to watch some Netflix. Knowing that Ayden wouldn't be home from her shift until after two, I was left to pout alone. I should be out and about, should have a phone full of friends I could call to spend a rare Friday night off with, but I didn't, and that was just sad. All I needed was a couple of cats and a pint of ice cream to make the pathetic picture complete. Sometime after my second romantic comedy and Chinese delivery I vowed to fully embrace whatever Ayden had in store for me for my birthday tomorrow because what I was doing now was depressing. My roomie was right; I needed some fun, needed to lighten up, and I was on board with however she decided to make that happen. I fell asleep watching yet another dorky girl get a fantastic makeover because for whatever reason the guy she longed for couldn't see how beautiful she was under her glasses and messy hair.

I woke up the next morning to happy birthday texts from Rome and my father. As usual, there was nothing from my mom and I hated to admit I was sad that Margot didn't send one. I decided to make breakfast and headed to the kitchen. I was surprised by a beautiful bouquet on the kitchen table and recoiled when I saw who the card was from. I was seriously going to have to do something about Gabe.

Ayden was an early riser and she went running every morning no matter how late she got in from work the night before. She motioned to the flowers with her mug and scowled. "They were on the porch when I got back from my run."

"I think I might have to get a restraining order."

"Isn't his dad a judge or something?"

I sighed. "Yeah." Getting Gabe to back off might be harder than I thought. "Do you want me to make breakfast?"

She shook her dark head and her eyes glittered at me with excitement. "No, I have the best birthday planned for you in the history of birthdays. First, we're going to Lucile's."

I loved Lucile's. It was a popular Cajun restaurant in Washington Park and probably one of the few places outside of New Orleans where you could find an honest-to-god beignet.

"Yay! Sounds good. What else is on the docket for today?"

"Shopping."

I made a face because I hate shopping. I lived in a ridiculous uniform for work and expensive, name-brand clothes that my parents insist I wear because I'm supposed to be dressing for the job I want and not the job I have—apparently doctors of any sort don't walk around in jeans and T-shirts even when they're off the clock.

Seeing my face, she grinned evilly. "No, we aren't going rich-girl shopping, we're going normal, everyday college-girl shopping. We're going to the mall, we're going to my favorite thrift store, we're going to that cool vintage store on Pearl Street, and you, my friend, are not allowed to spend more than fifty bucks on any one thing. There will be no two-hundred-dollar heels, no five-hundred-dollar cashmere sweater sets, and no perfectly tailored slacks that are hand-stitched by blind monks in the Andes or whatever. We're just going to be two normal friends spending a day blowing our tips on useless crap."

That actually sounded like fun and something I'd never done. "And then," she said, her whiskey-tinted eyes widening dramatically, "we're going to the salon and getting our hair done and mani-pedis. One of the girls in my inorganic chemistry class has this great hair—she looks like Rainbow Brite—she swears by this place. So we're going to get all pretty, put on our new, normal-girl clothes, and go have dinner at that Brazilian place we've both been dying to try."

It sounded awesome—all of it sounded awesome. I was about to launch myself at her in a huge hug of gratitude when she held up a hand. "I'm not done." She disappeared into her room for a minute and came back out with a card in a pink envelope. "Then you are going to take this very cool, very necessary birthday present I got you, and come out with me. I don't mean out to Dave and Buster's or Old Chicago, I mean *out* out. I will cram a good time down your pretty little throat if it freaking kills me."

I opened the card with mild trepidation. I didn't know what she meant by *out* out. Inside the card was a shiny wrapped present that at first glance looked like a credit card. After I read her sweet birthday wishes I carefully pulled the paper off and gasped when I saw what was looking back up at me. "Ayd, I can't use this."

The ID had my face on it, my birthday—only one year older—and looked exactly like a Colorado driver's license. In fact, it looked so much like the one in my wallet there was hardly any difference.

"Oh, yes you can. You've spent twenty years being everybody's good little girl, and I'm sick of you killing yourself

69

over it. Most girls your age go out, sneak into clubs, kiss boys, have sloppy one-night stands, get into ridiculous, drama-filled fights with their girlfriends, and you, Shaw, you don't do any of that. Tonight you are taking that ID and coming out with me and you will act like every idiot twenty-year-old I know. We're going to drink too much, act silly, and have fun—you deserve it. I can't remember the last time I saw you smile or laugh. You're letting your soul wither away trying to be someone you're just not and I can't stand by and watch it happen anymore."

"I turn twenty-one next year." I'm not sure why I thought that was a valid argument to all her more-than-accurate points, but for some reason it's what popped out of my mouth.

She shook her dark head. "Who cares? You're twenty today and you're living like you're fifty." It stung because on the last trip to Brookside, Rule had said pretty much the same thing. With a sigh I remembered my resolution last night to just turn myself over to Ayden's plan, to for once just let go. I tucked some hair behind my ears and squared my shoulders.

"Okay."

Ayden looked up under raised eyebrows. "Okay?"

"Yep. Let's do this. Let the birthday fun and debauchery commence."

She squealed loud enough to make my ears hurt and rushed around the table to wrap me up in a hug that squeezed the life out of me. "Trust me, Shaw, you will never forget today."

And she was right, because by the end of the night this birthday would prove to be life changing.

Breakfast was amazing. We stuffed ourselves so full of fried goodness that by the time we hit the mall I needed to do a few laps just to keep moving. I tried on a million pairs of jeans and ended up buying quite a few. I grabbed a pair of Chuck Taylors that I'd always wanted but had never had the nerve to buy because they would immediately be deemed inappropriate. I stocked up on boring old T-shirts and tank tops. At the thrift store I scooped up an awesome old-school leather jacket and a couple Western-style shirts with pearl buttons that I knew would look awesome with my new skinny jeans. At the vintage store I went a little crazier because I just fell in love with all the fifties- and sixties-style dresses. I looked like a character out of *Mad Men* in a few of them and like Bettie Page minus the height in a couple more. I bought a pair of heels that were peacock blue and had sequined feathers on the side and a sweet pillbox hat that I probably would never wear but adored. More important, I laughed with Ayden for hours while we tried on one thing after another. I felt like a giant weight was off my chest. It was fun, plain and simple, and the fact I had forgotten what that felt like was just sad.

At the salon I got a hot pink mani-pedi and, just for kicks, had them add little black stars. It was cool and totally unlike the normal pale and pearly colors I went for. The lady doing it had bright green dreadlocks and a tattoo across her forehead so I was thrilled when she grinned at me and told me she approved. Everyone who worked at this salon had a cool, rock-and-roll kind of vibe. I normally would have felt out of place and reserved, but they were all so nice and friendly that it was impossible to do anything but relax and have a good time. The guy in charge of my hair was a big, obviously gay African American with a shiny bald head with a big eye tattooed on it. He was dressed head to toe in leopard print and was wearing shoes that certainly cost more than mine. He was sweet and told me my hair was gorgeous and suggested I just put some layers

71

in it to give it body and life. I was all on board and even asked him if he could do something new with the color. My hair was so pale I normally avoided dying it simply because it would just be too extreme. His dark eyes gleamed in excitement when I asked for something kicky, but still respectable.

What I got was my normal ash blond with a shadow of chestnut brown underneath. It was awesome and different but understated enough not to be alarming. My favorite part was that he had bisected my superstraight bangs in half and added the darker color to one side. It was trendy and hip and so different from what my hair normally looked like. I hugged him hard in glee on my way out. He hugged me back, more than likely because I tipped him enough to take a weekend trip, but who cared, I looked awesome.

We ran back to the house to get dolled up for dinner. I put on one of my new outfits, a supertight pencil skirt and a sheer blue top with a black cami underneath. I curled my new hair, put on more makeup than I normally wore, and decided, just for the hell of it, to wear my awesome black boots that looked like something a Harley-Davidson model would wear. They gave my look a certain edge that I was feeling after a day of letting the real Shaw off her perpetual leash.

At the restaurant, Ayden's slinky red dress, which made her long legs look endless, had our waiter practically drooling into our water every time he stopped by to refill our glasses. She made me try out my new ID by ordering a drink, and it worked like a charm. Before I knew it we were both feeling no pain and having a great time bouncing from club to club in LoDo and hitting the hip dive bars in Capitol Hill. I was surprised that I didn't even need to show the fake ID at most places—turns out a tight skirt and exposed cleavage work just as well.

I was laughing hysterically at Ayden doing an impression of some guy flailing around on the dance floor. We had drawn a fair amount of attention everywhere we'd gone and had had to pay for very few drinks. At the moment a guy from CU–Boulder was telling me all about his illustrious football career, or rather he was telling my boobs about it since I don't think he had looked up from the girls once. Ayden was rolling her eyes and trying to avoid some guy in a banker suit who was offering to do her taxes for free if she gave him her number. It was silly and fun and I didn't have to work hard at the flirting or being charming. I was well on my way to being wasted, so conversation was out. All I had to do was smile and sit prettily on the bar stool, two things I was apparently getting really good at. Another cosmo, which I definitely didn't need, had just appeared before me and Mr. Football was leaning even closer to me when some sixth sense, or maybe it was my fight-or-flight response, suddenly kicked into overdrive.

I lifted my head and swiveled around on the stool, practically kneeing the leering football player. I looked around, craning my neck to see what had my skin suddenly feeling too tight, but all I saw was the regular bar crowd mixing and mingling. The football player was trying to get my attention back by running a finger up and down my bare arm; I guess it was supposed to be sexy, but now I was drunk and unnerved and I wanted him to get lost. I was suddenly ready to go, and looked around for Ayden so we could get a cab and get out of there. Before I could find her a warm hand slid under the heavy fall of my hair and settled on the back of my neck. A deep voice growled in my ear, "How in the fuck did you get in here, Casper? And what did you do to your hair?"

The football player's eyes went huge because, well, Rule

was Rule. Gone was the purple hair spiked up in a crazy mess. Now he had it all shaved on the sides and bleached out into a startling white Mohawk that was several inches tall. He had on a tight black shirt with a flaming skull in a Viking helmet on it, showing off both sleeves of tattoos, a pair of black jeans with a hole in the knee, and his heavy black motorcycle boots. He should have looked sloppy and unkempt next to the V-neck-sweater-wearing footballer, but he didn't. He looked hot and rumpled and clearly not someone to be messed with. The footballer pushed away from the bar in a hurry and vanished into the crowd.

I was drunk, admittedly probably not the best state to try to go toe-to-toe with Rule, but I liked my hair and he wasn't going to rain on all my birthday vibes, especially since he clearly didn't even remember what day it was. I shook his grip loose and sucked back the tart drink in one swallow.

"What are you doing here?"

He lifted an eyebrow at me and took up the same spot the football player had vacated, looking down my low-cut top. "This bar is right around the corner from the shop—Nash and I stop by all the time after work. I just finished with a client. I know they ID at the door, how did you get in?"

I flipped my hair over my shoulder like I had seen endless annoying girls do, only I practically fell off my stool because that last drink was letting me know just how bad an idea it had been to chug it. I grabbed the edge of the bar and Rule reached out a hand to steady me. I felt like it burned where he gripped my upper arm. Definitely should have listened to my flight response a minute ago. I put a hand on my forehead because it was warm and I suddenly felt clammy. "I need to go." It was too hot, too loud, and if I didn't get out into some fresh air, like now, I was pretty sure I was going to puke everywhere.

I tried to climb to my feet but the room started to spin around like crazy and I had to grab on to Rule's biceps just to stay upright. I was so glad I opted for my boots instead of heels—I would have ended up on my face otherwise.

"Who drove?" Rule's voice was coming from far away and he smelled really good. With a sigh I leaned into him and buried my nose in his throat. He was so tall I had to use my leverage on his arms to reach. "Seriously, Shaw, how did you get here?"

"Ayden and I, we took a cab."

"Where is she?"

"With a banker. I need to go home." I felt my boozy legs start to wobble and he locked a heavy arm around my waist to keep me anchored to his chest. It was nice. Not bothering to think about it, I wrapped both my arms up around his neck. He felt as good as I always knew he would.

"Her roommate is running around somewhere; wanna see if you can grab her? I'm gonna walk her to our place." I wasn't sure who he was talking to but a familiar voice rumbled an affirmative. The next thing I knew I was being half marched, half carried out the front door of the bar. The cold January air made me snap my head back and Rule moved me from the front of his body to his side, securing me with an arm around my shoulders. I hooked an arm around his lean waist and cuddled into him. I knew logically it was the vodka making me act crazy, but I couldn't stop it.

"We're only three blocks from my place. I'll pour a gallon of coffee down your throat and shove some chips or a frozen burrito in your face and get you a cab. You're even paler than normal and if you try to get in a car right now you're gonna puke everywhere. Why are you drunk and dressed all sexified tonight anyway?"

I shivered a little as the wind breezed across my bare legs. I turned my cold nose into his ribs and inhaled. He smelled like the antiseptic from the shop, like cigarettes from Nash, like the hair product in his Mohawk, and underneath it all the warm, earthy smell that was just Rule. In the six years I had known him, I'd never been this close to him for this long. It was enough to send my sex-deprived and alcohol-soaked system into overdrive.

"You think I look sexy?" That seemed like the important part of the conversation. We stopped at a stop sign and he looked down at me with exasperation clear in those pale eyes.

"Shaw, every guy in the bar was circling you like you were bait in the water during shark week. You know you look good, what I think shouldn't matter. What should matter is why you're suddenly dressing, looking, and acting like a different person. What's going on with you?"

I wanted to scowl up at him but that seemed too hard, especially when his T-shirt rode up in the back and my arm was brushing against nice, warm skin. I stumbled off the curb as we made our way down another block and his familiar Victorian apartment building came into sight. He pulled me in tighter to his side and I didn't even try to hide the soft sigh that fell out of me.

"Everyone thinks I need to act a certain way—you, my parents, your parents, the girls from work, Gabe. Everybody always wants me to be this, do that, walk this line, toe that line and I'm sick of it. Maybe for just once I just want to act how I want and feel how I want to feel without someone judging me and expecting something from me in return."

He was quiet as we walked up the front steps to the apartment. Maybe he was trying to translate my drunken speech because even I could hear that I was slurring between my chattering teeth. He pushed the door open and twisted the lock. It was warm inside so I shook off my jacket and pushed my shaking hands through my hair. I turned my blurry eyes on him and almost swallowed my tongue. He was leaning back against the door watching me with hooded eyes. He wasn't throwing sarcastic barbs at me or ignoring me, he was just watching me. I blew out a breath and tasted the tartness of the cranberry juice across my tongue.

I took a few unsteady steps toward him. He was so tall that I had to stand on the very tips of my toes to reach his ear. I put a hand on his shoulder and one on the door beside his head and whispered, "It's my birthday, Rule."

I expected him to move away, to gently shove me to the side, but he uncrossed his arms and placed his hands on either side of my waist. Those pale eyes flared for a second and his mouth twisted down, making the hoop on the side of his mouth glint at me. "I'm sorry, Shaw. I had no idea."

I shrugged it off and moved a step closer to him. "It's okay—my own family didn't even remember it." I pressed so close to him that my chest was flat against his. I could feel that the close proximity was having an effect on him. If I hadn't had to concentrate on my balance since I was on my toes I might have grinned at that. All I had ever wanted in life was to affect him, to get him to feel something, anything, other than simple tolerance for me.

"I know what you can do for me to make this officially the best birthday ever." I wanted to sound sure, to sound sexy and sultry, but I'm pretty sure I just sounded horny and drunk. I didn't care. I was here—the real me—the one who wanted him so desperately and always had. There was no chance at putting her back in her cage now.

I didn't think—didn't reason—just used the grip I had on him to pull myself up even taller and plant my mouth solidly over his. The ring in his lip was shockingly cold against my own; the rest of him was undeniably hot and hard. It was everything I had ever wanted, and even though he didn't kiss me back, I still ranked it up there as the best birthday gift ever. I went to settle back down on my booted feet when something shifted, something changed, and Rule went from a passive recipient to something else entirely.

CHAPTER 5

Rule

Shaw was drunk—really, really drunk. She was also dressed like something out of a retro fantasy and had on those boots that make me want to drool. I had been grumpy and moody all week—my friends had noticed, my clients had noticed, the chick I'd walked out on on Saturday night noticed. I couldn't put my finger on it. At first I thought it was Rome; I was pissed he wouldn't just tell Mom to grow the fuck up and get over her shit. I wanted him to spend time with me, to have some good times before shipping back out to the desert, but he wasn't ready to give up hope that he could fix our fractured family, and I didn't want to fight with my brother, the freaking war hero. I thought maybe I just needed to get laid, but the hot blonde I went home with on Saturday had started to annoy me in the car on the way to her place. By the time we got to her room the last thing I wanted was to see her naked, so I bolted. Sunday came and went and my mood got darker. The guys suggested going to the Goal Line, thinking maybe I needed a dose of verbal ass-kicking from an ice-cold blonde to get me out of my moodiness, but I refused and instead spent the day brooding and playing *Call of Duty*. I had no idea what my problem was, but now, with Shaw all but plastered to the front of me, I was starting to get an idea.

I hadn't been able to get the sight of Shaw and her ruffle-covered ass out of my head for days. Call me shallow, call me a chauvinistic pig, but there was just something about seeing her all sexed up and barely dressed that had made me look at her in an entirely new light. It was like being introduced to her all over again; the prim and proper little lady that Remy had worshipped overtaken by a sexy coed that had me up at night thinking X-rated thoughts.

Now with her looking at me all big-eyed and swaying unsteadily, I knew the right thing to do was fix her up and send her on her way. But then she kissed me and I was pretty sure I forgot my own name. I was too stunned to react at first—I mean, I had kissed hundreds of girls and there was always something nice about it, but Shaw kicked nice to the curb and went right into insanity inducing.

After I got enough blood back from below my belt, I realized that she was pulling away or, rather, falling away. And yes, I was a certified asshole because I knew she was sauced and I knew she was, for all intents and purposes, still my twin brother's girl. None of that stopped me because she tasted sweet and tangy and felt better than anything I could remember in my entire life. She had on some kind of slinky top that was rubbing erotically across my chest, plus her hands were wrapped around my neck and playing with the last pointy spike of my new haircut—it was all going right to my dick, which was screaming at me to do something. So like a bastard I did.

I picked her up because she was short and I was tired of bending over. Her skirt was tight so I had no problem moving it up her shapely calves so that she could get her legs wrapped around me. She made a gasping noise and I maybe, possibly, would have stopped what I was doing to her mouth if she hadn't used her new position to grind against my hard-on and get her hands up under my T-shirt. Of all the things I had ever thought about Shaw, the fact that she would go off like a bottle rocket when touched just right was not one of them. She always looked so cool and so collected, but now she was tugging my shirt off over my head and doing something with her tongue on my lip ring that was making my eyes cross. I knew—logically at least—that Nash was probably only a few minutes from walking in the door with her roommate and this had to stop. There was no way I would be able to live with myself if I let this get out of hand while she was drunk. I set her down on unsteady feet when I felt her push away from me, hoping that maybe, just maybe, even wasted she would be the voice of reason.

She just looked at me through hooded eyes the color of jade and licked her lips, which looked very thoroughly worked over—courtesy of yours truly. Nothing on this planet had ever been hotter.

She started pulling at the ties on her silky top and moved past me toward my bedroom. I forgot that she knew where my bedroom was, that she knew her way around my place— she had a damn key. It was on the tip of my tongue to tell her to stop, to tell her I would just put her to bed and she could just sleep whatever this was off, but as I followed behind her the blue top hit the floor followed by the black camisole and then the skirt that did amazing things to her ass. I picked up the discarded clothing and tried to talk myself off the ledge. I couldn't do this, wouldn't do this. It was bad enough I had kissed her like a sex-crazed lunatic. I needed to get control back, like yesterday. This was Shaw, not some bar bimbo. Not someone I could mercilessly kick out in the morning and never speak to again.

"Shaw." She turned to look at me over her shoulder and I think I blacked out for a second. I dropped the pile of clothes in my hands on the floor and tried to unstick my tongue from the roof of my mouth. I had seen a lot of girls naked, but none of them were this girl; none of them came anywhere close. Somehow she managed to get out of those tall motorcycle boots without falling on her face and she was staring at me with her big green eyes, clad in nothing more than a few scraps of black lace that were designed for aesthetics rather than function. Every good intention, every idea that I should be the good guy and do the right thing, went out the window.

She was all ice-cool hair, perfect pale skin, tiny little waist and high "touch me, please God, touch me" breasts. She had a body made to make men stupid and I wasn't immune. I took a fumbling step toward her after kicking the door closed behind me.

Somewhere my conscience was whispering I should just put her to bed and go find a giant bottle of Crown to crawl into and a cold shower to get my libido back in check, but none of that was going to happen because she met me halfway and her little hands went right to my belt buckle.

"Shaw," I tried again. I put my hands on her shoulders and where I thought I was going to push her away, my body betrayed me, and I ended up pushing the straps of that fancy bra off her shoulders. She pressed close to me, her hands making short work of the belt and the zipper on my pants. Her lips fluttered over the pulse pounding rapidly at my throat. Her hands trailed lightly over my chest and across my abs, which were tense with desire. One of her legs slid between mine and rubbed against the evidence that I wasn't going to stop her regardless of knowing it was the right thing to do.

"Stop thinking so hard." Her voice was all husky and cloudy with desire. She was the last person on earth I should be contemplating doing this with, but even as objections broke through my haze of lust I used one hand to unhook her bra and the other to tangle in her hair as I sealed my mouth over hers.

Kissing Shaw was a different experience from kissing any other girl. For one, she was really good at it. Most girls got lost or a little confused because of the lip ring and the metal barbell in the center of my tongue, but Shaw seemed oblivious to both of them and kissed me like she had been born to do it. She was also a lot shorter than most of the girls I normally hooked up with so there was an entire learning curve involved and I had to figure out a way to get all the best parts of us lined up. She didn't seem to care at all that I was a little rough, that I was suddenly impatient. I felt like if I gave myself too much time to get my head around what I was doing I would falter and stop. And man, I really, really didn't want to stop, because her hands had found their way into my pants and my dick would kill me if I pulled the plug now.

She tugged the denim down over my ass and I pulled her up so that we were pressed together chest to chest. I shrugged the pants the rest of the way off and gave her a little push so that she fell back onto my rumpled bed. It took some maneuvering and a few curse words to get my boots off and when I went to crawl up onto the bed my brain short-circuited because all she had on were the barely-there lace panties and a dreamy look on her face. A lot of girls had been in this bed; in fact, last weekend had been the first time in a long time I had spent the night alone. Even though I was in a haze of testicle-squeezing desire I knew that, beyond a shadow of a doubt, none of them had ever looked like Shaw looked against the dark sheets and comforter. She slid an appreciative eye over my naked form, not like she hadn't seen it before, but somehow now that I was sprawled out on top of her, the look was more "do me" and less "Rule, you're gross."

Her hand brushed over the tattoo of the sacred heart on the center of my chest and up along the two giant rib pieces that covered most of my torso. I had a lot of color and a lot of artwork decorating my skin and when I was naked it tended to be a lot to take in and had been overwhelming to some of my less adventurous bed partners. I mean, I'm not vain or conceited but I know I'm all right to look at. I'm tall and tend toward lean and fit and I go to the gym a few times a week, but none of that really mattered because she was looking at me like I was everything she'd ever wanted and it was doing weird things to my head. I also had a barbell pierced through the head of my penis, which meant I was both brave and idiotic, because half the chicks who saw it had no clue what to do with it. Shaw had walked in on me enough times to know that it was there, but she didn't seem to care either way. She let the pad of her thumb brush across the top ball of it, which made me suck in a breath.

I realized I was letting this girl call all the shots. I was about to have sex with her and we had barely said a word; she was touching me, making me go crazy and I was just letting her. I needed to get with the program, so I hooked my fingers in her tiny little underwear and pulled them down her legs. She shivered in response and now that she was finally fully naked and trapped under me there was a hint of trepidation in her mossy gaze.

"You're beautiful." I had said it to many others before her, but I think this was the first time I meant it.

She put her hands on either side of my head and I realized my new hairdo wasn't exactly an easy one to work with where sex was involved. There was nothing up there for her to hold on to, nothing up there for her to run her fingers through—it was all spiked up and manhandled into intimidating spikes—not that she seemed to care. She scraped her fingernails across my scalp and gave me a lopsided grin. I couldn't tell if the booze was wearing off or she was finally starting to realize we were naked in bed and about to cross a definite boundary, but a hint of the Shaw I was used to dealing with was starting to surface.

"So are you. You shouldn't be, but you always have been. I remember the first time I saw you I couldn't believe you were Remy's twin. He was so handsome, always so put together, but you . . . God, Rule, you are and were just perfect."

The fact that she brought Remy's name up while her hand was wrapped around my dick should have been like ice water on the moment. It wasn't. I kissed her below her ear and let my teeth nick her neck and she made a noise that did something to the center of my chest. She hooked a leg up over my hip so that all her heat was pressed up against my hardness. I blinked for a second because I felt like I was forgetting something. She was wrapping her arms around my shoulders and panting as I brushed kisses across her puckered nipples. Just as I was about to let her pull me in, a shiver of apprehension slammed across my spine and I pushed off her. "Condom." I'd been having sex since I was fourteen years old and it didn't matter who the girl was or how drunk I was—I never forgot. The fact that my head was spun around by her and I was so lost in what we were doing that I almost put both of us at risk scared the shit out of me.

"I have one in my purse."

I looked at her and blinked. "I have a box in the night-stand, Shaw. Come on, do you really want to do this? Think about it. You're wasted. You're probably going to regret it in the morning."

She sat up and her cool two-toned hair fell forward to cover the top of her swollen breasts. She looked like every naughty dream I had ever had of her and I couldn't believe I was trying to talk her out of doing this with me. Her eyes suddenly got glassy and I knew she was going to cry. She went to crawl past me off the bed but I trapped her in my arms and rolled her so that we were once again lined up.

"Don't cry."

"You never wanted me."

I was stunned I just let my mouth fall open. "Uh . . . I'm pretty sure you can feel the proof that that's not true. In fact, you just had your hot little hands all over it."

She shook her head and her silky blond hair rubbed across my chest. "That's not what I mean."

"What do you mean?" She wiggled a little against me and reached an arm up for my nightstand drawer. If it had been anyone else I would have freaked out, but this was Shaw. Anything that was in that drawer wouldn't surprise her or freak her out; including the loaded gun I kept in there. I heard the cellophane wrapper and felt her hands back below my waist. I wasn't sure I remembered ever having a condom put on me or it ever feeling so good.

"Rule, it's my birthday and my life is a freaking mess most of the time. Can you just for once do something nice for me, please?"

What red-blooded American male would turn down a dead-sexy, naked blonde who asked him to please do it to her? Not me, no way, no how, so I kissed her again, let my tongue slide against hers and lifted her leg up over my hip. I liked to think I knew what I was doing in this department—after all I had more practice than I cared to admit—but for some reason with her I felt like what I was doing was all new. She kissed me back and gasped softly as I started to slide in. She was tight and tiny, hot and wet, and I thought I was going to die if I didn't get to get all the way in in the next second.

She whispered my name across my neck and arched her back. Her nails dug into my shoulders as I lifted her up a little bit and tried to push all the way in. I swore and she froze as there was something most definitely in the way, but my momentum was too great and I had her too keyed up to stop. She snapped her wide eyes to mine as her mouth made a little O of surprised pain as I glared down at her.

"What the fuck, Shaw?"

She gave her head a little shake and lifted her other leg up around my hip and moved against me in a way that made me utter every swear word I knew. "Don't stop. Rule, please don't stop." She was breathy and it was too late for that to be an option anyway. She felt better than anything I had ever felt in my life and there was no way I was going to stop now, not unless I wanted to walk funny until I was thirty. I let the fingers of one hand tangle in her hair and propped my weight on the other so that I wasn't crushing her and went about having the best sex of my life with a goddamn lying virgin.

She moved just the way I wanted her to, touched me in ways that would wake me up in the middle of the night remembering them. She kissed me like she had been created to do it exactly the way I liked and matched my rhythm the way only people who've had lots and lots of sex together normally managed to do. Every time she whispered my name or made a sexy sound of satisfaction and delight it made me feel ten feet tall. I hadn't had sober sex in a long time and I hadn't had sex with someone I knew for more than a few hours in a long time, either. I couldn't believe the difference both those things made.

I wanted it to be good for her, wanted it to turn her inside-out like it was doing to me, and since it was her first time, I wanted to make sure that it was what she was going to have to compare every guy to after me.

As we moved together she arched her back and put her hands back on my head. "Oh my God, Rule." She was close; I could feel the little tremors all along my cock. There was no way I was going to ruin this for her so I touched her in a way that was guaranteed to make her shatter and was rewarded with big eyes and a gasp of surrender. I was super relieved because I wasn't going to last much longer. I buried my nose in her neck and followed her over the edge. By the time we were done my arms were shaking and I was breathing like I had run a marathon. I slid out of her and rolled to my side, all ready to have the regret and despair settle on me, but her eyes had drifted closed so I got up to go into my bathroom and clean up. I pulled on a pair of sweats and grabbed a washcloth for her. When I went back into the room she was curled up on her side with her cheek resting on her folded hands, which made her look all of sixteen years old. The steady rise and fall of her chest indicated that she was asleep, so I cleaned her up the best I could without waking her and settled on the bed next to her. I crossed my arms under my head and stared up at the ceiling.

What the hell had I done? And what in the hell had Remy been doing with her for all those years if he hadn't been sleeping with her? They had always claimed they were just friends, but no one had believed them. The love they had for each other, the protectiveness, the camaraderie they shared had often made me jealous, and now I didn't know what the hell to think. Shaw had been a girl who fell into the "girls I can't or won't have sex with" category for most of my life, but now I had blown that all to smithereens and I didn't know what to do about it. She wasn't just some chick I could never call again, that I could shove out the door the next morning. Add in the fact that it was probably the most intense, best sex of my life, and I felt like I was losing control. I shouldn't feel that way about Shaw; she shouldn't be the one to rock my world like it had never been rocked before. Frankly, it weirded me out that she was better and more turned on by my ink and piercings than the majority of girls I brought home. Now I had disarray on my hands and the wrong girl in my bed and I didn't have a clue what to do about it.

I fell asleep sometime after the sun started to come up and when I woke to the sound of my phone ringing the first thing I did was look on the other side of the bed. All the things from the night before slammed into my head. Shaw was gone. The pile of clothes I left on the floor last night were folded neatly on the end of the bed and none of her pretty little things were left. I groaned and threw an arm over my eyes while answering the call.

"What?"

My brother chuckled in my ear. "Did I interrupt something?"

When I moved to sit up, something crinkled under my hip, and I pulled it out. On a plain piece of sketch paper I'd had lying around for drawing up designs for clients she had written in her neat, girly script:

Best birthday gift ever! —Thanks!

She didn't sign it, didn't say she would call or ask me to call her. It was plain and simple, and I wasn't sure if it made me elated or furious. My brother was still waiting for a response, so I shook the cobwebs in my head loose and sat up in the bed. It smelled like sex and her.

"No, I just didn't sleep good last night."

"That's what happens when you bring strangers home with you—you have to make sure you sleep with one eye open so they don't rob you or stab you while you sleep."

I groaned. "Dude, you need to get out of the army. Not every stranger is an insurgent."

He muttered something under his breath that I didn't catch. "Hey, I'm gonna come to Denver for the week. My shoulder is acting up and I need to touch base with my orthopedic surgeon, plus Mom is getting on my last nerve. Shaw refused to come over for lunch today because Mom wouldn't invite you as well. Now she's convinced you've somehow corrupted her darling girl. I keep telling her she needs to see someone and Dad even agrees, but she's just so stubborn. I guess that's who we get it from."

I winced a little, glad the conversation was happening over the phone. I was sure guilt colored my face. My mom would freak out to extreme levels if she had any clue just how thoroughly I had corrupted Shaw.

"How much longer before you have to go?"

"I have to be medically cleared first and I'm supposed to meet with a VA counselor to make sure that I'm not suffering from PTSD because of the accident. I have to have a clean bill of health all the way around before I go back."

"Well, it'll be nice to finally get a chance to hang out without all the family drama."

"Yeah, I've been calling Shaw all morning to ask her if I can take her out to dinner or something for her birthday. I'm sure her moronic parents didn't do anything again and I hate the idea that she probably had to spend it alone. You should get off your lazy ass and come with us if I get a hold of her."

I started to choke a little. It was on the tip of my tongue to tell him that she most definitely hadn't been alone, but this was Shaw and, even as close I am to Rome, he didn't need to know what we had been doing last night.

"Naw, I think she's had enough of me. I ran into her a few weeks ago and I see her around here and there. I think it's a nice break for her not to have to deal with me every weekend."

He laughed a little. "You're probably right. I'm gonna crash with my buddy Drew since I don't think my shoulder is up to sleeping on your shitty couch and he has the room, but I'll hit you up when I roll into town. If I can't get in touch with Shaw, you and I can go grab dinner somewhere and you can disgust me with all the tales of your latest conquests."

I rubbed a hand over my tired face and shoved Shaw's note into the nightstand. I could still feel her hands moving all over me.

"You need to get off your butt and start having some conquests of your own. You're a hero, dude, chicks eat that stuff up."

"I'm not like you, Rule; I'm not twenty-two and living life by the seat of my pants. Right now I want to get healthy and finish up my tour without any more dead bodies. I've seen the worst humanity has to offer and in the last six years I've buried more friends than I've made. I get out of the army in less than two years and I don't know what the future holds for me so nailing every pretty girl in my path is pretty low on my priority ladder. One day you'll understand."

He wasn't wrong. My priorities were very different from his. I made good money, had a ton of savings, and drove a nice car. I was viscerally aware that the majority of my time was spent trying to outrun the shadow of my dead twin. I wallowed in superficial relationships so no one could get close to me, no one could judge me and find me lacking. I sought out girls who were easy, who had zero expectations beyond what I offered—a good time and a few mindless minutes of release. I have never had a girlfriend, and I've never let anyone all the way in because I was scared that I wouldn't be enough once they got down to the core of who I am. I knew it was messed up, knew I was an emotional train wreck, and the thing with Shaw was just bound to make it even worse.

"Whatever. A good time never killed anyone. Call me later."

I tossed the phone on the bed and went into the bathroom to take care of business. When I went into the living room Nash was sprawled out on the couch watching an early game on the flat-screen. He had a mug of coffee in one hand and a doughnut in the other.

"Morning."

He flicked his gaze up to me. "What's up?"

"Nothing. Did you see Shaw this morning?"

He nodded and held up the doughnut. "She left these. So what's the deal with that? She was in the kitchen this morning, so I assumed she stayed the night with you. I thought you were going to put her in a cab."

"Where did her roommate end up?" I tried to change the subject as I got my own coffee.

"I offered to bring her back here to wait for Shaw, but she was having a good time so we had a few more drinks, then I called her a cab. She seemed to think it was a brilliant idea that her very intoxicated friend was going home with you. Why is that?"

I grunted and sank down on the couch next to him.

"I dunno. Shaw and I have all kinds of twisted history, who knows?"

"But she spent the night with you?"

"Yeah."

"And I'm assuming—because I've known you since forever—that you didn't spend the night discussing politics and watching TV?"

I glowered over at him. "No."

He shook his head and made a *tsk-tsk* sound. "What were you thinking?"

"I wasn't, clearly."

"Dude, she's not one of those girls. You can't just have me escort her out in the morning and never talk to her again."

"Hey, I woke up alone this morning. I didn't make her go anywhere."

"But you would've and Shaw is way too classy and smart to do a walk of shame. Man, I can't believe you hooked up with your brother's girl. You really do have a problem. That's a whole mess I wouldn't even jump into no matter how hot the girl was."

I made a strangled noise and reached forward to put my elbows on my knees. "Let's just say I don't think there is any real reason to worry about tarnishing Remy's memory. I don't know what was going on between those two for all those years, but after last night there is undeniable proof that they weren't sleeping together."

Nash swore and his eyes got wide. "She was a virgin?"

I nodded. I probably shouldn't be sharing all this with Nash, but I was confused and he was my best friend. I was in over my head.

"She was a virgin and gave it up to *you*? Holy shit, bro, that's like a huge deal!"

I sighed. "That's what I thought, but then she was gone when I woke up. She was pretty trashed last night, so maybe it was just beer goggles and too many martinis that made the choice for her."

"She seemed fine this morning. I mean, she looked hungover and pretty worked over, but she wasn't nervous or weird or anything. She called Ayden for a ride and ran out for breakfast while she waited. I dunno, man, she didn't seem all swoony in love or stalker pissed-off, she just seemed

93

like normal Shaw. Granted, I always thought she kinda had a thing for you."

I turned to him with a look of bewilderment. "What?"

"She puts up with your shit no matter how bad it is. Don't you remember that one New Year's she showed up to get you and you brought home the redhead and her friend? That was a freak show and Shaw didn't even blink, she just tossed you your pants and told you to get it together. She lets you be all moody, surly, and grumpy and doesn't even bat an eye—and trust me, dude, that shit gets old superfast. She's willing to go to battle with the only parents she's known to show her any love because she wants them to treat you right and quit blaming you for Remy's death. She isn't doing any of that for Margot or Dale, and she sure ain't doing it for Remy. The only person any of that benefits is you. Even as stubborn and self-involved as you are, you have to be able to see that."

"But she's Shaw. Perfect Shaw. Even when she was little she was untouchable and aloof. She would be over at the house all the time with Remy and every time I said anything or did anything she would just look at me like I was an idiot."

He snorted. "You were an idiot. You don't remember being sixteen? We were a nightmare and never very nice to her. You made fun of her hair, teased Remy mercilessly about spending all his time with her, you were an ass."

"I was?"

"Dude, you still totally are. And Shaw is Shaw. She's so freaking beautiful it hurts to look at her sometimes, but she doesn't even know it. She's still untouchable because she's always going to be richer and smarter than we are, but she doesn't care about any of that. She's cool, she doesn't care that you're just you, and honestly, Rule, any chick who can put up with the headache that is you, well I'd put a goddamn diamond on her finger."

I punched him in the shoulder. "I'm not that bad."

He gave me a look. "Yeah, you are. Think about it; it only took seeing her dressed as a sexy referee to get you to notice she was an actual girl after all this time. You suck."

"But, man oh man, did she look good in that outfit."

"See, total suckage. So what are you going to do now, call her?"

"I don't know. Rome is coming to town, and since I like my privates located where they are I need to keep this on the down low. I don't think she'll say anything to him."

"Probably not. She knows it would drive your crazy mom right over the edge."

"Yeah."

"So." He paused and gave me a pointed look. "Was it worth screwing everything up?"

I let my head fall back on the couch and stared up at the ceiling. "It so totally was."

I had had the best sex of my life with a girl I had thought was way out of my league and in love with my dead brother. Yeah, Nash was probably right, if anybody could put up with all the crazy I was rocking I should probably lock her in quick because even I could see how seriously screwed up I am.

CHAPTER 6

Shaw

"Stop looking at me like that." I fiddled with my hair and adjusted the scarf I had around my neck. Rome was looking at me like he was trying to see inside my head and I didn't like it one bit. I ignored his calls all day Sunday because I was still trying to get my head around the fact that I had drunkenly demanded Rule take my virginity and I had been sore—from both the booze and the bed acrobatics. I had a test Monday and had to work a closing shift, and on Tuesday I did a volunteer shift at the children's hospital and suffered through an ungodly dinner with my father and his new wife. Rome had been forced to wait until today to take me on my belated birthday dinner. Ever since I'd sat down he had been peering at me intently and I had to keep checking to make sure that the scarf was covering the lovely hickey Rule had left Saturday night. I'd gotten enough flak from Ayden about it and I didn't need Rome joining in on the "Shaw Is an Idiot" bandwagon.

"It's the hair. It's nice but I'm just used to the all blond. You look different, more mature."

"Thanks, I like it."

"I don't think I've ever seen you in jeans, either."

"I went shopping for my birthday. I decided that the pearls and heels didn't need to be worn every time I left the house. I have plenty for when it's time to play society maven for the folks."

"Speaking of birthdays, I brought this from Mom and Dad." He handed me a little bag and I set it on the table between us.

"Your mom won't talk to me; I tried to call her the other day."

"She's having a hard time now that you laid down the law. She always viewed you as an ally in the 'Rule Needs to Get His Act Together' war. She just doesn't see what she's doing to him, to us."

I sighed. "I know. That's why I had to stop."

"This is from me." He gave me a gift certificate to my favorite bath and body store. I smiled and gave him a big hug. I just love this guy; he looks like a warrior, but he has such a good heart.

"Thank you, Rome, this is so sweet. I'm so glad you're home."

"Me, too, little girl. I tried to get Rule to come out but he had a late client. He was grumbling about having to draw yet another Harry Potter tattoo or something. I guess I forget he actually works."

I peeked inside the bag—it was a picture. Margot had found one of the very first pictures taken of me and Remy and put it in a lovely silver frame. I was so small and awkward and Remy was so tall and handsome—we looked ridiculous. It was a sweet gesture and it brought tears to my eyes. I showed it to Rome and slid it back into the bag.

"I miss him every day," I said.

"I do, too. I miss the way he made everyone act right."

I laughed a little and sipped some of my iced tea. "Yeah, he was good at policing the way everyone treated each other. He didn't tolerate any of the silliness we tend to allow."

"Rule said he's run into you a couple times, how was that?"

I cleared my throat and willed the scarlet blush that had been accompanying Rule's name all week to stay at bay. "Kinda weird. He came into the bar I work at with a bunch of friends on a game day. It's strange to interact with each other like normal people."

He nodded and I noticed the waitress openly checking him out when she dropped off our dinner. "He told me you've been having some issues with your ex."

I groaned and gave my head a shake. "He has a big mouth." Among other things, but I wasn't going to let my dirty mind go there.

"So what's the deal, little girl?"

I made a face and shoved a bite of pasta into my mouth. "Rule already talked to him, so did the enormous ex-marine who bounces at the bar. Gabe's just a spoiled guy who isn't used to rejection. He's having trouble hearing me say no."

"Is he still calling you?"

I didn't want to lie so I tried to change the subject. "What did the doctor say about your shoulder?"

He narrowed his eyes at me and picked at his own food. "He thinks I need to up my physical therapy and if that doesn't work I might need a second surgery; either way I'll be home longer than I thought."

"Well, that's good isn't it?"

He shrugged and I got the impression that he wasn't as excited about the prospect as I was.

"I guess."

"You want to go back?"

"I want to finish my tour; I don't want my tour to end like this. I hate leaving my platoon hanging. I've been in the army for six years, Shaw; I don't really know how to do anything else."

"You have a whole lot of people who love you, Rome. Getting out of the army and being safe shouldn't be what scares you."

"I know that, but it is what it is."

We lapsed into a minute of silence before he went back to Gabe. "What did Rule say to the ex?"

I lifted a shoulder and let it fall. "I dunno. He told him to leave me alone and Gabe immediately jumped to the conclusion that the reason I dumped him was because of Rule. Everyone always thinks that everything I do is because of Rule. It gets old."

Rome stared at me with eyes that looked so much like his brother's. I could tell by the twist in his mouth that I was not going to like what he had to say.

"Isn't it?"

I glared at him and poked at my plate. "No."

"Rule convinced Remy to move to Denver as soon as they graduated so you decided to move here, too. Rule acts like an ass, making things with Mom and Dad impossible, so you decided to play peacemaker and drag him home every weekend. Rule acts and everyone has no choice but to react and we've all been doing it for years, you included."

"I didn't break up with Gabe because of Rule." That wasn't entirely true but I didn't need Rome trying to pick it apart.

"Really?" His incredulous voice had me bristling. "I don't know all the ins and outs of your relationship with Remy—"

I interjected automatically, "We were just friends, best, best friends."

Rome went on like I hadn't even said a word. "But I do know that when you thought no one was looking you watched Rule like a hawk. I know that every time he came stumbling home drunk, reeking of sex and cheap perfume from whatever teenage tramp he talked into letting him in her pants, you looked like he had kicked you in the gut. I know that every Sunday you looked the same way when you brought him home, so, Shaw, are you really going to try to tell me that the choices you make don't involve Rule?"

I sighed and pushed the plate away, my appetite suddenly gone. "What do you want me to say, Rome? My life has been entangled with the Archer boys for as long as I can remember. How much truth do you really think you can handle? I mean, some of it just isn't anybody's business. You want to hear that from the second Remy brought me home I loved him but that I was *in* love with Rule? Do you want to hear that Remy knew and took that secret to his grave? Do you want to hear that I spent years and years being sad and alone with only Remy and you guys as friends, but it was okay because you guys were all I needed? Do you want to hear that every day my heart broke a little more because Rule had no idea I was alive? Do you want to hear that without your mom and dad I would have probably been forced into some boarding school and then some hallowed Ivy League college just so my parents didn't have to deal with me? Come on, Rome, what do you really want to know?"

By the time I was done my voice was bitter and I had twisted my napkin into a little ball on my lap.

"Why did Remy keep you so close if he knew you were all tangled up by Rule? He had to know that wasn't a match that was going to happen. Rule doesn't do anything that takes work, and as much as I love you, little girl, you aren't easy."

These were the questions that I wished Remy were around to answer. I sighed. "He had his reasons, one of which was to keep me as far away from my family as he could. He didn't want me to turn into a Stepford daughter, even though he was only partly successful. Sometimes I still don't feel I can get out from under all their expectations."

He tapped his fingers on the table. "So you've been in love with my brother since you were fourteen?"

I snorted. "Pretty much, and everyone else in the world seems to know it but him." I tried really hard to keep the memories from Saturday night at bay.

"Why don't you tell him?"

"Uh . . . you've met your brother, right? Mr. I'll Bang Anything with Big Boobs and a Negative IQ? Mr. I'll Do What I Want When I Want? Rule doesn't need to know because it won't change anything."

Rome shrugged his good shoulder and winked at the waitress as she dropped off our bill. "I don't know, maybe it would be good for him to know. He's lived his life as a substitute for Remy for so long, maybe it would wake him up to know someone as good as you, as kind and loving as you, has feelings for him and has for a long time. I know deep down he's a good guy, he just buries it under so much bullshit it can be hard to find."

My plan was to avoid Rule until hell froze over. I didn't regret sleeping with him; in fact, it had lived up to every expectation I had ever had of sex and, in all truthfulness, my ideas of sex with him. There wasn't any other person I could have imagined giving my virginity to. While I wish I had been sober and that it had been based more on emotion than physical attraction, the deed itself had been amazing and worth any twinge of remorse I had. I knew my relationship with Rule would never be the same and I had to be okay with that. I refused to be the girl who pined after him, who stalked him and called him a hundred times a day. I decided the morning after it was all said and done that I was lucky it had been as nice as it was and if that was all I was ever going to get from Rule it was going to be enough.

"No, his knowing wouldn't change anything; it would just make me feel worse. We both know I'm not his type and I've dealt with enough rejection from people who are supposed to love me to last a lifetime. Rule and I can just go on being uneasy companions when we're forced to spend time together and that'll just have to be how it is." Rome didn't need to know that things were bound to be even more strained and awkward between us now.

"Dinner with your dad was that bad this year?"

"He got married again; she's twenty-five." I rolled my eyes. "She spent the entire dinner telling me why I should rush the sorority she was in last year before she graduated. Dad spent the whole dinner trying to tell me that I needed to give Gabe another chance. He wrote me out a check for a grand after implying he would double it if I took Gabe back, so it was more like extortion and torture than dinner."

He chuckled without humor. "No word from your mom?"

"No."

"I don't know how someone as softhearted as you came from those two."

"Me, either. I'm just glad I only have to deal with them in limited doses anymore. Being a constant disappointment is exhausting."

He lifted a dark eyebrow. "My little brother probably knows a little bit about that."

"Clever."

"I try."

"What happens at birthday dinner stays at birthday dinner—right, Rome?"

"I'm not going to say anything. If he hasn't noticed it after all this time it's not my job to hit him over the head with it, but I do think there is a good chance the two of you might be really good for each other. Opposites attract and all that."

The problem with that was I didn't think Rule and I were really all that opposite. I mean, yes, he had ink from the top of his Mohawked head to his booted toes, and he was all metal barbells where I was pearls and antique cameos, but we were both people trying to live beyond the boundaries everyone else seemed to want to set for us. We both had deep, painful issues with our parents and we both loved the other Archer boys beyond measure. We both desperately wanted to be seen for the value we had without other people's expectations of what we should or shouldn't be doing, and after Saturday, I now knew we both wanted sex to be just a little bit rough and just a little bit dirty. Yeah, not as opposite as one would think at first glance.

"I've been trying to keep Rule from living in the dark ever since Remy died. It's only gotten worse, not better, and he just can't keep going down that path if there's never going to be an end," I said.

Rome sighed as we got up and headed out into the chilly air. "At the end of the day, little girl, we're all each other has, so no matter how tough it gets for any of us we just have to power through and keep it together."

I gave him a hug and rubbed my cold hands together. I clutched the picture close to my chest and shivered as the bitter night breeze got past my scarf. "That's easy for you to say because you're an ocean away. Most of the time it's just me and Rule in an uneasy truce, with your parents breathing down our necks and mine ignoring me."

"You said it yourself, Shaw—you're not a kid anymore. You can figure this out. I have faith in you."

That was just Rome. He was the protector, the one who ultimately wanted what was best for all of us. I told him to call me before he headed back to Brookside and made my way back to the apartment. It was a rare day that Ayden and I both had off so she was sprawled in the living room with books everywhere. She was studying so intently with the radio up so loud I don't think she heard me come in. She had been giving me crap all week about Rule. While she was all for me sowing wild oats and making decisions that made me happy— and believe me, he had made me oh-so-very happy—she knew that my feelings for Rule were more complicated than I tended to let on and was convinced I was courting an even more thoroughly broken heart.

I tiptoed behind her and tapped her on the shoulder, making her shriek and whirl around. The reaction was so dramatic it made me double over in laughter. I flopped on the couch with a groan and took off my coat and scarf. She scowled up at me as she reached over to turn down the radio. "Not cool. How was dinner?"

"Good."

"Just good?"

"He grilled me about Rule; he seems to think we can fix each other or some nonsense like that."

"Speaking of the troublemaker, have you heard from him?"

I shook my head. "No. I know how he works, Ayd. Do you know how many sad, bewildered girls I've seen him ditch the morning after? I refuse to be one of them."

"Yeah, but you guys know each other; you were kinda friends."

I shrugged a shoulder. "That doesn't matter to him. Women have always been interchangeable. It's been that way since we were young."

I ran a hand through my tangled hair and stifled a yawn. I had been studying extra hard because midterms were right around the corner and the extra weekend shift at work was starting to wear on me. Add in the fact I was waking up in the night all hot and bothered and I was a tired girl.

"I think I might go curl up with a book and crash out early."

"I'll keep the music down."

"No worries, have a good night."

"You, too, and hey, at least the hickey is starting to fade."

I stuck my tongue out at her and went into my room. I flopped face-first on the bed and swore under my breath when I heard my phone ringing from my purse. Normally, I would have ignored it but it was playing my mom's ringtone—Twisted Sister's "We're Not Gonna Take It." If I didn't answer she would just keep calling until I did. Her time was deemed just that valuable. I rolled over and dug it out.

"Hello, Mother."

"Shaw, I'm sorry it took me so long to get back to you about your birthday. We were in California. Jack had a business trip and since it's so cold here I thought the kids would like the beach."

I guess phones don't work in California. "No problem."

"I talked to your father. He said you seemed distracted and out of sorts. We discussed it and I really think whatever game you are playing with Gabe has to stop. You're a mature young woman now, Shaw; you need to start making smarter life decisions. Flitting from boy to boy will just not stand any longer."

She didn't even tell me happy birthday. "I'm not interested in Gabe, Mom, not at all."

"Interest is frivolous. He comes from a good family, he has a planned out future; those are things that a young woman of your lineage needs to look for in a partner."

I blew a hiss out through my teeth and squeezed my eyes shut. "So those are the things that drew Dad to Marissa? She comes from a good family? She has a secure future? Or maybe he just likes her big ole double-Ds and the fact she does whatever he says. Come on, Mom, you're being ridiculous. I most certainly am not going to spend time with a guy who makes my skin crawl just because you like him."

"Language, young lady! I don't know where you think all those smarts you have came from, but I'm neither foolish nor blind. I know that this has to do with that Archer boy. It always does."

I rubbed my forehead where I felt the beginning of a migraine starting; she brought them on faster than anything else. "So what if it does?"

"Oh, Shaw, when are you going to outgrow this silly crush?"

"Mom, I'm starting to get a headache. Can this wait until another time?"

She was silent for a long minute and I could feel the waves of censure over the phone.

"I'm going to invite the Davenports to dinner. You need to be there."

"No. Not if Gabe is going to be there."

"Yes, you will be there. Do not forget your father and I pay for your tuition."

Great, more parental extortion. Boy was I lucky. "Yeah, fine, whatever." I didn't even say bye; I just chucked the phone under the other pillow and hit the lights. I had no idea how Rome thought I could fix anyone, be good for anyone, when I didn't even have control over my own life and it was making me physically ill.

I spent the rest of the week and weekend being a good college student. I studied every chance I got, finished my lab project, got a head start on one of my papers that was due at midterm. I even managed to squeeze in some time to help Ayden study since she was struggling with I-chem and I had breezed through it. I was working on a piece for one of my prerequisite classes, a speech on why assisted suicide should be legal—superfun stuff—but the apartment was too quiet and I was tired of ignoring my phone every time it rang, fearing it would be one of my parents or Gabe. So I packed up my laptop and went down to Pikes Perk to finish it. Ayden had texted that I should just come to the bar because it was slow, but I needed a less stimulating environment and a coffee shop full of hipsters seemed to be just the ticket. I had a pile of research in front of me and a caramel latte cooling by my elbow. I was so into what I was doing that I didn't notice the chair across from me at the little round table get pulled back until the metal legs scraped across the floor.

In fact, I was so intent on the paperwork spread out before me it wasn't until a familiar hand with a snake tattoo and a name across the knuckles pushed shut the top of my computer that I realized I had company. I blinked in surprise and looked up to find those arctic-colored eyes watching me intently. He was still rocking the Mohawk, but now it was a shocking red and he looked ridiculously good in a tight long-sleeved T-shirt and jeans that were a little baggy. I didn't bother to hide the fact that I was openly checking him out.

"What if I hadn't saved any of that?"

"We've met, remember? I know you well enough to know you probably save after every sentence."

It was every paragraph, but whatever. "This is kind of out of the way for you. What are you doing here?" I hadn't seen him or spoken to him in exactly ten days. The idea that he had purposely sought me out just seemed too far-fetched, so I scolded myself not to read into his sudden appearance.

"I actually went by the bar. I ran into your roommate and she told me you were probably here working on home-work. Shaw, we need to talk." I had never heard him sound so serious. It made me nervous. I needed something to do with my hands so I picked up my drink and tried to hide behind it.

"I don't think we do." I was halfway certain he was going to say something that was going to make me want to chuck the lukewarm coffee at his head.

He raised the eyebrow that had the double silver bars in it and leaned forward so that he was resting his elbows on his knees and staring directly into my eyes. There were interesting shadows dancing and flashing in the silver depths of his eyes that I didn't know what to make of, but he had never looked more enticing than he did in that moment.

"Come on. You really think things can go down like they did and we just pretend like it never happened?"

"Why not? It's what we've been doing and it seems to be working just fine."

"Shaw." He sounded exasperated. "We are not going to have seriously awesome sex—especially since it was your first time—and not talk about it. First off, I want to know what you were doing with Remy for all those years if you weren't sleeping together. That just doesn't make any sense. I also want to know why you took off the next morning; you didn't even give me a chance to try to talk to you."

I set the coffee down and pushed some of my hair out of my face. I leaned toward him so that I was almost in the same position he was. We were so close I could see each of his eyelashes as they brushed against his cheek when he blinked.

"I told you guys until I was blue in the face that Remy and I were just friends. We never, ever had any kind of romantic relationship. Our friendship was deep. It was powerful and intimate in a way Neanderthal males fail to understand, but it was never physical, and I can't believe you thought I would stick around afterward just to have you rush me out the door the next morning. I've seen you in action more times than I care to admit Rule; I wasn't going to be another one of your morning-after headaches. I have more pride than that."

"But you were going to hold on to your virginity for twenty years and then just give it up to me for no apparent reason?" He sounded slightly put out, which made me grin.

"I had my reasons, Rule."

"And those would be?"

"For me to know. Look, I didn't ask you for anything after, I don't expect anything from you, so can't we just get over it?"

"No, we can't."

I reeled back a little bit and frowned at him. "What? Why not? We've known each other forever; this is just a thing that happened." I flipped my wrist in a way I hoped was dismissive and went stock-still as he grabbed my hand in his much larger one. I stared, fascinated, as the tattooed digits linked with my own.

"See, this thing that happened"—his voice dropped a few octaves and I was suddenly acutely aware that the coffee shop was full, and that for whatever reason, we had garnered enough interest from the fellow patrons who were watching our interaction with rapt attention—"it wasn't just some insignificant event that we can just ignore; believe me I tried. I went out Friday and met a smoking-hot redhead."

I felt my face fold into a scowl as I tried to pull away from him. He smiled at me and used my trapped hand to pull me even closer. "Sadly, it took maybe five minutes to realize that I was trying to use one girl to get another off my mind, so I thought Saturday I would try for a blonde or maybe a brunette—hell, maybe both—because my head was all twisted up by a chick it shouldn't be."

I tugged on my hand but he just pulled me even closer, so that he was practically whispering in my ear, and I was almost sitting on his lap. I had to use my free hand to brace myself on his hard thigh. It was way too intimate, way too familiar, to touch him this way when I was trying to put distance between us. "So Nash and I went out, and there were redheads and there were brunettes and there was even a superhot chick who looked kinda like Pink, but you think any of them did it for me? No, Shaw, not one, because they fucking weren't you. Ever since you walked out on Sunday all I've been thinking of is you. Now why is that?"

His words made me shiver from the inside out. "Because it was new, because we have history, and it makes it harder for you to keep me faceless and nameless. I don't know, Rule."

He lifted a hand and ran his thumb across the rise of my cheek. It made my breath catch and my heart start to trip over itself.

"Whatever the reason, it matters, Shaw. It matters a lot."

"What are you trying to say, Rule?"

"I don't know. All I know is other girls aren't you and that isn't cutting it for me. I think we need to figure out what's going on between us."

I shook my head a little and a silver flare lit up his pale gaze. "I'm not going to be one of many. Like I said, I had my reasons for letting things happen the way they did, but if you think I'm signing up to be a bed filler because no one else is fitting the bill right now, you are sadly mistaken. I know you, Rule; I've known you since you first figured out girls were more complicated than boys, and you've never wanted to put the work in."

The feather-light sweep of that thumb across my cheek almost had me melting into a puddle at his booted feet. "So this time I will. We'll hang out, do shit together. I mean, we've known each other forever but I honestly don't really know anything about you. Come on, Shaw, what do you really have to lose?"

Not my heart, because he already had it even though he didn't know it. "So you want to, like, date?"

He laughed. "I'm not really the dating type, but I swear that while we're trying to figure out what's going on I'll keep it in my pants. No screwing around, no other girls. I owe it to you and to me to see what's here or if it was just a fluke." He sounded so sincere; he looked serious and determined to make me believe what he was saying.

I cleared my throat and bit my bottom lip a little. Sure it was what I had dreamed of—Rule suddenly realizing I was a girl and wanting to be with me. Granted, in my fantasy, it always came with his profession of undying love and devotion. In reality, his curiosity and promise to at least feel things out was probably as good as I was ever going to get. I didn't know how much I trusted him, but I had always, always wanted him, and it just wasn't in me to turn that down when it was being offered up on a silver platter.

"If we do this—hang out, spend time together—your parents, my parents, Rome, none of them are going to like it very much."

"Who cares?"

I guess I did, but I always was the only one to worry about that stuff.

"Okay."

"Okay?"

I breathed out a soft breath and as it whispered across his mouth he briefly closed his eyes, so I did the only thing that was left to do. I leaned forward and pressed my lips to his. It wasn't with the same desperation as it had been the last time; there was no panic that he would change his mind, no years upon years of pent-up desire and frustration, no regret that it was only going to be a one-night thing—just the sweet press of my lips against his and the soft bite of his lip ring into my lower lip.

Kissing Rule would always be uniquely different from kissing anyone else. There was just something about it that put it in a class all its own. I felt his lips turn into a grin as audible sighs from several of the tables around us were heard. He pulled back and tapped a finger on the tip of my nose.

I sat back in my chair and cleared my throat. "Well, then."

He barked out a laugh. "Yeah, at least that part of it seems to be a no-brainer."

I shifted in my seat and motioned absently to the work still sprawled across the table between us. "As nice as this little visit was, I have to finish this presentation."

A quick flash of disappointment blazed across his eyes but he hid it behind his easy grin. "When do you work this weekend?"

"I work all weekend, but I'm first out on Saturday night. I just have to be in by ten on Sunday morning."

"Busy girl."

"You don't know the half of it."

"So, this hanging out thing might be harder than I thought?"

He said it lightheartedly but I knew Rule; he was an instant-gratification kind of guy. If my tight schedule made it hard for us to spend time together, I had no illusions that he would wait around for me to be free—he would move on to something easier and more manageable.

"I'll be out around ten on Saturday and usually I'm out by seven on Sunday. The Sunday shift is optional. I just picked it up because we stopped going to Brookside and I figured I might as well make a little extra money."

"My buddy Jet is playing at Cerberus this weekend, why don't you grab your roommate and come hang out Saturday night?"

"What kind of music is it?" Cerberus had a pretty rowdy

reputation in town. It was located in the warehouse district and had been shut down more than once for one thing or another. It wasn't the kind of place I would normally consider spending time. In fact, it was the kind of place I normally avoided at all costs on the off chance I would run into someone I knew and they would rat me out to my parents, but if I was going to commit and try to spend time with this boy I had wanted forever, then my horizons were going to have to expand.

"Metal."

I snorted a little. "Ayden is from Kentucky. She likes Taylor Swift and Carrie Underwood. I don't know that I could wrangle her into that."

"They're actually really good; they went on tour with a pretty famous band last year. Besides, Ayden seems like a pretty cool chick. I bet she would go just to be your wingman. If she doesn't come, just come alone. I won't leave you hanging."

"What about Rome?"

"He has to go to Fort Carson for the weekend. He has to set up meetings with his VA counselor. He's having a rough time since he isn't healing as fast as he thought he would be."

"That's too bad."

"I'm not going to hide this from anyone, Shaw. If you want to play those kinds of games maybe you need to rethink whether this is something you really want to do or not."

I grabbed his forearm and let the tips of my fingers dig into the body of the snake that was marked there. "No, I'm not going to hide. Just don't make me look like an idiot, Rule. This matters."

"It matters to me, too, Casper." He climbed to his feet so that he was towering over me. He bent down and pressed a soft kiss to the crown of my head. "By the way, you look good in jeans. Come to the show Saturday."

113

"All right." I watched him walk out of the coffee shop and it wasn't lost on me that so did every other girl in the place. I stifled a sigh and ruefully shook my head. I went to flip the top of my computer back open when the girl sitting directly across from me caught my eye. She was a little bit older than me, had long dreadlocks that were a startling ocean blue, and she was staring at me in open envy. I had to blink a little bit because I was so used to being the one who looked at the girls crawling out of his bed like that. She gave me a sheepish grin.

"You're going to have your hands full with that one."

Considering I wasn't even a hundred percent sure what we were doing, I had no doubt she was right. It wasn't like he asked me to be his girlfriend or even out on an honest-to-God date. He just said he wanted to hang out and spend time together. That wasn't defined or clear and I didn't even know what that meant to him. I appreciated that he told me he was willing to keep it in his pants, that he was aware that whatever was happening between us was important enough to try to figure out without the complication of other girls involved, but I was acutely aware that old habits tended to die hard, and Rule was not known to practice restraint. I huffed out a breath. "You're telling me."

The girl laughed a little. "He actually tattooed a giant lotus flower on my friend's leg; she spent all three sessions trying to get him to ask her out on a date. I guess I can tell her he has a girlfriend so it'll make her feel better."

I picked my coffee back up and tried to get my head out of the Rule fog it had descended into and back into good-college-student mode.

"I'm not his girlfriend."

"Really? It sure looked like it."

"We've known each other a long time; it's complicated."

She winked at me and gave me a saucy grin. "Oh, honey,

114

when they look like that and exude that kind of 'do-me' vibe, it always will be."

Well, there it was. If a perfect stranger could plainly see after only five minutes of watching us together that it was always going to be a battle to keep things with him on the level, what chance did I have of making anything between us work? With that depressing thought I went back to assisted suicide and tried to cheer myself up.

CHAPTER 7

Rule

The club was packed. Enmity was a pretty big local draw for metal heads and punk rockers, plus Jet had been in the scene since he was just a kid so he had a solid local following from just being around for so long. Some crappy wannabe Slayer band was opening up for them and already doing their warm-up. They were going to be followed by an all-girl punk band so the show was supposed to run late, which was good because it was well past eleven, and I couldn't stop looking at the display on my phone to check the time. Every time I did it Nash rolled his eyes and Jet laughed at me; granted, they were doing a bang-up job of polishing off a bottle of Patrón between them so I didn't take it personally. I had sent Shaw a text more than an hour ago to verify she was going to be here and I hadn't heard a thing back.

I was antsy and ill-tempered partly because I was navigating uncharted territory and, undeniably, because this whole monogamy thing was new to me. I was used to scratching an itch when I felt it, used to appealing to baser needs and letting my carnal instinct drive me. Behaving not because someone asked me to but because I wanted to was entirely new to me, and the side effects sucked—I was horny and irritable, plus I was sick of playing phone tag with her. I'd had no idea how busy Shaw's life was. The girl was bouncing from class, to work, to volunteer stuff all day long. When I saw her before on the weekends I had just assumed she had free time and was choosing to spend Sundays with my folks, but clearly that wasn't the case. Every minute of the girl's day was carefully planned and I was starting to see how much she had sacrificed to care for our fucked-up family. "Chill out. If she said she was coming, then she's coming."

Nash shoved an elbow in my ribs, making me jostle the phone I was glaring holes into. I shoved it back into my pocket and picked up the beer I had been nursing for more than an hour. I caught the eye of a smoking-hot blonde who had been scoping me out under the radar since we walked into the bar and had to do a quick mental rundown of why I thought spending time with Shaw and figuring out how she had gotten my head all twisted and turned was a good idea when easy as pie was right in front of me. The blonde gave me a smile that all but screamed "I want you to take my pants off with your teeth," and I almost choked when beer went down the wrong tube.

Jet snickered and rubbed a hand through his messy black hair. The guy looked like a rock star; he was lanky and had that permanent, freshly laid and right-outta-bed look that made girls stupid and dreamy-eyed with zero effort. He also had an awesome voice and could sing, like, really sing, which made the fact he chose to be in a heavy metal band ironic because most of his stuff with Enmity was screaming and loud. The guy was a consummate musician and could write a killer song as well as play pretty much any instrument he picked up. One night after a particularly nasty bout of beer pong, he had confessed that he liked metal because he couldn't deal with the fame and adulation of more popular styles of music. The guy wanted to be in a band, but for reasons that made sense only to him, had no interest in being a full-blown rock star—even though he had the look and the vocal chops to do it.

"I swear you pull more tail than me and I'm in a freaking band. All you have to do is blink and you have broads falling all over themselves to have at it."

I cleared my throat and set the beer down on the table. "Yeah, well, I told you guys I need to cut that shit out for a while."

Jet looked over his shoulder at the blonde, then back at me with a smirk. "Good luck with that."

Nash tossed back a shot and hissed out a breath through his teeth. "Cut him some slack, dude. He's got a good thing working."

"I'm just saying—he doesn't have to even work at it."

I pulled out my phone and checked the time for the hundredth time. "Something tells me that is about to be completely untrue."

Jet and Nash both did another shot and Jet gave a howl. "The first band is getting ready to start so I gotta go make sure the guys are ready to kick some ass. We're getting ready to finish the album we've been working on so we need to kill it tonight." A round of fist-banging went back and forth and I sighed as the blonde gave me another pointed look. I didn't mean to keep looking in her direction, but I guess old habits die hard.

"This blows."

"Seriously, chill. Shaw is awesome. She's a total babe, she's got enough balls to give you your shit right back, and she knows you and still is willing to give you a shot. She'll be here, so just calm down and tell your junk to freaking relax."

My hair was still up in the crazy Mohawk, so I couldn't

run my hands through it; instead I rubbed the back of my neck and tapped my fingers on the edge of the table.

"Why do you think she wants to give this a shot? I mean, logically she knows I'm a bad bet. She knows what my history is like and generally we don't have anything in common. I know I can't get her out of my head, but what do you think her reasons are for seeing what this is all about?"

"I think she's a superbright chick and, whatever her motivation is, she's thought a lot about it. I don't think she went to bed with you just because and I seriously doubt she agreed to kick it with you simply because you asked. I think if you can keep your head on straight and your dick in your pants you'll eventually find out why she's doing what she's doing, and I'm pretty sure the reasons will knock you on your ass."

"I think I'm certifiable for even thinking I'm going to be able to do this." I liked girls, no-strings-attached sex, going where I wanted when I wanted, and not having to answer to anyone but myself—hooking up with Shaw put all those things on ice. I sighed again and let my eyes wander back over to the blonde. She was still looking at me, only now her very pretty face was scrunched up into a scowl. Her mouth was pulled in like she had tasted something sour and I couldn't figure out what had changed in the minute since I had last caught her eye until I heard Nash mutter, "Damn," and realized that every guy seated around us had turned to watch Shaw and Ayden as they made their way past the bar and toward where we were seated.

They made a striking pair—by far the classiest girls in the place. It was clear neither one had ventured down to Cerberus before. Shaw's blond hair was loose and long, falling over shoulders that were bared in a black halter top. She had on skinny jeans that were so tight they looked like they would need to be surgically removed, and a pair of bright blue heels that should have looked ridiculous at a show like this, but instead had even old-school head bangers drooling in their pints. Ayden had her dark hair spiked up and sexy and was wearing a tiny little skirt and billowy purple top that completely fell off one shoulder. She was rocking a pair of black cowboy boots that had clearly seen some better days, but that didn't stop the two of them from turning every single head, male and female, as they slid up to our table.

I didn't know what to do so I just stared at Shaw while she stared back at me. I was pretty sure all the blood in my brain had been diverted south so I just blinked at her like an idiot while Nash chuckled and told both of them hello.

"Hey. Sorry we're late, we had a bachelor party run over and it took us longer to get out of there than we thought it would."

"I sent you a couple of texts to see what was going on." I should be asking her if she wanted a drink, doing something to let her know I was happy she was here, but instead I was being surly and weird.

She frowned. "My phone is off."

Ayden propped her elbows on the table and took the shot Nash offered her up. She glared at Shaw and pointed a finger at her. "Tell him why it's off." There was accusation there and I saw, even in the dim light of the bar, the way Shaw flushed.

I put a hand on her lower back and bent down so that my lips were touching her ear. I felt her tense but she leaned her hip into mine. "Why is your phone off, Casper?"

She shifted her weight from foot to foot. "Because Gabe is blowing it up. My mom invited his parents to Brookside Country Club for dinner next weekend and they expect us both to be there. He has it in his head that we should ride up there together and won't leave me alone about it, so I turned my phone off because he's making me crazy and I don't even want to go in the first place."

A cocktail waitress chose that moment to walk by so the girls ordered drinks and I got another beer. I pressed Shaw closer to my side and turned so that we were facing each other.

"So what are you going to do about it?"

She flattened a palm on the center of my chest right over my heart and looked up at me with sad, green eyes. "I don't know. I have to go or my mom will make my life hell, but I don't want to be anywhere near Gabe. I'm trying to just ignore the entire thing."

"That's not going to work for long." I liked the way she fit next to me, like she was custom-made to be right there.

"I know." The waitress dropped off drinks, and Ayden grimaced as the first band started. I laughed and poured her another shot.

"Just power through the first two; I promise Jet's band is really good."

She made a face. "I like stuff with a little more twang and a lot more banjo."

We all laughed a little. "Just help Nash finish the tequila, that'll get you through it and if it gets too bad I bet Jet has earplugs we can go snag for ya." She said something I didn't catch but made Nash laugh hysterically, so I turned back to Shaw. I gave an internal shiver when I noticed she was having some kind of girly stare down with the blonde from earlier. I curled my hand all the way around her waist and yanked until she was pressed full body against me.

"Hey, don't."

"It's not like she has to be so obvious about it."

"Shaw, look around. There are at least ten guys sitting no less than five feet away I can actually see undressing you with their eyes. It's cool. I'm hanging with you, not her, and you're here because of me, not them. That's what matters, right?"

She made a face at me, which made me want to suck on her bottom lip. I reached up and tucked a piece of her hair behind her ear. It felt like satin and immediately slipped back out. "I've never waited around for a week to spend time with a girl I'm into before; frankly it blows, and I want to spend time with you."

"I really am sorry we ran late. I had to do some work to get Ayden to agree to come. This really isn't her scene; mine either for that matter, but I'm glad we're here."

She ran her index finger over the tattoo of the phoenix that was sticking out of the sleeve of my T-shirt on my biceps. "I want to spend time with you, too, Rule. I'm sorry my life is so hectic."

"Don't worry about it." I slid my hand under the heavy fall of her hair and leaned down to whisper in her ear. "So, are you going to come home with me tonight or what?" If she said no there was a good chance I was going to have to take a cold shower before I could get my jeans off. Her green eyes were brilliant as they gazed back up at me. Never had a girl, especially a girl I had known for so long, been able to keep me guessing as to what she was thinking. Shaw was a hard one to read; her eyes just seemed to be reflecting back what I was feeling instead.

"We took a cab so as long as I make sure Ayden is cool that can definitely be an option." Her voice had dropped to an even huskier octave and I thought it was possible I had never heard anything sexier. I grunted in approval like the Neanderthal I was and let my hand fall from her waist to the curve of her ass.

The four of us chatted and had a couple more rounds while we all suffered through the first and second band. The second one would have been all right if the lead singer had focused more on trying to sing than looking a part, but mostly they just hollered and jumped around for an hour until Ayden was ready to jump onstage and wrestle the microphone from the poor girl. I was surprised how fun it was to just hang out. Ayden was funny and sarcastic and she and Nash bounced barbs back and forth like they had been friends for years. By the time Enmity was setting up, the Patrón was gone and the two of them were loaded.

Shaw was quieter and was watching everyone and everything around her. She asked questions and responded when engaged in conversation, but for the most part she just kept an eye on what was going on rather than fully participating in it. At one point I almost started a brawl. I had gone to the bathroom and Nash had slipped out to smoke. We were only gone for a minute, but by the time I got back to the table some sweaty metal head was trying to press up on Shaw.

I wasn't the type that got jealous. I mean I'd lived my entire life not being as good as my twin, so I couldn't understand the murderous rage that was suddenly flowing through me, the sudden need to claim something, to announce to the world that she was mine. Luckily, Nash got to the table first and sent the guy on his way in no uncertain terms, because chances are I would have pulverized him and ended up spending the night in jail. Still, when I got back to the table I yanked Shaw up to the tips of her fancy-ass blue shoes and planted a kiss on her pretty, pink mouth hard enough that my lip ring stung. I thought maybe she would pull back, maybe give me crap for acting like an idiot, but she just gripped my shirt in her tiny hands and let me do what I had to do. When I finally set her back down her eyes looked glassy and she was flushed. She slicked her tongue over her bottom lip and settled back into my side.

"Gotta tell you, Rule, I'm a fan of kissing with all that metal in your face. I never thought that was something I would be into, but you sure make it work."

Oh man, that was the hottest thing I had ever heard, ever. I hooked an arm around her shoulder.

I chuckled at her dry remark but didn't bother to deny what the overt action had been about. We continued to chat and have a great time, but by the time the house lights went down and Jet was ready to hit the stage, I had had enough of friend time and wanted alone time with just her. Unfortunately, Jet knew how to put on a good show and even though Ayden claimed that the racket the band was making could in no way be called music, it only took two songs to have her dragging Shaw up to the front of the stage with her.

The band was loud and aggressive and blazed from song to song, but Jet was a good-looking guy and knew how to work a crowd, so it didn't surprise me that when the girls ran off there had been a drunkenly interested gleam in Ayden's eyes. Unfortunately, it also left me alone to deal with my plastered best friend.

"You gonna make it?"

Nash's violet eyes were at half-mast and I was pretty sure that if the table wasn't available to hold him up he would be face-first down on the floor. This is what I normally looked like after a night of hard drinking, and it was slightly startling to see it from the other side.

"Huh?" His words were mumbled and unfocused and I saw visions of sexy time going up in smoke and replaced with the reality that I was going to have to manhandle him back to the apartment and get him in a bathroom, like, right now.

"Bro, you better not yak in my truck. Let me go find the girls and let them know we have to go."

"Smhhh . . ." Okay, it was mission critical to get him out of here before the tequila came back up. I sighed and started toward the stage only to be intercepted before I got there by the blonde from earlier. Now that Shaw was here and my head—not what was in my pants—was in control I could clearly see there was no comparison between the two. Shaw was flawless and pretty in a way that didn't require five pounds of makeup and clothes that exposed more than they covered. She was also charmingly unaware of the effect she had on the opposite sex, where this girl was here to be seen and appreciated. She put a finger on the center of my chest and blinked heavily lashed eyes at me.

"Hey."

"Uh . . . hi." I would have just stepped around her, but the bar was packed and the band was making the crowd go crazy. People were jumping up and down and banging their heads all around, so unless I walked right over her I wasn't going to be able to get by. Because I was so tall I had a clear sight of one dark head and one light bouncing along to the music right up front. While I was stoked that Shaw seemed to be having fun, I was also bummed she was practically impossible to get to.

"So I saw you earlier, you're friends with the band."

"Yep." Normally this was the kind of girl I sought out—easy, no strings, aware of where the night was going and what the morning was going to hold.

"So, do you maybe wanna get out of here, go somewhere quieter where we can . . . talk?"

My eyebrows shot up. When I was drunk maybe that sounded smoother, but now that I was sober it just seemed kind of sleazy and desperate. "Thanks, but I'm here with somebody."

Her bright red mouth pulled into a frown and she took

a step back. "Yeah I saw that, and I also saw that there is no way that she's going to be with you for long."

I was used to judgment, used to hearing that I wasn't up to par or good enough for whatever reason, but coming from a boozed-up barfly who had just tried to talk me into taking her to bed made me reel back a little.

"Okay." I didn't know what else to say to that.

The girl snorted and flipped her overprocessed hair over her shoulder. "That girl has money and status written all over her, you have ink and nothing but a good time spelled out bright and clear all over you. How long do you think she's going to think you've got more going on than that?"

I frowned, done with social courtesy. I physically moved her out of my way and called over my shoulder, "I don't know, but I'd be an idiot not to stick around until she figures it out."

Sweaty bodies got nudged and prodded until I got to the girls. Jet was right in front of them on both of his knees, his head was thrown back, his shirt was torn off and the massive angel of death I had tattooed across his torso was on full display. He was wailing like a true rock god and while Shaw looked fascinated, Ayden looked like she was about to melt into a pile of orgasmic goo. Looked like my buddy had turned the country mouse rock-and-roll for the night. I put a hand on Shaw's hip and bent low to tell her, "I gotta get Nash out of here, he's done for."

She looked at me with big eyes and nodded with no argument. She leaned over to holler something at Ayden, who hollered something back. The brunette wiggled her fingers at me in a wave, and the next thing I knew, Shaw's tiny frame was pulling me back through the crowd. Nash was now almost fully draped over the table and I didn't miss the bouncer giving him the eye.

"What about Ayden? You said we needed to make sure she got home okay."

"She promised to call when she was leaving. She said she would just get a cab."

"She'll be all right here by herself?"

"Yeah, she's a big girl and can take care of herself, plus I think she danced most of the booze out. I think she's sticking around to tell your friend how much she enjoyed the show."

"Jet has that effect on women."

"I can see why."

I wrestled Nash up and marched him out of the bar with an arm around his waist. He was solid, and maneuvering his sturdy bulk was difficult.

"You gonna change your mind and drop me for a rock star?"

She snorted and took the keys I tossed her to get the cab doors open so that I could shove Nash sideways across the backseat. "You better not get sick in here, dude," I warned.

There was no response, so I helped Shaw climb in and it occurred to me that she hadn't even hesitated to leave with me. That made something in the center of my chest get all slippery and warm.

"I'm just saying that he's pretty charismatic and even though I didn't understand half of what he was singing, it was still pretty powerful. He had that entire bar eating out of the palm of his hand; that kind of draw is impressive."

"Yeah, Jet was born to be a rock star. He just has a problem with the spotlight and recognition. He always has."

"You've known him a long time?"

"We used to go see him play when we were kids, back when he was into punk. Nash, Jet, and Rowdy have been my inner circle for a long time. Rowdy we met later, when he started working at the shop, but we all kick it like we are brothers from other mothers."

She settled in the leather seat and I adjusted the heat

when I noticed she was rubbing goose bumps on her arms. "It must be nice to have a lot of good friends. I was never like that."

I looked out of the corner of my eye at her. "What do you mean?"

"I'm shy and awkward. I never know how to just make friends like that. I was picked on a lot in high school. Remy was my only real friend and now only Ayden really. I have a hard time letting people in. I guess because I've seen how painful it is when the people who are the closest to you are the ones constantly disappointing you."

"What about me and Rome?"

"What about you?"

Nash groaned from the back and I looked over my shoulder apprehensively. He didn't sound good. "What about us? We were there, too. Weren't we your friends?"

She made a little humming noise that immediately made vital parts of my anatomy take notice.

"Rome has always been like a big brother. He looks out for me, he picks on me, he tries to keep things that hurt me and cause pain at bay. You, well, you were always something else, not a friend, not a brother, just something else."

"Is that bad, the something else?"

I felt rather than saw her shrug. "It has been, and then sometimes it's not." I didn't know what to make of that so I let the subject drop. I drove the rest of the way, keeping one eye on the road and one eye on Nash, who was making increasingly loud noises of distress in the back. When we got to the apartment I looked across the cab at Shaw but she was bent over the back of the seat rubbing Nash's bald head and uttering soothing words to him.

"Hey, I don't know how long it'll take to get him squared away, so you can just hang out and if you want me to run you home or whatever I will."

She looked at me over her shoulder and raised a pale brow. "Rule, it's fine. It's not like I don't know how you end up in the state you're normally in on Sunday morning. Like I told you, I just have to be at work on Sunday around ten. As long as you make that happen, we're good."

At a loss for words I just stared at her for a moment before Nash's gurgling made me move. "Have you always been this awesome?"

She shut all the doors behind us and helped me haul Nash up the steps. I noticed she didn't answer my question, but she did get Nash a huge glass of water and fished around in my bathroom until she found some painkillers. She left both on the bathroom sink in the hall that Nash used and gave me a pointed look. "Come find me when you're done."

I swore in a long litany under my breath as I helped Nash battle his thermal and jeans off. I was contemplating shoving his ass in a cold shower when the tequila started to take its revenge. His tattooed head disappeared inside the toilet and I spent the next hour making sure he didn't pass out and alternately cramming liquids down his throat and jumping out of the way as they came back up. When I was finally sure he wasn't going to get sick anymore I hauled him to his bed and made sure he was facedown before I did a quick cleanup of the bathroom and myself and then went to find Shaw.

The door to my room was cracked open and she had my TV on. I wasn't sure what I was going to find, the dirtier part of my imagination had all kinds of interesting scenarios laid out, but what awaited me wasn't one of them. She had my California king stripped to the mattress pad and was making short work of changing all the bedding. Her crazy blue shoes were in the center of the floor looking totally out of place next to my discarded T-shirts and jeans, and as

I propped myself up in the doorway all I could do was watch her. She seemed to be having some kind of conversation with herself but she was muttering too low for me to hear what she was saying. I waited a full five minutes for her to look up at me and notice me watching her but she never did, so I asked, "What are you doing?" which made her jump about a foot in the air.

She put a hand on her chest and had the good grace to look a little bit guilty.

"Changing your sheets."

"Why?"

"Uh . . . Why?"

"Yes, Shaw, why are you changing my sheets at nearly three o'clock in the morning?"

She was saved from answering when a Garth Brooks song rang from her pocket. I was starting to see she liked to pick songs for ringtones that fit the person calling. She had a brief conversation with someone I assumed was Ayden and left the phone on the nightstand next to the bed. She picked up the edge of my comforter and started to smooth it back over the big bed.

"Ayden got a ride home. I guess your friend in the band remembered her from the Goal Line and offered to take her."

"That's cool, though Jet isn't exactly known for being a one-girl kinda guy, so I hope she isn't reading anything into it."

"Like I said, she can take care of herself and honestly you aren't really known for that, either"—she waved a hand over the bed—"so I'll be damned if I'm going to sleep, let alone do anything else in a bed that has had more visitors than DIA without changing the sheets first." Her bottom lip stuck out and she sounded slightly defiant.

"Shaw." I moved out of the doorway, making sure to shut it and turn the lock on my way to her. "No one has been

130

in that bed since you. I told you I knew on that Saturday that something was happening between us that was different."

She shivered a little as I got close and I could see raw vulnerability in her eyes. It was scary to know how easily I could hurt this girl and how desperately I didn't want that to happen.

"I don't know how to do this with you, Rule. I drunkenly threw myself at you and was lucky you were willing to catch me, but sober it's hard to look at that bed and not see every single other girl who was there before me—sometimes more than one at a time."

She tried to make light of it but I could hear the genuine melancholy coloring her tone. I put both my hands on her face and tilted her head back so that we were eye to eye.

"I can't change the past, Casper, not any of it. I can't make any of those girls or the fact you walked in on them on Sunday mornings time and time again disappear. I can't bring Remy back or go back in time and not call him for a ride that night. There are probably a million and one regrets I have, and if they are going to be between us here or in bed, then let's just stop it now, because I'm not going to do combat over my past when my future is finally starting to be something I want to invest in."

She lifted her hands up and grasped my wrists; at first I thought she was going to push me away but she didn't. She leaned forward and let her forehead hit the center of my chest. "Rule, if this goes bad it's gonna be so, so bad." Her voice was just a husky whisper against my chest.

"True, but if it's good, it's going to be so very, very good." I tunneled my fingers through her hair and she let her hands fall to my shoulders. We weren't a perfect match; she was a lot shorter than me, and I had to admit that I knew logically we made an odd pair physically, but there was just something about her. Something about the way she curved into me, the way she sighed my name like a prayer, the way she smelled like sunshine and sweetness and everything yummy all wrapped into one bite that made none of that matter. It made her the only girl I could ever remember wanting to hold on to for more than a fleeting minute of time.

She started to pull my shirt over my head and I laughed a little when she got mad when it got stuck on my spiky hair. She made a face at me and tossed it over her shoulder onto the floor. She used a finger to poke the front tip of the spiked-up hawk and lifted an eyebrow. "You look hot with a Mohawk, Rule, but I gotta say this hair is more trouble than it's worth."

She trailed her hands over my ribs and stopped to look at the artwork imprinted there. On one side was a grim reaper that ran from under my armpit to the top of my thigh. On the other side was a beautiful angel and in between them on my back was a massive Gothic cross that went from shoulder blade to shoulder blade and ended at my tailbone, scrolling from shoulder to shoulder and on an elegant banner was "Remy" in bold script. I had more inked skin than not and although I normally didn't think anything about it, being naked next to her in all her pale, perfect-skinned glory it seemed slightly overwhelming. Her hands moved lower and before I had even kissed her she was messing with my belt buckle.

"Remy would have loved that piece, you know? He always used to tell me he was so glad when you started getting tattooed. He said someone having the same face as him was always too weird, but then you started looking so different. He was glad it was you because there was no way he could tolerate sitting still long enough to get anything done."

It was true. Remy was always moving, always fidgeting and twitching. He would have never been able to sit long enough for a session, and every time I had come home with a new piece I wanted to show off, he had been the first to see it. He had promised to let me draw up something for him once I completed my apprenticeship, but he died before I finished. It was one of those million regrets I had mentioned earlier.

Shaw was making short work of my pants and I had the sudden need to slow her down, so I picked her up like she was a little doll and tossed her onto the center of my bed. She bounced and ended up sprawled on her back spread-eagle. I toed off my boots and let my pants fall the rest of the way off, since I typically just went commando. When I crawled up over her I was naked and she was still fully dressed. Her eyes got big because I put my hands under her shirt and dropped down to plant a bunch of kisses along her throat.

"You're like good whiskey, Shaw. You go to a guy's head quick and smooth. Last time we blazed through a bunch of the good stuff. Why don't we slow it down a little this time?" I let my fingers brush over the halter top and felt her body get tight. She bent her legs so that I was cradled in between and, despite our size difference, we fit together just fine. She let her hands roam all across my back and I felt the edge of her nails bite into my skin and the press of her heels into the curve of my ass—it was awesome.

"I was afraid last time that if we slowed down to think you would stop and I felt like I would die if you stopped."

I had my hands under her top now and she was making little gasping noises that made me harder than I already was. I got her shirt off by untying the laces and letting it fall around her waist in a pool of fabric and sealed her mouth shut with mine. She didn't hesitate to kiss me back and I decided then and there that kissing Shaw was probably as close to heaven as I was ever going to get. There was just the right amount of give and take, just the right amount of tongue and teeth, just the right amount of breathless pull that made me see stars and want to tear her pants off and forge ahead like a marauder. She wasn't kidding about liking the jewelry in my mouth. She rubbed her tongue across the barbell and rubbed her bottom lip across the hoop in a way that had my eyes drifting closed and almost making me forget that I was supposed to be showing her that there were lots of good stuff we had flashed past last time.

"See, I don't think we spent any time here." I ran my thumb over her nipple and watched as it puckered instantly at my touch. "You are so pretty and pink, Shaw, and I don't think you even know the half of it." I let my tongue run across the base of her throat and down until I had one peak in my mouth. She tasted as sweet as she smelled, and the idea that I was the only one who got to do this to her, that she was mine, just mine, made it all even better. She muttered my name and arched up as I worked her over pretty good with my mouth on her breasts. She was undulating under me, pulling me closer to her with greedy hands and rubbing against the part of me that was fully agreeing with her that I was moving too slowly. I let go of the flesh I was torturing with a soft pop and kissed her breastbone. "See, good stuff."

She sighed. "Totally." I propped my weight up on an elbow and traced a path from her throat to her belly button. The taut skin on her belly quivered a little when I traced a pattern around the small indent. I liked the way my tattooed skin looked against her much clearer canvas. I also got a little kick out of the fact that when I flattened my palm against her belly that my name went from one side to the other, claiming what I was quickly starting to consider my very own. I let my thumb hook under the top of her jeans and rubbed a pattern that made her wiggle enticingly against me.

"Rule." There was a hitch in her voice. "What are you waiting for?"

"Nothing." I kissed her again and took my time about it. I wanted her to know that she affected me just as much as I seemed to be affecting her. Normally, when I was with a girl, I was all about instant gratification. There was no buildup, no anticipation. I mean, I liked to think that I had developed some pretty good moves over the years, but I was also a big fan of getting to the finish line in as little time as possible. I wasn't there to create memories; I was there for a mind-numbing orgasm and a minute of peace. But Shaw was different. With her I was different, and this thing happening between us was most definitely different.

I got under her supertight jeans and was surprised to find that she hadn't bothered with anything underneath. I pulled my head up and grinned down at her. "Commando?"

She shrugged and shifted a little when my fingers brushed over all her soft and warm parts. "What? These jeans are practically painted on and no matter how tiny the panties are, they show, so no underwear was the only option."

"I would never have pegged you for the type." She gasped my name out as I made my way into her damp heat. Her whole body bowed up against mine and I caught her across her back to keep her there under my ministrations. The friction between what I was doing and her tight jeans was making her quake in my arms and I knew it was only a matter of time before she came apart in my hands. "You're always so proper and put together, who knew underneath was such a naughty girl?" She was slick and fluttery, all the things I wanted a girl to be right before she made a sweet noise of surprise and flared her eyes open at me. Her hands clamped down on my neck and she tugged me down for another mind-bending kiss right before I felt her melt. I smiled against her mouth and shifted so that I could help her pull her jeans off, even though she was moving a lot slower than me. Once she was as naked as I was I took a minute to appreciate the view because a naked Shaw was something to appreciate, but a naked, luminously satisfied Shaw was something master artists would kill to capture on canvas.

She leaned over me to dig a condom out of the drawer. I settled on my back and let her crawl over the top of me. I stacked my hands behind my head and just watched as she tore the packet open with her teeth and set about suiting me up. She was gentle about it and I think afraid she might hurt me, but it was a good thing she took her time with it because the jewelry down there sometimes made getting protection on tricky.

Once everything was set and I was hard enough to pound nails she looked at me a little apprehensively and settled over my lap. "I don't think I know how to do it this way."

And wasn't that just amazing? I got to teach this beautiful, amazing, kick-ass girl all about sex and all about the great shit in between. I moved so that she was where she needed to be and helped her figure out how to slide down and glide back up. I gritted my teeth and let out some swear words because nothing had prepared me for her trying to find her rhythm. As she moved up and down, rocked back and forth, and pretty much turned my mind to mush I tried to keep some modicum of control but it was to no avail. When I felt her start to come apart again, I flipped her over on her back and drove into her like I was trying to bury myself inside her to live forever. She didn't seem to mind the manhandling too much; her nails scraped across the shaved part of my head and her tiny little teeth nipped into my shoulder. It only took another breath before I followed her over the edge, then lay in an annihilated heap on top of her. I felt her hands flow over my shoulders and her husky voice ask in my ear, "Have you *always* been this awesome?"

CHAPTER 8

Shaw

I was having a hard time concentrating in my study group, which wasn't a good thing because we were all expected to carry our own weight. I was pretty good with anatomy so I wasn't too worried about falling behind, but I didn't want anyone else to fall behind because I couldn't keep my head in the game. Trying to find time to work in Rule with my already busy schedule was proving to be a daunting and frustrating task. In the last two weeks I had only managed to squeeze in two lunch dates when he had time between clients, a Friday night when he came to the bar with his friends and hung out with me until I got off, and a subsequent Saturday night that, of course, led to Sunday morning. I had to work, so Sunday was just a brief kiss good-bye and then I was on my way out the door. We talked on the phone and texted back and forth, but it wasn't enough for me. Now that I was sleeping with him on a regular basis it wasn't enough for the me who wanted nothing more than to roll around in bed with him every chance she got.

I was blushing at a particularly hot memory when one of the girls had to tap me on the shoulder to get my attention. I'm sure my face was bright red so I cleared my throat and fanned myself down with the notebook I was using to take notes. "Sorry, what did you ask?"

She repeated the question and I stumbled through an answer, telling myself I had to stay focused for the remaining hour of the session. My phone went off a couple times in my pocket but like a good college student I ignored it and gritted my teeth through the rest of the question-and-answer portion of the meeting. As soon as time was up, I gathered my things and bolted out of the room we were using for the meeting. It was rude but I didn't even bother to say good-bye to my classmates. I wanted to see what was on my phone. Rule liked to send me dirty text messages when I least expected it. They made me get all breathless and silly and I couldn't wait to see what these might read. Only the name on my phone wasn't his, but Gabe's, and that made me want to toss the little device onto the ground. My mom was still insisting on a family get-together; luckily her schedule was so busy that I had managed to avoid it and Gabe for the last few weeks, but from the sounds of the messages he had left me that was no longer the case.

Shaw, I spoke to your mother today. She would like me to bring you to Brookside on Saturday night for dinner at the club. She would like you to stay the night there and then we are doing a big gathering at her house on Sunday for brunch. My parents will be there along with several other influential people.

I groaned out loud and scrolled down to the next message.

I know you are hesitant to spend time alone with me after my erratic behavior, but I assure you, my intentions are good. All I'm offering is a ride.

I most definitely didn't want to be stuck in a car with Gabe for an hour and I most certainly didn't want to deal with my mother for an entire weekend. Plus, Saturday night had proven the one night a week I actually got to spend with Rule and I absolutely didn't want to give that up, but I didn't see where I had a choice. I bit my lip and replied that I would be there but that I would be driving myself. There was no way in hell I was going to Brookside without a way to escape. He texted back that that would be fine and asked if I would mind giving him a ride. I wanted to say no but figured it wouldn't hurt anything to just take him and drop him off. We arranged to meet at a bakery that was between our two places on Saturday morning and I was just about to put the phone away when Black Rebel Motorcycle Club trilled from my hand. Rule's sneering face looked up at me from the display and I couldn't hold in a smile.

Ayden warned me every single day that I had to be careful. I was in love with Rule; Rule wasn't in love with me. We were having sex, really amazing, make-the-world-stop sex, but he never, ever mentioned anything about a relationship or how he felt. My roommate was sure I was standing on the cliff of an epic heartbreak, just waiting to fall over. For now I was okay taking what he was willing to give—I mean, it was more than he had ever given to anybody else—but in the back of my mind I knew it wouldn't be enough forever, and eventually something between us was going to have to change, or at the very least, be defined into clearer terms that I could live with.

"Hey, you, I thought you were working late tonight," I said.

"I am. I'm also starving and wondering if you've eaten yet."

"No. I just got out of my study group and have to go work on a project for my anatomy class."

"Is it something you can do here?"

I tucked a piece of hair behind my ear and stepped gingerly across the icy parking lot. "At the shop?"

"Yeah. We have Wi-Fi and it's just me and my client so it's quiet. You can grab some food and then work here for a couple hours until I'm done. We can go back to my place later if you want."

I so totally did want. I bit my lip and got into my car. "Are you sure you can work with me hanging around? I mean, I don't want to distract you or anything."

He gave a soft laugh that sent goose bumps running up and down my arms.

"While you are quite a distraction, Casper, my client is a fifty-five-year-old retired homicide detective who would gladly wring my neck if I screw his piece up. It's a memorial tattoo in honor of his son who died in Afghanistan. Feed me so that I can do a good job and not get my ass kicked."

I laughed and clamped the phone between my shoulder and ear. I hadn't ever been in Rule's shop. That seemed like a line that our previous relationship didn't cross, but I had to admit I was curious to see what the inside of a real tattoo parlor looked like. "What do you want me to bring you?"

"I don't care. I'm not picky, just make sure there is a lot of whatever it is."

"All right, I'm still at the school so give me a half hour or so."

"Cool."

He hung up without saying good-bye, something that drove me nuts because he always did it, but I was learning that he had a lot of weird quirks that I'd never noticed before. There was a lot I was learning about him, things that I had missed over the years that surprised me, like the fact that he was such a good friend. I had seen him interact with Rome and Remy so I knew he was giving and loving to

141

those he cared about, but he was the same way with his boys. Nash and Rule were most definitely a team. When one zigged the other zagged instinctively. They lived in sync, worked in sync, and it was clear to see that they just got each other, and as high maintenance and complicated as Rule was I had to admit it was fascinating to watch. They made each other laugh and made each other mad. Rule was kind of a slob and Nash was a neat freak, but they took care of each other in different ways. Nash tended to be quieter and let things slide—like the jerk across the street taking his parking spot even though it was snowy and cold, didn't bother him enough to make a fuss—but Rule was a born fighter, a hothead who refused to let anything ride. The guy in Nash's spot came out to find an elaborate scene of a big purple dinosaur getting head from what looked to be a perverted Yoda on the hood of his car in washable paint. Sure he was furious and wanted to call the cops, but Nash had talked him out of it by pointing out that he could have had the car impounded, which would cost more than a trip to the car wash. It showed how the boys just balanced each other out.

I decided on Chinese because I could grab a decent variety of things and I love sesame chicken. There was a line and I had to wait for what seemed like an eternity to get it. It was closer to an hour by the time I found the shop and a place to park that wouldn't take me an hour to walk there. Parking on Capitol Hill was a nightmare and walking on the crowded sidewalk with bags full of takeout and my laptop case proved to be an interesting challenge, but I made it, and the glass door painted with an interesting mélange of old-school sailor tattoos swung open before I had to figure out what to juggle in my full hands in order to pull it open. Rule took the food from me, pressed a quick, hard kiss on my startled mouth, and ushered me into the tattoo parlor. He flipped the sign on the door to CLOSED and guided me past a long marble counter that had a series of portfolios laid out across it and a massive high-tech computer system propped up on top.

Each of the workstations was divided by a waist-high wall and a mounted flat-screen TV. Everything was bright and shiny clean, and there was a myriad of different artwork and all kinds of interesting old-school tattoo designs for people to choose from plastering the available wall space. It was visually stimulating and there was old Bad Religion playing quietly on the house sound system. It was all very Rule, as if he had found a place to work that completely and totally embodied who he was as a person, and that was just really special to see. He led me to a back room that had a table and couch as well as a mini fridge and a bunch of different stations that had drafting tables and special lights for artists to use. Sitting at the table was a middle-aged man who could have easily been one of my father's golf buddies, except for the fact that he had his shirt off and the entire center of his chest was covered not in gray hair but a stark black outline of a bald eagle and an American flag.

Rule dumped the bags on the table and began digging through them. "Shaw, this is Mark Bradley, Mark this is Shaw. I hope you don't mind if she sticks around for a bit since she was nice enough to bring us dinner."

He started dishing stuff out onto plates that he pulled out of nowhere. "Sure thing. I didn't know you went out and got yourself a girl, Rule. A pretty one at that."

Rule winked at me over the guy's head and handed me a loaded plate that I probably wouldn't even put a small dent in. "She sure is that."

We ate in companionable silence for a few minutes but I kept checking out the bold outline on Mark's chest. It was huge and seemed like such a massive commitment for someone in his fifties to be making.

143

"That piece is pretty impressive," I said between bites.

He looked down at himself and then back up at Rule. "The kid has real talent. I looked all over town to find someone who would do what I wanted justice. Rule got it right away, and it didn't hurt that his brother is enlisted, so he understood the importance behind it all."

"He mentioned it was a memorial piece for your son."

"Unfortunately. Roadside bomb a few years ago. He was my oldest and nothing else seemed an appropriate way to honor how proud I am to be his father."

I felt tears well in my eyes. I was so used to parents being too thoughtless or lost in their own grief to really express their heartache in a healthy way. I reached out and squeezed the older man's hand while blinking away the moisture gathered in my eyes.

"I think that is beautiful."

"My kid was a sucker for a good old-school tattoo. I gave him crap every time he came home with something new. It would tickle him pink that this was the way I chose to keep his memory alive."

"You'll be finished with it today?" I asked Rule, who was eating while standing up and watching the interplay between me and his client intently.

"No. Something that big takes a few sessions. Today we'll hammer in the rest of the solid black and the gray, get some of the highlights and all the shading done. His next sitting will only be an hour or so and I'll get the color in it. It's going to be classic when it's all done."

We finished eating and I offered to clean up the mess while Rule went out to set up for Mark. I had just finished cleaning up and was pulling out my computer and books to set up in the back room when Rule poked his head into the room and crooked his finger at me. "Come out here and post up in one of the empty stations."

"I don't want to be in the way."

"Come on, Casper, you make the view better."

I rolled my eyes at him and moved to set up across from him. I settled into the surprisingly comfy chair and propped my computer on my lap. The music switched to a song by The Gaslight Anthem and I hummed along.

"What are you studying?"

I glanced up at Mark, who was making an interesting face as Rule bent over him, the constant buzz of the tattoo machine surprisingly lulling and comforting.

"I want to be a doctor. I would eventually like to work in emergency medicine."

"That's a pretty big goal. Why emergency medicine?"

I pulled my hair up into a sloppy knot on the top of my head. "I've always wanted to be a doctor. My dad is a heart surgeon, but I lost a really close friend a few years ago in a horrific car accident, and I guess I felt like maybe if he had had better care when he got to ER he would have made it. I want to make a difference when it matters most."

Rule looked up and we stared at each other for a long moment before he put his head down and went back to what he was doing. Mark grunted. "That's a pretty special girl you got there, kid. You better be doing right by her."

He muttered something I didn't hear and I turned my attention to the project I still had a bunch of work left to do on. I typed away and the machine buzzed for a solid two hours. We didn't really talk much—me because I was working and subtly watching Rule; Mark, because as time went on it was clear he was hurting; and Rule, because when he worked he was focused solely on what he was doing and it was extraordinary to watch. He was actually putting a little bit of himself into what he was leaving on Mark and he wouldn't settle for less than a perfect end product. I think watching him work, watching him diligently change this

145

man's body forever, made me fall just a little bit harder for him.

Mark had to take a couple breaks, and each time he got up, Rule made his way over to me. The first time he dropped a kiss on the top of my head. The second time he pulled me into a full-body make-out session that had me readjusting my shirt when Mark came back inside from smoking a cigarette. All in all it was a pretty nice way to spend an evening and I got plenty of work done. Four hours later Rule was wiping smears of black ink off Mark's angry red skin, and the image he had on his chest was a beautifully etched tattoo that was an honorable tribute to his fallen son. I told him again how beautiful I thought it was and that I would love to see it when it was all done, and he gave me a hug like a real dad would and told me to take care of myself. He also paid Rule, which made me balk. I had no idea how much getting tattooed cost and then he left him a gigantic tip on top of it.

Rule told me to pack up and then went about cleaning up his station and shutting the shop down for the night. It took us another hour to finally leave, and by then I was yawning and getting sleepy. My car was close enough that I decided to just leave it and not try for a spot closer to their apartment, and Rule promised to get up early in the morning and take me to it if I wanted. The walk was fast because it was cold; it helped that he pulled me close the entire way.

When we got back to his place, we said hi to Nash. I thought maybe Rule wanted to sit for a second and chat but he dropped my stuff on the coffee table, grabbed a couple beers out of the fridge, and hauled me into his room.

We didn't talk, didn't seem to need to. By now I was getting the hang of how the whole sex thing, or rather the whole sex-with-Rule thing, worked. He was very tactile, very hands-on, and I benefited from all of it. After rolling around not once but twice I was quite happily sprawled across his naked chest randomly tracing the scales of the snake on the arm next to my face. He was propped up on a pillow, drinking one of the beers and messing around on his phone while drawing some kind of pattern on my back with his finger. I was sated and almost asleep when his voice rattled through my head.

"Want to come to another show with me on Saturday? I tattoo one of the guys in Artifice and I got backstage passes."

I let my eyes snap open and went stiff, which he was bound to feel since I was using him as a body pillow. I pushed my hair out of my face and looked up at him. His eyes were droopy and sleepy as well, but I saw that he really wanted to know what my answer was. I gulped a little and bit down on my lip like I did when I was nervous.

"I have to go to my mother's for the weekend. I'm leaving on Saturday and won't be back until sometime Sunday afternoon."

Now he was the one who went stiff underneath me. "You going alone?"

"No." My voice was barely a whisper. "I told Gabe I would drop him off at his parents' on the way."

"You told the guy who has been stalking you and harassing you that you would give him a ride?" The incredulous tone made me nervous.

"Yes, I did."

"Why?"

"Because it was easier than dealing with the guilt trip and endless amounts of disappointment my mom would throw at me if I didn't. You don't understand."

"Oh, I understand perfectly. Your mom says jump and you do it right into that nut job's arms. I can't believe this, Shaw. I barely get to see you as it is. I go freaking insane half the time because I wake up in the middle of the night to reach for you and you aren't there, and now you're off planning a weekend getaway with your psycho ex-boyfriend. Unbelievable."

I rolled off him and pulled the sheet up around myself, feeling exposed and vulnerable, neither having to do with the fact I was naked. "It isn't like that and you know it. I don't want to go, don't want to spend time with Gabe, but letting my mother have her way is easier than trying to defy her."

"How would you know? Have you ever even tried to defy her?"

I sucked a cold breath in through my teeth. "She's my mom, Rule."

"Whatever. We can talk about it tomorrow." He rolled onto his side away from me and I knew Rule well enough to know that there would be no talking about it tomorrow.

In fact, as he dropped me off at my car the next morning there was zero talking, zero kissing, zero eye contact, zero anything from him to indicate that a conversation could fix what I had somehow done.

I texted him after work the next day that I was sorry and I wanted to see him, but he didn't respond. I called him on Tuesday to see if he wanted to get lunch and talk about things and was sent right to voice mail. By Wednesday I was practically frantic and ready to show up at the shop or at his apartment and demand that he talk to me, but Rome was back in town and commandeered me for dinner. He let it slip that he was crashing at Rule's for a few days because his other buddy had family in town for the week. My heart nearly devoured itself when I realized Rule hadn't even bothered to let me know Rome was in town. I very well could have shown up and made a complete ass out of myself in front of his brother and he didn't even care.

I spent Thursday and Friday sobbing onto Ayden's mostly

unsympathetic shoulder and tried to get through my shifts at work. I was a mess on Saturday morning when I stopped at the bakery to get Gabe and all I wanted to do was run his smug, smiling face over with my BMW.

He tried to lean in to kiss me on the cheek and I pulled away so violently I smacked my head on the driver's-side window.

"Don't." I could almost see the icicles hanging on my voice but I didn't care. I missed Rule, was mad that I was having to pick between him and yet another family, and pissed that he couldn't see why I had to do what I did. All week long I had been plagued with visions of his room turning back into a revolving door of sexual conquests and it made me hyperventilate. I could see why he was angry at me, but I hated that he was just shutting me out.

"Come on, Shaw, can't you at least try to make this weekend pleasant? Our parents would be thrilled if we could just work things out between us."

I turned the radio on and let Georgia rock from the Drive-By Truckers fill in the void where my conversation should go. I slapped Gabe's hand away when he reached for the volume control. "Don't even think about it."

"Come on, Shaw, we need to talk."

"No."

"Stop being so stubborn."

"Gabe, I'm involved with someone else. There is nothing we need to talk about. The only reason I'm going this weekend is to get my mom off my back."

"That tattooed punk? You can't think you have anything serious with him, Shaw. Seriously what are you thinking? You're going to come home after a seventy-two-hour shift at a hospital and he's just going to be sitting around waiting for you like some kind of house husband? You really think that's an accurate description of how your future looks with someone like that? More like you start your residency and as soon as he sees how much you're gone and how much time he has to spend alone he starts bringing all those girls that were there before you back around. Get real. Guys like that are not in it for the long haul, they're only there until the shine wears off."

I bristled because it was hitting a little too close to home for me right now so I just turned the music up louder and did my best to ignore him for the rest of the ride. I made great time, driving faster than I should have but desperate to get out of the confined space with Gabe. He had tried several times to pull me into conversation but each time I upped the volume on the radio until the Truckers were at an ear-splitting level, making it ridiculous to try to talk. He finally got the point and zipped his mouth shut. I practically shoved him out the door without stopping when I got to his house in Brookside. He motioned for me to roll the window down so he could talk to me, but I just gritted my teeth and pulled away with squealing tires.

My parents lived in another gated community in Brookside so as I tooled through town I decided to stop at the Starbucks where I had taken Rule last time I was here and pull myself together. Just to torture myself even further I pulled out my phone and died a little more when it showed no new messages or texts. I didn't know what to do and I felt like everything I had ever wanted was slipping right through my fingers.

"Shaw? Shaw Landon, is that you?" I looked up from my coffee and stifled a groan as Amy Rodgers barreled down on me. I should have remembered her and this Starbucks went hand in hand.

"It sure is, Amy. How are you?"

She air-kissed my face and gave me a toothy smile. She had never even pretended to be this nice to me in high school, so I was instantly on high alert.

"Oh, I'm good. I just finished beauty school and I'm working in a super trendy, super high-end salon in Denver. You're living there now, too, right?"

I nodded and I saw her eyes trail over my new and improved hair. "Well, I'm excited I ran into you. I was thinking about looking you up."

I lifted a brow. "Why?"

She flicked her hair over her shoulder. "Well, I was home a few weekends ago doing laundry and I ran into one of the Archer twins, the one with all the tattoos. Anyway, I remembered that you were close with them and I was wondering if I could get his number from you. I can't remember which one is which, but lordy was he gorgeous. I heard they moved to Denver, too, and I was hoping I might be able to start something up with him."

I felt everything inside me turn to ice. I almost threw my coffee in her pretty, perfect face but just barely, by the skin of my teeth, managed to restrain myself.

"Remy died, Amy. It's just Rule, has only been Rule for almost three years now, and I'm sure he would just looooove to hear from some idiot girl who didn't even know who he was, just one of the Archer twins. You make me want to vomit, and you're lucky we're in a public place or there's a really good chance I would be punching you repeatedly in the face right now."

She gaped at me in astonishment as I pushed past her and tossed my coffee in the trash, all taste for it gone. "I'm not giving you his number because he's mine and if you get anywhere near him I swear to God the things I'll do to you will be chronicled on Investigation Discovery for years to come."

I was shaking by the time I got back in the car and it only took a second for the tears to come. I missed Remy, I missed Rule, and I missed Margot and Dale. Rule was right;

I didn't know what it felt like to defy my mother because I never had and now she was just one more person trying to get between me and the person I wanted to be with. I had no trouble laying claim to him with a bimbo like Amy, but my mother, well that was a far bigger fish to fry. I had always known he was worth it—that's what I was waiting so desperately for his parents to see, but when the time had come to prove it I had done what everyone else did to him and let my mother pressure me into doing something that moved me away from him. I pressed my forehead against the steering wheel and picked my phone back up. I stared at it for a solid five minutes with the car running, trying to think of what to say to him and all I came up with was:

I really am sorry; I never meant to hurt you. I should've stayed. I really miss you.

I put it away before I made myself crazy seeing if he was going to text anything back and made my way to my parents' house. The house was more like some kind of elegant mountain chalet than an actual home. Everything past the gates was elegant and expensive, and as I parked and made my way to the front door I remembered how small I felt next to the grandeur. When Remy had come into my life and taken me under his wing, I had taken the opportunity to spend every second I could at the Archers'. For all their faults, they made a home where it was clear people were loved and cared for. Both my mother's and my father's homes had none of that; they were filled with servants and showpieces. As I was led into the living room I was struck again by how very much I didn't want to be here and how if I couldn't fix things with Rule after this weekend there was a good chance I was going to have to be committed because I just might lose my mind.

My mother in all her refined glory came at me with a critical eye. There was no hug, no "how was your drive?" no "sorry I missed your birthday, sweetie," just a quick sweep of her ice-cold gaze from the top of my head to the toes of my laced-up leather boots. Her already tight mouth pulled into a frown. "What have you done to your hair, Shaw? It looks dreadful and I hope you brought more appropriate clothes for the country club. We're going to dinner, not a potluck."

I was wearing leggings and a long oxford with a wide leather belt that matched my boots. It was way too fancy for a simple car ride home but I had been trying to avoid this exact scene. Once again I had failed to meet her exacting standards. My hands curled tighter around the bag I had refused to give to the maid who'd opened the door. My heart was in my throat—well, actually it was back in Denver currently ignoring me, but that was neither here nor there.

"I assume you and Gabe had time to talk on the way up here?"

"Not really. I've told you I don't have anything left to say to him."

If it were possible, her mouth pulled into an even tighter frown—she looked like she was sucking on a lemon. My mother was a beautiful woman—I got my fair hair and light coloring from her—but as I looked at her objectively, for possibly the first time in my life, I realized that all that beauty was harsh and encased in so much ice and bitterness that it was hard to see.

"I asked you to stop being ridiculous, young lady. You will be polite and charming this weekend. I will not tolerate any hostility or rudeness directed at Gabe or any of the Davenports, do you understand me?"

From somewhere deep inside me the Shaw that I was when I was with Rule, the Shaw that should have refused to come on this farce of a weekend, raised her head. I flicked the ends of my two-toned hair over my shoulder and brushed past my mother to head to the stairs where my room was located. "You ordered me to be here, Mother, so now you have to deal with that whether you like the outcome or not." She called something after me in a shrill voice but I tuned her out, calling over my shoulder, "Let me know when you're ready to leave for dinner."

I shut the door to the room that had never really felt like mine and let my bag drop on the floor. My mother's interior designer had done the room in a palette of grays and soft pinks. It was all very lovely, feminine and girly to the max with a million frilly pillows on the bed and even a lacy canopy draped over the white four-poster bed. It was the room a person who wanted to sleep in luxury and be surrounded by million-thread-count sheets would enjoy; for me it had always felt lifeless and dull. There were no personal pictures, no splashes of color, no TV or radio—simply nothing to describe a thing about the person who was supposed to live there. I settled cross-legged on the center of the big bed and sent Ayden a text. She had been acting a little weird since the night she had let Jet take her home from the bar, but she didn't want to talk about it, and since I was having my own boy drama I didn't want to fight to drag it out of her.

Wasn't even in the door two steps before she mentioned my hair and my outfit. So good to be home ☹

That sucks, honey.

Yeah and Rule still won't text me back.

Ummm . . .

154

What?

I don't know if I should tell you.

Tell me what?

You have to promise not to freak out.

Well now I'm bound to freak out!

Loren was talking about being out last night; she said she saw Rule and the boys at whatever club she was at.

Oh my God . . .

Yeah, well she mentioned she was going to try to talk to him or whatever because she's a clueless slut, but he had some redhead hanging all over him. She said she couldn't even get close to him.

Fuck.

Yeah, well, she also said he left with her, the redhead, I mean. She said the whole gang of them left together and she is a heinous gossip and likes to cause trouble but I figure you should have a heads-up since you can't get a hold of him.

Thanks.

You okay?

No, not at all.

Want me to hurt him for you?

Maybe. I'll call you later after I get through this stupid dinner. Love ya, girl.

You, too. xoxo

I swiped a finger across the screen and took a second to hold my breath before letting it out in a furious screech and chucking the expensive device against the wall with a satisfying crunch. I buried my head in my hands and tried to keep from throwing up. I couldn't believe this was happening. I had had everything I ever wanted for just a few seconds and all it took was one single bump, one tiny disagreement, to screw it all up. It shouldn't hurt that I was so easily and quickly replaced. I knew Rule, knew how he operated, but I still felt like someone was poking holes in the very fiber of my soul with a scalding-hot poker. Being in love with Rule had never been an easy thing to do, and now that I knew what it was like to actually *love* him I wasn't sure how to go back to before.

I spent the rest of the afternoon sequestered in my room. My mother sent one of the staff up to see if I wanted lunch but I refused to answer the door when they knocked. She sent her husband up around five to tell me that we were leaving in an hour for the club, and while a big part of me wanted nothing more than to wear skinny jeans and my motorcycle boots, I decided that having that fight with my mother in front of my half siblings would just make me seem childish and ridiculous, so I put on a long-sleeved white and purple A-line dress that hit me a few inches above my knees and spent a few minutes flat-ironing my hair so that it fell in a slick curtain around my shoulders. I had a pair of purple booties that had spiked heels and little studs on the back that completed the look. It wasn't exactly picture-perfect country club gear, but it should get me through the front door without too much trouble.

My mother gave me the evil eye as I came down the stairs, and Jack helped me into my gray pea coat. No one said anything as we piled into the family Escalade and headed to the country club. The kids jibber jabbered back and forth and I brooded about Rule and some unknown redhead, hoping it didn't mean what I thought it did and willed the car to get a flat tire so I could avoid Gabe and his family. It didn't happen, and when we got to the club and I had to force a smile and let Gabe kiss my cheek and pull out my chair, it literally took every single ounce of willpower I had not to run screaming in the other direction. I settled in between Gabe and my mother and prepared to suffer through the most awkward, awful dinner of my life.

CHAPTER 9

Rule

"So you want to come clean and tell me why you're acting like even more of an asshole this week than normal?" Rome was standing over me while I bench-pressed the weight up off my chest. He had asked me to go to the gym on Saturday because he was supposed to start rehabbing his shoulder. Even banged up my brother was cut, and working out with him put me to shame. I spent most of the workout trying not to flinch when I noticed how much more weight he was using than I normally did. Once the bar was locked in place I sat up and ran a towel over my sweaty face and newly shaved head. I hadn't cut it all the way to the scalp like Nash wore his, but the Mohawk was gone and all I was left with was dark stubble all across my head. With my eyebrow rings and the tattoos that climbed up my neck I thought it made me look a little like an escaped prisoner.

"Not really." I followed Rome as he moved over to the set of free weights and started hefting one back and forth with his bad arm. It still bothered him because he winced each time he retracted and extended but he didn't complain and just kept up the reps. I should tell him I was all bent out of shape over Shaw; he would probably have really good advice to give me, since I was pretty sure I was on a path bound to screw up something that was turning out to be amazingly good. When he'd left Wednesday to take her to dinner it had taken everything I could do not to tackle him and demand to know if she had asked about me and if she was doing okay. Then I remembered I was purposely not answering her text messages or returning her calls and figured I would just leave it be.

His eyes met mine in the mirror as his face twisted into a tight grimace of pain. "It wouldn't have anything to do with why Shaw looked like a freaking ghost on Wednesday when I saw her, would it?"

"Why would you think one thing had to do with the other?"

"Because I'm not stupid. She's had a thing for you for a while and I figured it was only a matter of time before you got your head far enough out of your ass to see it. Plus, both of you have been staring at your phones for the last week like they hold all the answers to the universe and looking like kicked puppies when they don't have on them whatever it was you're looking for."

I swore and worried my lip ring with my tongue. "You're really gonna be cool if I tell you Shaw and I have been hooking up? Or are you going to hurt me?"

"As long as it's more than hooking up I will be cool as hell. Shaw isn't one of your one-night stands, and if you're treating her like she is I'll break both your legs."

I scowled at him and flipped him off in the mirror. "What do you mean she's been into me for a while? She got hammered one night and things got heated and I couldn't stop it from happening, so I figured, why not roll with it? I like her. I mean I like spending time with her. She's fun but she's always so busy and this weekend she went back to Brookside with her weirdo ex because her mom told her to.

I just don't know if I can hang out with someone like that. She's twenty years old, she should be living her own life, not bowing down to her parents' every whim."

"So let me guess: Instead of having a rational, reasonable conversation with her about it where you laid out your concerns, you probably just shut her out and refused to talk to her while you seethed and festered in your own anger."

I shrugged a shoulder.

"Rule, Shaw has known you for a long time. Can you imagine what she's thinking you're out doing while you're ignoring her? Come on, brother, use your head for one bloody second. Is it worth it to ruin it all before you even get it started? That girl sees you, I mean really sees you, and I think she has since the very beginning when everyone was always looking around you to see Remy. You need to stop being stubborn and make things right with her."

"She went with her ex, Rome."

"Yeah, and you went out last night and let some skank shove her tongue down your throat. Not everyone operates off the same script, Rule. Most people want to make their parents happy, want to have them approve of what they are doing with their lives. Not everyone can burn every bridge the way you do. Most people want a way back home."

I cringed a little because his words hit right at the center of me. Had I been just a little drunker, just a little stupider, I probably would have made a mistake last night that there was no going back from. Luckily, the redhead had tasted like sticky sweet lip gloss and smelled like cheap floral perfume. She had none of the softness or perfectness of how it felt being lip-locked with Shaw, so I had sent her on her way and felt like shit for the rest of the night. I knew I was going to have to talk to Shaw. I couldn't keep going on like this or I was going to end up sabotaging everything that was building between us.

"It freaks me out, Rome."

"Why?"

"You know why. Once someone is in, it kills you when they leave."

"Come on, Rule, the people who care enough to get in normally don't want to leave. Just look around you: I'm still here, Nash hasn't gone anywhere. Jet and Rowdy would kill for you, and if you took a minute to think about it, Shaw has been there just as long. You might have thought she was there for Remy because he always watched out for her and protected her, but I think you're smart enough to realize now that maybe she was trying to take care of you for another reason altogether."

He let the weights clatter to the rack with a thud and turned to look at me out of cool eyes.

"Grow up, Rule. Stop acting like a spoiled brat who can't live outside his brother's shadow. You have an amazing, successful career, a solid group of friends, a family that might be broken but loves you nonetheless, and you have a pretty spectacular girl just waiting for you to realize she's yours for the taking."

"Man, when you go big brother you go all out."

He rolled his eyes at me as we made our way to the locker room. I shrugged back into my street clothes and shot a quick glance at my phone. My heart constricted in my chest when I saw the message she had sent. I could practically hear how sad she was in the words. I really was an asshole; I could have talked to her instead of sending her off with that jackass without a word. I was trying to think of something to text her back when Rome thunked me on the back of the head with his palm.

"Let's go."

161

"I have to be at work at noon anyway. Hey, Rome." I waited until he turned and looked me in the eye. "What about Mom and Dad?"

"What about them?"

"Me and Shaw. If I get it figured out, if I manage not to screw it up royally, what am I supposed to do about them? They would never understand."

"Who cares? You deserve to be happy and so does Shaw. Remy is gone and that's just the way it is."

I cleared my throat and ran my hand across the back of my neck. "Yeah, well, Shaw was never with Remy that way."

His eyes got big and his mouth sort of dropped open. "Do I want to know how you know that?"

"Probably not, but let's just say I know for a fact she and Remy didn't have a relationship like that."

"Well regardless, it isn't any of Mom and Dad's business."

I sighed again. "Yeah, I guess."

We parted ways and I made my way to the shop. I had a busy day with clients back to back and I was still committed to going to the show with the guys that night. Brent, the lead singer of the band, was a good client and I got a lot of good press out of having my work on him since Artifice had blown up over the last few years.

After work I went home and changed and got ready to roll out with the boys, but my mind was still on Shaw and the text she'd sent me this morning. She had hurt me and even though I was too hardheaded to admit it, that was the reason I had pulled away. I didn't want her around the ex because logically he was a better match for her and I didn't want to come up short. By shoving her away and not giving her a chance to talk about it, or a chance for us to work it through, I was cutting off any chance at rejection or being found lacking before it could start. I was an idiot. Of all the people in my life Shaw had never been one to make me feel like I was less than anything. Yeah, she could be judgmental and chilly when she was feeling pressured and cornered, but she never made me feel like I wasn't enough.

The show was awesome; we got treated like rock stars because we were backstage and knew the band. The girls who were around us were tempting and alluring, but when it came time for the after party I dipped out early and went home by myself. I took a shower and crawled into bed still staring at my phone. Not able to contain it anymore I finally sent her a text back.

I kissed some chick last night.

I held my breath because I didn't know what she was going to text back. I was fully prepared for her to tell me it was over, that I had gone too far, but nothing came. I stared at the screen for a good twenty minutes, my heart racing, and still nothing came through.

I'm sorry, I didn't do it to hurt you. I'm just an idiot and this is harder than I thought.

There still wasn't a response and I felt that weird slither in my chest that was tied to Shaw start to shatter. All I knew was I had to fix this, that I wasn't ready to let her go just yet. Rome was right, I needed to grow up. I hadn't even given this a fair shot—as usual my hot head was writing checks the rest of me wasn't prepared to cash. I tossed and turned all night. She never called or texted me back and I began to panic. I heard Nash stumble in at some point after four and I hoped Rome slept through it.

I got up the next morning and started moving around the apartment at a frantic pace. I brushed my teeth and shoved a bagel in my mouth. I tore through my closet to find the one shirt I owned that had buttons on it and found the single pair of black Dickie pants I had that weren't jeans. I put a black hoodie on and a pinstriped blazer over it and bounded out the door all while my brother and roommate looked at me like I had lost my mind.

"I'll be back later."

"Where are you going? To church?" Nash looked a little worse for wear and Rome was just watching me knowingly.

"I need to talk to Shaw."

"So call her."

"She isn't answering her phone."

"You think her mom's just gonna let you roll up to the house and let you in?"

"I don't care; I need to talk to her so I'm going to talk to her."

Rome winked at me and saluted me with his coffee cup. "Atta boy. Call me if they have you arrested and I will totally come get you out."

"Later."

I had to stop and put gas in the truck and for whatever reason there was a ton of traffic going out of town. I was impatient and ready to have a fit of serious road rage by the time I finally got to Brookside. I tried to call her one more time and was sent right to voice mail. I almost crushed the phone in my hand when her recorded greeting cheerily told me to just leave a message.

I knew where her mom lived because I had been forced to pick her up more than once and bring her to our house when I still shared a car with Remy. I followed the car in front of me through the gates and found the house with no problem. There was a menagerie of all kinds of expensive and fancy cars that seriously had no place being in Colorado parked out front the chalet-style mansion.

I jogged up the front steps and rang the doorbell. I was expecting a maid or maybe some fancy-ass butler to open the door; what I wasn't expecting was an older, harder version of Shaw. There was no doubt this woman was Shaw's mother; they had the same white-blond hair, the same piercing green eyes, but where Shaw was delicate and lovely, this woman looked like she had been carved out of a solid block of ice. I saw her eyes narrow and sharpen when she saw me but I was on a mission and I didn't care who this chick was—she wasn't going to stand in my way, even if I had to run her over.

"I need to talk to Shaw."

Her mouth pulled tight and she put her small body solidly in the doorway. "You're Margot and Dale's boy aren't you?"

"One of them." We weren't friends, were never going to be, and she was making that clear.

"What do you want with my daughter?"

"That's personal. I just need to speak with her for a minute and then I'll be on my way."

"You're interrupting a private gathering; Shaw is here with her boyfriend and I don't think she wants to see you."

I fought back an eye roll. The lady was manipulative and delivered it like it was fact, but I wasn't stupid so I just stared back at her.

"Davenport is a stalker not her boyfriend. Just get her for me, would ya?" I could see that my lack of respect was starting to get under her too tight skin.

"How do you presume to know what's going on in my daughter's private life? You've always just been a crush, and we all know you two aren't right for each other. It's time to stop playing childish games."

"Look, lady, what's going on between me and Shaw has nothing to do with you and I assure you it isn't a game. I don't mind making a scene if it gets me what I want, but something tells me that you wouldn't want all your guests to wonder what the commotion was about." I lifted my pierced brow. "Am I right?" I think she was about to tell me she was going to call the police or holler for her husband, but she didn't get the chance because the heavy door was yanked out of her death grip and suddenly Shaw's pale face appeared around the doorjamb.

"Rule? What are you doing here?"

Her hair was braided up in some fancy design that looked like it hurt. She had on a pearl necklace that looked like it was from the 1800s and a pink sweater that looked fuzzy and soft. She was also in a pair of loose cream-colored pants and had on a pair of pink heels that looked like they cost as much as my truck. She was so far removed from the Shaw that I was used to rolling around naked with I almost turned around and left without saying another word, but her green eyes were wide and sad and that slippery feeling in the center of my chest started to throb. I didn't care that her mother was watching me with an eagle eye—I grabbed her arm and pulled her onto the stoop with me. I held her face in my hands and peered straight into her eyes.

"I'm sorry," I said.

She put her hands over mine and blinked up at me. "What?"

"I sent you a text last night. I tried to call you back all night and you didn't answer me. I'm sorry. Sorry I pushed you away, sorry I acted like an idiot, sorry I don't know how to do this thing between us right, I'm just sorry."

"My phone is broken."

"What?" I asked it on a laugh. I wanted to kiss her, wanted

to scoop her up in my arms and take her somewhere so far away from here.

"I threw it against the wall because Ayden told me you went home with some girl Friday night. I shattered the screen on it."

"Shit. I'll buy you a new one." She closed her eyes and squeezed my hands.

"Did you do it, go home with her?"

"No, I kissed her, which sucks on my part and makes me an asshole, but I knew it was wrong so I stopped it. I swear if we get this straight between us I will never let it happen again. I'm trying to figure out how all this works, Shaw. I hate that you're the one who has to get hurt because of my learning curve."

"You shut me out, you left me alone in the dark, Rule. I don't think I've ever had anything hurt that bad."

"I know, Casper; I know, but don't give up on me now, okay?"

"You drove all the way here just to apologize?"

I nodded. "We have to fix this."

She gave me a lopsided grin. "We need to learn how not to break it in the first place." I gulped down the sudden surge of emotion in my throat and pulled her into a tight hug. It felt like coming home, a feeling I don't think I had ever actually experienced before. I kissed her softly behind her ear and whispered, "By the way, your mom hates me, like, HATES me."

She put her hands in the back pockets of my pants and stood on her tiptoes to kiss the underside of my jaw. "That's okay, she hates me, too. Why did you cut your hair all off? It looks good, you look good, but I liked the Mohawk."

I self-consciously ran a hand over my naked skull. "I don't know. I just needed to change it."

She looked at me with serious eyes and folded her hand

in mine. "It makes you look more like Remy than all your other hairstyles."

"Shaw, tell your friend good-bye and come back inside. We have guests and you're being very rude."

She peeked over my shoulder at her mother and I felt her grip on my hand tighten.

"I'm not coming in without Rule." Oh shit, she was doing it again, putting herself between me and another disapproving parent.

"Hey, it's cool. As long as we're good I'll just catch up with you when you get back to D-town. I can wait to see you later."

"No."

"Shaw." Her mother's voice was all whiplash warning. "This ends now. Send him on his way and come inside. You've made enough of a scene."

"No. I'm with him. If you want me to sit through another meal where you're going to blatantly ignore Gabe trying to grope me and purposely make me uncomfortable then I'm doing it with Rule there to keep him in check."

"Shaw, he does not belong in there with this group of people."

There it was, the judgment, the censure, the idea that because I lived on my own terms and in my own way I wasn't good enough for this girl. I pulled her to my side and met her mother's glare with one of my own. Remy might have protected her by giving her a safe haven, but I was a fighter by nature and this lady had pushed enough of my buttons to last for years.

"Right, but I'm the one she spent her birthday with, I'm the one who makes her happy, and I'm the one who is ready to protect her from the creep you keep shoving at her. I'm more than willing to take her with me and get out of your hair, but I doubt you want to try to explain her hasty exit to the Davenports, so why don't you just suck it up for once in your life and let your kid have something, just one thing, that makes her happy?"

"Shaw?" There was confusion in the woman's tone now.

"I go where he goes, so if you don't want him to come in then I'm outta here. I never should have come in the first place. I'm tired of being manipulated and used as a pawn and an accessory. I told you about Gabe and you refuse to listen."

"But you're perfect together."

"Right, only I want to be with him." She hooked her thumb in my direction.

"He openly admitted to cheating on you only a day ago, what kind of relationship do you honestly think you can have with him? Do you think your father will continue to pay for school when he hears about this?"

She shrugged and I put a hand on her hip to pull her back against me. "I'm sick to death of worrying about it. It gives me migraines and my relationship is mine to work out. He's not perfect and neither am I; if I choose to forgive him you don't get a say in it."

I felt like a heel. I shouldn't have assumed the redhead was just going to be forgotten, but Shaw was still letting me hold her, so I wasn't too worried about it.

"Fine. Come in, eat brunch, and try not to embarrass yourselves while you're at it. Shaw, I want you gone as soon as brunch is done and don't think for one single second that this is over. Just wait until I speak with your father about this circus."

She spun around and disappeared inside the massive house. I looked down at Shaw and ran a finger across her furrowed brow. "We okay?"

"Mostly. Let's just get through this, then worry about the rest later." She started to pull away from me but I caught her around the waist and pulled her back to me.

"Shaw."

"Yeah?"

I kissed her. I kissed her so that she could feel my regret, my desire to do right, the way that she had a piece of me now and I wasn't letting go. I kissed her because I had to and kissing her made me feel better. When I lifted my head her mouth looked puffy and damp and her eyes were glassy with banked passion.

"I missed you, too."

She giggled a little and hooked her elbow around my arm. "These are a bunch of country club people and Mom's political associates. You clean up nice, but don't expect them to welcome you with open arms. I don't think any of them have ever even seen a tattoo up close and personal so be prepared to be treated like half pariah and half zoo exhibit."

"It'll be fine. I can't promise to play nice if that douche bag tries to put his hands on you in front of me, though."

She shivered against my side. "He was awful last night. I kept trying to move farther and farther away and he just followed. My mother is insane if she thinks I'm spending one more minute with him."

"Don't you have to drive him back to school today?"

"I was planning on faking a headache and just letting him drive while I lay down in the backseat."

I didn't like that idea at all; she didn't need to be vulnerable and subjected to that nonsense.

"Just give him the keys to the BMW and you can ride back with me. Have him text you when he's home and Nash and I can go get your car later tonight."

"Really?"

"Yeah. Look, I know I messed up but I'm here for real now. We're going to do this and I promise I'll take care of you the best as I can. You're going to have to be patient with me because I'm flying blind, but this is the kind of

170

thing I should be doing for you. Plus, I don't want you anywhere near that guy. He has something going on under all that polo and khaki and I don't trust him one bit."

"All right. I'll set it up and if he refuses I'll just tell him he has to find his own way home."

She led me into a dining room that was packed with every real housewife of Brookside and every single person in the top-earning percentile of the state. There was a lot of money and power in this dining room, and Shaw was right, they were all looking at me like I was a wild animal let out of its cage. She tightened her grip on my arm and led me over to a table with all kinds of food spread out on it. Everyone gave us a wide berth for about three minutes, but as soon as Shaw tried to lead us to the table we were waylaid by Polo Shirt and the rest of the Junior League. He looked me up and down, then skimmed over Shaw in a way that made me want to hang him from a tree by his own intestines.

"This is a private function; I doubt you were invited."

I lifted an eyebrow and settled a hand on Shaw's lower back.

"He's with me." Her tone was cold and left no room for argument.

"For now."

"Leave it alone, Polo Shirt. This isn't the time or the place."

"You don't belong here. You're a thug and a loser. Shaw is going to get tired of living on the wild side and see reason."

"Here." She shoved her keys at him and dragged me behind her into the room where everyone was seated at a massive table. All eyes were on us as she stormed to the table calling over her shoulder, "I'm not spending one second more with you; you can take the Beamer home by yourself or find your own ride."

I heard him sputter but I was too busy pulling out Shaw's seat and settling in next to her to enjoy it. I could feel most of the eyes in the room on us and her mother's sour look from the head of the table. I was about to tell Shaw this was silly and was just making everyone uncomfortable when I heard a surprised voice say my name.

"Rule? Rule Archer is that you? What are you doing all the way out here for brunch?" The chair next to mine was pulled out and Alexander Carsten, a longtime client of mine, settled into the seat next to me. I gave him a grin and shook the hand he offered.

"What's up, Alex? Long time no see. How's the leg piece? Did it heal up all right?"

He laughed a big hearty laugh. Alex was a lawyer or something, in his early forties and pretty successful. I knew he drove a sweet Jag and had an awesome loft somewhere down in LoDo, but he was cool as hell for a buttoned-up kind of guy. I had done a couple big pieces on his leg and on his back, and under his pressed shirt and silk tie I knew he had two full sleeves, one Nash had done for him and one Rowdy had done. He paid big bucks and was an awesome tipper. Considering this was the last place on earth I would have planned on running into a client, I was stunned into momentary silence. I felt Shaw drop her hand onto my thigh and I covered it with my own.

"It healed perfect. I was actually thinking about swinging by in a few weeks and getting you to draw up something for my chest. So what are you doing out here?"

"I'm actually from Brookside, but I'm here particularly because my girl is stubborn and trying to prove a point." I inclined my head at Shaw and she narrowed her eyes at me. Alex looked around me at Shaw and snorted out a laugh.

"You're dating Eleanor Landon's daughter? I bet that went over like coal on Christmas." I guess Shaw's mom hadn't changed her name when she left Shaw's dad or maybe it was just a better name for her political agenda.

172

"Oh yeah, she's not a fan."

"Well, don't worry about it; she isn't a fan of much from what I hear. It's good to see a familiar face at one of these shindigs. I hope she keeps you around; these people can use the culture shock. This stuff is normally so boring."

We bumped fists and I turned back to Shaw to ask her how much longer we had to stay, but now everyone in the entire room was staring at me like I had grown an extra head.

"What?"

She laughed and pressed her head against my shoulder. "Do you have any idea who that is?"

I popped a piece of orange in my mouth and pressed her hand harder into my thigh. "Alex. I tattoo him—actually we all do. He's a regular at the shop."

She was laughing so hard there were tears running down her face. "That's Alex Carsten."

"I just said I know."

"Rule, Alex is the state attorney general. He's the most influential legal person in all of Colorado. My mother helped get him elected."

I ate another slice of orange and noticed Shaw's mom was looking at me totally differently now. "Weird. He's tatted up like crazy; under that suit and tie is some serious artwork."

"That's just too funny."

"Hey, how much longer do we have to stick around here?"

"Let's finish eating and then I need to pack my stuff up in my room. You can come up and help me."

"You think the queen of the castle is going to let me in the ivory tower?"

She leaned in closer to me and moved her hand up even higher on my thigh; it made me almost choke on the orange I was chewing.

"She might not want you in there"—her green eyes twinkled up at me with merriment—"but I sure do."

This stupid brunch couldn't end fast enough. I popped another piece of orange in my mouth and tried counting backward from a hundred to get my libido in check. I thought brunch with my folks was rough. I was starting to see why Shaw was so interested in pulling my fractured family back together. Even as messed up as we Archers were, these rich people had us beat in crazy and nasty by spades.

CHAPTER 10

Shaw

I was doing my best to get away from my mother's house but even though the plan had been to escape as soon as we were done eating, Alex had shown back up at the table and hijacked Rule. He claimed one of his coworkers was interested in some custom artwork for his man cave and he thought Rule might be the perfect person to produce it for him, so there I was again, the odd man out at one of my mother's awful events while my tattooed, pierced boyfriend was making the rounds like some kind of celebrity. It was kind of funny and I was secretly thrilled that it had to be getting under my mother's skin, but I wanted to go. I wanted to get him alone and make up for lost time. It felt like things had shifted dramatically between us and I needed time to put it in perspective, needed time to figure out what it meant to him exactly, because to me he had defined the relationship by showing up here to apologize and I needed to know he felt the same.

My mother was working the room, and Jack was tied up with the kids. Gabe was hanging out with the other future business leaders of America shooting killer looks at Rule, and my guy was in the middle of elegantly dressed men describing something with his hands that had them all nodding eagerly and chattering away at him. I saw my opportunity to escape for a minute so I slid through the kitchen and made my way up to my room. I shoved all my stuff into the bag I had brought and tossed my broken phone on top. I think I would hold Rule to buying me a new one, since he was the reason I had tossed it against the wall in the first place. I was looking around the bedroom for anything I might have forgotten when warm hands slid around my waist.

I knew Rule's touch and this wasn't it, so I jerked upright and shoved hard against Gabe's chest.

"What do you think you're doing?" He grabbed my arm, hard, and tried to pull me toward him. "Get out of my room, Gabe."

"I figured it all out, Shaw." He kept pulling on my arm hard enough that I knew there was going to be a bruise. I was trying to push him away from me but he was exerting a lot more force and he was stronger than me. "You dumped me so you could have sex with Archer. Well, by now you should have screwed him out of your system. You never gave me a shot to show you what I can do. I think you need a fair comparison before you totally shut me out."

I felt my eyes spring wide as I renewed my efforts to get free. "You've got to be kidding me! I didn't sleep with you because I'm not attracted to you. I didn't want to have sex with you then and I don't want to have sex with you now. You need to go or Rule is going to murder you."

He pulled my wrist tight behind my back so hard I yelped. He lowered his face until it was right in mine and grabbed my jaw with his other hand. I was starting to actually panic; my room was upstairs and on the other side of the big house. I was sure someone would hear me scream if I yelled, but I wasn't sure what the fallout from that kind of scene would be. I struggled to be released and he just laughed.

"I'm not scared of the street thug nor am I impressed by his artistic genius or whatever Carsten was going on about. He's trash and not going to get in the way of what I want, and Shaw, you belong to me, you should know that now." He gave me a hard shove back so that I fell onto the bed. I immediately scrambled across the other side so that the entire mass was between us. "You better get on board with this, Shaw, before it gets ugly."

I was breathing hard and had a hand to my throat. It was shaking and so was I. He threw my keys on the bed. "I'll get my own ride back to Denver. Wouldn't want you to spend any more time alone with Tattoo Boy than necessary, would I?"

He strolled out of the room like he hadn't just assaulted or threatened me. I shook myself out of the shock and gathered my stuff and bolted down the stairs. I found Rule wandering around the kitchen looking lost and clearly searching for me. I handed him my bags and hustled him out of the house without bothering to say good-bye to anyone, even my mom. It wasn't until we were on the highway headed home that I broke down. Out of the blue, broken sobs racked my whole body and I couldn't stop crying. I was shaking so hard and making such a hysterical fuss that Rule freaked out and pulled over to the side of the road. He kept asking me if it was my head but I couldn't answer so I just crawled into his lap and cried and cried.

It took a solid twenty minutes for the deluge to stop and by then Rule was frantic and threatening to take me to the nearest emergency room.

"No. It's fine, just give me a minute." He was rubbing my back and his blue eyes were crystal like frost. I pressed my forehead against his and pushed up the sleeves of my coat. Angry red welts and ugly purple bruises were encircling my entire wrist. "Gabe ambushed me in my room when I was grabbing my stuff. He shoved me around and threatened me. He said I needed to get on board with this, whatever that means, before it gets ugly. He really hurt me, Rule, and he scared me. I don't know what's wrong with him, but it's getting really bad."

He went still as a statue underneath me and he lifted one of his hands to grab my injured wrist. He turned his head to press a soft kiss against my pulse and breathed out in a tone that sent chills up my spine, "I'm going to kill him."

"I know." I let him soothe me for a minute before climbing off him and settling back in the passenger seat. "I have to go back to Brookside and get my car tomorrow."

"Don't worry about it. I'll take Rome and we'll go get it."

"Don't you have to work?"

"Not until one. I think I want to call Mark and ask him about getting you a restraining order."

"I can't believe this is happening."

"I can't believe you let us leave without confronting him. You should have raked his ass over the fire in front of his parents and all those people he was trying so hard to impress."

"I was freaking out and I just wanted to escape. I just wanted you." My voice trailed off in a whisper and he reached over to haul me up next to his side. Having bench seats in a big truck was nice.

"You have me, Shaw, any way you need me, any way you want me, you have me."

I pressed my face into the curve of his neck and exhaled. I think that was the nicest thing anyone had ever said to me. "How about you being the belle of the ball today? I bet that made my mother furious. She looked like she was going to have a coronary."

"I have a lot of clients who are out there in the business world. More and more of the general population is sporting some serious ink. She shouldn't be so judgmental."

178

"No, she shouldn't. I don't want you to get into trouble over Gabe. I just want him to leave me alone."

He gave me a one-armed hug. "Don't worry about me, Casper. I promise not to do anything overtly stupid. I just want him to leave you alone as well and I will make sure that happens. In the meantime, I don't think you should leave work alone so have Lou walk you out, and if we can figure something out with our crazy schedules I want you to stay with me or I'll be with you."

"You don't have to do that. I don't want you to re-arrange your whole life because some guy is being an asshole to me."

"Yes I do, and not because I have to but because I want to. He isn't getting his hands on you again, Shaw. Not ever again."

It was a nice thought, so I didn't want to argue. Instead I let him snuggle me into his side and absently ran my hand up and down his leg while he drove. I didn't ask if he was taking me home or to his place and I honestly didn't care until I remembered Rome was crashing on his couch.

"Hey, are we going downtown or to my place?"

"I figured mine since I need to get Rome to help me with your Beamer in the morning. Is that okay?"

"Uh . . . is it going to be weird walking in together with him there? I've had about enough drama for one day."

I felt him shake his head. "Naw, we talked about it yesterday. He knows we got something going on and it's cool. He did say that he would break both of my legs if I kept acting like a jackass though, so there is that."

"Hmm . . . Why did you do it?" I knew he would know what I was asking about without explaining.

"Because it's what I do." He swore under his breath. "Girls have always been easy and they usually smell good and taste good, so for just a second, things are simple and nice and all

179

the crap doing battle inside my head goes quiet. I knew I didn't want someone who wasn't you, but I was pissed off and confused so I just did what I always do, and thought maybe it would make me feel better. It didn't, it made me feel like absolute shit and made me see pretty clearly there is no substitute for you. I made a mistake but it could have been so much worse and I hope you can sincerely forgive me."

It made my heart hurt, but I understood it because I understood him. "I don't like it, but I get it. It just can't be your excuse for stepping out on me every time we fight. I don't have it in me to just look the other way every time you use another girl to work out your hurt feelings."

"I told you no more. I'll figure this out, Shaw, I swear."

"I hope so, because we're going to disagree, Rule. We argued before we started sleeping together so you know we're going to probably argue more now."

His hand stroked up and down my arm. "That's cool because I bet make-up sex with you is going to be out of this world."

I didn't deny it so I just stayed quiet and let him soothe me while he drove; he even picked Straylight Run to listen to instead of his normal blaring punk rock or heavy metal. By the time we parked in front of the Victorian I was back in control. He took my bag from me and led me into the apartment. Rome and Nash were on the couch yelling at the TV, and I assumed the Broncos were losing. They both looked up at me with twin faces full of relief.

"Thank God. Now maybe he'll stop acting like a cranky toddler who skipped nap time." Rule smacked Nash on the back of the head as Rome got up and wrapped me in a bear hug.

"Glad you gave him another chance, little girl."

When I was back on my feet I grinned sheepishly at both of them and turned back to Rule. "I need to call

Ayden and my phone is trashed, can I use yours?" I expected him to spend a minute erasing texts or clearing his search history but he just handed it over. I tried to hide how happy that made me, so I bit my lip and motioned down the hall. "I'll just go in your room so I can hear her over the game."

"Go ahead. I want to talk to the guys for a second anyway." The grimness of his tone let me know he wanted to fill them in on my situation with Gabe. "I'll be there in just a minute."

I resisted the temptation to scroll through his contacts and look at his text conversations and dialed Ayden. I didn't know if she would answer since she wouldn't recognize Rule's number, but she ended up picking up on the third ring.

"Hello?"

"Hey, it's me."

"What number is this?"

"I'm using Rule's phone because I'm a genius and threw mine against the wall."

She snickered at me. "It was because I told you about the girl at the club, wasn't it?"

"Yep."

"But now you have his phone so you must have worked things out somewhere along the way."

"He came to Brookside to apologize and then he crashed my mother's brunch and ended up being the star attraction. It was impossible not to forgive him."

"Good for you. Something tells me that one comes with a whole truckload of drama, so you might as well get used to it."

"Yeah, well, I'm not short on drama of my own." I went into the bathroom and leaned against the sink. The image looking back at me in the mirror was startling. I looked agitated and even paler than usual. "Gabe grabbed me and shoved me around. He cornered me in my room and threatened all kinds of crazy stuff. I just don't know what I'm going to do about it. Rule's all set to get together an old-fashioned lynching squad and I don't want him to get in trouble because of me. It's a mess."

"That asshole put his hands on you?"

I sighed. "Yeah, I have bruises."

"Then I say let Rule have at him. You better be looking into a restraining order."

"I am. Rule has a client who used to be a police officer and he's going to call him. He also said he wants to stay with me or have me stay here until the whole thing is resolved."

"Sounds like your boy is getting serious."

"He's trying."

"Well, I guess that's better than nothing for now. When are you going to get a new phone?"

"Probably tomorrow. Rule said he would buy me a new one."

"Man, I like a fella who knows how to apologize right. I'll see you tomorrow?" The last was asked as a question.

"I think so, I'll let you know for sure."

"Love ya, girl. Be safe, let Rule take care of you for a minute, you've earned it. You took pretty great care of him all this time, now it can be his turn."

"Isn't a relationship supposed to be about taking care of each other equally?"

She laughed but it sounded bitter. "You're asking the wrong person that, honey. My track record isn't anything to brag about."

"Ayden, do you want to talk about something? You seem, I dunno, sharper than usual."

"No, I'm good. Just worry about you right now, honey. I missed you this weekend."

"Missed you, too."

I hung up the phone and set it on the edge of the sink. I pushed the sleeves of my sweater up and splashed cold water on my face. I took the tie out of my hair and unwound the tight braid so that my hair fell down around my shoulders. I took off the pearls and kicked off my heels and started to feel a little bit more like myself. I heard the bedroom door open and close and Rule softly called my name.

"I'm in here."

I heard some shuffling and some swearing as he maneuvered through the stuff scattered on his floor. The bathroom door swung open and his eyes met mine in the mirror. The chilly depths of his were shadowed with concern as he crowded in behind me. "You okay?"

"Freaked out, but other than that, okay."

"Are you worried about your mom ratting you out to your dad?" He put a hand on either side of me, trapping me between him and the basin.

"I can't stop her, so if she does I'll deal with it then."

"What about school? She said he would stop paying if you didn't do what she wanted."

I leaned back so that I was pressed against his chest. "They both like to use that threat against me; it's their favorite extortion tool. I figure they're both actually more worried about trying to explain to people why their daughter is working at Subway instead of in medical school to actually stop paying tuition. And if they do"—I raised a shoulder and let it drop—"then I figure out a Plan B."

"Just like that?"

"Pretty much."

"I never knew you were so adaptable." I made a face that made him laugh and he moved his hands around so that they rested on my stomach. "The guys are going to order pizza

183

and watch the rest of the game. I told them I would check and see what you were thinking for the rest of the night."

I pushed my hair back and let my head fall onto his shoulder. "I want to take a hot shower and then I think I want to take a nap. This week has sucked. I've been stressed out and burned out from school. I can't remember the last time I got to just relax."

His dark eyebrows went up. "You won't mind if I kick it with them for a bit?"

I shook my head no. "Seriously, go bro-out. I'm good."

He watched me for a solid minute, waiting to see if I was just messing with him. To prove that I was fine with him spending time with his boys I pressed a kiss to his jaw. He pressed a kiss to my hair and backed out of the bathroom. "I'll grab your bag for you."

He set it on the toilet and gave me a hard kiss before searching my face for signs of something. I laughed and physically shoved him out the door before closing it firmly in his face. "Go be a guy. I'll be here when it's over." I waited until I heard the outside door shut and then stripped down and climbed in his shower. If I never had to suffer through one of my mother's functions again it would be too soon. I scrubbed every inch of my body until it was pink and shiny, laughing hysterically because I had to use Rule's dude soap and ended up smelling like a seventeen-year-old boy who'd just discovered AXE body spray. I had left my mom's so quickly I had forgotten to get my things from the shower. Even his shampoo and conditioner were designed for males only, so instead of my normal coconut and lime I ended up with hair that smelled like sandalwood and spice. I finger-combed my wet hair and put on a pair of yoga pants and a T-shirt and fell into his rumpled bed. For the first time in a week I felt like I could take a real breath. I burrowed into his side of the bed and fell asleep within seconds, even with the hooting and hollering coming from the living room.

Hot hands were traveling under my clothes in a lazy caress. I woke up already turned on and squirming under Rule's seductive touch as he tugged on the stretchy sleep clothes I went to bed in. I blinked to get my eyes used to the darkness but squeezed them shut again when his mouth landed high on my inner thigh after the thin cotton was out of his way. It was like the best dream ever, only now I was awake and wiggling in anticipation as his breath blew across the most sensitive parts of me. I reached for his head and giggled a little as my fingers skimmed over the buzzed surface. The stubble tickled across my sensitive fingertips.

"I really do miss the Mohawk."

"It'll grow back." I felt the slide of his lip ring over damp skin and sucked in a gasp so hard that it made my lungs hurt. He laughed against my skin and his hands moved to hold me where he wanted me. "I missed this. Nobody has ever been as sweet as you, Shaw."

I felt the press of the barbell in his tongue as he moved in and around the part of me that had woken up ready to take what he had to give. "I think the fact you're comparing me to the legions of girls who came before me should probably make me furious, but I think I'll choose to take it as a compliment." The last faded away on a tight moan as he pulled my hips up and settled his mouth at the burning point of my desire. I had heard tales from my coworkers and even from Ayden about how having a guy do this for you was often the best part of sexy, naked time, but I had always had my doubts because it seemed invasive and too intimate, but I was wrong. As he kissed and licked and maneuvered around all my damp folds and aching flesh I went a little crazy. There was nowhere to hide how he was affecting me while he was doing that and man, did he know what he was doing. At one point I wanted to scream his name but at the last second remembered his brother was just across the wall and shoved my fist in my mouth to stifle my reaction as the world kaleidoscoped into brilliant color in every direction. I didn't know how it was with other guys, but as with everything else I experienced with Rule, he just made it all so good.

I lay in a pile of worthless goo as he rose up off the bed and began to haphazardly pull his clothes off. The show was a delight in itself, so by the time he crawled in the bed beside me I was ready to purr and curl up around him like the satisfied sex kitten he was turning me into.

"That was certainly a nice way to wake up." I curled my hands up around his shoulders as he rolled over me and put his knee between my legs.

"You were out for most of the afternoon. I kept waiting for you to peek your head out and join us but it never happened." He dropped his head so that his nose rubbed against the side of my face. "I checked in on you and you just looked so perfect all sleepy and pretty in my bed I couldn't help myself." He laid a soft trail of kisses from behind my ear to the sensitive hollow of my throat. His fingers skimmed down my arm and lightly encircled my bruised wrist. Gabe had left a ring of black-and-blue marks that stood out in stark relief against my pale skin, and I couldn't help the emotion that clogged my throat when Rule lightly stroked the damaged flesh and lifted it up to press butterfly kisses around the circumference.

"This should have never happened. I'm so sorry."

I trailed a hand down over his flank and let my fingers spread out across the colorful surface of his ribs. "I shouldn't have gone in the first place. I need to learn to set boundaries with my parents and stick with them. It's not worth sacrificing things that matter to me in order to try to make them happy."

He took the hand he was holding and pinned it to the bed above my head, his pale eyes blazing into mine with a mixture of want and compassion. "Shaw, I'm the one who feels the need to burn the house down when the faucet springs a leak. I know I tend to go to the extreme and I need to back off. However, if you think I'm ever going to stand by and watch you purposely put yourself in danger with that asshole again, be prepared for us to do battle."

I didn't get a chance to reply because he kissed me, really kissed me, kissed me with an edge so that there was no mistaking he was serious and that I needed to pay attention to what was happening between us. There was a bite of teeth and the press of metal and all the goodness that was just Rule as our tongues slid together and hands began to roam. He caught my free hand and pinned it above my head with the other one so that I was stretched out beneath him. His eyes glittered with pure wicked intent as he leered down at me.

"I think I like you like this." His free hand twisted and wandered over sensitive skin and moist creases. I whimpered a little because it felt so good and because I wanted to move but he held me still with the press of his much bigger body into mine. "I like having you at my mercy. I can do whatever I want to you." He proved his point by taking the top of one breast in his mouth and sucking until it almost hurt. He'd left a hickey the first time we did this, too, but this one seemed different, more like a territorial marking, a claiming of sorts.

"Good thing for you I like all the things you want to do to me." He pulled my leg up and hooked it around his lean hips. I felt the hot press of him ready at my entrance and tried to shift so that he came inside. He pulled back and grinned down at me.

"Always so impatient."

I tugged at my trapped hands. "You have no idea."

He chuckled again as he kissed me. "So tell me."

I tried to pull him inside by sheer will alone but he kept moving just out of range with a taunting smirk. "Seriously, Shaw, tell me."

I squeezed my eyes shut because there was only so much truth I was ready to hand over to him in one day. He moved my other leg and pressed in just a millimeter or two, making me start to quiver. "Tell me why we all thought you and Remy had a serious thing going on but I'm the one who was your first. Tell me why Rome seems to think you've had a thing for me for a while now. Tell me why, when we do this, it's so much different than whenever I've done it before."

I wanted him to move, wanted him to let me move, but when I pried my eyes open he was watching me closely, clearly in control enough to wait me out. I met his pointed stare for a heartbeat before whispering, "Because it's always been you even when I didn't want it to be, even when it broke my heart over and over again. It's just always been you."

My words changed something in him; his eyes flashed with a sudden, bright spark and suddenly he was in and moving and the rest of the world just stopped and faded away. All that mattered was what was happening between us in that moment and that it mattered to him just as much as it mattered to me. His tempo changed with each thrust. He was always a little wild, a little uninhibited in bed, but it was like my words had broken something loose inside him and this was the real Rule, the guy who used crazy hair and a body full of ink to deflect anyone getting too close. I gasped and moaned, finally calling his name out in a shaky voice as we raced toward the end together. It felt different, like he said, more powerful, more intense, and when he finally dropped his forehead down to touch mine it felt complete.

I sighed in contentment and wrapped my arms around him. He pulled me over him and rolled so that I wasn't getting crushed. I closed my eyes and was about to go back into a very satisfied sleep when the entire length of his long body went board straight underneath me. My eyes popped open as I felt his hands tense in the ends of my hair and I forced my head up to look down at him.

"What's wrong?"

"The bed's wet."

I just stared at him blankly. "So?"

"So that means we didn't use protection. I haven't had sex without a condom since I was a teenager and an idiot. Geez, no wonder it felt so good."

"I'm on the pill."

"Why?"

I made a face and rolled off him. "Because my mother made me. She thought I was hooking up with one or both of you Archer twins long before it ever happened. I've just stayed on it because it makes my period less crazy, so we should be fine."

He pulled me back to his chest and brushed my hair away from my face. "With my history, you really wanna chance it?"

I exhaled. "You really know how to ruin a moment, Rule."

"Hey, I told you it's my job to protect you even if that means protecting you from me. We have to have clean health screens to work in the shop, since we work around bodily fluids, needles, and open skin, and my last one was crystal clear. And like I said, I never ever have unsafe sex unless it's with a high-maintenance blonde with killer green eyes that make me so crazy I forget."

I cuddled into the curve of his body and let him wrap his

arms around me. The hand that had his name inked across the knuckles ended up resting across my chest and I used my index finger to trace over the bold letters. "I trust you and I think we're good, so I'm not going to make an issue out of it."

"Yeah?"

"Yeah, because like I said it's always been you, Rule, even when I really wished it wasn't."

"I'm starting to wish I had paid closer attention."

I laced our fingers together. I liked the way they looked all tangled together. His were long and covered in brilliant designs, mine were small and tipped in boring pink polish, but next to each other they were more interesting, more vital. I fell back asleep listening to the steady inhale and exhale of his breath in my ear and thinking that even if I hadn't been on the pill, having a moment of wild, uninhibited, and totally unprotected sex with him was most definitely worth any of the risks that were involved with that. I could think of worse fates than bringing the next troublesome Archer into the world.

CHAPTER 11

Rule

"*The first time I came home and saw you sitting in the kitchen with Remy I remember thinking, what in the hell has he gotten himself into? You were so pale and scared, your eyes were twice as big as normal, and you looked like a little bird that had fallen out of the nest. Remy had always had a soft spot for the neglected so I wasn't surprised, but I was flabbergasted at how quickly the rest of the family took to you. I always thought it was going to be us Archers against the world forever and then there was you, and it all kind of broke apart and I became even more of the black sheep than I had been. Rome adored you, Mom and Dad just accepted you and Remy as a unit, and I was left out in the cold as usual. I think I just took all those feelings of separation and alienation and transferred them onto you. Remy and I were always two parts of a whole and when you came along that went away to some extent. I think I was jealous that he spent so much time and effort being your hero and not being my brother.*"*

"*The first time I saw you I was terrified. I had seen you and Remy around school and everyone always talked about the Archer twins like you were some kind of mythical creatures. Remy was so athletic and had all the right friends and the best grades, you were always in trouble, running around with older kids and constantly*" *getting called to the office for skipping class or whatever else you were up to. Remy saved me and brought me home. He made me laugh when nothing in my life seemed remotely funny and he was kind when no one in my life had ever even tried to be nice before. He sat me in the kitchen and told me not to worry when his brothers came home—he would keep them in line. Then you and Rome came barreling through the door. Rome looked at me and shook his head and asked Remy if I was another stray and you, you just looked right at me like I didn't matter and asked Remy if he wanted to go get pizza. I thought you were beautiful in such a different way from Remy. You guys looked so much alike but you turned your looks into something so interesting I couldn't look away. I stared at you for a full fifteen minutes and then when you and Rome left you looked at me and said, 'Geez, Rem, get her a cup of tea or something. She looks like Casper the Friendly Ghost.' Remy just shook his head and sat down across from me—he knew then, he always knew—and, he told me, 'Rule is a good guy, Shaw, the best actually. I love him more than anything in the world but he's also a sixteen-year-old guy and an Archer. Don't borrow heartache when you can avoid it.' For years and years he told me over and over that I was being foolish, that I shouldn't get wound up about you when your priorities were elsewhere. Then about a year before he died he changed his tune. When you moved to Denver together he was suddenly all about me going to DU after school, all about me getting to a point where I could tell you how I felt about you. Suddenly he was Remy the matchmaker. It was weird and then the accident happened and I never got a chance to ask what changed his mind."*

"Well, I'm glad I know now and I still think you look like Casper."

"I'm glad, too, and I don't mind when you call me Casper. It's kinda sweet. Besides, when you first started it I thought I was special; none of the other girls ever got a nickname, you just called them sweetie, or babe, or honey."

"You are special; you were special then, too. I was just too stupid to see it."

"I don't think I would have been ready for you then."
"Are you ready for me now?"
"Anytime."

The hushed conversation gave me a whole new insight into the girl who was starting to mean so much to me. It also brought up a lot of questions that I couldn't ask my deceased brother. I wanted to know why, if he had known she had a thing for me, he let me and the rest of the family happily believe they were an item for all those years. It seemed deceitful and shady and so not like Remy. I also wanted to know why he hadn't said anything to me about her. I thought we'd shared everything, and even though I hadn't been in a place in my early teens to offer Shaw anything, it still seemed odd he hadn't mentioned how she felt about me so that I might have treaded more carefully around her instead of trampling across her feelings like a herd of buffaloes.

The quiet conversation took place early in the morning while she was stumbling around my room trying to get ready for school. She only had a limited amount of clothes to pick from and didn't want to run back to her apartment so I told her to take one of my T-shirts out of the closet. It was fun to watch a hot chick scramble around half-naked and pick through my pretty basic guy wardrobe. She ended up in her leggings and boots and my Black Angels T-shirt, which hung almost to her knees, and suddenly getting up to take her to school seemed a lot more fun. She dodged my grabbing hands with a laugh while trying to pull her hair into a ponytail. This was the kind of interaction I had missed by only engaging in meaningless one-night stands. I liked playing with Shaw, liked having her using my bathroom and being all up in my stuff, and the more I thought about it the more I realized I had missed her in more areas of my life than my bed this last week.

She pressed a quick kiss to my mouth and told me she was going to make coffee and something for breakfast so I struggled to get up and searched around for my phone to call Mark. I wasn't going to waste any time trying to put as many roadblocks between Shaw and Davenport as I could. I pulled on a pair of dark jeans and a shirt and went into the bathroom to splash cold water on my face. The phone rang while I brushed my teeth and Mark picked up just as I was spitting into the sink.

"What's up, kid?" I was checking out my stubbly face in the mirror and decided since I didn't have any hair at the moment I was just gonna let it go, maybe try to grow it into a goatee or something.

"Hey, Mark, sorry to bother you, but I have a problem and I need some advice."

"You piss off that pretty girl of yours?"

I laughed and leaned against the sink. "Yeah, but I managed to fix that all on my own. But she is the reason I am calling. She has a lunatic ex who doesn't seem to want to take no for an answer. He's been showing up at her work, following her around, calling her a million times a day, but he's a friend of the family so her parents keep making excuses for her to be around him. This weekend he cornered her when she was alone and shook her up and grabbed her. He left bruises on her arms and made a bunch of threats about what he's going to do to her if she doesn't take him back."

"I'm surprised you're not in jail."

"Well, she didn't tell me about that until after we left her parents' house and I've already told him in no uncertain terms to leave her alone."

"What's his name?"

"Gabe Davenport."

There was a low whistle and I could practically see Mark

194

pacing back and forth. "He wouldn't happen to be Judge George Davenport's son, would he?"

"Probably. He keeps throwing around that there isn't anything I can do to him because of who his dad is."

"He might be right. I would say we need to get a personal protection order in place as soon as possible, but there is a good chance if Davenport sees his son is involved it might not get issued."

"That's bullshit."

"It is, but we still need to try; otherwise, there won't be anything on file. You need to keep a clear head about this, kid. The name Davenport is pretty powerful in our legal system and you don't want to end up on the wrong side of it."

I ran an agitated hand over my head. "I'm not going to let him anywhere near her, Mark, plain and simple."

"That's fine but don't go looking for trouble. She's going to be a sitting duck if you go after the son and end up locked up."

"I'm pissed, Mark, not stupid. I want her safe and this guy taken down a notch or two. I'm well aware that me rearranging his face isn't going to accomplish either of those things; however, if he comes at me I make no promises."

"If he comes at you, take him out, but remember, guys like this use laws and regulations to fight, not bare knuckles and fists. Tell Shaw to be extra careful, tell her to try and be around someone else at all times. Look at getting her a Taser or some mace and tell her if he shows up or put his hands on her again to call the police. She can get a harassment order in place if he keeps hounding her and once the police are involved there isn't much a judge can do to make the report go away. Give her my number just in case and tell her to call me if she has questions or just needs to talk. Like I said, that's a special girl you got there, kid. You wanna keep an eye on her."

"I'm doing my best."

"I know you are, and Rule . . ." I waited a moment while he finished. "It's good to see you finally settling down. You've always reminded me a little of my son, wild and carefree, but you needed something to give you purpose. For my son it was fighting for our freedom and protecting his country; for you I think it's figuring out you are worthy of the kind of love and affection a girl like that can offer. You two take care and I'll be in touch."

I hung up the phone just as the door swung open and Shaw stuck her head in. "Come on, let's eat so we can go."

I looked at her, I mean really looked at her, and that slippery stuff in my chest suddenly settled right in the center. Her green eyes got wide when I tugged her into the bathroom and pulled her between my spread legs so that she was up against my chest. I rested my chin on the top of her head. Sometimes the difference in our height was just delightful.

"Are you okay?" She put her hands around my waist and gave me a tight hug.

I let out a breath that I felt like I had been holding for a hundred years. Suddenly I knew that no matter how my parents felt, no matter what happened in the future—near or far—I was for once doing the absolute right thing. "Yeah, I'm good. Better than good, actually."

"Okay. Well, I don't want to be late so come eat some pancakes and take me to school." She gave my ass a little pat and bounded back out of the room. I shook my head on a little laugh and followed her out. Rome was up and sitting at the table listening to her tell him about the bizarre brunch yesterday but Nash was nowhere in sight. I had let both of them know what was going on with Polo Shirt yesterday and I think they were both on hyperalert so that I didn't go off the rails. My brother gave me a questioning look as I sat down, but I wasn't about to go into detail while Shaw was prancing around feeding us breakfast.

"You still good to go and get her car with me?"

"Yep, but I'm going to swing by Mom and Dad's while we're there. You wanna come?"

I flipped him off because he knew the last thing I wanted to do was see my folks. "Can't. Anyways, I have an appointment at noon."

Shaw placed plates in front of both of us and took a seat on my right. She gave me a warm smile and I knew, besides feeling right, that this is what I had been missing for so long. I felt at home; this girl, my brother, my friends, all the things that I had surrounded myself with suddenly made so much sense, and I had a clarity that had been missing since Remy's death. I loved my family, but I had never felt like I was part of them. This world I had developed, this life I was living, was a good one, filled with solid people who saw me for who I was and cared about me anyway. My throat got tight and I had to hide the swell of emotion behind a glass of orange juice or otherwise risk blubbering like a baby. I cleared my throat. "I'm gonna run Shaw to school then come back and get you, is that cool?"

"Sure. I'll go kick Nash and see if he wants to hit the gym with me while you're gone."

I glanced at Shaw. "You're going to have Ayden take you to work after school, right?" She nodded at me and continued to eat her breakfast. "Good. I'll come get you from the bar when your shift is done. Your car will be here so you can decide if you want to stay or go to your place later."

She lifted a shoulder and let it fall. "I don't get out until two. It's Monday night football so we're busy. I'll probably just stay here. Besides, you need to buy me a new phone tomorrow."

"Why does he owe you a phone?" I glared at my big brother but she answered before I could tell him to shut it.

"I broke mine by accident and Rule offered to replace it."

"He did? That doesn't sound like my little brother." I knew he was just trying to rile me up, but awesome sex and having Shaw close at hand with a plate of pancakes in front of me made that an impossible task. I smirked at him and leaned back in my chair to reach out and put my arm across the back of Shaw's.

"I'm turning over a new leaf."

He snorted, and eyes that were so similar to mine gleamed with repressed humor. "For you to be considering someone else like that is more like turning over a whole freaking tree, not just a leaf, but good for you. Being considerate is a nice change for you."

"Screw you."

Shaw rolled her eyes and let her fork clatter to her plate. "You're both ridiculous and I'm going to be late, so let's go."

I leaned over and kissed her on the cheek. "Let me grab shoes and we'll head out. Go grab your stuff. Thanks for breakfast."

"Sure." She ran out of the room and I pushed to my feet. I glowered at my brother.

"I do know how to be nice."

"Only when you want something."

"True enough. I want her."

"Looks to me like you got her."

"Now I just need to figure out how to not screw it up."

Rome got up as well. "You won't, Rule. When it matters you never do, just remember that. Hey, what did your cop buddy say?"

"That she needs to keep her eyes open and he wants me to get her a Taser or mace. He thinks the little punk is pretty insulated because of his old man, but he pretty much said if he tries anything with me I can lay him out. It sucks, he shouldn't be allowed to put his hands on her and live to tell about it."

"We'll keep her close and keep it under control; you know we got your back in this, lil' bro."

I made a face and lowered my voice because I heard Shaw coming back down the hall. "If anything happens to her, Rome, I'm going to lose it. I mean, I know I kind of went off the rails when Remy died, but something tells me if that girl ends up hurt or worse there won't be any recovering from that for me."

I think he was probably going to answer something back but Shaw popped up at my elbow and none too subtly tugged on me to let me know she was ready to go. She waved to Rome and hustled me out to the truck. It was cold out so I wrapped an arm around her and tugged her close to my side. She rubbed her cold nose on my neck and laughed when I swore at her.

"You need a hat." My newly shorn head was actually freezing but I was a tough guy so I just pulled the hood of my sweatshirt up and raised the eyebrow with the hoops in it at her.

"Better?"

"Whatever, macho man. Thanks for getting my car."

"No problem, just make sure you keep an eye out at school today. I don't want Polo Shirt waylaying you on your way to class or anything."

"Polo Shirt?"

"Davenport, he always has on a stupid polo."

She laughed so hard I had to hold her upright and give her a boost into the truck, not that I minded, because it meant I got to cop a feel of her superb backside.

"That he does. I'll make sure I walk to class with someone. This girl, Devlin, is in a bunch of the same classes as me and we have a couple study groups together so I'll just stick with her. I don't think she's a fan of Gabe, either, so that should make asking her easy."

"Cool. What kind of phone do you want? I don't want you to have to wait until tomorrow to get one. I'll go on my way back from Brookside and pick one up."

She shrugged and messed around with my iPod until the smoky sound of Lucero filled the cab. "I don't care. The same as my old one is fine. I need my contacts switched over, though."

"I'll take care of it."

She grinned at me and scooted over so that she could put her hand on my knee. Her fingers tapped out the rhythm of the country-tinged rock as we made our way across town to the university. It took about twenty minutes in light traffic, but it was getting ready to snow, and I could see having to push my first appointment back because of weather since I was driving out of town. She wanted me to just park on the street and drop her off, but I wanted to keep her in sight as long as possible, so I parked the truck at a meter and told her I was walking her to her first class. She rolled her eyes but didn't argue when I opened her door and helped her hop down.

I tucked her back in the curve of my body and walked across the campus with her, thinking this was the only time I had been on a college campus for a reason other than a party. Several people called out a greeting to her or waved hi. She replied in kind and I didn't miss the speculative looks we got. I'm sure we made an odd pair and her classmates probably weren't used to seeing her out of her normal rich-girl gear. We stopped outside an impressive-looking building and she tilted her head back so she was looking up at me. Her green eyes were bright, her hair was in a sexy tangle from me and from the brisk Colorado air, and her nose was a charming shade of pink; I don't think I had ever seen anything cuter.

"Drive safe. I agree with your brother, I think you should try to see your parents while you're there."

I didn't want to argue with her so I just kissed her hard and fierce with enough tongue and enough force to let her know she would be on my mind throughout the day. I thought maybe she would freak out about the public display of affection but it only took between one heartbeat and the next for her cold hands to climb up my chest and wrap around my neck. She kissed me back with just as much fervor and when she fell back to her feet, she was breathing hard and had a pretty flush under her pale cheeks.

"You be safe, too. I'll see you later. I'll bring your phone by the bar after work. Remember, don't be alone whenever you can avoid it. And Shaw"—she met my gaze with humor lighting up her own—"I like you going to school in my clothes, it's totally hot."

She stood back on her tiptoes and kissed the end of my chilly nose. "Agreed. And you suck for changing the subject, but I can take a hint so I'll see you later."

I watched her walk up the stairs of the building and she paused at the top, where a girl was seemingly waiting for her. She smiled at the girl and told her hello. I heard the other girl ask her in a surprised voice that was loud enough to carry down to where I was waiting, "Who was that?" I was curious as to what her answer would be, considering that wasn't something we had ever really talked about.

Her laugh carried sharp and clear through the winter air. "That's Rule."

"I didn't know you had a new boyfriend."

"Well, he isn't exactly new, but yeah."

I was her boyfriend. She was my girlfriend. How weird was that? I hadn't had any girl in my life long enough in twenty-two years to call a girlfriend; I didn't even really have friends who were girls. Shaw was the closest thing that had ever come to filling that role as well. I was her boyfriend and that made me want to dance a jig and pump my fist in the air. Instead, I winked at her when she turned back to look at me and laughed when she in turn stuck out her tongue at me. Why hadn't I realized before that letting someone in would make me happy, that she made me happy? I couldn't remember the last time I had laughed so much and even in bed she made it fun. She made things better and I knew I wanted to do the same for her.

I sent Rome a text that I was on my way and he replied back that he and Nash had just finished up at the gym so he would be ready to go when I got home. I changed the music to the Bloody Hollies and rocked out on the way back to the Victorian. I ran in to grab Shaw's phone out of her bag and collected my brother and in no time we were on the highway headed to Brookside. The first few flurries of snow started to pelt the windshield as we were just entering the interstate and I swore, knowing what it was going to do to the commute and my schedule for the rest of the day. In fact, before we even got to Brookside, Nash called and told me both my noon and two o'clock appointments wanted to reschedule because of the weather, so I no longer had the work excuse as a reason to bolt home without trying to see my folks.

Rome, not being stupid, blatantly listened in on the call and looked across the cab of the truck expectantly. "It won't kill you to stop by and just say hi for a minute. We can even go there first so they don't ask why we have Shaw's car with us."

"I just don't see the point."

"The point is that no matter how you feel they're still our parents and you don't just get to give up on them."

202

"Why not? They gave up on me the minute the good twin was pronounced DOA."

"Stop it and grow a pair. You can tough out a five-minute visit with Mom and Dad if only to say you tried. It'll make Shaw happy to know you made a minimal effort. Remember they're more like her parents than her real parents so if the two of you are going to do what you're doing for the long term, you're going to have to show her that even if Mom isn't going to budge that at least you tried."

He was right and it totally made my stomach turn over. Right now, Shaw was all about building a bridge and forcing my mom's hand when it came to dealing with me and accepting me, but after seeing how awful her biological mother treated her I had no doubt the divide between her and my parents wouldn't be longstanding, which meant I had to figure out how I fit into that puzzle. Trying wouldn't kill me, but it was sure as hell going to be awkward and uncomfortable for all of us I was sure.

"Fine, we can stop by but don't get your hopes up. I haven't heard from either one of them since I left brunch that day."

"Archer pride is a dangerous thing. If we aren't careful it's going to destroy our entire family."

I just grunted in response and tried to tell myself that doing this was not only going to make Shaw happy, but clearly it meant something to Rome as well and if there was anyone in the world who I would do anything for, it was my brother. Rome never asked me for anything and had given me his support and his approval endlessly, even when it put him at odds with the rest of the family, and I owed him at least the opportunity to try to mend what was fractured. We drove the rest of the way to their house in silence but I could see Rome giving me surreptitious looks out of the corner of his eye the entire way. I think he was waiting for me to drive past the exit or freak out and change my mind, but I kept telling myself that I didn't need my parents to look at me the same way they looked at him to go home and be okay. Before, that tore me apart and made me act like a troubled adolescent with a chip on his shoulder, but now I knew I was going home to a kick-ass job, a rock-star brother, a smoking-hot girl who happened to be totally into me—issues and all—and to a solid group of friends who were willing to put up with me and have my back no matter what. And while the hole that Remy's death left would never really be filled, I was living a good life and they should be proud of me. If they weren't, they could just piss off.

Both my folks' cars were in the driveway when we pulled onto their street. I hissed a breath out between my teeth and tried not to flinch when Rome clapped me on the shoulder and gave me a little shove. "Come on, we'll be quick."

I jumped out of the truck and my boots sent little tufts of snow scattering. I could see my breath in the air, indicating the weather was going to get worse before we headed home, which was kind of how I felt about my situation here. I knew Rome had a key, but since I was with him he stopped at the front door and knocked, relegating himself to visitor status just like me. I heard shuffling around and it took a few minutes for my dad to come to the door. He peered out at us in surprise and I had to admit I was secretly pleased that he looked equally surprised to see Rome as he was to see me.

"Boys? What are you doing here?"

He pushed open the screen door and motioned us into the warm house. I was rubbing my hands together to warm them up so he didn't even try to give me a hug after he embraced Rome, which was fine by me because I wasn't sure we were at the hugging phase of our relationship anymore.

"Rule had to run an errand before work out this way so

I thought we'd stop by and say hi. You guys aren't busy are you?"

"No, your mom's in the living room." His gaze settled on me. "I'm surprised to see you, son."

I wanted to throw out something flippant but in the vein of trying to make peace I gave a lopsided grin and answered, "Yeah, I bet. Rome thought it would be cool."

"Rule, this is your home, you are always welcome here."

I wanted to say I hadn't felt welcome in well over three years but I just nodded and said, "Thanks for that, Dad."

"What kind of errand did you have to do an hour away in the snow?"

I rubbed a hand over my head and looked at Rome sideways. "Uh . . . I actually told Shaw I would come get her car for her. She left it here when she was visiting her folks."

"Shaw was in Brookside this weekend? You might not want to let your mom know that. She's having a hard time with the line Shaw drew in the sand. That little gal is just as stubborn as you boys, and I don't think Margot was prepared for her to stick to her guns the way she has. It's awful nice of you to help her out, Rome."

I rolled my eyes at the automatic assumption that Rome was the one she called on even though he had already told him it was my errand. I wasn't going to say anything, but Rome chuckled and patted my dad on the back.

"Not me, old-timer. Shaw and Rule have called a truce. You should see them; they actually act civil and spend time together like normal people do. He's the one who told her he would get the car, I just got roped into being the second driver."

My dad looked over Rome's broad shoulder at me with shock clear on his face. "Really? You two were always at odds, even when you were young."

I shrugged. "I'm trying to grow up a little bit. She's been

205

in my life a long time and I'm trying to put that into a new perspective. We get along fine." Plus, spending time with her naked as often as possible was my new top priority in life, and doing things that made her happy and kept her safe also had the bonus of making me happy, which was such a new feeling I wasn't sure what to do with it yet.

"Well, maybe you can tell her how hard it's been for your mom without her around. Getting her to come by for a visit would be lovely."

"She has her reasons for staying away, Dad." My tone sharpened reflexively, but I kept my face smoothed out, trying to belie the tension that was growing as we walked into the living room where my mom was watching TV on the sofa. Her eyes snapped from Rome to me and then back. Even from across the room I could feel the displeasure radiating off her.

"What are you doing here?" She didn't even look at Rome; her eyes were glued to me, and her anger was like a whip across my skin. I shoved my hands in my pockets and met her gaze with a level one of my own. I wasn't going to let her get under my skin this time—I owed it to my brother and to my girl.

"Just came by to say hi and see how you're doing."

"I don't want you here." Rome went stiff beside me and I heard my dad take in a quick breath, but I wasn't surprised.

"I know, but I thought it wouldn't kill me to try and fix things."

"Why bother? You just ruin everything." Her voice was raspy and I swore I could see the hatred she harbored hanging off each syllable. My dad took a step forward but Rome pulled him back. "Margot, that's enough. The boy is our son, not a stranger we're going to just put out on the street because you're unhappy with him right now."

"Dad, it's cool. I know how she feels and she's never hidden it."

"What do you expect, Rule? Because of you your brother is in a box in the ground and the girl I think of as a daughter won't have anything to do with me. You're a poison to this family."

Well, that was a little harsher and a little blunter than she normally went for, but it was finally out in the open. I rubbed my fists in my eyes and let out a sigh. My dad and Rome were trying to talk over each other, both trying to get her to retract her awful statements and telling her that none of it was true, but it was to no avail.

"Hey, hey, everybody stop. It's okay. Come on, Rome, don't act like you're shocked. She's always blamed me because I called him that night for a ride. It's cool, I get it. In fact, I blamed myself for a long time, too, until I realized it could have been a million other reasons. It was an accident, an accident that took someone we all loved, but still an accident. She could blame the truck driver, she could blame Remy for speeding, she could blame God for the rain or even the doctor in the ER for not being good enough at his job, but no, she blames me and always will, and it's fine if that's what she needs to do in order to keep it together. I can shoulder that load." All three of them were looking at me with wide eyes. It was probably the most I had said to my parents in one sitting in more than five years, and there was no yelling and no temper tantrums.

"Shaw is a smart girl and has strong convictions, so I refuse to let you put your actions and consequences with her on me. She told you straight up what you needed to do in order to maintain your relationship with her and you refused. No one is to blame for that but you."

"You don't know anything about Shaw. She is in a totally different league from you. She and Remy were both on a far better path than you ever dreamed to walk."

I just shook my head sadly and jerked my head toward

207

the door. "Mom, you have no clue. Shaw's the most loving, kind, compassionate person in the world. She would chew off her own arm before trying to put herself above someone she cares about. She doesn't give a flip about this path or that path as long as everyone she loves is going somewhere and at the end they're happy. I'm outta here. I have shit to do. Dad, it was good seeing you. Rome, I'll be in the truck."

I turned to walk back down the hall and out the front door but her chilly voice stopped me cold. "Stay away from Shaw, Rule. You'll just end up hurting her like you did your brother."

I wanted to tell her it was way too late for that warning. That I was beginning to know Shaw inside and out and that she was becoming a critical part of me, but I just met her cold gaze with one that I'm sure held resigned sadness. "Good luck ever getting her back into the Archer family fold with that kind of attitude, Mom. Keep it up and it'll be a cold day in hell before Shaw ever steps foot in this house again."

"Why she would choose you over this family is beyond me."

I gave her the only answer there was. "Because she thinks I'm worth it."

I gave Rome a bland look and moved around him, being careful to avoid my dad. I didn't look back to see if either of them followed me but when I got outside I let out a pent-up breath and looked at the street blanketed in snow. Her words hurt, they always had, but instead of feeling self-destructive and alone like I normally did, I could fully see now that the issues were all hers and there was nothing I could do to change her mind unless she actively sought out help. Too much time had passed with me playing the role of the accused for me to offer any form of clarity to her.

"Son." I was startled at the sound of my dad's voice. He had stopped to grab a jacket but had followed me to the driveway. Rome was nowhere to be seen. I shifted my feet in the powder and shoved my hands deep inside the pockets of my hoodie. "We need to talk about this."

"So much for this always being my home, huh, Dad?" I regretted it as soon as I said it. There was still a little boy somewhere deep inside me who wanted his parents' approval and no matter how hard I tried I just couldn't get him to shut up. "Sorry, that was stupid."

My dad shook his head, and for once, I saw genuine remorse in his gaze. "I had no idea it had gotten this bad with your mother, Rule. I'm not a fan of the crazy hair or the obsessive tattoos all over every part of your body, and it bugs me to no end that you purposely dress like a hoodlum just to annoy us, but I've never blamed you for what happened to Remy. You were two very different boys, always were, but I loved you both the same. I heard what your mother said at the funeral but I convinced myself it was just grief, just a mother's overreaction to losing a child too young. I honestly thought she would find her way clear of the sorrow and depression, but after today I see where Rome is coming from. We need help; she needs help. I would never ban a child from my home—pink hair, blue hair, green hair—none of it ultimately matters because I love you and I just want you to be happy and live a good life. I would prefer you stop aggravating an old man every chance you got while doing it, but I don't want you to think that I ever wish it was you and not Remy that night. It should have never happened to this family, but it did, and you are absolutely right that it was an accident."

I stared at my dad like he was a stranger. It was cold and I could barely feel my toes but my blood was pumping fast and hard in my veins. "You've never said any of that to me before. You normally just get mad and leave the room or let Mom tear me apart at every turn."

"You've always been hard for me to relate to, Rule. Rome

209

was my buddy, Remy was everybody's best friend, and you, well, you made your own path when you were just a little fella and I never felt like you needed any kind of guidance from me to get where you wanted to go. Your mother is fragile, more so than I thought, and while I knew that what's been happening over the last few years hasn't done us any good as a family, I guess I kept hoping she would just snap out of it. The harsher we were, the more you fought back. You never let her get to you the way I think she wanted, and while I should have stopped it years ago, I guess I see now how much damage what we were doing could have done to you."

"She wants me to be Remy." Saying it out loud to him felt like letting go of a lifetime of tightly held secrets.

He coughed and rubbed his thick hands together. "She wants the easy relationship she had with Remy with you. Remy wasn't argumentative or problematic, he just went with the flow. Rome knew we didn't want him to join the military, but he did it anyway because he's stubborn and determined to make a difference in the world. You were never easygoing and complacent. You hated curfew and any rule we imposed on you. You were always creative and quirky, but hard to relate to—we said go left and you went backward—she doesn't have a son left that she can just dictate and manage. She misses having someone to mother and Remy never minded her doing it for him and neither did Shaw, but now Shaw has chosen a side and Margot is deteriorating rapidly."

"Dad, I can't come back here, not like this. I appreciate everything you said today; in fact I wish you had said it years ago, and maybe I wouldn't have a litany of bad behavior and questionable choices littering my history the way I do now, but I'm not going to be her scapegoat anymore."

He sighed and looked at the door as Rome came out

looking thunderous. "Something tells me you aren't the only Archer who is making that call."

"Shaw, too. I'm not going to let Mom use her as a pawn in this mess."

"Yeah, neither am I. She's like a daughter to me."

Rome joined our little huddle and, boy, did he look pissed. My eyes tended to be light and go silver or gray whenever I felt a strong emotion, but my brother's blazed a bright blue, the color of the base of a flame.

"She's out of her damn mind. Seriously, Dad, she needs therapy and possibly drugs. I can't believe she said that shit to Rule."

My dad sighed again and shifted, sending tufts of snow that had gathered on the shoulders of his jacket drifting to the ground.

"I know, son. I just told Rule I recognize the problem is worse than I thought."

"I only have a few weeks' leave left; you better let her know I won't be back unless she gets her head on right. I tried to tell her and she just started spouting nonsense about Rule brainwashing everybody she cares about. She has straight up vilified him, her own child. I refuse to support her treating him that way."

"You're both good boys. For right now you two take care of each other and I'll work on your mother. I love you both. Don't give up on us yet."

We all shared a back-pounding round of hugs before Rome and I climbed back into the truck. I had to let the massive motor run a few minutes before the heater would pump out warm air, so while we waited I stared out the snowy windshield in contemplation while Rome rattled on about our mom. He was repulsed by her reaction to our surprise visit, but I wasn't. I was, however, stunned by everything my dad had told me. I couldn't remember the last time anyone told me they loved me besides my brothers. I had forgotten how nice it made me feel.

"You wanna take the Beamer or the truck since it's coming down pretty good now?"

"The BMW. I've seen you drive, little brother. You won't make it back to Denver in one piece in that sports car."

He had a point. I wanted to get back in one piece because I wanted to get Shaw a phone and pick her up from work and spend the night in bed with her wrapped around me. I wanted to make her whisper my name over and over in that husky voice. I wasn't sure, but this slippery feeling in my chest sure felt a hell of a lot like love.

CHAPTER 12

Shaw

I was still trying to figure out my new phone. Instead of replacing my broken one with the same model, Rule had gotten me the brand-new version with all the bells and whistles, and the thing was ten times smarter than me. I was trying to text Ayden that I was running late for our coffee date because one of my classes had run over. I hadn't seen her for more than a few minutes at a time in the last couple of weeks so we were meeting to catch up. She was still acting a little off. Between staying at Rule's place or him crashing at ours, and being constantly vigilant to avoid a run-in with Gabe, pinning her down and making her talk to me hadn't been possible.

I was developing a pretty good rhythm. On the days I worked, I stayed on the Hill with Rule, since his place was closer to the bar and he didn't mind coming in for a drink while waiting for me to get off; he and Lou were best pals now. On the days I was at school or volunteered, he would show up sometimes around dinner but often right before bedtime and spend the night at my apartment. I had decided to drop my Saturday shift in order to have one weekend night off to spend with him. He liked to go out on Friday and

Saturday nights with his friends so I figured it was cool to let him have a night to get his bro-time in while I was working. Plus it was fun to have a weekend day off to go shopping or watch a movie when I was so used to being busy all the time. Being with Rule was teaching me that my time was precious and I needed to spend it doing things I wanted as well as the things that were required of me. That was partly why I felt justified in ignoring the calls from my parents that had been coming in nonstop since the trip to Brookside.

I finally got the text sent and got one back saying she already had a seat and had ordered for us. When I got to the coffeehouse the place was packed, but Ayden had secured a spot by one of the windows and was messing around on her phone. A table full of geeky-looking guys was trying to get her attention by talking and laughing loudly, but she seemed oblivious. I missed our girl time and I wished she would talk to me about what had been bothering her the last month, but with so much on my own plate I was well aware that I hadn't been the best friend as of late. I flopped in the seat across from her and gratefully scooped up the frothy drink she had ordered for me. She made a face at me and put her phone away. "I almost saw your boyfriend naked this morning."

I laughed at the look on her face. "I don't know what to say to that—you're welcome?"

She crinkled her nose at me. "He doesn't have much shame, does he?"

"You've met Rule, right?"

She picked up her own drink and peered at me over the top of the cup. "I guess he doesn't really have much to worry about, does he? I don't know how you don't get distracted by all that stuff inked all over him. I think I would spend all my time looking at his tattoos rather than getting down to business."

"It's fun."

"I bet." She had a faraway look in her pretty eyes that I just couldn't let slide anymore.

"Come on, Ayden; tell me what's going on with you lately. I know I've been wrapped up in my own stuff but I can see the change in you. You look so sad all the time and that's just not like you."

Her whiskey-toned gaze shifted from one side to another before settling on the table between us. She set her coffee down and traced the rim of the cup with her finger.

"I don't know. I mean, I know, but not really." I just watched her because I wasn't sure what she was talking about. "I used to think I had it all figured out—school, boys, my future, all of it. I knew that coming from nothing and no one didn't matter because I was on the right track and I was going to be something great, and now I just don't know."

"What brought this on?"

"The night at the rock bar, the night I had Jet take me home, I practically threw myself at him." I saw her flinch a little. "He was polite enough about it all but said I wasn't really his type and that nice girls like me deserved better."

"Well, that seems chivalrous and nice of him, not life-altering."

"That's the thing, Shaw. I'm a nice girl now but you have no idea about the life I lived before I moved to Colorado. When I was in Kentucky, I was out of control. I partied, messed around in all kinds of bad stuff, played around with too many guys, and I was a mess inside and out. It took a miracle to get me into this school and away from all of that, but part of me is still that girl, and when Jet turned me down it just made both parts of me go a little sideways. He's cute and in a band, and I was mad, really mad, when he rejected me on the basis of being a good girl. That's just not who I think I want to be. I've been struggling with it ever since."

I set my coffee down and looked at her out of narrowed eyes. "You let a guy get all up in your head after one brief encounter? That doesn't sound like you at all."

"There was something about this guy, Shaw. I don't know what it was."

"Ayden, you're amazing. I don't care what your life was like before, because now you're loyal and kind, you make me laugh, you're smarter than practically anyone I know, you're ridiculously beautiful, and we both know that there have been times in the last couple of years when the only thing holding me together was you. I've met Jet a few times and he is nice and definitely a babe, but he's also a rock-and-roll guy who comes with legions of rock-and-roll groupies fawning all over him, so whatever moment you had with him is not worth this mopey self-doubt he seems to have spawned in you."

"This from the girl who pined over her guy in silence for half a decade?" Her sarcasm was biting, but well deserved.

"Yes, and look how miserable and lonely it made me. All I'm saying is that if a guy can't appreciate you for how wonderful you are, then he isn't worth it, and if he doesn't want to sully your good image, whether it is real or not, then I hate to say it but that just sounds like maybe he wasn't interested. You are pretty country and he is pretty rock. I mean, I know I've been drowning in opposites attract and all that nonsense for my whole life with Rule, but maybe they really don't and you just weren't his type. I've seen the girls who gravitate to these guys when they go out. Heck, I've walked in on Rule with them over and over again, and trust me, big brains, self-confidence, and ambition are not things these women bring to the table."

She exhaled loudly. "Maybe. It just made me wonder

about what I'm doing. I date, I have a pretty good time, I love living with you, and I'm awesome at school, but I feel like something is missing. And when I see your superhot, half-dressed boyfriend covered in tattoos looking all sleepy and satisfied I get a little burn near my heart that hurts. I think I'm lonely and not for something casual and simple. Trust me, I had plenty of that when I was younger."

I laughed a little and scraped some of the foam off my drink with my finger and popped it in my mouth. I think the table of geeks gasped but I wasn't sure, because when I looked back up at them they were all frantically typing away on their laptops.

"So you pick a heavy-metal singer to get all mushy and sentimental over? Man, we've got marvelous taste in men."

She laughed with me and leaned back to cross her long legs at the ankle. "I think it'll probably fade away, but in the meantime I need to figure out how to move forward without totally forgetting who I am. I mean, look at you, you're not suddenly covered head to toe in ink and sporting a face full of extreme piercings. You took Rule's make-your-own-rules philosophy and used it to mellow out and take control of your destiny, not turn into a different person."

She was partly right. I figured it was probably too much information to tell her I had been seriously considering getting my nipples pierced. Rule was always telling me how sensitive they were, how easy it was to get me turned on and all worked up and ready to blow by just playing with them. After having intimate contact on a repeated basis with someone who had piercings through strategic parts of his anatomy, I knew exactly how the little pieces of jewelry could enhance the experience. It had always been Rule for me, so I didn't know what it was like to be with anyone who didn't have barbells in his cock and through his tongue, but as good as it was with him, I had no desire to find out how it was with someone unadorned. I didn't want them for him; I wanted them for me, but I wasn't sure I was ready to commit to something that big yet.

"He influences me, he always has, but I don't want to be with someone who wants to be with me just to change me."

"I know, and neither would I. I think when I left home I had the idea that if I didn't change, I was just going to be stuck in that endless rut forever, and somehow I lost everything, even the good stuff, about the pre-Denver Ayden."

I reached out and squeezed the hand she had resting on the table. "Maybe you're just entering a new phase; maybe this isn't new Ayden or old Ayden but an excellent new incarnation of both. You're fine; whoever and whatever you want to be is just fine."

"I sure hope so. So, have you seen or heard anything from Gabe?"

I shook my head and kicked back in the seat. "No. I've seen him on campus coming and going but he keeps his distance. Rule's retired cop friend says he heard that Judge Davenport wasn't happy to have his son's name come up in open court, so maybe he put a leash on him. The guys have been really good about keeping me close, so I don't think he has the nerve to go up against Rule or Rome. I'm purposely avoiding all contact with my parents, so if he's trying to enlist them it isn't doing him any good."

"So, what's your long-term plan? Rome has to go back to playing soldier soon, and as much as I'm sure Rule likes keeping you close, eventually it's gonna get old. The honeymoon phase won't last forever."

I was worried about that myself. Right now he seemed to like hanging out at the bar and didn't seem to mind juggling our hectic schedules back and forth to see each other and to keep his eye on me, but I agreed with her that it couldn't last much longer.

"I don't know what to do. If the legal system can't help and my own parents are working against me, I just don't know. I wish he would find another girl who is socially acceptable and forget about me."

"I don't know, either, but I'm glad you aren't trying to handle this all on your own."

"Rule is good for me. I feel like my life is finally my own with him in it."

"Have you told him that you're in love with him and have been for eternity?"

I gulped down some of my drink and it went down the wrong tube. I hacked for a second until tears filled my eyes. "No! Are you nuts? Why would I do that? He already knows that I've had a crush on him since forever and I think that just weirds him out. I don't want to put all kinds of pressure on him to feel the same about me. He wants to be together and he's making a true and honest effort to be in this relationship with me, and for now that's good enough."

She clicked her tongue at me and waved a finger back and forth. "If you think you hide the way you feel about him at all, you're so wrong. The feelings you have for that boy radiate out of you like a bright light. He has to see it every time he looks at you."

I fiddled nervously with the ends of my hair. "Well, he's never said anything about it and that's just fine by me."

"You are so silly. You've been in love with this guy since you were a teenager and now you have him and you're still worried about being open and honest with him? It just seems to me like you wouldn't want to waste any more time."

"This is Rule we're talking about. He's unpredictable and doesn't deal with emotions in a typical way. I don't want to scare him off by getting too intense, too quickly. I've seen what he does to people who push him and it isn't pretty."

"For what it's worth, I think he's just as sprung on you

as you are on him. That glow you have, well he has it, too, just in a darker, slightly more confused way."

"Well, that's nice to hear. I don't know that I believe it, but still, it's a nice thought."

We spent another hour and one more coffee each catching up. We talked about school and I told her a little about Margot's breakdown when Rule went to get my car. We talked about work and how ridiculous Loren seemed to be every time she opened her mouth and we made plans to go shopping the following weekend after another trip to the salon. By the time we were done talking, she had to run to get ready for work. We left on a hug, which I'm pretty sure caused the table of geeks to spontaneously break into juvenile erection territory, and I headed up to Capitol Hill. Since I was off and Rome was back in the Springs for another checkup, I had promised Rule I would meet him at the tattoo shop and wait until he was done with his last client.

I hadn't been in the shop during business hours so when I pushed open the door I was slightly taken aback at how busy it was. There was a girl behind the counter with supershort hair bleached out as white as mine and spiked up all over the place. She was answering the phone, handling the people milling about the waiting area, and pointing prospective clients in the directions of the appropriate portfolios. There were three other artists set up in the stations not filled by Nash, Rowdy, and Rule. I noticed one of them was a very pretty girl with black and green hair that looked like something out of a comic book. There were also six clients in varying positions getting all kinds of designs and making all manner of awful sounding noises and looks of discomfort that had their friends and the artists laughing and making lighthearted comments. Against Me! was blasting over the sound system and the entire vibe was energetic and exciting. I couldn't fathom how anyone earned such a good living in such a crazy environment, but it seemed to suit Rule's personality to a tee.

I stood unsure in the doorway for a full minute just taking it all in until I was jostled to the side by a girl in too-tight pants and disgusting UGGs. Her hair was teased up and I could see she had swirling sleeves of ink under her supertiny T-shirt. I guess she was good-looking in a trashy, desperate kind of way, but the girl behind the counter apparently had no time for her because her voice, loud and clear with a hint of an East Coast burr, told her none too graciously, "Fuck off, Liza. I already told you over the phone that he was booked up for the next two weeks and he has no interest in working late to touch your shit up."

The girl mumbled something I couldn't hear and leaned over the counter. The receptionist or whatever her title was rolled her eyes dramatically. "Look, let me break this down for you: he is not interested in you. You are a client—you give him money to tattoo you, not to date you and not to flirt with you. He's busy, and I mean busy, so if you want work done, you will get put in the book like everyone else and come in for your scheduled appointment. Besides, he's got a girlfriend now and has no interest in the little ink bunnies anymore."

I blinked rapidly in surprise when I realized she was more than likely talking about Rule and that I was more than likely the girlfriend she was referring to. How strange was that? The girl continued to have a little bit of a fit until it became clear she wasn't going to get past the blond fireball. She shoved past me on the way out the door, and a clean-cut college guy took her place at the desk. He made his appointment with no fuss and I continued to watch the ebb and flow of business for a while until the girl's attention finally landed on me.

"Can I help you with something?" She wasn't exactly friendly, more like matter-of-fact, so I started a little bit.

"I'm just waiting for someone."

"Well, you can have a seat over there if you're waiting for a client."

I tucked my hair behind my ears and cocked my head to the side and regarded her carefully. "I'm actually waiting for Rule."

Now that she was looking at me I could see she had really unusual-colored eyes; one was dark brown and the other was a swirl of green and blue. She gave a really heavy sigh and narrowed her eyes at me. "Like I told the other tattoo tramp, Rule is busy. If you want to see him, you have to have an appointment just like every other client."

I snickered against my will. "Tattoo tramp? Is that what you call them?"

She seemed surprised by my question. "Yeah. You have no idea how many poor girls are walking around this town with stupid lower-back tattoos just because they wanted to pull their pants down for one of the guys."

"Oh, I would totally believe it."

She leaned her elbows on the counter and sized me up and down. "What did you say your name was?"

"I didn't, but then again you didn't ask. I'm Shaw. I'm not a tramp of any persuasion and I don't have any tattoos, so neither of those things apply to me."

As soon as I said my name her jaw dropped open and she shoved off the big leather chair she was sitting on. Her wicked-colored eyes went wide and she smacked her hands down hard on the marble surface separating us.

"Holy shit! *You're* Shaw? You're freaking real? Unbelievable! Guys, Rule's girl is here and she's like an actual girl with an actual brain. Un-freaking-believable. The terrible trio has been talking about you for weeks and I just didn't believe it, but here you really are."

Like something out of a movie all eyes in the shop suddenly swiveled up to where I was standing. I had spent plenty of time with Nash and Rowdy over the last few weeks, so they both just offered up brief "heys" and went back to what they were working on. Rule's look turned my insides out and he gave me a wink before saying something to the kid he was working on and sitting back to wipe the excess ink off. The other three artists stared at me openly, which would have made me uncomfortable, but the blonde had sprinted around the counter and was now standing right in front of me. She was almost the same height as me but weighed a good thirty pounds less, though somehow her wild hair made her look taller and it was hard to believe that loud voice came out of such a tiny package. She was like a punk-rock pixie.

"Do you have any idea how long I've waited for one of those guys to land a serious girlfriend? Forever! Sending away the ink bunnies has never been as satisfying as it is now and I never ever would have pegged Rule as the one to go down first."

She waved a hand over her shoulder toward the opposite side of the shop, where the three artists I didn't know were working and pointed to each one. "Bixie, she's married to a firefighter so she's never caused too much fuss with weirdo client stalkers. Mase has an on again-off again girlfriend so he can behave, but when they're off he can give Rule a run for his money in the manwhore department. Jasper, well, we call him Jaz, keeps his liaisons quiet because he's got ties with the Kings of Sorrow, the local biker club, and apparently that's supposed to be hush-hush so the bunnies don't hover around for him too much. But the terrible trio, man oh man, I show those bitches outta here all day every day, and even with Rule being hooked up with you it still seems like it's my full-time job."

She talked so loud and so fast I had a hard time tracking everything she was telling me. Plus, Rule had snapped off his gloves and was prowling toward me in the way that made my legs go all gooey. He moved with a limber ease that was just sexy and confident; also his hair was starting to grow back in and I liked the near black fuzz covering his scalp.

"Are you telling my girl stories, Cora? I told you Shaw's been around for a long time—you aren't going to be able to scare her." He came around the corner and before I could get myself all worried about whether it was appropriate to touch him at work he had me all wound up with his hands in my hair and his mouth slanted across mine. He tasted like coffee and peppermint, and he didn't seem to mind that all eyes remained on us while he thoroughly devoured me, like we hadn't seen each other in weeks rather than just a few hours. He gave his tongue one last flick, clicking his tongue ring against the back of my teeth. When he pulled away I'm sure my eyes were glassy and I was breathing hard. I cleared my throat and put a shaky hand on his chest until I regained my composure. "I've got, like, a half an hour left. Are you cool to hang out that long? You can come chill in the back and do your school shit or whatever." I nodded and took a step back from him. He was potent and went to my head fast.

"No, let her stay up here and hang out with me. I'm dying to know all about this mystical creature that got you to act human for once."

He shot an annoyed glance over his shoulder at the pixie. "Shaw, this is Cora Lewis. She's the shop manager and our resident body modification expert."

She wiggled her eyebrows up and down and gave me a

224

leer. She twirled a finger in Rule's direction. "Since you're with this guy I'm sure you're familiar with my work."

I choked back a laugh and put a hand to my mouth as a hot flush worked up Rule's neck. "Seriously, Cora?"

She shrugged a tiny shoulder. "What? It's true, isn't it?"

His arctic eyes landed back on me and the chagrin in them made me laugh out loud. "She's from Brooklyn. None of us know where Uncle Phil found her and they refuse to tell us but she keeps the shop running like a well-oiled machine. Most of us wouldn't know if we were coming or going without her."

"I can stay up here and wait for you. I'm hungry, though, so you need to feed me when you're done."

He bent down and put his lips right next to my ear. "Oh, I'll feed you when I'm done all right."

A hot shiver shot through me so I gave him a heavy-lidded look. "Goody." He kissed my cheek and made his way back to his waiting client. I shifted my gaze to Cora and blushed when I noticed she was grinning like a demented Cheshire Cat.

"So it's like that, is it?"

I blinked and shifted from foot to foot. She grabbed my hand and pulled me around the counter, actually shoving me into another leather chair that was stashed back there.

"Like what?"

She swiveled her chair so we were facing each other and gave me a level look. "It's like all hot and bothered but sweet and fuzzy, too. I didn't know the asshat had any of that in him. You make him human."

That was the second time she had mentioned something like that but I had to wait until she fielded a couple phone calls to question her about it. "What do you mean about that, exactly?"

"I've worked with Rule for the last five years. I was here

225

when he and Nash started their internships right outta high school. Phil and I go way back so I've known the boys for a while. I adore Rule. I think it's genetically impossible not to be kind of in love with him when you come equipped with a vagina. It's just something about all that angsty, moody swagger he has that makes you want to cuddle him up and make him feel better."

I knew exactly what she was talking about so I just nodded in agreement. "But he's also arrogant and explosive, he treats women like crap because too many of them let him get away with it, and for a long time after his brother died I watched him just go through the motions of living his life. He came to work, he hung out with his boys, he gave me shit on a daily basis, and he screwed his way through the entire Front Range. But he was doing it all locked inside this bubble that none of us who loved him could get through. He was cold and unreachable but then all of a sudden there were cracks, and some of the old Rule was showing through. The robot version of himself he had been operating from for so long started to fade and the good ole human Rule was back, and I think it has to do with you."

"That's a really nice thing to say."

"It's not nice if it's the truth. So tell me how a vanilla girl like you, all virgin skin and no piercings, gets into a guy like Rule. From first appearances I would never peg him as your type; you look more Brooks Brothers than Dickies if you know what I mean."

I twirled a piece of hair around my finger and watched as she typed a bunch of stuff in the computer. She was freakishly efficient and fast and I wasn't sure I wanted to talk about how sexy I found Rule with someone who already had intimate knowledge of my boyfriend's junk.

"When he was sixteen he came home one day with an awful tattoo of a horseshoe and a shamrock on his forearm.

226

Phil had given Nash a tattoo machine and some ink for his sixteenth birthday and instead of trying to learn on pigs or melons they decided that they would try to learn on each other. Both of them were always really gifted artistically. Nash was more into street art and graffiti-type stuff where Rule just fiddled around with it and happened to learn he had some real talent.

"Anyway, I was over at his house and I don't know if you ever got a chance to meet Remy, but identical doesn't even come close to how those two looked: the same eyes, the same dark hair, and the same innate sense that they were out-of-this-world good-looking. So Rule came home with that terrible tattoo and suddenly he was a new guy. He claimed his skin as his own, made the mark to define who he was and how he was different from Remy, and it was just beautiful how much he loved what changing his outer appearance did for his inner sense of self. He's always been a babe, but when he started to customize the hotness it just made it better and better. Without all the tattoos and piercings he just wouldn't be Rule."

"And what about you? You're not into any of it?"

"I don't really know. I had really particular parents growing up and if I had come home with a tattoo or any kind of extreme piercing they would have grounded me until graduation, so I never even thought about it."

"How old are you now?"

"I just turned twenty."

"You still live at home?"

"Nope."

"Then shouldn't you be allowed to do whatever you want with your body without fear of their reaction?"

I sighed and swiveled my chair back and forth. "Yeah. I've actually been thinking about getting a little something done."

"A tattoo? You know Rule would give you something beautiful, especially since he's the one who would have to look at it all the time."

We shared a laugh that had the guys in the shop looking at us curiously.

"No, I was thinking about getting my nipples pierced." I wasn't normally so open but I figured since she did it for a living it was kind of like talking to a doctor about a health problem. Her unusual-colored eyes widened and she gave me a huge grin.

"That's superhot."

I shrugged and continued to twirl my hair. "I like the way it looks and like you said, I'm familiar with your work so I know it can be awesome. I just don't know that I'm ready for something so extreme."

"They take a bit to heal but when they do it's amazing. If you decide to go through with it let me know and I'll do it for you for free, I'll just charge you for the jewelry."

"Well, Rule's birthday is next month so if I do it, it'll be before then."

She clapped her hands together and giggled like a little girl. She was kind of crazy but I think I liked her. I had always had such a hard time making friends and just being at ease around new people, so it was a testament to all the positive ways Rule was influencing me that I could talk with this wacky girl with no reservations or inhibitions.

"Oh, a sexy surprise, I just love that idea. Like I said, just let me know and we can work something out. I like seeing my boys happy and doing right by a good girl."

"Thanks, I think."

We chatted easily for another hour because whatever Rule was working on was taking longer than he thought. I watched her process out the clients who were finished getting their designs done and watched her help a few people come in who had questions and were interested in setting up consultations. She chased off another girl who came in looking for Rowdy, and by the time Rule walked up to the counter with his freshly bandaged canvas, I felt like I had made a new friend. She was sarcastic and witty as hell but her insights into the way my guy's head worked were clear and coming from a different perspective than I had ever heard before.

Rule's client looked like he was barely old enough to drive but he was sporting some major artwork and had his entire upper arm wrapped up and shiny with ink and salve. I didn't miss the appreciative look he gave me as he was walking out and apparently neither did Rule. He flicked the kid in the back of the head and told him that if he wanted his sleeve finished he better keep his eyes to himself. He told me to give him just ten more minutes so he could clean up his station and then we could go. I watched him walk away and noticed that the female client Nash was working on and the young girl that the artist they called Mase was working on both did the same thing. Cora was right, it was just some kind of magnetic pull he had over the opposite sex, and as long as I was with him I was just going to have to learn to deal with it.

He moved quickly and came back to collect me in no time at all. He handed Cora a bank bag and hollered out good-bye to no one in particular and pulled me out with him into the now frigid evening air. I shivered involuntarily and huddled into his side while he adjusted the hood of his sweatshirt over his still mostly naked head and shoved his arms through the sleeves of a black mechanic-style work coat that had the tattoo shop's logo and name embroidered in a bright design on the back.

"Do you want to order something for delivery or go somewhere?" He rubbed his hands together roughly and then pushed them under the fall of my hair to clasp the back of my neck. They felt like blocks of ice so I shivered even harder until he pulled me to his chest and tucked my head under his chin.

"Delivery so I don't have to move my car."

"Cool, what are you in the mood for? I'll call on the way home."

"Anything, really. I'm just hungry."

"Pizza?"

"Sure, but no green peppers or mushrooms on my half."

I hooked an arm through his and tried to keep up with his long strides as we made our way to the Victorian. My phone vibrated in my pocket and I frowned as I saw it was once again my father. I was sure whatever story my mother had spun about my last visit had him all riled up, but I just didn't have the patience to get a lecture on morality and suitable romantic partners from a guy whose new wife was only a few years older than me. I sent the call to voice mail and let go of Rule to sidestep a particularly dangerous and icy patch on the sidewalk.

He scowled at me and snatched my hand back up. He tugged me around so that I was pressed up against his front while he walked forward and guided me backward. "I wouldn't let you fall."

I reached up to put my hands on his shoulders and gazed up into his eyes, which were just as frosty as the snow coating the ground all around us. "No?"

"No. You don't trust me?"

"Most of the time I do."

"Why not all the time?" We stopped in front of the Victorian and I moved my hands from his shoulders to the back of his neck, which made his hood fall off.

"Because I've never trusted anyone all the time. It's the people I care about the most who always seem to do the most damage."

230

"I'm not going to be one of those people, Shaw." If only he knew how bad it had hurt my heart each time I had to see him with one of his conquests he wouldn't be saying that. I forced a small smile and brushed my fingers over the soft black hair starting to grow on his head.

"I hope not."

He just shook his head and hauled me into the apartment because it was way too cold to keep messing around outside. He shrugged out of his coat and hoodie while motioning for me to hand my stuff over. "Nash has a date tonight so he won't be home until later, if at all." He disappeared down the hall to drop the armful in his room and came back talking on the phone with the pizza place. I took down a couple plates and handed him a beer while looking in a futile attempt to see if the boys had anything in the fridge to make a salad with. I needed to get some normal food in this place if I was going to keep spending time here or I was going to end up the size of a baby hippo.

"I think he's probably done with having me around in the man-zone. I know Ayden mentioned that she almost got an eyeful while you were over this morning. They're undoubtedly sick of us."

He laughed and took a chug out of the beer bottle. "I didn't mean to surprise Ayden this morning. I thought she was gone. I didn't know she just went running."

"Yeah, she goes every morning and it's not like she was complaining; in fact she complimented the view."

He snorted. "Nash doesn't mind having you here. He likes that you actually cook and that we don't have to get delivery or bring stuff home every single night. Plus, you smell good and always pick up the random stuff we leave lying around. If having you here got on his nerves he would say something to me and more than likely to you as well. He has no problem letting Rome know when he has overstayed his welcome."

I leaned back against the counter and twisted the cap off a bottle of water. "So, Cora was telling me all about your ink bunnies, or tattoo tramps, as she calls them. I had no idea just how far your appeal reached. Girls get work that they aren't going to love in ten years just to spend time with you. That's pretty crazy."

"Cora has a big mouth and exaggerates, but getting tattooed is pretty intimate no matter who the client is. When they leave they're leaving with something you put on their skin forever. They trust you to capture their vision and execute it perfectly, so sometimes that means you have to invest in them as a person to some degree. Some girls, especially younger ones, get really wrapped up in the process and turn it into more than it is. I have my fair share of clients who have little crushes on me and come back for work. Not because I'm awesome but because they want to spend time in the setting, but it's my job so I keep it professional. I'm not going to lie, I've hooked up with a client or two, but never after work or never while I was in the process of doing a piece. Sex and work don't belong in the same place."

I sucked back some of the water and mulled that over for a minute. "Does it bother you that I don't look like the typical girls you find attractive?"

"What in the hell are you talking about?"

I hopped up on the counter and let my legs dangle. I tapped the tips of my nails on the tiled surface and cocked my head to the side while I studied him closely. "I don't have tattoos or piercings. I don't have sex hair or wear clothes that are impossible to breathe in. I'm just, you know, a normal girl. I've seen enough, been around enough of your morning-afters to know that I'm not what you typically gravitate toward. When you look at me, do you wonder if you would like it better if I looked more like you and your crew?"

He put the beer down on the dining room table and locked

his eyes on mine while he stalked toward me. Before, that would have made me nervous and panicky but now it made me all warm and breathless. He didn't stop until he was pressed right up against me, between my legs with our hips aligned in a perfect position to make me forget my own name.

"When I look at you I don't see anything but you, and Shaw, you are perfect. I don't care what color your hair is, if you're pale or tan, if you have makeup on or just woke up—all I care about is that when I look at you, you always look back and see me. You're beautiful inside and out and if you wanted to tattoo all that pretty white skin from head to toe, I would be honored to put it there for you, but if not, I'll take you all smooth and milky white any chance I get."

It was heart-wrenchingly romantic. It was the most thoughtful thing anyone has ever said to me, and I was about to go all weepy female on him and blubber about how wonderful everything he said was and how much he meant to me. Either that or I was going to yank off his clothes and have at him right there in the kitchen. I was waffling between the two reactions when the doorbell rang and shattered the mood. He pushed away from me and went to collect dinner, and I took a minute to get my composure back. The boy was potent, all right, and I planned to enjoy every single minute that it was directed at me.

CHAPTER 13

Rule

There had been a few moments during the last week that had been so perfect, so poignant, that they froze me with fear and made me want to run the other way as fast and as far as I could. Sitting on the couch in my living room, eating pizza and knocking back a few cold ones while I watched *SportsCenter* and she did schoolwork on her computer was one of them. Watching her *just be* had me suddenly feeling like I was suffocating in the rightness of it all, and I had to escape to a burning-hot shower before I did something stupid like ask her to marry me or tell her to take a hike. She just fit. She filled every hole I had in my life and the idea of her not being there, of it going away, terrified me like nothing I had ever felt before. I didn't want to rely on her, didn't want to build a mountain out of what might just be an early-in-the-relationship infatuation, but there was something that made me think that if this all went away I would never be the same.

The last few weeks had been amazing. I liked having her in my house and in my life, and I enjoyed making a place for myself in hers. My friends all adored her, and I couldn't begrudge them the little crushes they'd developed. She was just so endearingly oblivious to her appeal; it was hard not to fall for. I could tell when we left the shop that Cora was a fan. That meant a lot because she was kind of like a big sister, and I trusted her instincts when it came to people. It was what made her such a good shop manager. Shaw was already part of my family, and after I gave her the rundown of what happened on my visit home, she wasted no time in firing off a scathing email to my mother, letting her know in no uncertain terms that she wouldn't stand for that behavior and pleading with her to seek help. She had my back, and I wondered again how long she had been fighting for me before I pulled my head out and noticed. It always made me feel like shit.

The quiet moments were settling, and made me feel like I was building a foundation for something great. The passionate moments, the moments where she looked at me like I was a present she had always wanted to unwrap, were enough to make me think I had found the one person who would never bore me in bed. The thing about being the only guy she had ever been with was that I got to teach her everything, and Shaw had always been an A-plus student. Whether it was fast or slow, gentle or rough, a quickie that blew my mind or an all-night session that had her running late for class the next morning—there was no doubt that we were sexually compatible. She was starting to figure out her own preferences; she liked it a little rougher and dirtier than I would have figured her to, for instance. She also managed to find humor in the act when it was awkward or not going the way one of us intended. I couldn't remember ever having as much fun in bed in my life. I didn't know it was possible, but she even made sex better and the thought of losing any of it just made me want to fall into a hole and never climb out.

I was trying to shake off the fear. After all, it was just a nice night at home and Nash was gone, so I should be doing my best to make her scream my name over and over again at the top of her lungs. But the doubt lingered and I stayed in the shower until the water ran cold, forcing me to get out. I ran a fuzzy towel over my head and face and secured another one loosely around my waist. I left my clothes in a heap on the floor and wandered into my room, figuring she would still be out in the living room doing her homework and I would have a couple more minutes to get my shit together. Only the TV was off and she was sitting in the middle of my big bed, sipping on the beer I had abandoned when I bolted earlier. As if that wasn't enough, she was only wearing my T-shirt that had the tattoo shop's logo on it. It looked better on her than it ever had on me, and she was watching me with very serious eyes the color of new grass.

"What's going on?"

I cleared my throat and tried to play it off. "Nothing. Why?" Only this was Shaw and she knew my bullshit better than almost anyone. She scooted to the edge of the bed and set the beer down on the nightstand.

"Because you were in there forever and you already took a shower this morning. Something spooked you and you ran. I want to know what it was."

I considered lying to her, considered telling her that she was just imagining things, but in the end knew that I just needed to come clean and hope that she didn't freak out because I was so emotionally screwed up.

"All this." I waved a hand between the two of us. "It's so easy, so smooth and simple, that sometimes it freaks me out. I'm not used to normal and ordinary, so it makes me nervous. My life was always about trying to grab on to fleeting moments of pleasure, of feeling good, and now I have that all the time with you, and I get lost in my head wondering what I'm going to do to screw it up, or how I'm going to

236

keep it together if you decide to take it away. Sometimes I get sucked into my visions of what could happen and I have a really difficult time staying in the present. Watching TV with you, just being with you, soothes something inside me that I didn't even know needed soothing, but it also makes something in there cower in fear. I'm sorry."

She just watched me and I prepared myself for her to get up off the bed and walk out the door. If she did I was pretty sure that, towel or not, I would chase her into the cold and beg until she came back. Instead, she unfolded from the bed and came up to me on bare feet. My shirt covered all the good stuff but just barely. She stopped so that we weren't touching but we were close enough to share a breath.

"It scares me, too, Rule. I'm not used to ordinary, either, and I never thought I would have that with you, never thought I would have anything with you at all, so it's okay to get a little lost in your head, as long as you come back and we can talk about it. I'm not going to ask you to give anything you aren't comfortable with. People have done that to me my entire life and I'm sick of it."

I exhaled a hard breath and unclenched the fists I hadn't been aware I had curled up at my sides.

"What if I ask you to give me everything, Shaw? What if I want it all? Won't that make me just like all the rest of them?"

She made a noise in her throat and then broke into a smile that nearly killed me on the spot. She was just so lovely and pure. "No, because you don't have to ask for anything. All of it is already yours. You're the only one I've ever wanted to give it to."

This girl was going to be the end of me. She put a hand on each of my sides, one splayed over the angel, one splayed over the reaper, and I thought my heart was going to pound out of my chest.

237

"You have to promise not to bail on me when I get lost, Shaw. You have to promise to just wait it out until I can find my way back. I need to know you're at the end of the tunnel when everything goes black."

"I know how to wait for you, Rule, and I don't mind doing it as long as you promise not to shut me out. I can't do this with you, be so wrapped up in you and what's happening between us, if you're going to close the door on me when it gets to be too much. My heart can't take that."

"I know." But I wasn't sure that was a promise I could keep. My default was to return to what I knew, and that was distance and space, so that I could protect myself. "I can do my best, Shaw, but I told you all along I'm not real sure how to do this whole relationship thing and I'm scared shitless I'm going to do something to screw it up."

She leaned forward and let her hands glide up around my back and across my shoulders. She pressed a soft, open-mouthed kiss to the center of my chest and it made my entire life zero in on that tiny point of contact.

"Well, you can be scared alone or we can be scared together. I prefer the second option, but if you need some space to get your head around it and figure out what you want, I can make that happen. I want to be with you, Rule, but I'm not going to be here with you if it makes you hurt and makes you freak out. We both deserve better than that."

I wasn't sure at this point if it was about what I deserved or not, but I wasn't stupid enough to let what I had with her get demolished under the weight of doubt I couldn't control. I finally reached out and pulled her to me in a suffocating hug that pressed her length against all my bare skin. I had spent plenty of time with her this morning, making her beg, turning myself inside out, but that didn't seem to matter, my cock reacted under the towel, letting

238

her know that whatever was going on inside my head had no bearing on how my body felt about her.

"I'm just messed up, Shaw. I'm sorry that I get this way but the last thing I want is to chase my tail all alone." I kissed her, letting her feel the things I couldn't say as they burned through my blood. I wanted her always and the idea of that made my knees weak.

She let me devour her mouth, let me get my hands all tangled up rough in her hair, let me press her up against the closest wall and push an insistent erection against her all without complaint or argument. There was no gentleness, no concern for skill or whether or not I was making it feel good for her, all that existed was a blinding need to get inside her, to make her feel the emotion that was making me go crazy. I needed to syphon off some of the want and need, and the only way to do it was to get it out of me and into her. Her head made a dull thunk against the wall and I felt her suck in a tense breath and still none of it gave me pause. The towel hit the floor and my T-shirt offered no resistance as I rushed through getting both of us naked. Somewhere in my head I knew I needed to slow down, needed to get control back, that my hands were too hard on her, that my mouth was going to leave marks, but I couldn't rein it in.

She whispered my name, tried to get me to slow down, but I didn't care. I was ready to just move in her, to bury all the fear and uncertainty blindly inside her warm body, but this was a girl who knew all my tricks, knew that I was operating from a place where I probably wouldn't even remember what I was doing in the morning, and she wasn't going to let me turn her into another faceless conquest that I used to find silence. Since I no longer had hair and was so much bigger than her, she had to resort to digging her nails into my scalp and pressing her teeth down on my invading tongue to get me to jerk back and give her some breathing room. She struggled to catch her breath and pushed away from the wall by planting her hands in the center of my chest and giving me a hard shove.

I stumbled back a step and shook my head back and forth. "Casper." I wanted to apologize, wanted to tell her I would never devalue all that she was coming to mean to me on purpose, but she didn't give me a chance. She stood up on her tiptoes and put a small hand over my mouth. Her green eyes were big and there was a mixture of desire and trepidation in them that twisted my heart into a knot. This girl just simply understood me and wasn't going to blame me for all the crazy that I had built up inside me.

"Just don't, Rule." She moved her hand and kissed me with a million more levels of care than I had just shown her. "You need me to take care of you right now and I'm going to do it, but I'll be damned if you don't know it's me."

"I know it's you, Shaw."

"Good, because for a minute there I wasn't sure, and I can't even begin to tell you how much that pissed me off. Now shut up and let me help you out of the dark."

I went to grab for her, to wrap her up and hold her close, but she evaded my hands and slithered around so that she was on her knees in front of me. I stopped breathing for a second when her lips landed somewhere below my navel, and my abs contracted hard enough that it hurt. We had messed around plenty, but this wasn't an area she had seemed ready to venture into before now. My dick quivered in anticipation as the tip of her tongue traced the outline of the mermaid I had inked down there, the long tail curling right around the base of my cock. I didn't know how far she was willing to take it so I gingerly placed my hands on the top of her head. Her hair felt like silk against my fingertips and I stopped moving just in case anything I did was going to make her stop.

"Shaw." I wasn't sure if I was going to ask her to keep going or to stop, because I wasn't sure how much I could take. I felt wound up too tight and too ready to break as it was. "You don't have to do this." I meant it when I said it but I also knew there was a good chance I would die if she decided to stop. Her mouth was damp and warm and the apadravya piercing I had through the tip of my dick and the Jacob's ladder that was spaced out on the underside pulled the sensitive skin taut when she closed it over the eager flesh. My eyes squeezed shut as I hit the back of her throat and every sensation I had ever experienced up to this point in my life ceased to exist.

I had received head from a bunch of different girls in my lifetime, and had enjoyed it pretty much every single time, but there was something about having Shaw on her knees before me, having her suck and pull me into her pretty mouth, that made this experience better than all the rest. I was breathing hard and my knees were suddenly feeling like they weren't going to hold me up anymore. My cock throbbed in time to my heartbeat, and flesh that was sensitive suddenly felt too tight and ready to split into pieces. I didn't have the words to encourage her or to tell her what I liked and didn't like, not that it mattered because, just like with everything else we did in the dark, she seemed to have a natural aptitude for it. She played with my piercings, her quick little tongue darting in and around metal that heated and cooled as she moved her mouth around it. I sucked in a breath and tried to stave off the impending orgasm but there was no controlling it. I gasped her name in warning, tried to tug at her long hair to let her know that she might want to get out of firing range, but she wasn't having any of it. She finished me off like a champ, placed a kiss on my quivering stomach while I tried to get my mind back in working order, and glided to her feet in all her naked glory.

She lifted a blond brow and flipped her now tangled and messy hair over her shoulder.

"I'll always take care of you, Rule. In fact, I like doing it because it makes me happy and it feels good, but I'm not ever going to let you use me to work out your demons like you did with all those girls who came before me, so you better learn the difference."

I didn't answer her because she was right. Instead, I picked her up by the waist and tossed her on the bed. I didn't need to give her time to get ready for me. I was pretty sure that working me over—better than anyone ever had—had done a good job of turning her on and making her wet and slippery. Her folds were already slick and ready for whatever I had to give. When I moved inside I made sure the top ball of my piercing rubbed against her most sensitive parts. Now that we had sex with nothing between us I knew even if I wasn't particularly stellar in the sack that having all that jewelry down there could and would create a sensation that got her off regardless, not that I didn't always make it my goal to make her lose her mind. She hooked her legs up around my hips as I moved in and out of her and let her eyes fall to half-mast. I was braced up above her and her hands were wrapped around my biceps. I was pretty sure I could die a happy man having her look up like that at me, with having her moan and writhe beneath me as pleasure shot through her body and made it clench around mine.

I had never really given much thought to monogamy and committing to having sex with only one person over and over again because I had never really seen that as a path I was going to take. With her, I knew it to the bottom of my soul that I would be happy just having her, making her fragment and break apart. When she moaned my name low and needy, it triggered my own release and I buried my face in the delicate curve of her neck and growled like a feral animal. After we were both wrung out, I collapsed on top of her in a boneless heap and felt her wrap her slender arms around me. I kept my face pressed into her neck and gave her a series of butterfly kisses with my eyes closed.

"You make me think everything will be okay."

She turned her head to give me better access to her neck and rubbed her hands lightly up and down my spine. "All we can do is try, Rule. I'm willing as long as you are. I'm not delusional—I've known you a long time and I know it isn't always going to be easy and fun; that things like pizza and a quiet night at home have the ability to send you into a tailspin—but I'm here as long as you recognize what is happening and agree to try."

I snickered a little against her damp skin, which made her shiver. "If freaking out means you go down on me to get me to stop acting like an idiot, I can't promise to knock it off anytime soon."

She swore and swatted me on my ass. I fell asleep with her wrapped up in my arms and her soft laughter in my ear. The tunnel was long and dark, and sometimes no matter how good my intentions were, the walls tended to close in on me, but if Shaw was willing to be my light at the end, then there was no way I wasn't going to try.

We were both quiet the next morning when we got up to go back to her car. We stopped at the corner coffee shop for breakfast and neither one of us seemed overly eager to rehash the events of the night before. After a solid night's sleep and waking up to her peaceful and innocent face I had my head back on straight and was calling myself all kinds of names for letting my usual hang-ups pull me in such a dark direction the night before. Pizza and quiet time on the couch was nothing compared to all the heavy shit I had rattling around in my brain since she made me come clean. I was ashamed that she knew I had been trying to use her body to escape, to take something that was so different with her and on such another level, and drag it down to where every other sexual encounter had begun and ended. If Shaw hadn't called me on my shit and just let me go, it would have been the end for us. I knew it and I was pretty sure she knew it. Allowing me to put her in a box with all the rest was something she wouldn't stand for and I was eternally grateful.

It had warmed up just a tad from last night and the icy spots on the sidewalks were now mushy puddles of dirty slush. We navigated around them while balancing hot coffee and trying to stay warm. She had parked her car off the street, a couple blocks over from the shop in one of the neighborhoods. I was getting ready to ask her if she was all right, if everything was still cool between us, but she came to a grinding halt and I almost ran into the back of her. I swore softly as the hot coffee splashed over my hand. "What the hell, Shaw?"

She didn't move and I had to jump back when her coffee slid out of a suddenly lifeless hand and clattered on the snowy ground. She lifted a shaking hand to her mouth and before I could ask again what was wrong a pickup truck that was waiting to make a left-hand turn moved and I caught sight of her car.

All the windows were smashed out, the headlights had been shattered; all four tires were on the metal rim on the ground, the slashed rubber sitting lifelessly around them like tattered material. The pristine black paint job was now marred with ugly red spray paint that had even uglier words blazed across the surface. The hood had the word *whore* in huge letters and along each side of the car from front to trunk were variations of the same thing. It was bad and, considering what kind of car she drove, it was also going to be extremely costly to fix.

I could see that she was shaking, so I put an arm around

her shoulders and tugged her to my chest. At first she resisted, standing stone still, eyes locked on the senseless destruction, but when I applied just a little more pressure she came willingly and I tucked her head up under my chin.

"We should probably call the cops."

She shuddered against me and I felt her head move "no" against my throat. "No. What's the point? His dad will just cover for him again and make it all go away. Besides, it's not like there is any proof he did it."

I hated that she was probably right. "Do you want me to take you to school? I can get this taken care of for you while you're there."

"No. I need to call the insurance company and have it towed somewhere. Why can't he just leave me alone?"

I ran a hand lightly from the crown of her head to the ends of her almost-white hair. "Because you're kind of impossible to get over."

She sighed against my neck and just let me hold her until she stopped shaking. "I guess I need to go back to your place and get this taken care of."

"Of course." I handed her what was left of my coffee and made sure I kept her tucked in close to my side on the way back to the Victorian. We were both quiet—now for different reasons—but I knew I needed to keep the rage that was practically choking me at bay until I got her somewhere safe and where she felt secure. Having something destroyed like that must have been a violation like I couldn't imagine. Even though Gabe had been quiet the last few weeks it was clear now he had no intention of letting go of his obsession with my girl.

When we got back inside, she started calling around, getting things in place for an adjuster to check out the damage and have the car towed to a body shop. She needed a rental in the meantime and wasted no time in setting that up as well. After about an hour or two, during which I just watched her like a hawk, all the adrenaline finally wore her out and she mentioned that she wanted to take a shower and lie down. I sent her off to my room with gritted teeth and a kiss, hoping she couldn't feel the fury that was burning in every cell of my body.

Nash came crawling in a few minutes after I heard the hot water turn on. He looked a little worse for the wear but he had a shit-eating grin on his face and his shirt was on inside out so I assumed the date had served its purpose. He took one look at the way my jaw was clenched and the way I'm sure my eyes were flashing with platinum fire and asked, "Bad night?"

"Bad morning. Shaw's car got trashed last night."

"You think it was Polo Shirt?"

"Who else would do something like that to her?"

"I dunno. One of your legions of one-night stands who's pissed you're off the market? You both have some pretty heavy baggage floating around out there."

I hadn't even considered that I might be the cause of retaliation against her. That just made me even angrier. I inclined my head toward my bedroom.

"Can you keep an eye on her until I get back? She seemed okay but I could tell she was pretty shaken up."

"Where are you going? I have to be at the shop at one."

"I'll be back before then."

"Rule . . ."

"Just don't, Nash; it's long past time for me to lose my shit. This asshole is going to hear it from me that if he keeps messing with her I'm going to annihilate him."

"You're asking for trouble and not in a good way."

"I don't care. I'll be back in a few. Just keep an eye on Shaw and if she asks where I am make something up. She doesn't need to worry about anything else today."

He grudgingly agreed, but I could tell he was not stoked with what I was about to do.

I jumped in the truck and drove to the school. I knew that Shaw had class the same time as Gabe on Mondays, Wednesdays, and Fridays so after I found a place to park it only took a nod at one coed and a wink at another to find my way to where all the political science classes were held. It was cold outside and students were hurrying from building to building with their heads down, so no one really paid any attention to me as I lurked around the building that I was sure Gabe would eventually come out of. Fortunately, I didn't have to wait long, and campus security had already passed by without so much as a pause. Twenty minutes into my vigil the doors opened and a group of dudes who looked like they had emptied out a J.Crew store and topped it off with L.L.Bean's winter line came pouring out. They were all laughing and talking about something and Davenport looked so self-satisfied I wanted to knock his pearly whites down his throat.

I waited until the group dispersed and it was just Davenport by himself. He pulled the collar of his Patagonia jacket up around his ears and pulled out his cell phone. I pushed off the wall of the building I was leaning against and silently followed him until he reached the parking lot. When he stopped by the Lexus, I reached out and grabbed the back of his neck and shoved him forward so that his face was smashed against the freezing metal of the roof. He let out a surprised sound and the bag with his books and computer in it clattered to the ground. He struggled but I had a good grip and was fueled by a burning fury so he didn't have a chance. I leaned forward so that my elbow ground painfully into the base of his neck and tightened my fingers until I felt his skin start to resist.

"You want to harass someone, scare someone, terrorize

someone, you might want to pick someone who doesn't have a pissed-off boyfriend waiting around the corner, preppy boy. This is the last time I'm going to tell you to leave Shaw the hell alone. If you don't, that fancy Ken Doll face you seem so fond of is going to end up like hamburger." I gave him another shove so that the metal smacked unforgivingly against his cheek. People were wandering around the parking lot and stopped to stare at us but I didn't care. "Are we clear?"

He grunted and got his hands under his chest so that he could lever himself off the side of the car. I let him go and stepped back, hands hanging loose at my sides in case he decided he wanted to throw down right then and there. He smoothed down the hair my rough handling had messed up and glared at me while working his jaw back and forth.

"We both know my father can keep me out of jail, what can yours do for you? Change a tire, help you move?" He laughed bitterly and spit out a mouthful of blood that narrowly missed the toe of my boot. "You aren't a match for me in the real world. You can call yourself her boyfriend all you want but the fact of the matter is she simply isn't allowed to walk away from me for someone like you. It sets a bad precedent."

I thought he was just spoiled and annoying, but the more he talked the more I started to wonder about his sanity. The guy talked like a lunatic.

"Dude, go fuck someone else. Shaw isn't into you, she never will be, and harassing her is just pissing everyone off. If you think I'm scared of what your dad or anyone else can do to me, if it means protecting her, then you're in for a shock. Even if you manage to get me out of the way, there is a whole group of people out there ready to take my place. You aren't going to get anywhere messing with her and if you ever touch her again, I'm going to snap every single one of your fingers off and cram them down your throat."

He scoffed at me and poked a finger in my chest. He was lucky I didn't knock him in the mouth. "You're so stupid, so uneducated, and low class to think it has anything to do with sex. I can get sex anywhere. You really think I let Shaw dangle her ass in front of me for six months and didn't get some on the side? Sex is irrelevant and if she's giving it up to you I don't want to go near her with a ten-foot pole. This is business and image; she can't set a precedent that I'm replaceable with a tattooed punk who has nothing to offer. I can't have people remembering that."

I grabbed the wrist of the hand that was poking me and shoved him back into the car. "If you think sex with Shaw is irrelevant, then you're the one who's uneducated, jackass. Get over yourself. If I can prove that you had anything to do with her car, we're pressing charges. If you keep harassing her, we'll keep going to court and eventually someone will notice your old man covering your ass. I'm telling you this stops now or you can go to the hospital and I can spend some time in jail, got it?"

We stared each other down. By now there was a sizable crowd gathered around while we sized each other up. I didn't see the security guard until he was getting between the two of us. Before he could start asking questions, I flipped Gabe off and headed back to the side street where I had parked the truck. The guard called something after me and I heard Davenport's raised voice, but I didn't stop until I was back in the truck and had the heater blasting. I flexed my hands repeatedly on the steering wheel and took a few deep breaths to get myself back under control. The last time I had felt this amount of impotent anger, this unfinished need to destroy something, was when I had watched them put my brother in the ground. I wanted to tear Polo Shirt's perfectly tailored

249

body apart seam by seam and watch him suffer. Pushing him around and making him uncomfortable just wasn't enough. The darkness, the unpredictability that lurked inside me reared up again and wanted unbridled vengeance, but I had to put it back in the box because I wasn't going to make Shaw wrestle with it again so soon.

It took me a solid half hour before I felt like I was ready to go home and face her. When I walked in the door, Nash was playing one of the game units and screaming a mouthful of obscenities through the headset at whomever he was playing with. He ripped the gear off and gave me a once-over as I shut the door and climbed to his feet.

"I don't see any blood or gore."

I shrugged and tossed my jacket on the back of the couch. "Too many people around. Plus, I think kicking his ass would only encourage him. The guy has a whole toolbox of screws loose. It isn't even about Shaw; it's all about how it looks that she dumped him and is hanging out with me. His ego is out of this world. I seriously don't know what we're going to do about it because he's right about his dad being able to cover for him; he already proved it once."

Nash jerked his head in the direction of my room. "She hasn't made a sound. She never surfaced after the shower so I don't know how she's doing, but I have to go or I'm going to be late for my appointment and I still need to tweak the drawing a little."

"It's cool, I got her. Maybe she was just so stressed out she slept the whole time."

"You could only be so lucky, bro."

I snorted and waved him off as I headed toward my room. The door was closed and everything was dark when I pushed it open. Shaw was curled up in a fetal position in the center of the bed and it didn't take a genius to tell she was wide awake and had been crying. She had her

hands tucked up under her cheek and was staring sight-
lessly at the blank TV.

"What did you do to him?" Her voice was raw and even
more husky than normal from crying. I sat on the edge of
the bed and reached out to run a hand over her thigh.

"I told him to back off and that it wasn't smart to piss off
someone who had me as a boyfriend. I don't know what
his deal is, Shaw—I think the dude is certifiable. He just
doesn't relate on any kind of logical level."

"I thought you were going to hurt him."

"Well, I might have but it was broad daylight and there
was an entire college of students walking around. I pushed
him around a little and we tossed some crap at each other,
but I just mostly wanted him to know you aren't alone,
that if he hurts you there are plenty of people waiting in
the wings to hurt him back."

Silent tears ran down her face and I had to lean all the
way over her supine form to wipe them away with my
thumbs.

"I just want him to go away. I never did anything to
deserve this. All I ever do is what everyone else wants. Why
I am being punished for doing the one thing in life I want
for myself?"

"I don't know, Casper, I just don't know." I didn't know
how to make her feel better so I just scooted up on the bed
behind her and gathered her up in my arms while she cried.
I didn't consider myself an empathetic or even a compassionate guy. I was usually too wrapped up in my own head
and my own spiral of emotional nonsense to pay much
attention to anyone else's, but holding Shaw while she cried
changed something in me on a fundamental level. I felt like
there was nothing on earth I wouldn't do or wouldn't give
to make this better for her. I felt like a failure for not stopping it from happening in the first place, and I knew that

251

from this point on, keeping an eye on her and keeping her relatively safe from just Davenport wasn't enough.

Suddenly, with blinding clarity, I knew that I wanted to keep her safe from anything that could hurt her, and that just sucked, because I had a sneaking suspicion that somewhere along the line I had been the source of just as much distress as Polo Shirt was proving to be. That made me want to break things all over again.

CHAPTER 14

Shaw

"Are you sure you want to do this?" Ayden sounded nervous and she wasn't thrilled I had dragged her to Marked so early in the morning. We were sitting in a little room at the shop I had never seen before, even though I was spending more and more time at the shop waiting for Rule to get off or dropping off dinner for him if he had to work late. The room had clearly been decorated by a female; Cora's funky sense of style was all over the place and it smelled a little less antiseptic than the rest of the shop. I was sitting on a chair that looked an awful lot like the one you would find in a gynecologist's office, and nervously fidgeting with everything in sight.

"I'm sure."

"I just don't understand why you want to do something that's going to hurt."

"It'll only hurt for a minute and I trust Cora." I did. Whenever I was at the shop we ended up spending hours talking, and had even taken our budding friendship out of the building. When Rule or Rome were unable to pull "eyes on Shaw" duty Cora didn't seem to mind hanging out with me until one of my many watchdogs was free. I really liked

253

her and having someone I was comfortable with pierce me was the only way I was going to go through with it. Cora had even agreed to come in when the shop was closed while Rule and Nash were at the gym so that I could keep it a surprise.

"I just want to make sure you're doing it for you and not for Rule. What if you guys break up and the next guy you date is all straitlaced and proper? Pierced nipples might not work for your next boyfriend."

I gave her a bored look and tried to calm my nerves. The truth was, doing it had nothing to do with Rule. I was back to feeling like I had no control over my life again. The thing with my car and the way Gabe was still influencing my day-to-day life, the pressure from my parents about everything from my hair to Rule, the way Rule disappeared inside himself when I started to get too close—it was all closing in on me and I needed something that was just for me. I wanted this little something that was my choice, a decision to alter my body that no one else had any say in. I was having migraines more frequently, three in the last two weeks, and if I didn't do something I was going to shatter apart into too many pieces to put back together.

"If Rule and I break up, you really think the next guy in my life is going to be all clean-cut and preppy?"

"I don't see why not. You dated Gabe for six months and he's about as opposite from Rule as one can get. I bet pierced nipples would send him into cardiac arrest."

"I'm never dating anyone just because I'm supposed to again, and I'm not planning on dating anyone besides Rule for the foreseeable future anyway, so let's not get ahead of ourselves."

The truth was things had been strained between Rule and me for the last week. I didn't know what it was but he was treating me like I was spun sugar and going to break apart at any moment. When he didn't think I was paying attention I would catch him staring at me with a confused look in his eyes, like he was trying to figure out what I was still doing there, or why he was still around. He was obsessively concerned about my safety and made sure I was never alone. We still spent every night together at alternating homes, and the time we spent in bed had morphed from passionate and out of control, to tender and fleeting. While it was nice, it didn't feel like him and it was starting to really concern me. I didn't know how to address it because it wasn't like there was anything actually wrong. He was still emotionally present, still attentive and clearly willing to try like I'd asked him, but something was off. I just couldn't put my finger on what it was.

"If your father finds out, he really will make good on pulling his tuition check for next year."

My dad had finally gotten tired of me ignoring his calls and had ambushed me at the apartment last weekend. I had tried to explain the situation with the car, tried to make him understand about Gabe and his threats, but none of it did any good. All my dad was concerned about was how things looked for him and Mom. The requisite threat about tuition had been leveled, but it held no weight with me. I told him if he pulled my tuition I would gladly get a job as a stripper to pay my way through med school, and he hadn't liked it one bit. I knew the threat would only keep him off my case briefly, but for now that was all I needed if he wasn't going to have my back against what was going on with Gabe.

I hadn't seen hide nor hair of Gabe, but I don't think Rule pushing him around had really sent him to ground. Ayden mentioned she had heard some girls in one of her classes talking about me, and from the sounds of it, his new mission was to trash my reputation on campus with a series of foul lies and outrageous stories. Luckily, I was pretty immune to hearing awful stuff about myself from growing up in such a judgmental and hateful household. Otherwise I would have been freaking out even more and contemplating changing schools just to get away from it all.

"Yeah, he would. Good thing that's not something he ever has any opportunity to see."

Cora opened the door with a little metal tray in her hand that looked sterilized and smelled like hospital-grade antiseptic.

"You ready?"

I swung my legs up and around so I was lying back in the chair and tried to control my rapid breathing.

"As I'll ever be."

"I'm fast, so it'll be over quick. Just remember you have to keep them clean so for the first three to four weeks don't play with them or let you-know-who play with them. He should know the rules by now."

I laughed as she told me to strip out of my tight V-neck henley and bra. I shivered involuntarily at being so exposed but Cora was reassuring, and even though I knew she was uncomfortable, Ayden held my hand and watched what was happening with rapt attention.

"First, I gotta mark you to make sure they're even and straight on both sides." It was weird to have someone, even though that someone was a friend, handle my body in such a way. The tip of the marker was cold and it made me shiver but not nearly as much as when she put the metal clamp on the first light-pink tip. Her two-toned eyes stared into mine and I felt my nails dig into Ayden's palm. "Okay, babe, take a really deep breath and when I tell you, let it out slow and even. You're going to feel a lot of pressure from the needle pressing through and then the jewelry being put in place. Just keep your eyes on me and keep breathing."

I did what she said and after the initial pain, which

admittedly had a couple of surprised tears welling in my eyes, it was more uncomfortable than painful. She repeated the process on the other side and then it was over and I was pierced. She asked me if I wanted a mirror. I took it and admired her handiwork.

I had pretty nice breasts already; they weren't huge or anything outrageous, but they were firm and high and my nipples were always a nice, pretty pink. The silver hoops were similar to the ones in Rule's eyebrow and the one in his lip, but the ball at the center of mine was a bright aquamarine globe. They were sexy and feminine and I freaking loved the way it looked. I took the aftercare instructions and climbed back into my clothes. I felt the little piece of me that had been flailing over the last weeks lock back down, and I smiled at Cora and gave her a hug.

"I love it."

"You should. It's over-the-top hot."

Ayden nodded as she pulled on her coat. "I didn't think it would suit you, but I was wrong. They look really girly and sexy. I can see now why you wanted to get it done."

Cora lifted her superblond eyebrows as I shoved money into her hands. "I know you said you would do it for free but I want to pay you."

She shook her head and tried to hand it back but I refused to take it. "I consider us friends now and I don't take advantage of friends, so please just take it."

She frowned at me and moved around to pick up all her equipment. "If you wanted a tattoo and Rule or Nash offered to do it for free, would you let them?"

"Rule yes, Nash no."

She sighed in defeat then. "Well, fine then. Let me know what loverboy thinks, not that I think he'll be able to hide his shit-eating grin. I swear his mood entirely revolves around how the two of you are going at it."

I pulled my long hair out of the collar of my coat and tried not to wince as the movement caused my new additions to move uncomfortably against my bra. "So, how's he been lately?" I really wanted to know.

"Fine, more mellow and maybe more quiet than usual, but good."

"Well, that's good, I guess."

"You don't sound so sure about that."

I shrugged, not sure how to explain it. "Rule has never really been a mellow guy."

"No, he hasn't, but maybe you have given him a reason to be. Maybe he's happy and has everything he wants, so there isn't a reason to be all angsty and aggro all the time anymore."

I would have been thrilled if I thought she was right, but I knew Rule and none of it sat right with me. "Maybe."

She gave me another hug, careful of my chest, and ushered us out of the shop. "Don't get your panties all wadded up over it. There is nothing wrong with mellow."

"Thanks, Cora."

"Anytime. Now scram so I can clean this up before regular business shows up and the guys get here to set up."

Ayden gave me a searching look as we exited into the cold. "How did you get the guard dogs to let you off the tether this morning? Rule has a fit whenever you try to gallivant around without someone on your heels."

"I told him I had a hair appointment and that you were going with me and wouldn't let me out of your sight. No guy wants to go spend an hour in a salon, especially a guy like Rule." She lifted her brows at me when we got to the rental I was currently driving.

"So are we actually going to go get our hair done?"

Since I wasn't a liar and hated being dishonest with him I had indeed made both of us an appointment to get the works done. "We are, only it's my treat this time because we have to make a stop first and it's kinda out of the way."

"Where at?"

I pulled out onto Colfax and headed to the highway in the direction of Brookside.

"Where are we going?" I knew Ayden was curious but when I woke up this morning and Rule had been so cloyingly polite and kind there were two things that I knew I had to accomplish today. The first was done and the second, well I wasn't sure, but I felt like the second might end up being even more painful.

"I just need to swing by and see an old friend really quick."

"In Brookside?"

"Just outside. Let me just get through it first and then I'll explain." I drove silently through the mountains until we got to the small cemetery on the outskirts of Evergreen, listening to Dawes play melancholy songs that fit my mood perfectly. I had always thought it ironic that Remy was buried so far out of the city on such a quiet piece of land, when he had been so buoyant and so full of energy and life. I parked in the visitors' lot and pulled on a pair of gloves and a hat because I wasn't sure how long I was going to be, and it was even colder up here at the higher elevation than it was in the city.

"I'll leave the keys so you can run the heater and mess with the radio. I'm not sure how long I'm going to be."

Ayden's amber gaze was liquid with sadness and understanding. She gave me a quick one-armed hug and shooed me off. "I'll be fine. You take as long as you need. You can spring for a hot-stone massage if it takes you too long."

"Deal." That's why I loved this girl.

My boots crunched on the snow as I made my way to the back of the lot where the gravestone sat so cold and sterile, just one more shade of gray on the barren winter landscape. There was a bright spray of red roses lying on top of the stark white plot and it made me smile. Remy loved red, loved things that were vibrant and eye-catching, anything that suited his personality. Not caring that the ground was frozen and covered in snow I knelt down and traced his name with a gloved finger. Tears immediately filled my eyes. I moved my hand along to glide over the huge horseshoe that both the surviving Archer boys had insisted go on their sibling's headstone. Turned upward, it was said to keep all the good luck in. Rome liked the symbolism, and Rule liked that it was a visual representation that tied the two of them together for eternity.

"Hey, handsome. I'm sorry it's been so long since my last visit but things have been . . . intense." I laughed humorlessly. "I have a feeling if you were here you would be laughing your ass off at everyone and shaking your head at all of us. I miss you so much and every single day I think it would make things so much better if I could just call you, that you would make sense of everything and keep it all together. Doing this is a million times harder without you."

I was crying in earnest now and couldn't really see the headstone clearly anymore. I flattened my palm over his name and concentrated on taking deep breaths in and out. "I'm sleeping with your brother, and if you thought I was a silly lovesick fool before, you should see me now. I'm freaking out because he's being too nice. I know, only I would worry about my boyfriend being too nice, but we both know Rule and something is up. He won't talk to me about it. By the way, how weird is it that I'm calling Rule my boyfriend? My heart turns over every time I do it and sometimes I feel like my entire world is in his eyes and yet he still closes me out, still shuts down and makes it so very hard to *just love* him. If you were here I would make you pull it out of him and he would tell you because he always did."

I sighed and let my head fall forward. "I wish you had told them, Rule and Rome. I wish you had trusted them enough to let them in like you did me. Your mother has gone off her rocker because Rule still refuses to be your carbon copy, and as a result your family is in tatters. Maybe if everyone knew, if you had tried to let them know everyone deserves to be loved no matter how they choose to live their lives, it wouldn't be like this. Your dad is coming around but still trying to keep Margot out of the loony bin. And Rome, poor Rome is just a giant Ping-Pong ball trying to protect everybody and make everything okay but he has no one to help him. He needs you to be the mediator like you always were."

My knees were freezing and my pants had long since soaked through. My teeth were chattering and I had quickly learned that supercold weather and nipple piercings were not exactly a great combo.

"I have a crazy ex who is in turn stalking and harassing me; it's making my life hell. My parents are convinced I should marry him and move to Cherry Hills. Rule hates him and there's a good chance if the ex keeps it up he's going to murder him and it just makes things that are already complicated even more awful. I have a sneaking suspicion that if you had been around you would have seen through all Gabe's polish and shine to the tarnish underneath and I wouldn't have ended up in this situation in the first place. I miss having you protect me from myself. Your brother is all about keeping me safe and I think he really honestly cares, but he's so busy keeping me safe from everyone, himself included, that I don't think he sees that I can be my own worst enemy. He keeps talking about messing things up between us and I don't have the heart to tell him that he can't ever mess up bad enough to make me stop loving him. There is a good chance that, like everyone else, he's going to see what I have to offer isn't all that great and want more than I can give. It's so convoluted and twisted I can't even believe we've gotten as far as we have."

I laughed a little, real laughter this time, and a couple standing by a grave a few feet away gave me a dirty look.

"I got drunk on my birthday and threw myself at him. I was terrified the entire time he was going to turn me down, to claim that he was taking advantage of me because I was drunk, but it happened and I totally gave up the V-card to your twin. Somehow I know you would find that hysterical and never let me live it down. You were right. I was always just waiting for him to get with the program and now that he has, well, let me just say the program is amazing and I have a hard time seeing a future without it or without him."

I pressed a kiss to the stiff leather of the glove and placed it on his name. "Every day, Rem, every single day something reminds me of you, makes me think of things I want to tell you, makes me want to cry because of what happened to you. Every day I miss you and right now when I need you more than ever, I try to make decisions, try to go in a direction that I know would make you proud, would make you smile for me, but it's hard."

I stayed for a few more minutes until the tears were nothing more than icy trails on my cheeks, then climbed to my feet. I rested a hand on the top of the gravestone and said a final good-bye while trying to regain my composure. When I got into the car, Ayden had hijacked the radio and Lady Antebellum was twanging it up. She turned it all the way down as I got behind the steering wheel and peeled off my gloves.

"Everything okay?"

I nodded and held my frozen hands over the heater, wishing I had one big enough to dry the legs of my jeans. "Yeah, it's just sad. I miss him a lot. We used to talk every single day, sometimes for hours and hours. I feel lost without him. So much of the time I think he's the only one who would make sense of how hard it is to get a handle on Rule. They were very different, but still essentially the same at the core, good men with a strong sense of self and loyalty."

"It's obvious you cared deeply for him, so why didn't the two of you ever hook up? It seems like it would have been an obvious match."

I smiled ruefully and headed back toward the city. "Because we didn't feel that way about each other. He knew I was in love with Rule. At times he encouraged it, at times he tried everything to talk me out of it, but he knew it, and for the most part respected it. As for Remy, he was in love with someone else, someone very unlike me. Remy was the life of the party; he had a million friends and everyone wanted to be around him all the time, but he was really private when it came to his love life. Rome and Rule burned through girls at a rate that is honestly alarming, but Remy played it close to the vest. I think he let people believe we had a thing going because it kept them from asking questions he didn't want to answer. He didn't want the comparison to his brothers, and his parents loved me so it was just easier for him to play along than deal with the hassle."

"That doesn't seem like it was very fair to you. If he knew you were in love with Rule the whole time, why would he let him believe you and he were a couple?"

Rule asked me that same question all the time, even though he wasn't armed with the knowledge that I had been in love with him for so long. I hated that I couldn't answer it for him. Remy's secrets weren't mine to tell, even if it strained things between Rule and me.

"He had his reasons. At the time I understood them; I guess I didn't see how damaging they could be. At the end of the day, he saved me from a high school life that would have been miserable and a family that treats me like furniture, so I don't mind suffering for him in the slightest. You would have liked him; everyone did. As moody and difficult as Rule can be, Rem was just the opposite. He was always affable, smiling, and happy. He just wanted to have a good time and make sure everyone else did, too.

"When he graduated, he was supposed to go to California on a football scholarship. He was good, better than good, but he turned it down because if he had to play in order to stay in school, then that took the fun out of the game for him. Rule moved to Denver with Nash, and Remy left with them. The guys went to work in the shop as soon as they had their diplomas, and Remy screwed around trying to figure out what he wanted to do. Eventually, he got hooked up with a high-end event planning company throwing swanky parties and doing black-tie events. He had found his niche and he never talked about college again. He made good money, loved living in the city, had a great relationship with his brothers and his family. He got involved in a relationship with someone who made him smile and act like a giddy kid. I had just moved here for freshman year when he died. It sucked and it totally wasn't fair; everything was right where he wanted it, and he was taken away from it all because of a stupid accident."

"That's just tragic." I could hear the emotion in her voice.

"It is," I agreed because that was all I could do. By the time we got to the salon, we were both beyond ready for a little pick-me-up and I decided that a hot-stone massage was definitely in order.

We got pampered and all loosened up. Maybe too loose, because when it came time to touch up my hair, I had him take the chunk in my bangs and make it almost black instead of the subtle light brown it had been. He did the same to the underside of my long hair so that I had almost a checkerboard effect. It was edgy and dramatic; there was no way to miss it, and the black made the green of my eyes iridescent. I really liked it and so did everyone else. As soon as we got out of the salon, a group of girls around our age stopped to ask where I had it done.

Ayden and I went to get lunch and decided to grab a cocktail at a bar close to the apartment. I glanced at my phone and noticed Rule had texted to ask how I was doing. I frowned and shot back that everything was fine. I waited for him to demand to know where I had been all day, to ask what I was up to, but instead he said that was good and wanted to know what time to come over tonight. My stomach knotted and I felt something awful rise up in the back of my throat. He was only being thoughtful, but I hated it and I wanted it to stop. I texted:

I think I have a migraine coming on. Ayden isn't working tonight so I think we'll just have a girls' night at home with a stupid movie and some popcorn so you can go out with your friends or whatever.

I wanted him to tell me that was stupid. That of course he would come over, but I got back:

All right. Let me know if you need anything for your head. Keep your door locked. I still don't trust Davenport.

I wanted my Rule back. I wanted him to get mad at me. I wanted him to throw all that attitude he normally toted around at me, but I got none of it. All I got was quiet acquiescence and easy agreeability, things that my Rule knew nothing about. Angry and not sure why or what to do about it, I tossed the phone into my purse and ordered us another round of drinks.

"What's wrong now?"

"Nothing."

"Come on, Shaw. I've been with you all day; tell me what's really going on. The boobs, the hair, the freezing visit to the grave—something is behind it all. You make me talk when I don't want to, so spill it."

I sighed dejectedly and twirled the straw around in my drink. "I told Rule not to come over tonight because I was getting a migraine."

"Which I assume is not true."

"No, and I don't really want him to stay away. I just want him to do what he normally does and throw a fit, to act temperamental and bossy, to tell me he's coming over whether I like it or not. Instead, he just says okay like it's no big deal, and I don't know what to do with it. It's not like he can't be sweet and nice when he wants to, but that's just not his default. He's complicated and argumentative, but lately all he wants to do is smile and nod like I can do no wrong. It just isn't like him, and it weirds me out."

"Maybe try being stoked that your boyfriend sounds awesome?"

I tried to smile because I knew she was just kidding, but I didn't have the heart for it. "It's not just when we talk or I ask him to do things, it's in bed, too. Normally, it's all out-of-control passion and mind-numbing orgasm after orgasm, but lately it's been a lot more like 'May I do this?' and 'Is it okay if I do that?' and 'How does this make you feel?' He's never been the type to ask for permission, he takes what he wants and by the end makes sure you want it twice as bad. It's starting to freak me out because I don't know how to talk to him about it without sounding like a paranoid lunatic."

"Well, you have to talk to him about it. You can't just keep expecting him to act one way while he's doing something entirely different or you're both going to be disappointed."

I knew she was right but that didn't mean I had the first clue how to go about it. "Whatever happened between him and Gabe after my car got trashed is what started it. He left the apartment one way and came back as a stranger."

"I know a couple people who were walking to class when it happened. They said it looked like Rule was going to tear Gabe apart, but then he let him go and a security guard broke it up. I don't know what could have triggered such a strange reaction in him."

"I don't, either, but I hate it and it's just one more reason to curse Gabe and how he has managed to interfere in my life."

I was feeling pretty down so we had a few more cocktails than we'd planned. Ayden decided that since we were already bombed, we should make good on the girls' night. We ordered wings to go from the bar and hiked home since we were only four blocks away. We stumbled in and crashed on the couch. We watched three sappy, romantic comedies back to back, polished off the wings with a bottle of wine, indulged in ice cream and popcorn, and laughed hysterically at things that were not remotely funny. It wasn't until I finally crawled into bed hours later that I realized that I hadn't called Rule or even sent a message to let him know what I was doing all night long. I think my heart cracked a little when I looked at the screen of my phone and it reflected back no missed calls or new messages. He hadn't even bothered with a "good night" or "miss you."

I tossed the phone somewhere on the floor, careful this time not to hurl it at the wall, and crawled under the covers. I assumed that since I was pretty plastered, sleep would suck me under in no time, but I was wrong. I tossed and turned for more than two hours until I finally gave up and realized

I wasn't going to sleep unless I changed something. I had spent the last month cozied up next to Rule's solid bulk, and sleeping in an empty bed when I was feeling shitty just didn't hold the same appeal. I shoved the covers aside and rummaged through one of the dresser drawers that Rule had started stashing some of his things in when he stayed over. I found his favorite Defiance Ohio T-shirt and stripped down and put it on. It was worn and soft and it reminded me of him, so when I crawled back into bed I finally fell into a fitful rest, knowing that I had to get a handle on things before I went crazy or turned into a sleepless lush.

CHAPTER 15

Rule

"Hey, you got a minute?"

I looked up from the drawing of an old-school pirate ship I was working on when my brother's voice surprised me from the doorway of my room. I was concentrating so hard that I hadn't heard him come in, and my mind was a million miles away because for the second night in a row, Shaw had come up with some lame-ass excuse to hang by herself and it was pissing me off.

I was actively making an effort to behave in a way I thought good boyfriends were supposed to act. I was being considerate, attentive, deferring to her wishes and not pushing for anything—so generally being a giant pussy—and letting her call all the shots. It wasn't getting me a damn thing, even in bed. I wanted to be a guy who wouldn't give her a reason to walk away, who would make her happy so that she didn't have to battle my mood swings and outbursts of crazy. I was trying, with limited success, to be a guy she wanted to keep around—especially since Davenport was still floating around unhinged, but my new and improved attitude seemed to be achieving the opposite result. I had spent the last two nights tossing and turning because I was used to her soft form curled up next to mine. I was too irritated to just call her and tell her I was over it and coming over anyway because I knew it was what we both wanted.

I tossed my pencil at Rome's head and indicated he could come in if he wanted. "What's up?"

He threw the pencil back at me and dropped heavily on the bed. He stuck his long legs out in front of him and crossed his ankles while reclining back on his elbows, making himself right at home.

"Still no word from Shaw?"

I bit back a growl because just thinking about it made me want to hurt things. "She says she has too much homework due tomorrow, so she's just going to head home after work and do it."

"Huh."

"What's that supposed to mean?"

"Nothing just . . . huh."

"Shut up, Rome. Your 'huh' never means nothing."

"Well, it's just odd that she hasn't been around much the last couple days. Did you have a fight you didn't tell me about?"

"No."

"Are you sure?"

I scowled at him. "Yes, I'm sure we didn't have a fight. Did you just come in here to harass me or did you actually want something?"

"Trying to change the subject?" I called him a nasty name and spun back around in my chair.

"If you're just going to be annoying I have to finish this back piece I'm working on for a client."

"I got my medical release today. The doc from Carson called a little while ago. That means I'm going wheels-up at the beginning of next week."

I spun back around. He was trying to look relaxed but I could see the tension around his mouth and eyes.

"Your shoulder is going to be up to it?"

"That's what they tell me."

"How about you? Are you up to going back?"

"I guess I don't really have a choice. I would feel better leaving if I knew things with you and Shaw were straight and she didn't have some lunatic stalking her, and that Mom had agreed to get some help, but I guess miracles only happen in the movies."

I grunted and rubbed my hands over my hair, which seemed to be getting longer by the minute. I was tempted to shave the Mohawk back, but in my head I knew Shaw shouldn't be with a guy rocking hair like that, so I was keeping it normal and natural, though she told me on a regular basis how much she missed the hawk.

"Shaw and I are fine, so don't worry about it. As for Mom, well, there's nothing I can really do to help you with that. Promise me that you're going to be safe. No more driving over bombs."

"That wasn't in the plan the first time. Look, I'm going to tell Mom and Dad. You know they're going to want to do something since no one knows when I'll be back or what condition I'm going to be in."

"Rome, I can't go through that with Mom again."

"I'll tell Dad to set something up at a restaurant or something. I'll make sure he knows it has to be a family event, which means you will be there and so will Shaw. I'm not asking, little brother, I'm telling you. I'm about to go back to the desert for who knows how long, and I deserve a good family memory to take with me. Everyone can just suck it up for one night. I deserve that."

"You saw how well it went last time and I wasn't even provoking her."

He sighed and pushed to his feet. "Do this for me, Rule, please."

I didn't want to, not when things with Shaw were weird and not after my mom had made her feelings about me so clear, but there wasn't much I would deny my brother, and there was nothing I wouldn't do for him when he said please. I growled a lot of really dirty words and let my head fall backward.

"Let me know when and where. I'll tell Shaw, but you can't get pissed and go back to the war all mad if Mom does what she tends to do and makes it ugly."

"I don't understand why we can't all just be a goddamn family for once. I really don't feel like that's too much to ask."

"You're right, it's not and I will do my part. Okay?"

"Thanks, bro, you're only half as bad as everyone thinks."

"Shut up." I laughed and went back to my drawing. "Just so you know, I'm going to miss having your bossy ass around."

He walked over to me and put me in a headlock. I struggled in vain trying to get loose but he was just too big and easily manhandled me.

"I'm going to miss your smart mouth and shitty attitude as well. Though this hair you have going on is stupid and not at all you, so I won't miss that one bit." He finally released me when I got a solid fist into his ribs. He let me go with a grunt and I pushed the nondescript locks off my forehead.

"You're just worried that when I have normal-looking hair that people will start to realize that I'm much better looking than you."

He lunged for me again and we wrestled around for a little bit like we used to do when we were kids, only now Rome was a giant with a solid fifty pounds on me, so it wasn't much of a fight. He left with a promise to call and order something for dinner and it gave me a small measure of satisfaction to notice he was rubbing his ribs on his way out.

I pulled my phone out and stared at the screen. I hated that I was struggling with what I wanted to say to Shaw, that I was worrying over what words to use. I was so used to just saying and doing whatever I wanted, that this controlled and locked-down version of myself was getting old before it even started. I wrote out a quick message:

Rome just got his medical release. He's going back to the desert on Monday.

I figured since she was working that she wouldn't respond right away. It wasn't like we had been engaging in any kind of deep philosophical conversations as of late.

Oh no! Are you okay?

I'd already lost one brother, so the idea that my remaining one had a job that constantly placed him in jeopardy most definitely meant I was not okay, but there wasn't anything I could do about it. Rome's sense of duty was part of what made him who he was, and I respected it and him far too much to let my feelings taint any of the fleeting time we spent together.

I've been better but he seems okay with it so what else is there to do?

Do you need me to come over after work?

I thought you had homework.

I do, but if you need me it can wait.

I did need her. I wanted to hold her and love all up on

273

her, but not because she was feeling sorry for me, but because she wanted to be with me, too. I glared at the phone and at how complicated things seemed to have turned overnight.

Naw, I'm straight, but he wants to do a family dinner with EVERYBODY before he leaves. He's going to have Dad set it up.

How's that going to work with things between you and Margot?

Not just me, you're coming, too.

I'm not worried about me.

Rome seems to think that since he's shipping back out she'll behave if he asks her to, but I have my doubts. He thinks if we do it someplace public she'll behave.

It's so sad you guys even have to worry about that in the first place.

Not the only one with family problems, Casper.

No, you're not.

Have a good night.

There was a long pause and I didn't think she was going to say anything back but after about five minutes my phone beeped with a new message.

I miss you, Rule.

I didn't know what to say to that because I wasn't the one pulling away this time. I clicked the screen off and went back to my drawing.

The next night, I was the one blowing off spending time with Shaw because I decided it was a great idea to take Rome out and at least attempt to get him laid before he went back overseas. Somehow, I ended up facedown in a fifth of Crown, so I'm pretty sure I failed and ended up being the worst wingman ever. Rome and Nash dropped me on the bed after practically carrying me home. It wasn't until well after eleven the next morning, when I was attempting to shower and fake being human enough to show for work, that I noticed I had three missed calls and five missed messages from Shaw. They were all variations on the same thing: Where are you? What are you doing? Why aren't you answering? Should I come by? Are you going to come by? They all made me cringe and swear. I felt guilty as hell because had things not been so strained between us I would have called her before I left or asked her to come with us. Instead, I had enjoyed just being my normal self and not putting any effort into being anybody's perfect anything.

I was about to try to call her to explain when Rome came out of the hallway bathroom running a towel over his head. "You alive?"

"Barely. I need to call Shaw. I was too messed up last night to let her know what was going on."

He gave me a sharp look. "I already called her. She texted me last night wondering what you were up to so I told her you were loaded and out of control. She sounds sad, worse than that, she sounds sad because of you."

I growled a little and rested my elbows on the kitchen counter. "I know but I don't know what I did wrong. I almost beat her ex to death in a parking lot but realized if I was going to act like a caveman I was going to lose her and not be around to protect her. I've been minding all my p's and q's and, let me tell ya, I had no idea how many of those little fuckers there were. But ever since I started, she's been acting like I cheated on her or did some other horrible thing."

"Rule, she liked you just fine when your p's and q's were all over the map. Stop trying to be something you aren't and just let her love you. It's not hard. Dad called and dinner is tonight at Ruth's Chris downtown at six. I already told Shaw, so unless you want to grovel and apologize, you don't need to call her."

"They're coming here?"

"Dad thought it would be good for Mom. He thought maybe getting her out of Brookside would break some of that hold the past has on her."

"I guess we'll see."

"Rule." I turned to look at him and was struck by the sincerity in his eyes. "Thank you for doing this for me. I know it isn't easy for you."

"I'm learning easy things never really pay off. It's the things that make you work that really matter."

"You're still a little punk who can't hold his liquor, but somewhere along the line you really did turn into a man I'm proud to call my brother."

We stared at each other for a long moment—and I would kill before I admitted it—but my eyes totally welled up. I cleared my throat and pushed off the counter.

"Thanks, Rome. Now I gotta go see if I still have a girl-friend or if I managed to drink myself single last night."

I was thinking about his words as I dialed Shaw's number only to be sent to voice mail. I just had to let her love me; I wasn't sure how to go about that but I knew whatever I was doing now wasn't working. After her recorded greeting I left a gruff message.

"Hey, it's me. I suck and I'm sorry. I should have called.

I'm sure you were worried and if you had pulled that shit with me, I would have been climbing the walls. Really, I don't have an excuse other than things have been off with us for a little bit and I'm trying to figure it out. Call me when you get this if you want. I'll see you later tonight. I'm really sorry and I promise to stop trying to do things different when the old way was working just fine."

I didn't know what her response was going to be, I only knew that I had screwed up and I hoped it wasn't too late to fix it. I finished getting ready for work without hearing from her. I burned through my first two appointments with no word from Shaw and I was starting to worry. I knew she had class today, but that didn't normally stop her from hitting me up between sessions. I was tempted to call her again, but worried what getting sent to voice mail again would do to me, since I was already hanging on by a thread. I was cleaning up my final appointment of the day when I finally got a text from her:

I'll see you at dinner.

That's was all. There was no "I forgive you," no "Yes, you suck, now let's kiss and make up," no "Everybody makes mistakes," no "I'm so glad we're getting things back to normal," just "I'll see you at dinner." What was I supposed to do with that? This having a girlfriend business was starting to make my head hurt and I longed for the days when we were cordial enemies who only spent a few hours a week together. That wasn't remotely true, but it made me feel a little better as I plodded home and changed into something that wouldn't give my mom a fit.

I put on gray Dickies and a button-down plaid shirt with pearl snaps on it and changed out my studded leather belt for a plain black one. I left my boots on and made sure my unruly hair had just enough product in it to keep it a semi-styled mess. I still looked like me, just a me that my dad wouldn't razz and my mom wouldn't bitch about. I had to admit that I wanted Shaw to see that I could clean it up when the occasion called for it, but my head was so twisted where she was concerned, I tried not to spend too much time thinking about what her reaction would be when we finally saw each other.

Rome and I climbed into the truck to head to dinner. I could tell he was nervous by his silence on the ride down to the restaurant and I honestly couldn't blame him since the last family get-together had gone so smashingly. To date, Mom still didn't believe that she held any responsibility for the family rift. I wasn't sure that meeting in public and having all this extra tension between Shaw and me was going to be a recipe for success, but I was determined to give Rome the send-off he deserved, and not let him leave disappointed in me or with too many reasons to worry about those he loved.

We parked in a crowded lot and shoved a couple dollars in the payment kiosk. As we made our way to the busy restaurant, we could see Mom and Dad waiting out front with Shaw. My breath quickened and something in my chest flipped over at the sight of her. It had only been a few days, but seeing her now I suddenly felt like we had spent years apart. She had changed her hair in the time that had passed; it was now drastically two-toned and looked badass next to her pale skin and bright eyes. Her cheeks were red from the cold and her green eyes were guarded as we got close. I could see my mom had a near death grip on Shaw's arm and that she wasn't exactly overjoyed with our arrival. Rome leaned in and kissed both of them on the cheek and shook Dad's hand before moving to pull open the door. I opted for a chin lift and a raised eyebrow in Shaw's direction.

"Hey."

The corners of her mouth pulled down and my mom flat-out ignored me. "Hey. Let's go inside, I'm freezing." She let my mom pull her along and a little sliver of anger started to spark under my skin, but this wasn't about me so I tried to tamp it down as my dad cupped me on the back of the neck and gave me a little shake. It was a gesture that made me feel like I was ten years old again, which was funny since I was about six inches taller than him now.

"This is a good thing for all of us, kiddo. Just be patient and we'll all get better at being a unit again."

"It's just dinner, Dad. Let's not get ahead of ourselves."

"Well, we have to walk before we run, son, and as of now the Archers are barely managing a staggering limp. All we can do is move forward."

I didn't know what to say to that so I just kept my mouth shut and watched Shaw's shapely form as the hostess guided our group to a table in the back of the building. My mom was jabbering nonstop at Shaw and she was occasionally nodding and making noises of agreement, but what she wasn't doing at all was looking at me or acknowledging me in any way. The anger was starting to turn from a smolder to a burn. If something didn't give soon, I was bound to do something I would regret later.

At the table, I ended up sandwiched between my brother and my girlfriend. One was looking at me warningly, and the other was watching me with eyes shrouded in sadness and accusation—two things I didn't understand. I was ready to say the hell with it to get some answers. I didn't get the chance because as soon as I turned to Shaw, the waitress appeared and we were busy ordering drinks. My mom once again hijacked all Shaw's attention.

Just to test the waters, I put a hand on her thigh under the table and felt her tense at my touch. I waited for her to move or to pry it off with her own hand but she didn't even stop the flow of conversation with my mom. It was obvious that they had missed each other. I felt a stab of guilt that, because of her loyalty and feelings for me, Shaw had missed out on a relationship she obviously appreciated. I let my dad and brother draw me into a conversation about the Broncos and kept an eye on Shaw as we ordered dinner. She never moved my hand but she never once looked my way, either. I didn't know what to make of it. I was grateful, however, that as long as my mom was focused on her she didn't so much as bat an eyelash in my direction, allowing the dinner to go as smoothly as it could, considering the circumstances. Dad ordered a bottle of champagne with dessert and before it showed up my mom went to use the restroom, finally giving Shaw a chance to turn and look at me. When she did her mouth was tight and her superlight eyebrows were furrowed over her eyes.

"We need to talk."

My own eyebrows shot up so hard they pulled against the hoops pierced there. "That's kind of hard to do when you won't answer the phone when I call and you make up lame-ass excuses to avoid spending time with me."

I saw her flinch and she leaned closer so that our heads were bent near each other. She hissed in a tone low enough that only I could hear, "Well, excuse me for not knowing what to say to you, considering the last time we didn't talk for a few days you stuck your tongue down the first willing girl's throat. I don't know what's going on with you, but I feel like you're turning into a stranger and I hate it."

I scowled at her and tightened my fingers on her leg. "Do you trust me at all? Geez, Shaw, maybe I was just trying to be a better boyfriend—one who doesn't flip out over stupid shit all the time and one who isn't in jail while your psycho ex is still on the prowl? Maybe I was trying to act right for a change. I was trying to be the kind of guy you deserve."

She blew out a hard breath through her clenched teeth and her emerald-colored eyes sharpened with an anger that I was surprised to see burned as hot as mine. "Maybe you should have asked me before deciding what I deserve, Rule. Maybe I liked the you that flips out over stupid shit. Maybe I miss the you that is passionate enough about me, about my safety, to risk going to jail over my psycho ex, and I sure as hell never asked for you to be a better boyfriend. In fact, the boyfriend you've been the last week has done nothing but make me confused and sad."

I don't think either of us realized that we had raised our voices or that we now had a captive audience. In fact, it took my mom making a noise low in her throat like a wounded animal as she wobbled on her heels to get our attention. She was looking from me to Shaw with huge eyes, and had a hand pressed hard into her chest. My dad looked far less surprised, but worried about my mom as usual.

"What did you just call him?"

Shaw looked at my mom, then back at me. She sighed and answered softly like she was afraid the news would shatter the woman before her. "Rule and I have been seeing each other for a little over a month now. I told him to stop acting like he needed to be someone else to be a good boyfriend." She turned to look at me and I could see her doing some kind of internal warfare with herself. Finally, she sucked in a deep breath and turned back to my mom. "I've been in love with him since I was fourteen, Margot."

I went still at her confession and felt everything inside me turn to jelly. She loves me. This perfect, wonderful, kind young woman loves me and had for a long time. I didn't know where to put that because my mom started blinking back tears, and for the first time that night turned her attention to me.

"It's not enough that you took Remy's life? You had to take the girl he loved from him, too?"

Stunned silence landed on the table like a ton of bricks. My instinct was to push away from the table and storm out of the restaurant, but I couldn't because Shaw clamped a hand over mine on her leg. My dad and Rome both leapt to their feet in outrage. "Margot!" "Mom!" Voices were raised and the other patrons in the restaurant were starting to pay all kinds of attention to the scene we were making, but I was too stunned to care. I heard Shaw say my name, felt my brother put his hand on my shoulder, but I just wasn't there. At least I wasn't there until Shaw climbed to her feet, put her fingers in her mouth, and let out a whistle that had us all looking at her in shock. She put her hands on the table and leaned forward so that she was talking directly to my mom, but she made eye contact with all of us.

"Everyone shut up." She pointed a finger at my mom and narrowed her eyes. "Listen to me, Margot, and for once you need to hear what I'm saying. I loved Remy, still do, but we were never *in* love. He knew how I felt about Rule and at times both encouraged and discouraged it, but at the end of the day he agreed that we don't necessarily get to choose who we fall in love with."

She took a deep breath and I watched her chest rise and fall. She was struggling with something, something big, if the flush on her face and the way her hands balled into fists were any indication.

"Remy had secrets. I know you boys were close, that you all loved and respected each other, but Remy was different from the two of you and he just didn't know how to tell you. He thought that maybe it was best for everyone to just let all of you assume we were a couple because of how hard

Dale and Margot were on Rule—and all he did was tattoo himself and wear his hair all crazy."

She turned so that she was fully facing me and I saw she had tears in her eyes and that her bottom lip was trembling. I wanted to wrap her up in a hug and make it all better but even in the emotional shell shock I was experiencing, I knew her words were about to change my world forever.

"I promised him and I owed him so much. I swore on my life I would never tell anyone." She let her gaze skip around the table and land on all of us. "But he would want his family healthy and whole more than he would want me to keep his secret." She took a deep breath. "Remy was gay. He was my best friend, my surrogate family, but he was a homosexual. He was involved in a serious relationship with a guy named Orlando Fredrick that he met his last year playing ball. That was the real reason he moved to Denver after school. Lando goes to DU as well."

Disbelief, foreign and cold, snaked up my spine. Rome let out a string of nasty words and my mom started bawling in earnest. Shaw turned sad eyes in my direction and I looked at her like I had never seen her before.

"No way. He would have told me."

She shook her head, sending white and black hair sliding across her shoulders. "He wanted to, but he was worried you wouldn't understand his desire to keep it quiet. He was scared you would push him to come out. It was never about worrying how you would react, he just knew it would kill Margot."

"We were twins, goddamn it. He would have told me."

"Rule."

I pushed away from the table and glared down at her. "This is bullshit."

Rome got to his feet as well and I noticed he was also looking at Shaw with hard eyes. "You don't need to make up lies about the deceased to try to fix things for Rule. That's desperate and uncalled for, Shaw."

Tears trailed down her face as she looked back and forth between us. She opened her mouth to say something but was cut off by my dad clicking his spoon against the side of his champagne glass.

"All right everybody, sit down and shut the hell up." He cut a hard look at my mom and pointed to the seat she had vacated moments before. She looked like she was going to faint, and about as happy to sit next to Shaw as she did when I stopped by a few weeks ago. I sat back down grudgingly but, surprisingly, Rome was the holdout. He hovered by the back of his chair until my dad glared at him and pointed. "Ass in the chair, soldier."

Shaw was crying next to me and now instead of wanting to comfort her, all I wanted to do was get as far away from her as possible. My dad cleared his throat and crossed his arms on the table.

"Things in this family have been in shambles for a long time. There has been too much dishonesty and too much subterfuge for everyone's sake and I'm done trying to sweep it all under the rug just to keep my wife happy, because she isn't. None of us are."

He rubbed a hand over his chin and suddenly he looked a hundred years older than he actually was. "Margot, don't pretend to not know that the way you've been treating Rule these last few years is cruel and uncalled for. I lost my son the same as you and I'm done watching you try to turn his twin into a stranger or someone who hates us. He's a good boy; he works hard, loves his family, and clearly has qualities that are good enough for our girl to appreciate. I'm finished freezing him out. We both know Shaw has been in love with him since she was a kid. We saw the way she watched him, the way she defended him, and don't think for one second I didn't notice that's why you were always trying to shove her in Remy's direction."

He heaved a sigh that seemed like it came all the way from my youth and looked at me and Rome. "Shaw isn't lying to you, boys. Your brother was a homosexual. He might not have wanted your mother and me to know about it, but teenagers are crap liars and he wasn't exactly as discreet as he might have thought." He slid a sideways look at my mom while Rome and I gave each other shocked looks. "Margot thought it was a phase; that's the main reason she was so eager to welcome Shaw into our home and family. At first she was convinced you were going to change him, make him like girls or, more specifically, like you, but like I said, it was pretty obvious your interest was in Rule. After a while, we just adored you so much and saw how much love you were missing and how much you had to give that we couldn't let you go, even though I never approved of the way Remy let everyone just believe there was more between you two than friendship."

I growled. "He would have told me." I smacked the flat of my hand on the table and my dad glared at me.

"No, son, he wouldn't have. Remy struggled with it. He struggled with who he was supposed to be versus who everyone else thought he was, and that's not something you've ever done. You've always owned you, and screw anyone who didn't like it."

I looked at Shaw and then at the table. I had tried to change for her and it had been an epic failure. I climbed to my feet again and let my gaze fall on my mom.

"I don't understand why you've never been able to love me the way I am when you obviously had the capacity to love him regardless of his choice not to tell everyone the truth. He lied to all of us for years. It just doesn't make sense. I need to get out of here."

"I'm with you." Rome looked as wild as I was feeling on the inside. I looked down when a soft hand clasped around my forearm. I flinched involuntarily and I think I actually saw her heartbreak in her eyes.

"Rule." Her voice was a broken whisper. "I'm sorry." She let me go and I almost couldn't talk over the lump in my throat.

"I understand what you meant about those closest to you hurting you the most now. I'll be in touch." But as Rome and I hurried out of the restaurant, I wasn't sure I was telling her the truth and I refused to think about how much walking away from her like this hurt.

CHAPTER 16

Shaw

It had been three weeks, give or take a day, with no contact from Rule. No text messages, no phone calls, no emails, no carrier pigeons, just a whole lot of silence and heartbreak on my end. Rome hadn't even returned my calls or texts telling him good-bye and that I would miss him while he was gone. He left for the desert mad at me, and as upsetting as that was, the daily battle I had with myself about whether to call Rule and beg him to forgive me was soul crushing. I wanted to plead with him to understand that it was never my secret to tell regardless of our relationship. Ayden kept saying he would cool off and come around while Margot and Dale firmly believed he wasn't going to speak to any of us ever again. They were in the same boat as me; neither of the boys was speaking to them, and Margot had nearly had a nervous breakdown when Rome had refused to allow them to drive him down to Fort Carson for his send-off. Instead, the brothers went together, leaving the rest of us out in the cold.

I was hurting but I was also sick and tired of my love and affection not being enough for anybody. I had loved Rule longer and harder than anyone else in my life and that still wasn't enough for him to look beyond his own hurt feelings and sense of betrayal to work things out with me. I was still pissed that he had spent the week prior to the bomb being dropped trying to act and behave in a way I had never asked for or wanted, but when I was alone at night and crying in bed I had to admit that it was a sweet—if misguided—gesture. I remembered telling him to be aware of how bad things could be if we tried to do this and it didn't work. Somehow, even finding him in bed time and time again with every skanky girl this side of the Platte River couldn't hold a candle to this complete freeze-out.

I tried really hard not to worry about what he was doing or who he was doing it with, but every day that passed I became more and more fatalistic. Whatever he had felt for me wasn't enough to get him past the hurt he was feeling, and it obviously came nowhere near the heart-wrenching emotion I felt for him. As much as it pained me to let it go, I had to get over him. I had to work at moving on because, even if he did get back in touch with me, there was just too great a chance he had relapsed into his old ways, and there was simply no way I would survive that kind of betrayal from someone I cared so deeply about. So instead of languishing, I forced a smile every day, picked back up the shifts I had dropped at work, threw myself into my studies, and spent as much time as I could with Ayden and Cora. I was careful around Cora to give nothing away and she was just as careful to never, ever mention Rule or anything having to do with him.

To say my parents were excited that Rule was no longer in the picture was an understatement. Unfortunately, I had let it slip that we were no longer seeing each other during a less-than-friendly conversation with my mom. My dad was so happy he took my newly repainted BMW and traded it in for a Porsche Cayenne because I had mentioned wanting an SUV for the snow. I tried to refuse it. I didn't need to be bribed, considering Rule had effectively left me, but the title was in my name and the BMW was already gone, so I reluctantly accepted it. My mom was even worse. She called every day to check on me. The woman who had never had the time of day for me was suddenly overly interested in everything I did and everyone I spent time with. I think she was trying to subtly let me know that as long as I kept unsavory characters out my life, I would eventually gain her approval.

The funny thing was now that Rule was gone, I didn't want it. I would have taken being disowned and disinherited a million times over if it meant I could just get him to talk to me, just get him to feel one-half of what I had always felt for him. I think my disinterest made both my parents nervous. They were so used to dangling approval and acceptance in front of me like a golden carrot, they didn't know what to do now that it held no appeal for me. Having the power now should have felt exhilarating, but instead it just left me hollow. I should have fought them sooner. I should have felt this way as soon as Rule and I started whatever it was we had been doing. I had wasted so much time, and it just piled more sadness and regret on top of what I was already managing.

"Thanks, Lou." I gave him one of the strained smiles that I was becoming a pro at and let him scoop me up in a bear hug as he walked me to my car after my shift. I hadn't heard a word from Gabe in weeks, but it made me feel better to know someone cared enough to make sure I was safe, so I never turned Lou down when he offered to see me to my car. This was an odd night on for me, meaning I had just picked up a shift because one of the girls was sick, so Ayden wasn't working and I was alone. In fact, my roommate seemed to have shaken out of her funk and was on a date with a very cute physics major who just happened to be as different from a rock-and-roller as one could get. She had gone out with him twice this week and seemed a little more like her old self. I was happy for her even if it meant one more night I spent wallowing in misery by myself. No one said the road to recovery was pretty, after all.

Lou set me back on my feet and gave me a peck on the forehead. "I miss that young man of yours, Shaw. He was a smartass, but a good kid."

I sighed because I kept having this same conversation with Lou. "I know. I miss him, too."

"Take care, girly."

"I always try."

My new car was awesome; I'm not going to lie. It purred like all good sports cars should, but had no trouble navigating the icy downtown streets as I made my way across town to my apartment. I listened to the Avett Brothers sing me sad songs about broken hearts all the way. It was well after midnight on a weekday, so there wasn't really anybody out on the road. A dog barked somewhere, it was cold and dark, and I shivered involuntarily. I hated this part of the drive home; it just hammered home the fact that I was really and truly on my own now. I was lucky to get a spot right in front of the building and sprinted to the security door because my uniform wasn't meant to be worn outside at the tail end of a Denver winter. I heard the familiar click of the lock when I punched in my code, and ran inside.

I blew a warm breath on my fingers and dug around in my purse for my house keys, since I still hadn't added the new key for my SUV to the set. Normally, I had them out and ready to go, but lately I had been so distracted by all the noise in my head and the heavy weight in my chest, that maintaining my personal safety had fallen somewhere toward the bottom of the priority list. I had just pushed the key in the lock and was getting ready to turn the deadbolt when a deep voice said my name from over my shoulder. For a split second I was excited. Unbridled relief flooded through me, because the only guy who would be waiting for me at my apartment was Rule. Before I could turn around and throw my arms around him, hard hands grabbed me by the back of the neck and shoved me face-first into the door. I gasped in shock, some part of my brain flashing that I should be screaming for help right now, but the door swung open with the flick of a wrist decked out in an all-too-familiar Tag Heuer watch, and I went stumbling forward as rough hands pushed me inside.

My purse went flying and I was stunned to see Gabe standing before me. He looked as pressed and polished as usual, except his eyes were crazy and he had a demented grin on his face that terrified me. I couldn't move.

"How did you get in here?" I knew this wasn't good. I wasn't safe with him, didn't want to be alone with him at all, but the apartment was tiny and there wasn't anywhere to run. My mace was in my purse on the floor, and the Taser that Rule had bought for me was resting uselessly in my new car. I was really regretting not letting Rule leave his gun over here all the times he had asked when we were seeing each other.

Gabe ran obviously agitated hands through his dark hair and watched me like any other predator watched its intended prey. "I told your mother that we were working toward reconciliation and wanted to surprise you. She gave me the code. I followed you home from work since the freak is obviously out of the picture and the military monkey hasn't been around. I figured now was as good a time as any for us to get on the same page."

He was so cold, so matter-of-fact, that I didn't even think he understood he had just forced his way into my apartment and that I was trembling in fear. I crossed my arms over my chest to try to bluff away some of the terror I was feeling but he just continued to watch me like he was mentally taking me apart.

"We aren't even reading from the same book, Gabe. You need to go because in like two seconds I'm about to start screaming my damn head off."

He shook his head and made a *tsk-tsk* sound. "Well, you see, Shaw, things have really gone to shit for me. Ever since your thug of a boyfriend made me look like a pansy and my dad pulled the plug on my credit cards because of that little stunt you pulled with the restraining order, things have been going downhill. I'm failing my political theory class, my fraternity wants me out because apparently it's not okay to let some guy with the IQ of a sewer rat make you look like a sucker on your own campus, my parents are furious with me over the restraining order, and the internship I wanted with your mother's campaign fell through because she simply didn't have time to get it together. So you see, Shaw, ever since you decided to be a selfish whore and turn your back on all the great things we could have had, I've been having to work double time to get what I deserve."

He was crazy, flat-out off his freaking rocker. I was trying to edge away from him because I knew if he moved close enough to get his hands on me things were going to go from terrifying to unimaginably horrible.

"I'm sorry you're having a hard time with things, Gabe, but you shouldn't have messed with my car. It pushed Rule over the edge. I told you to leave me alone or you wouldn't like what he was going to do."

I shrieked because apparently bringing up Rule was the wrong thing to do. Gabe moved faster than I would have thought he was able to. He chased me as I pedaled backward, keeping as much space between us as I could. Unfortunately, he caught me in the living room, and even though I fought, he was just bigger and stronger. He grabbed me by the throat and we struggled all the way to the floor. I kicked an end table over, which made a huge racket, and earned me a backhand across the cheek that split the side of my lip open. He sat all the way across my middle, pinning my arms to my sides and wrapped a hand around my throat. My eyes were watering from the tears of fear and the struggle to breathe. I clawed at his squeezing hands and flailed my legs but he just bent over me and continued to tighten his hands around my neck.

"You think I care what that loser thinks? You think I give a single fuck what that degenerate wants to do to me? He's nothing. I told you all along that he wouldn't stick around. Now look at you—all alone and finally doing things my way. I told you I would get my way. I always do."

I needed to get away from Gabe. He was going to kill me, seriously kill me. My vision was starting to blur in and out and my lungs were on fire. He kept squeezing and sitting on me while telling me all about how we were getting back together and how I was going to call my mother and have her reconsider her actions about his internship now that we were a couple. I shook my head back and forth, gasping for any air, and managed to get my hands between us enough that I jabbed my nails hard into the underside of his biceps, making him wince and reel up enough that I could crawl a little bit away from him. I sliced my hand open on a piece of the broken lamp as I scrambled to get my feet under me only to be dragged back down by a cruel hand in my hair. I grunted as his weight landed squarely on my back and had to blink away a steady flow of blood as the side of my head made contact with the leg of the overturned table.

"Ayden is going to be home any minute." My voice was thready and thin from the pressure he had put on my neck, but it didn't matter anyway; he simply jerked me back to my feet and pressed me so that I was folded in half over the back of the couch. I was trying desperately not to think about how little of a barrier my work uniform offered in the way of deterring him but he bent his face low to mine, not seeming to mind in the slightest that blood was getting everywhere.

"Who cares? You're my girlfriend, Shaw. You belong to me. If your roommate comes home you're just going to tell her things got out of hand while we were making up."

He'd put so much of his weight on my back that the way he had my hand wrenched up behind me couldn't take the torque and with a sickening *pop* that made both of us jerk my shoulder found its way out of its socket. I screeched in pain and went limp on that side. Fear and panic rose up hard and fast in my throat as I struggled. I knew that I had to get to my purse for the mace or to the kitchen for some kind of weapon to use against him. He let go of my hands now that one was totally useless and put one of his on the back of my neck to keep me bent over the couch while he used the other to start tugging and pulling at the bottom half of my uniform. He was muttering all kinds of broken sentences and talking about how he was going to make sure that I understood we were a couple. He was rambling about getting married and making our families one. I started to cry in earnest because I didn't know how to stop him from violating me this way. Fortunately, part of the lamp I had kicked over landed close to the couch and a piece was imbedded in one of the cushions. While Gabe was busy tugging and pulling at my clothes I wrapped the fingers of my good hand around it. I could feel the little ruffly shorts I wore under the uniform start to rip, and that was enough to spur me into action. The only thing I could reach from my prone position was the meaty part of his thigh and I wasn't sure that I had enough strength to do any real damage, but I swung the glass shard as hard as I could and heard him swear as he suddenly jerked back. I slumped to my hands and knees and screamed bloody murder as my weight landed on my injured arm. I crawled across the floor while he struggled to get the glass out and managed to get to my purse. I was just struggling back to my feet as he was thundering toward me, but I got the mace out and the nozzle turned toward him and gave him a full dose right in the face while he bellowed like an injured bear. I squeezed the canister in my good hand and bolted out the door. I was sure I looked like an escapee from an insane asylum. I was crying hysterically, had blood all over my face, and could barely talk because of the damage to my throat. I raced to the security door and I ran smack into Ayden as she was coming in. I collapsed into a blubbering mess as she caught me.

She was screaming my name, demanding to know what happened and I heard her dialing 911 on the phone, but between the shock and pain I just shut down. I blinked up at her through the blood trailing down over my face and was aware dimly of a crowd coming out of some of the other apartments. It was just too much and everything faded to black. I was pretty sure she caught me before I hit the ground but the next time I was cognizant of anything I was strapped to a stretcher and being loaded into the back of an ambulance. The lights and the sirens were making my head throb and a young paramedic was firing a million and one questions at Ayden as she scrambled up into the back with me. She immediately grabbed my hand and squeezed it. I noticed she was crying almost as hard as I had been.

"Gabe?" My throat was on fire and talking made it feel like I was speaking through a forest of razor blades.

Ayden brushed away her tears with shaking hands and I winced as the paramedic turned his attention to me.

"The cops have him. His dad showed up as they were putting him in the back of the police car. The mace you used on him was hard to miss so he couldn't really deny he was in our apartment. How did he get in through the security gate?"

I flinched as the paramedic prodded at my shoulder. He turned sympathetic eyes to me. "You're going to have to get it reset. It's dislocated and I think the cut on your forehead is going to be deep enough that it's going to need to be glued or sewed shut. Sorry."

I wanted to tell him it was okay because I was alive and at least Gabe hadn't gotten away with the ultimate violation, but talking hurt too much. When he asked about needing a sexual assault exam I shook my head no and squeezed Ayden's hand as she started crying again.

"My mom." The words were broken and not just because of my throat. "She gave him the code because he told her we were getting back together."

Ayden let loose with a string of swear words that would have made Rule proud and we spent the rest of the short ride just clinging to one another. The next two hours were a blur of doctors and police officers. After the first fifteen minutes, it was clear I wasn't going to keep up my end of the conversation with my vocal cords being as abused as they were. I had to resort to writing everything down. Gabe was in lock-up, at least for the night, and there wasn't anything his dad could do to get him out. The detective who took my statement let me know there was a good chance his family would post his bail in the morning and he would be out, but there was now a mandatory restraining order in place and there wasn't a thing his dad could do about it. Not that it mattered; they were keeping me at least a night in the hospital to see how bad the damage to my throat really was, and I needed superstrong painkillers to dull the migraine I was battling on top of the pain of having my shoulder shoved back into the socket.

My mom and Jack showed up sometime near dawn and my dad came as well. I told Ayden I didn't want to see any of them, which caused a huge scene. When my mom started screaming that it was probably one of the thugs I had met while I was dating Rule, Ayden totally lost her cool and informed all of them that if it hadn't been for my mother giving Gabe the code to the security door of the apartment this would have never happened. That shut everyone right up. My dad forced his way in using his medical connections and I spent a solid hour ignoring him and glaring while he apologized profusely. When he tried to kiss my cheek I turned my head away and made sure he could see the absolute disgust in my eyes. Part of Gabe's obsession had to do with all the things these people represented and I just couldn't abide having it around me right now. They all left after a nurse threatened to call security if they didn't stop disturbing me.

Ayden pulled up a chair and propped her feet on the edge of the bed, and we both fell into a fitful sleep as morning rolled around. I would only doze on and off, needing more pain meds as my shoulder started to ache and various other parts of me that had been abused made themselves known. Ayden vanished somewhere around noon, which was fine because another round of doctors and detectives came by.

Gabe's dad had managed to get him out on bail, but there was no dispute about how bad he had hurt me and the police were looking at charging him with attempted murder. They made me tell my story over and over again, and I never wavered from the brutal facts. Gabe was sick and needed help, but more than that he needed to be somewhere where he wasn't able to do this to someone else. Feeling entitled enough to own another person despite their feelings in the matter was beyond mentally unstable.

297

Ayden came back in with yogurt and some granola, looking sheepish. "I called Cora to let her know what was going on. I didn't even think about the fact that she would freak out while she was at work."

I went completely still and turned wide eyes to my friend.

"Apparently Rule threw a major fit when he heard what happened and, needless to say, he'll be here in, like, five minutes. Sorry, but I figured you should know. I guess I could ask the hospital staff to keep him out if you want, though I have a feeling stopping him when he's all worked up might be a chore. There'd be another ex you'd have to send to the slammer for the night."

I wasn't sure how I felt about him coming here. On the one hand, all I had wanted for the last month was to see him, to have him acknowledge me, but on the other, it shouldn't have taken a vicious and violent wake-up call to make that happen. I sighed and rocked my head back and forth. She was right, anyway: keeping him out if he had made his mind up to storm the castle was going to be more of a hassle than I needed right now.

"It's fine. I can handle him." My voice was still raw and scratchy but at least it hurt marginally less to use it now.

"You don't look like you're in any kind of shape to handle anything." She wasn't wrong. My arm was in a sling, I had a three-inch gash glued shut and wrapped in a white bandage on my forehead, matching the setup on my hand, my lip was split open and crusted with blood, and I had a wicked ring of black-and-blue bruises circling the pale skin of my throat. To top it all off, I was sporting a dandy set of black eyes from being shoved face-first into both the door and the floor.

"It'll be fine. He can come see that I'm all right, then go about his day, which I'm sure is all he wants to do."

She gave me a skeptical look and patted my feet where they were stacked up under the itchy hospital blanket. "All right then. If you swear you're going to be okay I'm gonna run and find someplace with coffee that doesn't taste like tar, and I'll be back."

I wasn't going to ever really be okay again. I didn't think anyone who had been through what I had in the last few months would, but I wasn't scared of Rule. Almost being raped by a lunatic had given me a whole new perspective on what was missing from my life and what I was going to do differently from this point on. I wanted to fidget with my hair, but it was snaggled together with dried blood and who knew what else and it wasn't like there was going to be any fixing my face. Rule was just going to have to face the horror show full-on and deal with it.

I was messing around on my phone, returning texts from Cora and most of Rule's boys, letting them know I was fine, when the door opened and he came in. I looked up and watched him, so I saw the initial anger that was stamped all across his handsome face quickly bleed into horror at the sight of me all battered and bruised. I saw his chest inflate and deflate as he sucked in an audible breath and moved to the end of the bed. We stared at each other in silence and I noticed absently that his hair was still normal, if unruly, as well as its natural dark brown color. I still hated it because it made him look like a stranger. His eyes looked wild and too big for his face; a full-blown blizzard was sweeping out of the cold depths. He was messing with his lip ring like he did when he was nervous and I realized if I didn't say anything there was a good chance we would spend the rest of the afternoon watching each other warily.

"You didn't have to come. I'm fine, just a little banged up."

His big hands tightened on the end of the bed and I watched the snake head bend and flex with his aggravation.

"I wanted to see for myself that you were all right. You could have called to let me know you were hurt."

I refused to look away from him and he seemed infuriated each time his gaze landed on another part of me that was broken. "Well, considering you haven't spoken to me for weeks, it didn't seem very logical to let you know what was going on."

His mouth tightened. "You're right. I should have been there. You shouldn't have been alone."

I sighed and clenched my hands in the blanket. "You're right, you should've been there, but not because Gabe is crazy and not because I needed protecting from him. You should have been there because you care about me as much as I care about you, but that isn't the case. No one is to blame for this mess but Gabe; he's sick and broken and chances are, even if someone had been with me, he still would have gone all stalker crazy, so it is what it is. I don't hold anyone accountable but him. Besides, my body is already on the mend; it's my heart that still feels like it went through a food processor."

"Shaw." He tried to interject something but I held up my good hand and looked him right in the eye. "I'm tired of my love not being good enough. I thought when this started with you I would be okay with whatever it was you were willing to give. I thought I could love you enough for the both of us since I had been suffocating in it for so long, but I realize now that I deserve more."

I blinked back tears that snuck up on me. "I deserve it all because I'm willing to give it all. I would have worked through the darkness with you, Rule. What I won't do is watch you walk away from me every time something happens that has the potential to hurt you. I'm sorry I never talked to you about Remy, but I told you all time and time again he and I weren't a couple. You had the undeniable proof on my birthday. You should be mad at him for keeping it a secret, not me. You were right all along; we don't trust each other enough to ever have had a chance at making this work. I think I wanted it too much and you didn't want it enough."

I was surprised to see moisture in his eyes when I was done talking. The only time I had ever seen Rule cry was at Remy's funeral. He reached out a hand like he was going to lay it on my leg but retracted it before he ever made contact.

"Shaw, what if I did love you?" His voice was just a hint above a whisper. "Seeing you like this makes me want to murder Davenport with my bare hands, but it makes something deep inside me hurt. I've missed you these last few weeks, but I was also furious with you. I couldn't get the two to ever line up."

I gave my head a sad little shake and let the tears gathered in my eyes fall. "That isn't enough. I've spent my entire life trying to live up to unreachable expectations. You were the only thing I ever wanted for myself, and once I got you, you felt like you had to entirely change who you were in order to be with me. I refuse to put the same kind of expectations I always struggled with on someone else, even if I didn't ask that of them. Parts of us are great together, Rule, but other parts of us just don't work. All this"—I waved my good hand over my reclining form—"will knit itself back together. It'll be fine and we'll just go back to whatever it was we were doing before." I made sure that he understood I was talking about everything from the gash on my head to my broken heart. I would get over him. There just wasn't another option.

"You've always been in my life, Shaw. We should've been able to make this work." I wanted to shrug but I only had one working shoulder so that wasn't an option. Instead I swiped at my tears with the back of a hand and offered him up a shaky smile.

"There are a lot of things that maybe should have gone one way and didn't. I know most people thought you and I being together was a long shot, so we should just be grateful for what we had."

"I feel like I'm letting you down, letting everyone down, and for once it's bothering the hell out of me. I just don't know how to work around what's going on up here." He tapped his temple with a finger.

I was crying in earnest now and it was on the tip of my tongue to tell him that if he could just love me, just learn to let me love him the way he deserved, the way I desperately wanted to, then it would all be fine, but that wasn't the case. We needed to believe in ourselves, needed to trust that we were each enough without trying to be other people. That just wasn't happening, so I closed my eyes and for once I was the one to shut *him* out and fall into the dark.

"Some things just aren't meant to be. I'm getting tired. Can you send a nurse in on your way out? I think the painkillers are starting to wear off."

"Shaw, I'm so sorry."

"Me, too, Rule, really. I am, too." I had spent a lifetime in love with him, and as much as I wanted to be strong and put it all behind me, letting go of what I felt for him was going to be the hardest thing I ever did. We stared at each other for a long, sad minute, then he turned and left. When Ayden came back in the room I was crying inconsolably and she had to crawl up on the bed to wrap her arms around me. I cried longer than I ever had before. I cried until there was nothing left inside me to cry out. I let my best friend hold me as I fell apart. The nurse came in with a painkiller, but when she saw the state I was in she turned right back around and came back with a sedative.

I spent one more day in the hospital, and when I was released I realized there was no way on this earth I was going back to my apartment with Gabe out on bail—restraining order or not. Luckily, Cora had an extra couple rooms open in the house she rented in the Washington Park area because both of her roommates had recently gotten engaged to each other and had moved to their own place. Ayden dropped me off at her place and returned a couple hours later with all my essentials packed up for an extended stay. She said the property management company was working on getting our place cleaned up but it gave her the creeps to be there alone. It didn't take more than a week for her to ask Cora if she could crash in the other vacant room at her house as well. Our apartment manager had even agreed to let us break the lease without paying a penalty because of what happened to me.

Being around the girls did wonders for both my mental health and my physical state. They never let me get down and someone was always there to remind me that everything I was feeling was temporary. They also refused to let me freak out over pressing charges against Gabe.

Things were moving fast, and a few times it looked like Gabe's father was going to use every trick he had to get him off. Alex Carsten had stepped in and now Gabe was on an ankle monitor and being charged with not only aggravated assault, but breaking and entering as well. I didn't think for one second that was a favor my mother called in, but Rule and I were back to radio silence so I never called to ask him or to thank him. Of course, the Davenports had the best defense lawyer in town on their payroll, but all signs pointed to a slam dunk for me, so I tried to stay positive.

I was refusing to talk to both of my parents. In fact, I hadn't told either one of them I had moved and I had changed my phone number within hours of leaving the hospital. The fact of the matter was I had nothing to say to them; all the things I had said to Rule held true for them as well. I deserved better and if they weren't willing to give me the love I showed them, without restrictions or demands, I didn't want them in my life. I knew my mom was struggling with the fact that she had to be accountable for giving Gabe my security code but, like I told Rule, the only person I blamed was Gabe. It was more important to me that she recognize that she should have never pushed him on me when I told her I was in love with someone else in the first place. If they couldn't figure out how to love and appreciate me for me, I would make do without them.

Ayden and I were settling into a new routine and we both adored Cora. It was nice to be living in a house rather than an apartment, and as each day went by it got a little easier to breathe around the hole in my chest where my heart had once been. It had only been a little over a month but it felt like a lifetime we had been apart. This time, faking it to make it was so much harder—maybe because I knew for real it was the end. This time there was no fake smiling, no pretending to glide through life. I was struggling and I was struggling hard. I missed him. I loved him. I couldn't have him and it was killing me in an entirely different way from when I had loved him from afar without him knowing it. Cora was back to keeping all talk of work and the guys at bay, but every now and then she would let something about him slip, and every time it felt like a shard of glass in an open wound. It should have made me feel better that he didn't sound like he was doing much better than I was, but it didn't. We both deserved happiness; it just sucked that we couldn't seem to find it together.

It was a couple days before Saint Patrick's Day, which not only fell on a weekend this year but also happened to be Rule's birthday. The girls had decided that instead of sitting around being sullen and grousing about things that we needed to go out and have fun. I didn't want to go. I mean

I really didn't want to go, and not only because my face wasn't entirely pretty again, but because I didn't think I could handle being in a crowd just yet. I was almost certain that I was going to have an awful time, but because I loved them, I let them badger me into agreeing to go. To my surprise, after a few martinis at an out-of-the-way lounge Cora knew about I relaxed and actually started having a good time. Strike that, I had a *fantastic* time, which I totally needed.

Getting up for school the next morning was awful and I was tempted to skip, but I had missed so much because of the attack that I couldn't afford to. I was standing in front of the mirror doing my hair and trying in vain to cover up the yellowish remnant of my black eye when I had a startling revelation: Loving Rule had never been easy. It was always hard and painful and the payoff had been years coming, but I had never decided he wasn't worth it. To me, loving him had never been a choice; it was just something I had decided was inevitable, just like I had decided that him ever coming to care about me was never going to happen. Last night I had been so sure I wouldn't have any fun, that going out was going to be miserable and awful, but after doing it I'd had a blast and it was totally worth the risk. I had done with Rule what I swore I never would: I had walked away because there was no guarantee in the end, no guaranteed happy ending for us.

I set my curling iron down on the sink and stared at myself in the mirror. All the sadness and loneliness was clear in the reflection staring back at me. Rule was the one thing I had always wanted and when it got hard to hold on to him, I had just let go rather than fight to keep a hold of him. That wasn't right. I deserved love but I also deserved him and whatever form his love came in. Rule wasn't a normal guy; there was never going to be hearts and flowers or poetry

305

flowing with words that made me blush. What there was always going to be was give-and-take, ups and downs, and a passion that burned both of us to the core. When he asked me at the hospital "What if I did love you?" my answer should have been: "If you're asking, you already do."

I knew it now, could see it as clearly as I could see my own face in the mirror: Rule loved me. He just didn't know that's what it was. Neither one of us really had shining examples of healthy, loving relationships to draw from, but the second he told me he wanted to try, I should have known he was falling in love with me. He never tried for anyone.

There was a knock on the bathroom door and Ayden popped her head in the room. "We have to head out soon. Are you almost ready?"

Considering I only had the right side of my head curled, I think the answer was obvious. I turned to her with huge eyes. "We need to go dress shopping after school."

She propped a hip in the doorway and lifted a dark eyebrow at me. "Any particular reason why?"

"Rule's birthday is this weekend."

"Cora might've mentioned that."

"He's gotta be having a birthday party."

"She might've mentioned something about that as well."

"Well, we have to go."

"Why? I thought you were done with all that noise, or is this the martinis from last night talking?"

I shook my head and picked the curling iron back up. "I have to give him a present."

"Oh yeah? What if he's there with someone?"

I cut her a look. That possibility hadn't even occurred to me. "Is that likely?"

She muttered something under her breath and brushed her long bangs out of her face. "No. Cora said he's been pretty much a hermit since you guys split, that and his temper is on fire, so everyone who doesn't want to be flayed alive is pretty much staying the hell out of his way. What are you planning on giving him anyway?"

"The only thing I think he wants."

She snickered. "More jewelry for his face?"

I laughed a little. "No . . . me. I think the only thing he really wants is me. We were both just too messed up to realize it."

She rubbed her hands together. "Well, it should be interesting either way."

Interesting didn't even begin to cover it, but my new leaf was all about self-gratification, and Rule was ultimately what I wanted to be gratified with. I could only hope he hadn't gone so far down the tunnel that I couldn't pull him out.

CHAPTER 17

Rule

"Hey, dude, happy birthday." I traced a finger over the horseshoe that I had insisted be on the headstone, and cleared away the emotion that was clogging my throat. I didn't come here enough, but every year on our birthday I made sure to stop by and let Remy know I was thinking about him. It was hard, being reminded that he wouldn't be turning twenty-three right alongside me, that I was getting older and he was stuck in time at twenty, his life cut way too short.

"I'm pretty pissed off at you right now. My life is all upside down and I can't seem to find my footing, and all the stupid shit I normally do to ignore the hurt and confusion just doesn't hold any appeal. I don't understand why you didn't just talk to me, why you used Shaw the way you did, and I really don't get how you just let me act like a total asshole to her for years and years knowing she had feelings for me. Well, here's a newsflash, bro: I have feelings for her, too. And now things are so jacked up, I can't see any way to make it right. Everyone always gave me hell for being difficult, for being temperamental and complicated; turns out you had more going on under the surface than Rome and

308

I could ever imagine, and yet you were still the favorite. Isn't that just a kick in the balls?"

For the second time in a few short weeks, I felt tears well up in my eyes. "Shaw kept your secret. All this time, even when things got intense between us, she kept your secret. She loves you, but she loves me, too. I just didn't know what to do with it, so I got mad and I shut her out and as a result, she got hurt and wouldn't let me back in when that's all I wanted. It sucks—love sucks—and I feel like if you were here none of this would have ever happened in the first place, so you suck, too."

There was no answer, just the sound of my shallow breathing and the wind moving the trees. I felt really alone for the first time in a long time, and the loss of my twin was really pressing down heavily on me. The last month and a half had been rough; everything with Shaw had left me strung up and stripped bare. My normal response to that overwhelming flood of emotion would have been to drink my liver into submission and screw any and every girl who looked my way. Neither of those things had been on my agenda. Booze wasn't enough to make my conscience stop screaming at me that I should have tried harder, should have handled my shock and anger better. And the idea of taking anyone to bed who wasn't Shaw made everything I had below the belt freeze up.

I was working a ton, trying to keep tabs on Gabe through Mark and Alex—I was determined to keep him away from her permanently, even if she didn't know I was doing it—and I was spending a lot of time with the boys, licking my wounds. Even though Shaw had been upset with me for trying to change, to be better for her, I think I had effected some major changes on my own, in spite of myself, and that wasn't bad. I was allowing myself to feel everything, and while the feelings tied up in the failure of my relationship with Shaw burned, at least I was processing them and not drowning them in bad habits.

I was getting ready to say good-bye when footsteps crunching on the thin layer of snow still covering the ground made me lift my head up. I felt my eyes narrow involuntarily and the corners of my mouth pull down when I recognized the figure making her way toward me. Every instinct I had was to get out of there before she could ruin my day, but I stayed put because she was looking right at me, and for once, there wasn't contempt or hatred shining out of her eyes.

"Mom."

"Happy birthday, Rule."

I cleared my throat because I had no clue what to say to her. I knocked my knuckles on the hard headstone and gave my brother a silent good-bye. "I'll take off so you can have some time with him. I'm sure today is hard for you."

I nearly fell over when she reached out a hand and put it on my forearm. My mom hadn't touched me voluntarily in years and it was enough to stun me into silence.

"It's hard for all of us, but that's not why I'm here. I actually called your work to see if I could maybe take you to lunch for your birthday. I figured you wouldn't answer if I called your cell, so I asked your roommate where I might find you and he pointed me here. I guess if I hadn't been so busy trying to shut you out all these years, I might have figured that out on my own."

I took a step away from her because I was pretty sure aliens had abducted my mom and that this creature before me wasn't real. The things coming out of her mouth were almost too much for me to take in. "Where's Dad?"

"Home. He's working on getting through to your brother, and after all that's happened, I needed to be the one to come to you. Can I take you to lunch or maybe for coffee?"

I didn't want to go. I didn't trust her or her motivations but it was my birthday and we were standing at my dead brother's grave, so turning her down just didn't seem like a viable option or one I could live with later on.

"Coffee would be all right." She gave me a smile that was sad. I mean, really, truly sad, and I realized for the first time that my mom had a dark tunnel she disappeared into as well, that maybe it was a trait I'd learned from her. We walked back to the parking lot in silence and I followed her back to Brookside, even though all I wanted to do was keep driving back to Denver. We stopped at the Starbucks I always hit, and I let her buy me a coffee while I settled into a semi-secluded corner and stretched out my legs. I could tell she was nervous, so I tried to relax and not be as guarded as I always was around her.

"I've been talking to a specialist. Your dad found someone here in town who deals with grief and family issues. I think it's been really helpful."

I blinked. "That's a change."

She smiled ruefully and I caught a glimpse of the woman who had raised me before our relationship had been tainted with tragedy.

"After the way things went at dinner, your dad had reached his breaking point. It was go and get help or watch my husband of thirty-six years walk away from me. Dale has always been the only constant in my life. I wouldn't make it without him and it took realizing how alone I would be if he walked out the door to make me see what I've done to my family."

I could only stare at her in shock. I didn't know what to say or do so I just kept sipping on my coffee and watching her.

"You asked me how I could love Remy, knowing how different he was while I always had such a hard time with

311

you, and I want to try to explain things. It's not an excuse; our relationship has never been easy. We've never been as close as I was with your brother and it started when you were both born. You guys were early, which is pretty common with twins, only you came out strong and healthy, bawling your little head off; Remy wasn't so lucky. He had his cord around his neck and was breech. It took a lot of work and effort to get him here alive, and well, from the start I think I focused more on him than on you, which makes me a terrible mother but doesn't mean I didn't love you both. Remy breast-fed; you wanted a bottle, and when you were both old enough to walk, Remy held on to my fingers and tottered all over the house, but you pulled yourself up using Rome as a lever and then just took off on your own. Your brother always needed me, always wanted me, and you, well, you were like you are now: independent, fierce, and determined to blaze your own way in the world, and I just let you go. Your dad and I both just let you slip away."

I was having a hard time breathing but I was so focused on what she was saying that it didn't seem to matter. "When Remy brought Shaw home I was so excited. He hadn't ever shown any interest in other girls, and meanwhile your dad caught at least one girl a week sneaking out of your window. We were starting to put the pieces together about him, but I was convinced he was just waiting for the right girl, and Shaw had it all—she's lovely, well educated, comes from money. It never occurred to me that she was too delicate, too broken down by her own family to be with someone as gentle and sweet as Remy. She needed someone strong, someone not afraid of all the things that tormented her day in and day out, so of course she picked you. She's loved you forever. I saw it, your dad saw it, and even with that we let Remy use her and snow everyone into thinking they were an item because it was just easier than dealing with the truth."

She stopped fidgeting with her cup and met my stunned gaze. She had tears in her eyes, which were nothing new, but for once these seemed generated by actual regret, not overbearing anger and blame directed at me.

"The night of Remy's accident he called me. I knew he was on his way to pick you up and I told him not to go, that you were a grown man who could find his own way home. He got really mad at me, told me I needed to get over whatever it was that kept me from embracing you, from loving you as openly and fully as I loved him. I got angry back and told him he had no place to lecture me on how I interacted with you if he was going to keep living a lie. We had a huge fight. It was ugly and I threatened him. I told him I was going to let you and Rome know exactly who their brother was and he freaked out. He hung up and left to get you, and those were the last words I said to my baby."

She was crying openly now and all I could do was sit there and let everything she said flow over me.

"I said it should have been you—I put all my grief and responsibility on your shoulders because I was too weak to be accountable for my part in what happened to Remy. Out of all of us, you're the strongest and you're the one who handled it the best. It was easier to blame you than to look at you and realize what I had done. You never loved me the way Remy did and the further away I pushed you the easier it was to feel less guilt. I'm sorry I did it; you never deserved it. I felt like you were already lost to me so the idea of losing you wasn't as crippling as it was with Rome, but I realize now you were never lost—I had just shoved you as far and as hard away as I could, and that's not healthy or acceptable."

We sat in silence while I tried to work through all of it. I couldn't just accept her apology; too much time and too many hurtful words and actions had been exchanged for that. But I could recognize that we were all human and prone to making careless mistakes with people we cared about, and that we could try to work toward a resolution from there.

"That's a lot to take in, Mom, and I'm not sure what you expect from me after telling me all that."

She swiped at her cheeks with the back of her hand and gave me a rueful grin. "I don't expect anything. I do want you to know that your dad and I are committed to putting this family back together, including Shaw. I know you're mad she didn't tell you about Remy, but I also saw the way you two were looking at each other. I saw the way you were with her, Rule, and I know you have never been like that with anyone else. She has always thought that you were worthy and in need of love, even when you did your absolute best to convince the rest of the world that you weren't interested in being loved. I just think you should consider that before deciding to walk away from her for good."

Was my mom, the woman who had made it her mission for the last three years to make sure I knew I was the lowest form of humanity, trying to give me relationship advice? Was she seriously telling me to try again with Shaw?

"She actually walked away from me. She told me that trying wasn't enough, that she needed to know that I loved her for sure and I just couldn't do that. I don't know if we're ultimately good for each other."

My mom reached across the table and grabbed my hand, which was resting by the cup. I nearly jumped out of my skin.

"She needs your strength and you need her to teach you how to love. She comes from a really awful group of people, Rule. She needs someone who can stand by her while she deals with that, and you need someone who's not scared of you, someone who can love all the different parts of you and not ask you to change any of them. She's done it for years even if you didn't know it. She was loyal to your brother, she kept his secret even though it caused problems between the two of you, and she'll be loyal to you, too."

We sat in silence while her words washed over me. I just didn't know what to say but I did know that things weren't the same without Shaw in my life. The last few weeks had been hollow. I didn't just miss her in my bed, which I did . . . *a lot*. I missed her in the morning when I had breakfast. I missed hearing from her in the afternoon and sending her naughty little text messages that I knew made her blush. I missed her coming by the shop for dinner and hanging out while she did her homework. I just missed her, and things weren't as good as they were when she was around.

"I have to say this is one of the more surprising birthdays I've ever had."

"You deserve some peace and I need to be responsible for the part I've played in making it so hard for you to recognize true and honest love when it's staring you in the face."

"I need to go." I pushed away from the table and looked down at her. I was grateful she didn't get to her feet and try to hug me because I was nowhere near ready for that, but when she offered me up a small smile I didn't hesitate to grin back at her.

"Thanks, Mom."

"You should have great things, Rule, including a happy and whole family."

"One step at a time, Mom."

I was walking out of the shop when I almost plowed over

the tiny brunette who had been checking me out the last time I was here. I grabbed her upper arms to steady her and let her go so I could move past her. What I needed to do, who I needed to get to, was suddenly so clear it was like a light at the end of the tunnel and I knew, just knew, that if I could make it right, the darkness wouldn't pull me under anymore.

"Sorry." I was going to move around her but she counteracted my move and put herself back squarely in my path. I frowned down at her while she batted her long eyelashes up at me.

"No girlfriend this time, isn't that just a shame?" I recoiled because this is what was out there—girls who would flirt with me, girls who would go home with me knowing I was seeing someone. It wasn't enough anymore. I deserved better.

"I'm actually on my way to go get her now."

The brunette tried to pout prettily but it did nothing for me.

"I would never have guessed you and Shaw would end up as a thing. She's been frigid since high school and I thought she was in love with your brother. Doesn't it freak you out being his replacement?"

Normally, something like that would have made me see red, would have made my damn head explode, but I got it now—this girl was nothing. Her opinion didn't matter and her misinformation was just laughable. I was done letting anyone, including a clueless stranger, use Remy as a weapon against me.

"I gotta run. Next time I'll be sure to go in the opposite direction if I see you coming." She gasped in outrage but I didn't care. I was too busy sliding around her and sending a text to Cora to find out if Shaw was still hanging around her house.

I wasn't guaranteed an answer back, because the girls had bonded, and Cora was all for me staying the hell away from Shaw, but maybe because it was my birthday she shot back that Shaw and Ayden had both worked a day shift today so they should be at the house. I would prefer to say what I had to say to Shaw without an audience, considering Ayden wasn't exactly my biggest fan right now. I was, however, willing to pick her up and move her out of my way if she didn't let me get to my girl.

It was late afternoon by the time I got back to the city. I was glad I had taken the day off, considering all the unexpected and life-changing revelations I had been fielding all day. I was supposed to meet up with the guys for dinner and then I was having a little party at Cerberus. Jet's band was playing and all my friends and some of my regular clients were swinging by for a drink or two. It was lame that Rome was already gone, but we had grown so much closer while he was here. I told him repeatedly I would just drink his share so that he could be here in spirit. All I knew was that it wouldn't be any kind of celebration until I got to Shaw and told her what I had to say.

When I got to Cora's house my nerves started to act up. If this was the last chance I had to make this work and she still sent me on my way, I wasn't sure how I would handle it. There was a good chance that Shaw was going to break my heart and that was big and scary because I didn't even know I had a heart to break before she came along. I skirted past a brand-spanking-new Porsche SUV and was relieved to see that Ayden's Jeep was nowhere in sight. I could hear music coming from inside the house. She was listening to the Heartless Bastards and the sentiment made me chuckle as I rang the doorbell. I had to wait a good five minutes before the music went down and I saw the blinds next to the door twitch. I was proud of her for not just opening it without checking to see who it was, but my nerves ratcheted up even higher when the door didn't open immediately.

When it did, I stopped breathing and forgot everything I wanted to say. She was obviously on her way out somewhere. She had on a supertight, supershort black dress that made the green in her eyes electric and the pale blond of her hair glow around her head like a halo. I had obviously interrupted her because she was barefoot and didn't have any makeup on but had her hair all curled up in a complicated style. She looked so perfect, it was enough to make my eyes hurt. The idea that she might be going on a date with someone else immediately crashed into all my hard-won resolve and made my back teeth snap together.

"Hey." It wasn't eloquent or romantic but I was having a hard time not overthinking this, and she didn't seem to mind. She shivered in her almost nonexistent outfit and took a step away from the door.

"Come in. It's cold out."

I followed her into the house and was relieved when she went into the kitchen and pulled out a beer for me. It gave me something to do with my hands and a minute to get my head together.

"It's not much of a present, but it's the best I can do on short notice. Happy birthday, Rule."

"Thanks. Are you . . . uh . . . headed out somewhere?" I let my hungry gaze travel from the top of her shiny head to the tips of her bright red painted toes. She was working toward being all healed up and looked like everything I ever wanted, with a few bruises and bumps thrown in to remind me how close I had come to losing her altogether. "You look very nice."

She grinned sheepishly and twirled the ends of her hair around her finger. "I was getting ready to go out later."

"Oh, well, I won't take up too much of your time then. I just wanted to talk to you real quick."

She leaned up against the kitchen counter while I took a seat at the kitchen table.

"Ayden forgot about something she had to do for her I-chem class so she won't be back for a couple hours and Cora doesn't get off until seven. We're going to dinner."

I was so happy to hear that she didn't have a date with another guy that I let out an audible sigh that had her raising a pale eyebrow at me.

"What did you want to talk to me about, Rule? It's nice to see you and all, but I have to say I'm kinda surprised you're here."

I wanted to tell her that I needed her, that I wasn't the same without her, that she was my entire world, but what fell out of my mouth was "I had coffee with my mom today."

I saw her eyes get big. "Wow. That's huge."

"She found me at Remy's grave. I was alternately chewing him out and telling him how much I miss him. I go every year on our birthday. Did you know that Dad threatened to leave Mom if she didn't go get some help?"

She bit her bottom lip and it took every ounce of self-control I had not to climb up and replace her teeth with my own.

"I didn't know that's what Dale told her, but I knew it was bad. They're used to you pulling away, but having Rome shut them out and refuse to let them see him off really did some damage. I'm glad it's helping. You guys are a family, you need each other."

"That's the thing, Shaw; I never thought I did until you. I never thought I needed anyone or anything until you got into my head and started breaking down all the walls I had built around all my feelings."

We stared at each other in a tense silence. Until she sighed softly and uttered, "I'm not sorry. It's not a bad thing to feel, it's not awful to care about other people."

I watched her carefully. I couldn't tell how she was feeling and it made laying it all out on the line for her even more frightening. "No, it's not bad, but it scares the hell out of me. I never had anything to lose before and losing you nearly undid me."

She sucked in a sharp breath and I saw a myriad of emotions in her eyes and face. "It undid me, too."

I shoved my hands through my hair and met her gaze, trying to let her see everything I was feeling. I wasn't good at expressing this kind of emotion and it was frustrating me. "I want you to know that there's been no one but you, Shaw. You've got me running in circles and so wound up, there could never be anyone but you. I miss you. I know you want undying declarations of love. I know trying isn't an option and that I just have to do it, but I want you. I need you, and more important, I get that you need me, too. Not some watered-down synthetic version of me that makes being together easier but the fully leaded, hard-to-handle me that you can lean on because I'm strong, Shaw. I'm not going to let anyone, your family especially, devalue all the wonderful things you have to give."

I got to my feet and walked to where she was leaning. Her eyes were enormous and I could see her chest moving up and down with rapid breaths. She still hadn't said anything so I pulled out the pen I had stashed in my back pocket and put my hand out.

"I'm not Jet, so I can't write you a song that makes you understand how important you are to me. I'm not Nash, so I can't find a building and paint you a mural that makes you see that it all starts and ends for me with you." She placed her hand palm-up in mine and didn't look away as I bent my head and began to do a quick sketch with the ballpoint across her superpale skin. "I'm a tattoo artist. I'll probably always be a tattoo artist, and I don't know how that plays into your future or the future you have planned after school and, frankly, I don't care. This is what I have to offer you, Shaw, and just like you let me be your first, I'm letting you be mine."

I covered her entire palm with a detailed drawing of a sacred heart; it matched the one I had inked on the center of my chest. It had flames dancing up the back, a crown of thorns on top of it, a spray of roses along the bottom, and in the center I drew a scrolling banner with my name in the center. "Here's my heart, Shaw. You have it in your hands, and I promise you're the first and last person to ever touch it. You need to be careful with it because it's far more fragile than I ever thought, and if you try to give it back I'm not taking it. I don't know enough about love to know for sure that's what this is between us, but I know that for me it's you and only you from here on out. I can only promise to be careful and not push you away again. Life without you in it is doable, but if I have a choice I want to do it with you by my side, and I'm telling you I'm not running away from the work it takes to make that happen. Shaw, I'm not scared of us anymore."

When I was done I was breathless but I felt like a huge weight had been lifted off my shoulders, because even if she rejected me at least she knew how I felt. I let go of her hand and she curled her fingers around the drawing that covered her palm. When I lifted my eyes to hers I was a little surprised to see tears shining in the emerald depths. She put the hand that I didn't draw all over on the side on my face and ran her thumb over my bottom lip, pausing at the hoop. Her mouth crooked up on one side, and just like that I knew everything was going to be all right.

"I was going to crash your birthday party tonight." We

321

were close but still separated by a few feet. I couldn't look away from her and she opened her other hand and put it on my chest over where the heart matching the one I just gave her lay. "That's where I was going later."

"I would have been happy to see you."

She smiled a little brighter. "I resolved the other day that I had to stop deciding how things were going to happen before giving them a chance to play out. You shut me out, Rule, but only because I let you. I was so worried about what you were doing, about what would happen, I just let you close the door, and when you wanted to pull it back open, I was so scared of how bad being without you hurt that I didn't want to give it space to happen again. That wasn't fair to either of us. I'm not afraid of the work or us anymore, either. I promise to not let you shove me away again. I do need you, Rule, and you are the only thing I have ever wanted just for me. I should have tried harder to hold on to you because you're right, I need to be careful with this." She tapped her palm with the heart on it against the one pounding under my skin. "It's precious and the best gift I could ever ask for."

I wrapped my arms tightly around her and lifted her off her feet. I wanted to kiss her, wanted to do all the things I had spent weeks missing out on doing to her. I wanted to make her forget Davenport's cruel hands and imprint on her every single thing I felt about her, but just as I was about to put my mouth on hers she pulled back and shook her head.

"If you start that, there is no way you're going to make dinner and your party tonight."

She was right but I didn't care. I had her and that was the only present I wanted. It must have shown on my face because she pressed a boring, closemouthed kiss on my lips and wiggled out of my grasp. "I love you, Rule, I really do.

I have something I want to give you for your birthday, but it has to wait until later, when we're alone and the threat of Ayden or Cora bounding in isn't a likely scenario, so go have fun with the guys. I'll see you at the bar later and then we can celebrate in private."

I pouted. That's right, I pouted like a little kid denied his favorite toy, which in a way I was. We had been apart too long. I needed to touch her, needed to get my hands on her, but she wasn't cooperating at all. "Come on, Shaw, just a little kiss. It's my birthday and I missed you so bad." I sounded whiny and not badass at all, but I could tell she was about to cave in by the way she slithered a little closer to me. But then the moment was ruined when the lock on the front door clicked and Ayden came sweeping through in all her long-legged, dark-haired glory. She took one look at me and Shaw and grinned.

"Hallelujah! It's about time you two idiots figured out that you were made for each other."

Shaw laughed and shook her head. She gave me another brief kiss and moved away. "Tonight. I promise it'll be worth the wait."

I agreed under protest. I still wanted to make out, but she clearly wouldn't be swayed, and I had to admit my curiosity was piqued as to what kind of gift she wanted to give me in private. I went home and took a shower—a freezing-cold one—and got ready for the night. I didn't want to drink too much because there was no way I was letting booze inhibit my reunion with my girl. I had never given much credence to the idea that being with someone you cared about made sex so much better, but it was true.

The guys took me to the Buckhorn Exchange so we could gnaw on giant pieces of wild game like cavemen and act like a bunch of jackasses. Now that things were back on track with Shaw, I felt lighter and happier than I had in months, and they could tell. They all gave me shit about my chronic bad mood and advanced levels of dickheadedness, but I could tell they were relieved and grateful that I was back where I needed to be. Dinner was fun, but I was ready to get on with the night so I could take Shaw home and have some proper make-up sex to cement this as the best birthday ever.

The bar was packed wall-to-wall with people wishing me a happy birthday. Even Uncle Phil had come out for the occasion. I accepted pats on the back and hugs as I looked for a particular blond head in the crowd. It took some skill to avoid shot after shot getting shoved in my direction but I managed to do it. I caught sight of a shimmer of white and black near the stage. Shaw was posted up front with Ayden and Cora and it irked me to no end that Jet was already at the table getting his flirt on with the beautiful brunette. Ignoring everyone else calling my name and clamoring for my attention, I scooped my girl up, even though she was in really tall heels and, for once, closer in height to me, and sealed my mouth over hers. I didn't care that she muttered a startled protest. I wanted a kiss and it was my birthday, so I was getting a damn kiss from this girl who was my world.

She wiggled a little until she could get her hands in my hair and I made sure it was worth her while as I stroked across her yielding tongue with my own. She gave a little moan and I moved a hand to her ass, pressing as hard into her as I could until I became aware of the roar of catcalls and applause surrounding us. I lifted my head, which left us both breathless and panting, and was greeted by a standing ovation from the bar. I shared a shocked look with Shaw and we simultaneously burst out laughing. I took a brief bow and she curtsied, making everyone else laugh along with us. She pressed back up against me to give me another kiss that turned my head to mush. The combination of a few beers, her soft mouth, and that ridiculously short dress was enough to have me cutting out of my own party early. We hung out long enough for Jet to get onstage and sing "Happy Birthday" to me and for me to instruct Nash to maintain a low profile when he came home. I grabbed whatever gifts I had been given and hustled Shaw out the door well before midnight.

We held hands in the truck on the way home and made small talk about what we had been up to during our time apart. I was glad to hear that she had pretty much been doing the same things I had, and that she was handling the situation with Gabe in a professional and no-nonsense matter. She was amazing and I was truly lucky to have her as mine.

When I let her into the apartment I was ready to just drag her to the bedroom and have my way with her, but she kicked off her sexy heels and padded to the kitchen to grab us a couple drinks. I was anxious and aroused but I didn't want to push her, so I followed her to the couch and took the beer she handed me. She sat facing me and reached out to put her hands in my hair. It felt nice but there were plenty of other places I wanted her hands, so I asked her, "Why are you always playing with my hair?"

"Because you change it so much and it always feels different. This is the first time it's all natural and I can't believe how soft it is."

"I thought you liked the hawk?"

"I do. I like it however it is, but when it's normal like this it makes you look more approachable."

She seemed nervous, which was weird. This was an area we had never had any issues with before so I wasn't sure what to do to put her at ease. I clicked the neck of my beer against hers and gave her a lopsided grin. "Happy birthday to me."

She smiled back and shifted so that her hair slid forward. "So, I need to tell you something before you get your present."

Her tone was pretty serious so my mind immediately went to all the worst possibilities: there had been someone else while we were apart, Gabe had hurt her worse than anyone knew and she wasn't ready for intimacy yet, she didn't really want to be in a relationship with me, she was moving to Peru. It took every single ounce of self-control I had not to freak out and ruin whatever progress we'd made today.

"Alrighty, hit me with it."

"It's kind of embarrassing."

"Shaw, I'm dying here. Just talk to me." She put her beer down and scooted closer to me on the couch, which pulled the hem of her dress tantalizingly up her pale thighs. If she didn't spit it out soon, I was taking her to bed regardless and we could just hash it out in the morning. She put a hand on either side of my face and pulled me down so that we were literally eye to eye.

"All that stuff about being nice and trying to be someone different to make being together easier applies to the bedroom, too, right?"

I felt my eyebrows shoot up and I tugged on her tiny waist until she was straddling my lap. "What are you getting at, Casper? Just spit it out."

She made a face and I saw her skin heat to a pretty shade of hot pink. "Nice Rule, the Rule that goes with this hair, is boring in bed. I don't like him. I just want normal Rule back and everything that comes with him. It's been a while so I just wanted to make sure we're on the same page."

I barked out a laugh and gave her a squeeze while working my hands up under the material of her dress to get a handful of her very bitable ass. "I can't decide if I should be thrilled or insulted."

She leaned forward so that our mouths were almost touching. "I just want you."

I grunted in response and decided the time for talk was over. She gave a squeal of surprise when I climbed to my feet with her still in my arms. She shifted her legs so she was wrapped around my waist and twined her arms around my neck in a loose hold.

"The present-giving can take place in the bedroom, I assume?" She didn't answer but instead started to kiss all along the side of my neck. It made my blood thunder in my ears and I wasn't sure I was going to make it to the bed when her sharp little teeth clamped down on my ear and she started whispering every dirty thing I ever wanted to hear. I kicked the door shut with the heel of my boot and kissed her all the way down to the black comforter on my bed. Her legs parted and I found myself cradled in the only place I wanted to be ever again. I hooked a finger in her very tiny panties and stripped them off. Had I known how little she was wearing under that short dress, I wouldn't have made it even halfway through the party. We both groaned at the first press of skin on skin as she grabbed the back of my T-shirt and pulled it over my head. We still had on enough clothes that I could kiss her and rub against her with delicious friction, while winding us both up to the point we were panting and straining against each other in the most enjoyable way. I was glad she didn't want it soft and gentle, glad she could take whatever I threw at her, because it had been too long and I felt like the top of my head was going to come off. I made a guttural noise of protest when she maneuvered free and pushed me over onto my back. Knowing she was naked under her dress had me itching to get my hands on everything that was damp and achy, but she had other ideas.

She was messing with my belt buckle and telling me to

take my boots off, but apparently I was too slow to comply because she had it all handled and I was spread out below her in nothing but my birthday suit in no time flat. She turned her back to me and asked me to undo the zipper that ran from her shoulder blades to the base of her spine. I was eager to oblige her, especially when all the black material covering her satiny skin puddled on the floor at her ankles. I ran my fingers along the pronounced ridge of her spine and was pleased to watch a trail of goose bumps follow in the wake. She looked over her shoulder at me and I felt my heart turn over at the mischief in her gaze.

"So I actually got your present a while ago, before we started having problems. That was lucky, I guess, because now they're healed and you can actually touch them." She pulled her long hair up in one hand and turned to face me as my curiosity piqued because she had her other arm across her naked chest. She climbed back up on the bed so that she was straddling my waist, which was fun to watch and had my erection sticking up like a lead pipe between the two of us. She dropped her arm and my eyes snapped as wide as they could. I was pretty sure I was drooling because, while Shaw was the most beautiful woman in the world to me, Shaw sporting nipple rings, naked and on top of me, was enough to make my brain short-circuit and all the remaining blood in my body shoot right between my legs.

"Oh, man, that is so fucking hot."

She laughed a little, which turned to a whimper when I circled the cool metal with a finger. "That's my birthstone." The jewel in the center of the ring was a shiny, pretty bluish-green aquamarine, delicate and pretty just like her.

She hissed out a breath when I tugged on the ring softly and I saw her eyes droop a little in pure unadulterated desire. I knew better than anyone how much intimate piercings could enhance a sexual experience and I would make it my personal mission in life to show Shaw everything I had ever learned. She bent down for a kiss.

"Happy birthday, Rule. I'm giving you me for now and forever, and if you want to give me back, I'm not going."

I flipped us over and kissed her like it was the end of the world, kissed her like we would never get to kiss again, kissed her like, well, like I loved her and was never going to let her go. The slide of tongues and press of my lip ring imprinted on her how much I had missed her. The bite of teeth left marks that let the world know we were claimed and the press of nails into tender skin had both of us breathing hard.

By the time I got my hands between her legs and my mouth on that pretty jewelry decorating even prettier nipples, we were both a wild tangle of grasping need and less-than-tender groping. I felt her nails break skin on the curve above my ass as I worked her into a frenzy with my hands and mouth, but I wasn't nearly done. We had been apart too long, and the weeks before when I was trying so hard to be something I wasn't, I had tainted something that was amazing between us and now I wanted to erase all of that. My girl had other ideas.

"Rule." She had one hand pulling on my hair and the other reaching between us in search of my cock, which was throbbing insistently between our stomachs. "While I appreciate the foreplay and the fact that nice Rule is clearly gone, if you don't fuck me in the next two seconds I'm going to scream. It's been too long."

Her eyes were bright and shiny and even though I would have liked to get her off at least once before unleashing all my pent-up sexual frustration on her, it didn't look like she was going to give me a choice in the matter. I grunted because her fingers curled around my dick and slid across the skin stretched tight by the barbells and my rampant erection. She wasn't playing fair so I lifted myself up in a vertical push-up so that I was poised at her burning-hot entrance and let her guide me home. We both went still at the initial contact; the absolute perfection of the two of us together like this was just a lot to take in and we had to give it a minute to sink in. She hitched her hips up and I slid all the way in until both of us let out a different swear word.

It wasn't slow and sweet, more like frantic and wild, but it was wonderful and so damn hot I thought we were going to burn each other up. The metal in her tight nipples made me growl every time they brushed against my chest, and I could feel it every time the top ball on the head of my cock hit her clit because her body bowed up and her breathing got choppy and wild. It was the kind of sex I could only have with her, and when I felt her come apart around me I realized I might not really know what love was on my end, but I recognized it clearly shining out of her when she looked at me like that. I couldn't help but feel she had to see the same thing when I looked at her. I picked up the pace, felt her run her hands up and down my back and grab on to my ass, and then shattered into a brilliant mess that I didn't ever want to put back together.

She turned her head and kissed me on the temple. "Love you."

I pressed my face into the curve where her neck met her shoulder and sucked the skin between my teeth. "I'm going to love you, Shaw."

Her eyes crinkled at the sides. "You already do."

I didn't have to say anything because I figured she was probably right. Me and this girl had spent too much time trying to be too many different things to too many people for too many wrong reasons. Now it was up to us to be ourselves for each other and love each other for all the right reasons. As she curled up next to me and threw her leg across my waist I knew that somehow this is how it was always supposed to be and maybe, just maybe, this was a gift I could share with Remy because I was happy, Shaw was happy, and ultimately, that's all he would have wanted for either of us.

About eight months later

"If you don't lie still and quit wiggling around I'm going to stop."

"But it hurts."

"You always say that. We do this enough that you know exactly what you're getting into. I'm almost done so stop complaining."

"You could be gentler."

"You don't like it when I'm gentle. Seriously, Casper, you are the worst client ever, which is a shame because all this white skin takes ink like a dream." I glared at Rowdy as he peered over the short wall again and leveled him with a death glare. "If you don't stop trying to get a look at my girlfriend's ass you're going to need to find a new career because I'm going to break all your fingers."

Shaw giggled and turned her head where it was resting on her crossed arms propped up on the table she was lying on before me. The current piece I was working on for her covered her entire right side from the base of her armpit to the bottom curve where her sweet ass met her thigh and everything in between. It was huge and graphic and arched all along her delicate rib cage. I still had about three hours of color and shading to add to it, but since the canvas practically lived at my apartment I wasn't worried about finding time to finish it up. But while I was working on it now she was practically naked, covered only by my hoodie and a very tiny pair of shorts. I knew the guys in the shop were digging the view—they always did when I worked on her—but it was hard to concentrate and keep the lurkers at bay at the same time.

Rowdy flipped me off but grinned in good humor. My friends loved Shaw, loved that she made me tone my crazy down and become an easier guy to live with and be around. It was almost a year in and while I still wasn't the easiest person in the world to get along with, I was making real strides in at least being a more tolerable human being. "That could be the very best piece I've ever seen you do. Are you going to put it in your portfolio when it's done?"

The piece was a very intricate, very colorful Day of the Dead–inspired grim reaper. The face on the woman was beautiful and tragic and she held on to an exact replica of the heart I had initially drawn on Shaw's palm all those months ago. Shaw had insisted on two things in the design— she wanted the sacred heart represented and she wanted it to resemble the grim reaper on my side. I never would have thought Shaw was going to get as interested in body modification as I was, but after only a month of us being an official couple she had asked me to draw her a bunch of tiny snowflakes in different colors of blue, gray, and white. When I asked her why, she said my eyes reminded her of winter and she wanted something to keep with her that reminded her of me, so she now had a snowstorm that started behind her left ear and trailed across the back of her neck to the base of her right shoulder. It was one of my favorite places on her body to trace over with my tongue, and I loved not only that she got something that reminded her of me, but that I was the one to put it on her. A couple of months after that she wanted me to draw her up a horse-shoe with Remy's name in it so she was also rocking a memorial tattoo for my brother that made me feel good every time I saw it on her inner arm when she hugged me or we held hands.

The piece I was working on today was a hundred times bigger and more detailed than either of those. It made a statement and I had to admit I loved it, loved the design, loved that she trusted me enough to permanently alter her, and loved that I was the one who was going to see it every day when she got into bed beside me.

I ran the paper towel I was using to wipe away excess ink and blood off her over her hip and cleaned her up. I gave her a light tap on the ass and snapped off my gloves.

"That's up to Shaw. If she wants it in there, I will. If not, it's cool." I flexed my fingers as she swung her legs around the table so I could slime tattoo goo all over her and wrap her up so she didn't ooze blood and ink all over the place until I could get her home. The hand that had her name inked across the knuckles folded up and brushed against her cheek as I snuck a kiss. As a professional tattoo artist I knew all the mojo and all the warnings about tattooing a significant other's name anywhere on your body, but I didn't care. I liked looking down and seeing her name there, liked that when I held my hands next to each other our names were side by side forever on my skin. I had also had Nash ink a perfect little replica of Casper the Friendly Ghost behind my left ear so that I had something that reminded me of her in the same place she had something that reminded her of me. It was kind of cheesy but she thought it was sweet and the way she had showed her appreciation was enough to keep me smiling for days, so who gave a fuck.

"It's beautiful. Thanks, love."

"So are you." I kissed her again as she hopped off the table, careful to keep all the good stuff covered up as she went into the bathroom to get dressed. She trailed a finger across the bald side of my head where I had it shaved. The Mohawk was back at alternating intervals and she hadn't been lying—she never cared what my hair looked like. As long she could get her hands in it or around it, she didn't care what style it was or what color I picked for the month.

Rowdy shook his head and gave me a sour look. "You are one lucky bastard, Archer."

I laughed and started to clean my station up. "I know it."

Things weren't always perfect. We were still two very different people on two very different paths but we always managed to take time to work it out. The trial against Davenport had been hard and I hated watching her have to relive it all. There was just too much influence for him to get as harsh a sentence as he deserved, but she stayed strong. When her parents had encouraged her to just drop the charges and let Davenport's dad deal with him, she had pressed forward and done the right thing. Gabe was getting punished, just not as harshly as any of us would have liked. Her parents weren't any kind of fan of our relationship, but once it was clear that Shaw and I were a package deal or they weren't welcome anywhere near her, they relented slightly. Personally, I think it was guilt from the attack and their general shitty parenting that kept them paying her tuition and grudgingly accepting me in her life. I didn't care because I was here to protect her from them. Whatever the reason, as long as they behaved it was all good, or at least good enough.

Things with my folks were better, not perfect, but better. My mom and I had reached an understanding. We were never going to have the close relationship she shared with

Remy, but we at least could talk now. I had even gone along to a couple of her therapy appointments and I had a better understanding of how she was wired. Much to my surprise we were far more alike than I had ever imagined. Shaw and I made it a point to go back home every Sunday for brunch again but now I was an active participant, and it was one of my favorite times of the week. Unfortunately, Rome was the Archer brother being difficult now. He still refused to talk to Mom and Dad and he only thawed toward Shaw when I let it be known that if he didn't I was going to beat his ass when he came home in a couple months. Things were rocky on that front. He felt lied to and betrayed, but I had faith in him. If I could see the light, then my brother, who was already a way better man than I was, would come around eventually.

Shaw came out of the bathroom pulling her hair up into a messy ponytail. Cora turned from the front desk to scowl at her. "I can't believe you're leaving me for that asshole. I'm going to miss you so much."

"Awwww . . . I'm going to miss you, too, girl, but I'm never there and I'm sick and tired of having my stuff in two different places." Shaw was moving in with me and Nash this weekend. We had put it off even though she was there five to six nights a week because I didn't want to burden Nash. It had been my best friend who finally told her over breakfast one morning that if she agreed to do most of the cooking then she was welcome to just move in. We were both grateful because I liked our place, it was superconvenient for work, and I really didn't want to move or ask Nash to leave. The three of us got along great and Nash was gone enough nights that we never really got on one another's nerves. The girls were bummed she was going and I knew she was really going to miss Ayden and Cora, but they hung out enough and had declared every Thursday girls' night, so I wasn't worried at all about her regretting her decision.

Cora screwed up her face, looking like an angry Tinker Bell. "I just hate the idea of moving a stranger in. You and Ayden were, like, the perfect roommates ever and after what happened to you I don't trust some random stranger off the street to move in."

Shaw sat in the chair I had vacated to clean up and I hid a grin as she sneakily ran her fingers up the inside of my thigh. Nash looked up from the owl he was working on and looked back and forth between me and Rowdy. "Isn't Jet coming back from tour soon?"

"Yeah. So what?" Artifice had hit the big-time, booking a slot on Metalfest and had tapped Jet's band, Enmity, to be on the opening stage for them. He had been gone for more than six months and while he was on the road, the girl he had been shacking up with had hooked up with some ex-con, so Jet was out on his ass. We all just figured he would crash with Rowdy or one of the other guys in the band.

"You can rent the room out to him." Nash said it like it was perfectly reasonable. "He's cool with Ayden and he's always on tour or whatever anyway. I bet he would be a good fit."

Shaw and I shared a raised-eyebrow look. Jet was cool with Ayden; in fact they had developed an independent friendship outside the rest of us that often left us all questioning how close the country girl and the metal boy were. They were close, but so opposite it was hard to understand how they ever had anything to talk about. If anyone asked me, Jet moving under the same roof as the dark-haired beauty was just asking for trouble, or a really good time depending on how you looked at it. I cleared my throat and reached out for Shaw's hand.

"My older brother will be back in a few months, too. He's

gonna need a place to crash until he figures out what he's doing. That might be another option you want to consider." Cora nodded and turned back to whatever it was she was messing with on the computer. I turned to Shaw. "You ready to go home?"

I loved asking her that. I loved that she knew I loved asking her that. She smiled at me and gingerly reached up to give me a quick peck. I knew her side had to be hurting her. Four hours of getting drilled was a lot and she normally sat like a champ, still as stone. I was going to put her in a hot shower and make her feel all better.

"Yep."

We walked out of the shop hand in hand and headed toward the Victorian. She liked to run her thumb back and forth across her name on my knuckles and it never failed to make me smile.

"Do you want to put me in your portfolio, Rule?"

I wasn't expecting that question so I looked at her in surprise. "Why do you ask?"

She shrugged. "I dunno. You put all your really big pieces in there. I just didn't know why you would want to leave this one out."

I wrapped an arm around her neck and pulled her to me so I could kiss the top of her head. "Because those are work. I put them on people and then they go out into the world where they are hopefully appreciated and loved by other people. Anything I do for you, anything between us isn't work and it's for you and me to appreciate. When I work on you I do it knowing what I put on you will be with us forever. Like I said, if you want it in there I'll be happy to put it in, but if not, then I'll be happy to be the one to admire all my handiwork every day."

She stared at me in silence for a second and then burst out laughing. "You give the most backasswards compliments

338

in the world but that was lovely and you're absolutely right. The only person that I really want to see it is you."

I growled and tugged on her hair. "That thing covers half your butt cheek. I better be the only one looking at it, Casper."

Her green eyes glowed in a way that only I could make them. "I do love you, Rule Archer."

Every time she said it I had an easier time telling her "I love you back" and that's all it was. I didn't have to question, didn't have to worry, didn't have to fall into the tunnel of darkness, because whatever Shaw felt for me I just gave it to her back and knew that was enough. I didn't have to try; I just did. And every single day I did it better than the day before.

"So what about Jet or Rome going to live with Cora and Ayd?"

She snuggled into my side as we approached the Victorian.

"I can't wait to see how that plays out."

I snorted. "That's what everyone said about us."

"And look at the show we gave them."

"True enough, and opposites don't just attract, they freaking catch fire and burn the entire city down."

"Don't I know it."

Whatever was on the agenda I knew one thing. If any of my boys were lucky enough to find a girl who made them feel the way Shaw made me feel, I would do whatever it took to make sure they saw it through to the end. Love like this wasn't to be missed, even for those of us who had never realized it was out there. Look at me being all optimistic and shit.

Remy would be so proud.

If this story had a soundtrack this is what it would be

The Civil Wars: *"Falling"*
Social Distortion: *"Like an Outlaw (For You)"*
Twisted Sister: *"We're Not Gonna Take It"*
Garth Brooks: *"I Got Friends in Low Places"*
Black Rebel Motorcycle Club: *"Ain't No Easy Way"*
Bad Religion: *"American Jesus"*
The Gaslight Anthem: *"Film Noir"*
Drive-By Truckers: *"Decoration Day"*
Straylight Run: *"Hands in the Sky (Big Shot)"*
The Black Angels: *"Better Off Alone"*
Lucero: *"Kiss the Bottle"*
The Bloody Hollies: *"Raised by Wolves"*
Against Me!: *"Borne on the FM Waves of the Heart"*
Dawes: *"If I Wanted Someone"*
Lady Antebellum: *"Need You Now"*
Defiance Ohio: *"Anxious and Worrying"*
The Avett Brothers: *"I Would Be Sad"*
Heartless Bastards: *"Only for You"*

About me

First of all I am a girl . . . Yes, I know, I didn't think I needed to say that either, but after a few interesting emails of late I thought I would put that out there. Jay is short for Jennifer.

I live in Colorado, which is lovely, and offers up all kinds of interesting people to draw inspiration from. I love tattoos and body modification so I love that more and more stories out there now are featuring heroes and heroines who reflect what I see when I look around the world. I love to read and just love any kind of great story that engages; of course a pretty, tatted-up bad boy always makes it better. This year was life-changing for me, so I woke up one morning and decided that I was finally going to finish one of the millions of stories I was always fiddling around with. I love to write and for a long time have been pondering what I should be doing with my life. So consider yourself a valued part of me figuring out my new life plan. I hope you enjoyed this story and if you would like to contact me please feel free to email me. I love feedback in all forms, but if you're mean we might have to box.

So let me clarify a little. I wrote this book in a frantic state of trying to pull my life together. I just wanted to prove that I could, that I could finish and do something I promised myself I always would. It was a personal challenge that I had NO IDEA would take off. That's why it wasn't edited perfectly or all shiny and spot-on. This copy has since been edited, but I'm still not going to claim perfection, because that just isn't my style. For those of you who read the first copy and loved the story underneath the typos I adore you, thank you so much. For those of you who feel like you got cheated I'm sincerely sorry, but all I can do is learn about editing and how fast a book can go viral and promise to put forth a better effort next time around.

jaycrownover@gmail.com
Later, JC

Can't get enough of the Marked Men series?
Good news, there's much more to come!
Turn the page for a sneak peek at . . .

Jet

With his tight leather pants and a sharp edge that makes him dangerous, Jet Keller is every girl's rock-and-roll fantasy. But Ayden Cross is done walking on the wild side with bad boys. She doesn't want to give in to the heat she sees in Jet's dark, haunted eyes. She's afraid of getting burned from the sparks of their spontaneous combustion, even as his touch sets her on fire.

Jet can't resist the Southern belle with mile-long legs in cowboy boots who defies his every expectation. Yet the closer he feels to Ayden, the less he seems to know her. While he's tempted to get under her skin and undo her in every way, he knows firsthand what happens to two people with very different ideas about relationships.

Will the blaze burn into an enduring love . . . or will it consume their dreams and turn them to ashes?

**Available now in ebook, coming soon
in paperback from Harper**

Ayden

It was totally against everything I was supposed to be doing in my new life—to ask a really cute boy in a band to take me home. There were rules. There were standards. There were simply things I did now to avoid ever going back to being the way I was—and sticking around to wait for Jet Keller was right on the top of the no-no list. There was just something about him, watching him wail and engage the crowd while he was on stage that turned my normally sensible brain to mush.

I knew better than to ask my bestie what was wrong with me.

She was all about boys covered head-to-toe in ink and littered with jewelry in places the Lord never intended boys to be pierced. She would just say it was the allure of someone so different, someone so obviously not my type, but I knew that wasn't it.

He was entrancing. Every single person in the packed bar had their eyes on him and couldn't look away. He was making the crowd feel—I mean really feel—whatever it was he was screeching, and that was amazing.

I hated heavy metal. To me, all it sounded like was yelling

and screaming over even louder instruments. But the show, the intensity, and the undeniable vibe of power he was unleashing with just his voice—there was just something about it that drove me to drag Shaw to the front of the stage. I couldn't look away.

Sure, he was good looking. All the guys who Shaw's boyfriend ran around with were. I wasn't immune to a pretty face and a nice body; in fact, at one point those things had proven to be weaknesses that had gotten me in more trouble than I cared to think about. Now I tended toward guys who I was attracted to on a more intellectual level.

However, one too many shots of Patrón and whatever crazy pheromone this guy was emitting right now had me forgetting all about my new and improved standards in men.

His hair looked like he had just shaken off whatever girl had messed it up. At some point during the set he had peeled off his wife-beater to reveal a lean and tightly muscled torso that was covered, from the base of his throat to somewhere below his belt buckle, in a giant black and gray tattoo of an angel of death. He had on the tightest black jeans I had ever seen a guy wear, decorated with a variety of chains hanging from his belt to his back pocket, and they left little to the imagination.

That might have been why Shaw and I were nowhere near the only female fans at the front of the stage.

I had seen Jet before, of course. He came into the bar where I worked on a pretty regular basis. I knew that the eyes, now squeezed shut as he bellowed a note that was enough to have the girl to my left spontaneously orgasm, were a dark, deep brown that gleamed with easygoing humor. I knew of his penchant for outrageous flirtation. Jet was the charmer of the group and had no qualms about using that, combined with his heartbreaking grin, to get what he wanted.

I felt a warm hand land on my shoulder and turned to

look up at Shaw's boyfriend, Rule. He towered over the rest of the crowd and I could tell by the twist of his mouth that he was ready to go. Shaw didn't even wait for him to ask, before turning to me with guileless green eyes.

"I'm going with him. Are you ready?"

Shaw and I had a "leave no man behind" policy, but I was far from ready to call it a night. We had to scream over the blaring guitars and the ear-splitting vocals bombarding us from our prime location, so I bent down to holler in her ear.

"I'm gonna hang out for a bit. I think I'll see if Rule's friend can give me a ride."

I saw her speculative look, but Shaw had her own boy drama to handle, so I knew she wasn't about to try to tell me any differently. She hooked her hand through Rule's arm and gave me a rueful grin.

"Call me if you need me."

"You know it."

I wasn't the kind of girl who needed a wingman or wing-woman. I was used to flying solo and I had been taking care of myself for so long it was really second nature. I knew Shaw would swoop in to grab me if I couldn't get a ride home or if calling a cab took too long, and knowing she was there was enough.

I watched the rest of the show in rapt fascination, and I was pretty sure that when Jet threw the microphone down after his final song, he winked at me before slamming back a shot of Jameson. Even with all of the things I knew I should be doing pounding in my head, that wink sealed the deal.

I hadn't been on the wild side in too long and Jet was the perfect tour guide for a quick refresher course.

He disappeared off the stage with the rest of the guys in the band, and I wandered back over toward the bar where everyone had been posted before the band had started playing. Rule's roommate, Nash, had apparently been dragged home by the lovebirds. There was no way he was making it out of the bar under his own steam. Rowdy, Jet's BFF, was busy sucking face with some random girl who had been giving Shaw and me the evil eye all night. I gave him a *you could do better* look when he came up for air, and then found an empty stool by the bar.

The thing about heavy-metal bars is that there are heavy-metal guys in every corner.

I spent the next hour fending off come-ons and free drink offers from guys who looked like they hadn't seen a shower or a razor in years. I was starting to get annoyed and, in turn, nasty when a familiar hand with a plethora of heavy silver rings landed on my knee. I turned to look up at laughing dark eyes as Jet ordered me another Patrón, but got water for himself.

"Got ditched, did ya? The way those two were looking at each other, I'm surprised they made it halfway through the set."

I clicked the tiny shot glass against the rim of his glass, and gave him the smile that I had always used in the past to get whatever I wanted. "I think Nash had a fight with the tequila and the tequila won."

He laughed and turned to talk to a couple guys who wanted to congratulate him on the show. When he turned back to me, he looked a little embarrassed.

"I always think that's so weird."

I lifted a dark eyebrow and leaned a little closer to him, as I caught sight of a redhead in too-tight clothes circling. "Why? You guys are great and obviously people like it."

He tossed back his head and laughed and I noticed for the first time he had a barbell through the center of his tongue.

"People, but not you?"

I made a face and shrugged. "I'm from Kentucky." I figured that would explain it all.

"Rule sent me a text saying you needed a lift home. I have to go pull Rowdy off that chick and help the guys load the van, but if you can chill for, like, thirty, I'll totally give you a ride."

I didn't want to seem too eager. I didn't want to let him know how much I wanted him to give me a ride of an entirely different kind, so I shrugged again.

"Sure. That would be nice."

He squeezed my knee and I had to suppress the shudder that moved through me from head to toe. There was most definitely something up if just a little touch like that could make me quiver.

I turned back to the bar, ordered myself a glass of water, and tried to close my tab. I was surprised when the bartender told me it was already taken care of and a little annoyed that I didn't know who to thank. I swiveled around on the stool and watched closely as people fought their way through a bar full of overly enthusiastic guys and overly obvious girls. I wasn't a saint by any stretch of the imagination, but I really had no respect for any girl who was willing to degrade herself, to offer herself up for a single night of pleasure, just because Jet looked hot in tight pants.

Whatever was happening to me went deeper than that; I just couldn't name it. And tonight I was drunk enough—and missing some of my old self enough—to ignore it for now.

By the time Jet came back, I was faking interest in a conversation that some guy who looked like he had raided Glenn Danzig's closet was forcing on me. He was telling me all about the different genres of metal and why the people who listened to each different kind either sucked or ruled.

It was all I could do not to shove a stick of gum in his mouth to stop him from breathing heavy, boozy fumes all over me.

Jet gave the guy a fist bump and hooked a thumb over his shoulder.

"Let's roll, Legs."

I made a face at the generic nickname because I had heard variations on it my whole life. I was tall, not as tall as his six-two, but I towered over Shaw's five-three and I did indeed have very long, very nice legs. At the moment they were a little wobbly and a little unsteady, but I pulled it together and followed Jet to the parking lot.

The rest of the band and Rowdy were piling into a huge Econoline van, and shouting all kinds of interesting things out the window at us while they peeled out of the parking lot. Jet just shook his head and used the control on his keys to pop the locks on a sleek black Dodge Challenger that looked mean and fast. I was surprised when he opened the door for me, which made him grin, so I folded into the seat and tried to plan my attack. After all, he was a guy who was used to groupies and band sluts throwing themselves at him on a daily basis, and the last thing I wanted was to be just one more.

He turned down the music blasting from the obviously expensive sound system and wheeled out of the parking lot without saying a word to me. He had found the time to put his shirt back on and it was now covered by an obviously well-loved leather jacket, complete with metal studs and a patch of some band I had never heard of. The combination of cute rocker boy, too much tequila, and the heady scent of leather and sweat was starting to make my head spin. I rolled down the window a little and watched as the lights of downtown bled by.

"You okay?"

I tilted my head in his direction and noticed the real

concern in his dark gaze. In the dim light of the dash, the gleaming gold circle that rimmed the outer ridge of his eyes looked just like a divine halo.

"Fine. I shouldn't have tried to keep up with Nash for the first hour."

"Yeah, that's not a good idea. Those boys can put it away."

I didn't answer because generally I could hold my own with anyone when it came to matching shot for shot, but that wasn't something I liked to talk about. I changed the subject by running a finger over the obviously new and pristine interior of the car.

"This is a supernice ride. I had no idea screaming into a microphone paid so well."

He snorted a laugh and gave me a sideways look. "You need to branch out from cookie-cutter country, Ayd. There are all kinds of great indie country bands and even some amazing Americana bands I bet you would totally dig."

I just shrugged. "I like what I like. Seriously, is your band famous enough that you can afford a car like this? Rule said you guys were popular in town, which was clear after tonight, but even with that crowd it doesn't seem like you would make enough to live on just playing music."

I was prying, but it had suddenly occurred to me I didn't really know anything about this guy other than he was making my heart race. He was also making my head create all kinds of interesting scenarios that involved both of us and a whole lot less clothing.

He was tapping out a rhythm on the steering wheel with his black-tipped fingers and I couldn't look away.

"I run a recording studio here in town. I've been around a long time so I know a bunch of bands and guys in the scene. I write a lot of music that other people end up recording and Enmity is big enough that I don't ever have to worry about starving. Lots of people make a living just playing music. It's just hard and you have to be dedicated to it, but I would rather be broke and do something I love, than be wealthy working a nine-to-five job any day."

That was something that just didn't make any sense to me.

I craved security and a future with a foundation rooted in safety. I wanted to know that I was going to be able to support myself; that I would never have to rely on anyone else for life's basic needs. Happiness had nothing to do with it at all.

I was going to ask more questions but the apartment I shared with Shaw was quickly coming into view, and I hadn't even tried to let him know that I was interested in more than a lift home.

I turned my entire body in the seat so I was fully facing him, and plastered my best *do me* smile on my face. He lifted an eyebrow in my direction but didn't say anything, even when I leaned over the center console and put my hand on his hard thigh. I saw the pulse in his throat jump, which made me grin. It had been a long time since I had been so overtly interested in anyone and it was nice to know that he wasn't immune to me, either.

"Want to come up and have a drink with me? Shaw is staying with Rule, so I'm sure she'll be out of commission for at least a couple days."

His dark eyes grew even darker with something I didn't recognize, because we really were strangers, but he put his hand over mine and gave it a gentle squeeze.

I wanted to inhale him; I wanted to get inside him and never come back out. There was just something there, something special about him that pulled on all the strings I thought I had neatly trimmed away when I had left my old life behind.

"That sounds like a bad plan, Ayd." His voice was low and had undercurrents floating through that I couldn't identify.

I sat up straighter in the seat and turned his face with my other hand to look at me. "Why? I'm single, you're single, and we're consenting adults. I think it sounds like a fabulous plan."

He sighed and took both of my hands and placed them back in my lap. I was watching him carefully now because, while I might have undergone a dramatic life change over the last few years, I was still smart enough to know I was way better looking than most of the bar trash who had been circling him all night. That—and *no* guy ever turned down no-strings sex.

"We have friends who are dating. You drank half a bottle of tequila tonight, and let's be real—you're not the type of girl who takes a guy she barely knows home for the night. You're smart and ambitious, and you have no fucking idea what that Southern drawl does to me or how fast it would cause us to end up naked and tangled up. You're just a good girl all around.

"Don't get me wrong. You're beautiful, and in the morning when I replay this conversation over and over in my head, I'm going to absolutely want to kick my own ass, but you don't want to do this. Maybe if I knew for a fact we would never have to see each other again, never have to spend time around each other, I could do it with a clean conscience, but I actually like you, Ayden, so I choose not to mess that up."

He was so very wrong.

I totally wanted to do this; to do him, but something about him thinking he knew what kind of girl I was shocked my libido like a bucket of cold water. I jerked my head back so hard that it hit the passenger window and the car suddenly felt like a coffin. I scrambled to open the latch and bolted out. I heard Jet call my name, heard him ask if I was all right, but all I needed to do was get away from him. I jabbed the security code into the door and ran into the apartment.

It wasn't until I had the doors locked and had a hot shower pouring over me that I realized how close I had come to letting everything I had worked for unravel around me. Whatever it was that Jet made me feel tonight, it was far too dangerous to try to act on. Not only had it ended in humiliation and panic, but I had also risked all the things that mattered to me now, and I just couldn't allow that.

I was going to have to keep Jet Keller locked in the box where I kept pre-Colorado Ayden. Only now, I was going to make sure that the lid was on so tight, there wouldn't ever be a chance of it coming off. The risk just wasn't worth it.

Up next . . .

Rome

Cora Lewis is a whole lot of fun, and she knows how to keep her tattooed bad boy friends in line. But all that flash and sass hide the fact that she never got over her first broken heart. Now she has a plan to make sure that never happens again: she's only going to fall in love with someone perfect.

Rome Archer is as far from perfect as a man can be. He's stubborn, rigid and bossy and has come back from his final tour of duty fundamentally broken. Rome's used to filling a role: big brother, doting son, super soldier; and now none of these fit anymore. Now he's just a man trying to figure out what to do with the rest of his life while keeping the demons of war at bay. He would have been glad to suffer it alone, until Cora comes sweeping into his life and becomes the only colour on his bleak horizon.

Perfect isn't in the cards for these two, but imperfect might just last forever . . .

Out now in ebook, coming soon in paperback

The W6 Book Café

Who's your favourite #bookboyfriend?

Who do you wish was taking you out tonight? Tweet us at **@W6BookCafe** using hashtag **#bookboyfriend** and join the conversation.

Follow us to be the first to know about competitions and read exclusive extracts before the books are even in the shops!

 Find us on Facebook **W6BookCafe**

 Follow us on Twitter **@W6BookCafe**